B W "good"

Praise for William Deverell and *Slander*

"*Slander* takes risks in crossing the quicksands of
the gender wars, and, in Elizabeth Finnegan,
Deverell has created a strong female character of
intelligence and moral complexity."
— Marilyn Bowering

"A page-turner, all right, and much more than that;
it is a fine exploration of our 'surfaces' and the
darkness that so often lies beneath them."
— Audrey Thomas

"Once again, Deverell has stepped bravely into
the minefield of sexual politics to challenge the
reader to examine closely held assumptions.
In Deverell's world there are no moral certainties;
no absolute black, nor is there pure white,
and the truth plays hide and seek behind
all the shades of gray."
— Alison Gordon

"An imaginative and ingenious treatment of
serious issues. Deverell has outdone himself."
— Graeme Gibson

"Entertaining and intriguing ... The characters are
so well written and believable, the reader feels
part of the action."
— St

"Will keep yo
the

D1007526

"Stirring ... Ingeniously plotted."

— *Hamilton Spectator*

"Deverell can move a plot ahead like
no one else in this country."

— *The Gazette* (Montreal)

"Raises important issues and the resolution is
a real surprise, a very clever piece of work."

— *London Free Press*

"Deverell gets the ring of female truth ...
comes up with an ending that at
first makes the reader go, no way!
This is followed almost immediately
with another, more lasting reaction:
Yes, yes, I see it, I believe it!"

— *Toronto Star*

"Fast-paced, slick."

— *Times-Colonist* (Victoria)

"Deverell is a brilliant craftsman of suspense.
Not since Ross MacDonald have
I read an ending with such a
breathtakingly unpredictable twist."

— *Kitchener-Waterloo Record*

"Deverell fans get the full monty with *Slander*."

— *Quill & Quire*

Slander

BOOKS BY WILLIAM DEVERELL

FICTION

Needles
High Crimes
Mecca
The Dance of Shiva
Platinum Blues
Mindfield
Kill All the Lawyers
Street Legal: The Betrayal
Trial of Passion
Slander

NON-FICTION

Fatal Cruise

Slander

WILLIAM DEVERELL

Seal Books

Seal Books and colophon are trademarks of
Random House of Canada Limited.

SLANDER
Seal Books/published by arrangement with
McClelland & Stewart, Inc.
McClelland & Stewart, Inc. edition published 1999
Seal Books edition / September 2000

For information: McClelland & Stewart, Inc.
The Canadian Publishers
481 University Avenue, Toronto, Ontario M5G 2E9

ISBN 0-7704-2856-8

Seal Books are published by Doubleday Canada, a division of
Random House of Canada Limited. "Seal Books" and the portrayal
of a seal, are the property of Random House of Canada Limited.

Cover image composed by Ingrid Fraser
Image of man by Benn Mitchell/Image Bank
Image of clouds by Siede Preis/Photodisc

PRINTED AND BOUND IN CANADA

TRANS 10 9 8 7 6 5 4 3 2 1

Author's Note

Bruce Johnson, a Seattle libel lawyer of formidable talent, assisted with local lore and law and offered keen commentary throughout. Judge William L. Downing, of the Superior Court of Washington, gave not merely judicious advice but invariably wise and witty literary insights. Judith Lonnquist contributed from her perspective as Seattle's pre-eminent lawyer on gender-equity issues. Dr. Martha McMahon provided sharp critiques from the viewpoint of a feminist writer and sociologist; Tekla Deverell as a psychologist; Dr. Catherine Milsum as a Rhodes Scholar in literature; and novelist Ann Ireland reviewed the work-in-progress with her discerning eye for detail. I thank Margaret Atwood for her gracious advice at the fine-tuning stage.

Slander

PART ONE

September 1998

. . . Let my shame
  Go where it doth deserve.
And know you not, sayes Love, who bore the blame?
  My deare, then I will serve.
You must sit downe, sayes Love, and taste my meat:
  So I did sit and eat.

– GEORGE HERBERT, 1633

1 | Tuesday . . .

I can almost feel it stick to my skin, the hot mist of pious energy wafting from the true believers hunched behind me, whispering, suspicious: what new tricks has the system devised for its secret plot to kill babies? Such rage is beyond my understanding. I have never hated anyone, so I've only a vague idea how the emotion operates. I've been pissed off, but that's different. There are some whom I have never forgiven, but I don't *hate* them.

No, what I feel for you sentinels of morality is a lesser emotion: pity. I sense you are frightened − society is moving beyond the firm boundaries you have set; you feel lost, displaced. I have anti-abortion friends: my own mother, if one were to start a list. But you're different from them, obsessive, unbending, unfunny: how many of you are complicit in this latest bombing?

A more comradely energy flows from the front rows, where sit a dozen friends, clients, sisters from the abortion movement and (to give them credit) a few brothers, Curtis Kaplan among them, my omnipresent shadow. I would never have gone to bed with him if he hadn't seemed so needy. *Quelle erreur.*

On this day of the autumnal equinox, we've drawn Judge Larry Wong, who can be gracious or grumpy depending on the state of his hemorrhoids. Today, they're sore. He is sitting on one cheek, glowering at the gallery as he summons them to silence; he then addresses me. "Ms. Finnegan, I have read all the material. What is it you want?"

"An expanded no-go zone. Your Honor, this is the second abortion clinic in the last four months −"

"I know that, but you are asking for an injunction to

stop *all* picketing, *all* leafleting, *and* engaging in peaceful persuasion within an entire city block. When I last checked, the First Amendment hadn't been repealed."

"I suspect if we were dealing with a pederast on a playground, an injunction would fly out of this court."

Judge Wong's scowl tells me he is peeved at my effrontery. Derek Reilly, a small fussy man of sixty, rises for his lifers, complaining, forcing me almost to shout, "It's a different situation only by a slight degree."

"That's the most irresponsible —"

"Oh, please sit down, Derek. Your Honor, the people Mr. Reilly represents — by their presence, by their acts, and by their language — are encouraging shamefully anti-Christian acts like last Sunday's bombing. It's only a miracle no one was killed or injured —"

"Can I be heard?" Reilly says.

"Not now, counsel." Judge Wong is at least even-handed in his surliness — he is definitely hurting, doesn't want to sit long. "Finish, Ms. Finnegan."

"They were passing out leaflets advocating terrorist acts. Encouraging criminal behavior is speech that falls outside the First Amendment just as much as falsely shouting fire in a crowded theater."

I carry on as boldly as I dare, bidding for my expanded no-go zone instead of the current fifty feet, a block in any direction from all clinics, the protesters outside it free to exercise that hallowed right of free expression. I have as much hope of winning this as the Olympic steeplechase, but my speech has to be made, even if it is in the form of sound bites. The bigger trial is before a wider public — I talk not to the judge but for the eagerly scribbling pens of reporters, here in goodly numbers.

And maybe I hope the publicity will goad the police to put more zap into their search for the bombers. The

Seattle Police Department hasn't a suspect for either arson attack, both of them sudden, smashed windows, Molotov cocktails, a vehicle heard accelerating away. The Second Avenue Clinic half gutted at four a.m. on Sunday, the All-Women's Co-op burned last June; in both cases security persons could have been killed, volunteers sleeping on foam mattresses.

I have been up since four-thirty working on this restraining order with my staff, and it's . . . what? Only eleven o'clock? I'm drained, put me on life support. And since Judge Wong is squirming, I take pity on him, summarize quickly, and rest my case. Reilly takes the floor, harrumphing, waving aloft the Constitution, accusing me of various slanders and abuses, demanding justice for the unborn, playing to the smaller audience, his people, the converted.

When I moil away like this in a courtroom I almost feel I am bartering a piece of my soul. Though women have forced their way in after centuries of disempowerment, the court is still an arena devised to suit the so-called demands of the male ego, a kind of sweaty forensic gym, a place of combat instead of conciliation, of wounding instead of healing. So you play by their rules and in doing so you lose something of yourself, you buy in, you accommodate.

You don't want to sell yourself to the system like a mercenary, but you do sometimes end up betraying yourself as a feminist, which I try to be in my backsliding way. I've never quite untied those tangled bonds of patriarchal conditioning. I'm still enmeshed in the superficial fluff: outward appearances matter, let's make sure our pantyhose isn't bagged at the ankle.

I often worry I am more into the theater than the substance of law and politics. Sure, I know what the deeper struggle is about, but I am cursed with too robust an ego. Love to win, hate to lose. Where my drive as a lawyer comes from I have no idea. My father was a mechanic and my mom, widowed early, runs a beauty parlor in a little town in the Idaho Rockies.

So here I am, at twenty-six, doing what she always said I would do: Darling, I'd better send you to law school so you can exercise that big mouth of yours. I was what the folks back home in Coalsack called a smart little whipper-snapper. For a girl. Skipped two grades. Two degrees from the University of Washington at twenty-one. Mom calls me her brain child.

She's fairly conventional, but father was a shit disturber, a leftie, a brave thing to be in the rhubarbs of Idaho, where Pat Buchanan is on a plane with Jesus. Dad passed on to me his bent for radical politics. ACLU, Greenpeace, anti-poverty: you name it, I'm in it. My feminist awakening was inspired by a sociology professor I thoroughly worshipped – and still do.

"I will reserve ruling until tomorrow at ten o'clock," says Larry Wong, who then rises and departs with his pillow.

I linger awhile, dallying with friends, hoping Curtis Kaplan might leave. But he waits me out, staring at me with eyes that warn of matters that must be dealt with. Why is it some men feel such necessity, after sharing a bed with a woman, to fall in love? It was just a sex thing, Curtis.

"Let's grab a coffee," he says. "I'm buying."

I pack up my papers and we wait silently at the huge bank of elevators, find one that's still functioning, slide silently down to ground level. Outside, the September sky is murky and damp, the long rainy season soon to begin: Seattle, the wet coast of America. But surely we will yet have an Indian summer. I must steal some time then, go up into the mountains, get naked.

And when the snows of winter carpet those mountains I will definitely get out on the boards for more than the five weekends I spent skiing last winter. J.J. owns a chalet near Crystal Mountain – we're free to use it if we can find a nanosecond of spare time. I say J.J. owns it, not the firm. He *is* the firm. "J.J. Plum and Company," that's what the business card says: there's J.J. and there's us, the company, his loyal sweatshop workers, two dozen lawyers, another thirty support staff. J.J. is a legend. We call him God.

But we keep a fair cut of fees, and the ambience is relaxed, although you have to sidestep all the prickly trial-lawyer egos. We are hired guns, mostly young, and mainly do referral work. At J.J. Plum, no musty wills are to be probated, no tax dodges to be advised – but we'll be happy to take the falsely claiming nephew to court and to defend the dodger at our usual rates. Civil and criminal courts, boards of arbitration, state-capitol hearings: when a tongue is needed, J.J. will deliver.

I do sex-equity cases. Last year, three hundred thousand dollars for a nineteen-year-old supply clerk, sexual harassment; everyone was buzzing about it, and I'm afraid the ego became deformed for a while. And recently, a big settlement in a pay-equity class action and a pocket-emptying judgment (still too low) against a wife-abusing stockbroker.

So I am gaining a reputation. I'm fairly happy doing what I do. Most of the time. . . . Yet why do I persistently feel that sense of anomie, those whispered urgings from deep within that something isn't right in my shiny little world, and never has been? Why do I often feel displaced, adrift, astray?

Curtis leads me to the nearest Starbucks, gently pushing me along like a reluctant child, and I am forced to remove his hand from my back. I hope we can make this quick, because I want to be in court for a sentencing: a white-collar predator who should be looking at ten years for a second-degree rape.

As I sip my latte, I ask myself if there isn't some humane way to pilot Curtis through his maze of distress — he is a gentle-hearted man, and he does work at being non-sexist. Medium height and build, balding in front, a lean intellectual face. At thirty-eight, he is rather immature, I think, and suffers such an excruciating sensitivity that sometimes I want to beg for mercy. But what I really cannot stand is his constant hovering. You can't turn without bumping into him.

"Curtis, the reason I didn't meet you for drinks last evening was . . . well, I really got tangled up in work, I was up late because of this hearing, and . . ."

Curtis holds up a restraining hand. "No problem."

"That's great. I'm sorry, I should have phoned."

"Nor is there a problem over the fact that for the last week you have traveled several miles out of your way to avoid me in the office. I was puzzled, but now I think I understand. You want your space." He enfolds my hand gently in his. "Liz, I can live with that — I can give you your space."

It is meant, I suppose, as a benign gesture. He is giving me *my* space.

I had intended to level with him over a quick drink last night but contracted a bad case of avoidance. The erotically incorrect episode occurred three weeks ago at his apartment. I had gone up there with my eyes open and a condom in my purse. Beware men still suffering the effects of marriage breakdown.

After that, he was like a ghost around the office, haunting my footsteps, sending me yearning looks. I went to the theater with him on a let's-just-be-friends basis, and dropped him at his door with a quick kiss with a message: this is over. He was on the machine when I got home, a twenty-minute dissertation about how he understood where I was at.

I ask, "How's the Ignacio case going?" He specializes in personal injuries, or what the crude around the office call leg-off cases.

"Might settle it." He won't be diverted: "Elizabeth, I don't want to own you. I'm willing to share you. You can have other lovers. I just want to borrow you a little bit. It's not the sex. The sex isn't that important right now."

It wasn't that sensational, either. He was *so* polite, so shy, so . . . unadventurous. I slip my fingers from under his. "Curtis . . ."

"I love you, Elizabeth."

His face wrenches painfully. Oh, God, is he going to cry?

"You're not over your wife yet. This is just something on the bounce."

He lightens up – maybe he heard too much sympathy in my voice. "No, she's gone. Totally. I've worked that through, Liz, along with a lot of other things. I've joined a more challenging group, by the way. Divorced men, mostly in mid-life. Some of the guys were trying to help me out with my feelings about you – they said I was pushing too hard. Back away a little and just let her get to know you, they said. She's a feminist: she'll appreciate the fact you're liberated from false historic roles."

He has been learning this language from the books he reads, SNAG manuals, as in Sensitive New Age Guy. He is determined to the point of dreariness to avoid seeming ego-testicle.

"You don't want me, Curtis, I have a very brittle temperament. I can hardly stand myself sometimes. Look, I've got to go. Curtis, this is not only over, it never was."

He sits back, ashen, working through his endless pain.

"What don't you like about me?"

I finish my coffee and rise.

"No, just before you go, what do you find so offensive about me?"

I am shrugging into my coat as he wallows in his sulk. Avoid being baited, Liz. Leave with kind words and a smile.

"I think you're a very nice man, Curtis. Empathic, sensitive, and obviously capable of being very devoted. There are women out there who'd just love to spread you with butter and eat you alive. You're wasted on me. I'm just . . . not your type."

"Tell me what you *want* in a man." His voice has raised; antennae are being turned our way.

"Curtis, it's not there. You don't engulf me in flames. I'm sorry. I have to be blunt. I want you to get over it."

Now he rises, shouting: "I'm losing my hair? I'm Jewish? My armpits smell? What is it?" He is still yelling as I move to the door. "Okay, goodbye, I'm out of your life! Have a good one! Don't worry, I won't kill myself!"

How awkward, a public spectacle. It has put me in a frazzled state: Curtis has somehow succeeded in his task of making me feel guilty.

As I make my way back to the courthouse, I ask myself: what is it with relationships? Why do they become so complicated and distorted? I really am too much of a small-town naïf, untrained in the complexities of amity between woman and man.

Again that sense of loss, of anomie, intrudes. It isn't a lack of love: I have glowed to its flame now and then, but each time it guttered. I am not a lonely person, I have friends. Mostly women, several men.

Only one affair with a married man, for which I plead diminished responsibility. I was seventeen, he was a visiting French professor from Paris, enough said. Well, a lot older, too.

Most of the other men were of more mature age as

well. It does not take a Sigmund Freud to figure out why. Desperately seeking father. He died when I was six, under a dump truck. An ancillary trauma: I can't change a tire, I always become anxious that the jack will give way. His picture sits on my desk: brawny and handsome, a sly half-winking smile as if he holds some intriguing secret. I remember him in hazy flashbacks: piggybacking me across the living room, walking me to Sunday school, lifting me up to pick apples from a tree. He used to rail on relentlessly about the government; the clowns in Washington, he called them. I kept imagining a circus or a scene from *Sesame Street*.

But reality blurs when precious memories are thumbed through too often, like pictures in the family album. Do I remember only what I want to? To be honest, my father often descended into moods of bitterness. He had survived Vietnam.

I trudge back up through City Hall Park, dispensing pocket money along the way – it's not really a park; call it a cobblestoned rest stop for luckless vagabonds. The courthouse just up the hill occupies an entire block between upscale downtown with its shiny massive monoliths and a seedy area down the hill toward Pioneer Square. It's a squat, frumpy fortress, a twelve-story jumble of marble floors, oak accouterments, and bland wallboard, acoustic tile, and plastic trim. My roommate calls it an architectural fiasco.

The prurient have gathered outside the door of room 746, where Judge Hugh Vandergraaf will presently be sending away the vice-president for sales of a company that makes food-processing equipment: convicted yesterday of a nasty rape at last year's convention of the Kitchenware Association of America.

I take a seat in front, on the counsel bench, where I can give Vandergraaf the evil eye if he doesn't do his duty. The defendant, one Tyler J. Henderson, is sitting with his lawyer and a small troop of friends, including his wife. Henderson, late forties, looks like your average anonymous businessperson in a fresh-pressed suit, white shirt, dark tie. I try to picture him in prison fatigues.

The doors open, the court fills, and the clerk announces a sitting of the Superior Court of the State of Washington for King County, Judge Hugh Vandergraaf presiding. He strides in frowning, sits, then surveys the room as it slowly settles into stillness. His eyes hold with mine for a couple of seconds, and I am treated to the briefest hint of a smile.

My totally vacuous reaction is to cross my legs. Immediately I feel foolish. I am displaying. Woman as object. I often give unthinking messages to men I find appealing, an ingrained habit I haven't been able to unlearn.

Hugh Vandergraaf is attractive, though, and I must admit to having had some fantasies about him. Late forties, tall, lean, hard sharp features, eyes that bring Svengali to mind, though of intense blue. And that flowing silver-streaked golden mane cascading over his shoulders, down his back, a proud statement: I don't give a shit about convention, I'm a damn good judge and I'll prove it.

Hugh Vandergraaf is something of an enigma to most of us toilers in the trenches – despite his displays of scholarship, panache, and wit, he's erratic in his decision-making. You never know what he'll come up with. Too forgiving a heart, which worries me when it comes to a guy like Tyler Henderson. Vandergraaf made quite a name for himself as counsel on rights issues. He was elected to the bench a couple of years ago, in 1996. Despite a few haphazard excursions to the wrong side of the political tracks, he is usually eloquently impressive on social issues, unlike many of the starchy conservatives who inhabit the bench.

Judge Vandergraaf looks gravely down upon the perpetrator. "Mr. Henderson, yesterday you suffered a well-deserved tragedy that I hope and expect will affect the rest of your life." Vandergraaf's diction is almost startling in its clarity, every word precisely sounded. He is not using notes.

"The jury has found, contrary to your story, that Ms. Bachello's bruise to the head was not self-inflicted, that the bite marks on your foreskin were not occasioned during consensual lovemaking, and that she did not act in a suicidal fashion when you asked her to get dressed and leave your room. As a pertinent aside, may I suggest that some of the attempts made during the trial to discredit your accuser have only resulted in discredit to you. For that, however, I think I shall be content to place most of the blame on your counsel."

His lawyer, a supposed flash from San Francisco, turns a light shade of purple. I like the way this is going.

"But I don't think it necessarily follows that I must accept Ms. Bachello's version that she went to your room solely to examine your new line of food processors. While I reject the notion that Ms. Bachello was, as you put it, coming on to you, it seems quite compelling that she was enjoying your company, and on that issue I accept the testimony of the two persons at the cocktail party who saw you in the act of kissing."

I am thinking: so what?

"There was a considerable amount to drink on both your parts, and the victim suffered no damage other than the slight bruise and the tearing of some undergarments . . ."

No *damage*? Oh-oh, where are we heading?

"I have been provided with a string of testimonials to your good reputation, so many I tired of reading them. They all use the same words: 'out of character.' I think I must accept that. You had enough to drink, I suppose, to have lost much of your hold on reality. You know, Mr. Henderson, there is a group of citizens out there who would like to see you chained to the rack until kingdom come. Were I to bow to this kind of outside pressure, however, I would no longer have faith in myself as a judge. You had farther to fall than most, and no penalty I impose can be harsher than that of a shattered career and a lifetime of being unable to look former friends in the face. I sentence you to six months' home detention, a year of community service, and I place you on a further five years' probation with a direction that you continue psychiatric counseling."

As court recesses, I am immobile, in utter shock. The only muscle I am able to move is my jaw, which has dropped. That line about "outside pressure" came with a hard look in my direction: a shot to *my* head. This Henderson character had assaulted a woman, almost knocked her out, then raped her.

I gain my feet and push my way past the defendant's well-wishers out to the corridor, where I am waylaid by a barrage of media microphones. Still flustered by that ridiculous scene at the coffee shop, now enraged over this travesty of justice, I let fly: "'Farther to fall than most' . . . if this guy had been a deprived person, someone without advantages, rather than a white Anglo-Saxon male with stock options, he'd never walk out of Walla Walla. Poor, poor man, the pain of not being able to look friends in the face as he counts up the month's sales receipts — it must be almost unbearable. That's a sentence? What kind of message does it send? It's okay to smash the base of a lamp over someone's head and rape her as long as you pay your dues to the Chamber of Commerce? It's the old boys' club sticking together, isn't it? How can you jail some guy for doing what comes naturally? It's the damn *judge* who should be seeing a shrink."

"Ms. Finnegan, what do you think the sentence should have been?"

I scowl into a camera. "Oh, probably castration. Of Judge Vandergraaf's brain."

Strapped into backpack and helmet, I pedal grimly through the six o'clock traffic from office to home. There have been heated consultations: the pressure is on the King County Prosecutor to appeal that sentence. And surely he will: it makes a joke of the sentencing guidelines.

A truck driver gives me a surly honk as I cut across his lane. I answer him with a finger. I am in that kind of mood.

I can sail down to my place by bike; the run takes a couple of minutes, Madison to Second, squeezing the brakes all the way, then a gentler descent the five blocks to Yesler Way, which is Seattle's old skid road, and finally to Pioneer Square – this is my 'hood, the heart of the old city, at Occidental and Jackson: galleries, trendy eateries, great pubs, the whole rich city scene. I can't get enough of it. (I'm from Coalsack, Idaho, population 847.)

Home is the fourth-story loft of what we call the Washington Shoe Building, a factory once, maybe a century ago, with an antique store and a live theater on the ground floor, and several galleries above. Nick has set up half of our area as a studio: drafting boards and miles of sample fabrics. Nicholson Jones, my roommate, is an interior designer (quite successful) and visual artist (quite undiscovered), and he's my best friend. We've been together ever since I answered his classified four years ago.

"Person of impeccable taste required to share space with hysterical artist in historic building," ran the ad in *Seattle Weekly*. "Must have a life."

I had rather hoped the author was a woman, and upon hearing the name Nick Jones I summoned a picture of a van Goghian brute smeared with paint. But reality was a tall, elegant, and charmingly fey thirty-year-old Adonis. "You're just what I want, a filthy-rich lawyer."

I was hesitant, but he showed me around. Two bedrooms, a guestroom, the remaining area open, with a large kitchen screened from the living area and an adjoining studio. He had been creative with the space: dozens of hanging plants, big splashy cushions and bright rugs and lampshades, and everywhere huge canvases, mostly energetic human forms: running, walking, jumping, even making love.

"I'm a master chef, compulsively tidy, I don't smoke, rarely drink to excess, and won't wear your clothes."

"Stayovers?"

"Would there be a lot of those, dear?"

"Just occasionally. My mother, for one."

"Oh, my goodness, yes. Your mother. With arms outstretched. I was thinking of the other kind. But those, too. You give me notice, and I'll be out of your hair. Which, frankly, you should be wearing shorter. That look is just too *démodé*."

I have since had my mother cut it. Now Nick's not sure about the long bangs. It has been a successful arrangement, though he can often be trying: when he promised hysteria, he wasn't playing with words. As he grew more comfortable in my company, he allowed himself to be more outrageous – though he has always managed to be Monsieur Suave when we are out with friends. He's a flake – no insult; I am often called that, too.

After I lock my bicycle to the stairwell banister, I work my way up the spooky wooden staircase to the fourth floor. The doorway opens to a hall leading first to the kitchen. As I pass by, I see Nick spooning reheated casserole onto a plate and happily humming a tune. I don't want to drag him down to my low level, so I just wave, hasten to the living room, kick my shoes off, and sink sulkily into a swing chair by a window.

This is my view: skyscrapers hover like beacons in the darkening distance above the budding plane trees on Occidental walkway; to the west, a glimpse of Puget Sound with its cranes and bustle of boats and barges. The ugly Kingdome – a monstrous concrete mound with the Stars and Stripes stuck on top like a birthday candle – is behind our building, and we don't have to look at it. Soon it is to be torn down and replaced with another elephantine monstrosity.

"Was there a cave-in at the mines today, princess?" Nick has come up behind me; he offers me my daily dry martini. "How many lives were lost?"

"I had a hopeless day: a no-win situation with my injunction – I can barely talk about it – and then Curtis Kaplan laid a guilt trip on me."

"I think you'll find more of the same on the answering machine, pet. You apparently don't understand where he's coming from."

"And then Judge Vandergraaf loosed a psychopathic monster onto the streets."

"Don't you just hate it when that happens?"

Nick quietly allows me to vent, and I spill forth the whole shabby day, but I am annoyed that he begins to chuckle as I tell of my impromptu press conference.

"I don't find this funny."

"Oh, we ardent feminists are *so* humorless and strident, aren't we? But it's absolutely hilarious." And he does a horrid imitation of me screeching at the cameras, ordering my troops to woman the barricades – he knows he can easily prompt me to laughter. "But, princess, I do think a public call for the castration of a judge's brain might be a *little* close to the line."

"God, I hope he doesn't take it personally."

For some reason we both succumb to a spate of

giggling, a tension release for me, but I realize Nick has forced me to face the absurdity of it all, a farcical day in an imperfect world. Laughter does not mean forgiveness, but it softens the fall. I frequently suffer such lurching mood swings, depressive to manic. Nick is the same way: don't come near us when we're both in the sinkhole, it's like the Chernobyl disaster.

He knots his tie and slips on his jacket. Cool. Sharp. Wide lapels, colors that should clash but don't – he dresses like a Fauvist art piece. He is such a handsome man, tall and sinewy, long ponytailed hair. What a waste, in a way, though I suppose it's sexist to think so.

"Stephane and I are off to sit through what will probably be an utterly *boring* film from Slovenia, but one which apparently must be seen if we are to maintain face within our cultural milieu. I am tired of films. I want to see a *movie*. With Sylvester Stallone's half-naked body in it. I may be late if Stephane doesn't have to go home."

Dr. Stephane Vradjik: he's the current love of Nick's life, but there have been so many that I worry. One little slip . . . It is not that Nick is promiscuous, but I wish he would settle down with someone, lead a normal life. Stephane would be an excellent candidate but for the fact he has an *abnormal* life, wife and two kids. As Nicholson puts it, he won't let go of the closet doorknob.

"Wear a condom."

"Oh, always, princess. There's still plenty of casserole. Shoot it up with a few rays."

From my backpack I remove my homework – tomes about the new reproductive so-called technologies (three months of commission hearings start in January; I'm counsel for the Planned Parenthood Association). While I wait for a bath to fill, I watch a rerun of my *coup de théâtre* on the KOMO news. Here's Little Miss Sniff looking right at you with those bright blue eyes, jabbing away with her finger and, yes, urging a castration of Vandergraaf's brain. There will be substantial fallout from this.

In the bathroom I peel off my clothes, strike a pose before the mirror, try to look tall and willowy, fail the tall part. (At a little over five foot three, I'm not actually a towering presence in the courtroom.) But otherwise I pass the physical rather well, I think: no slack in tit or tummy, some muscle in those twenty-four-speed thighs. I need to trim the streaky blonde bangs falling over my self-admiring eyes.

As I ease myself into the tub, I recall with remorse how I flashed my legs at Hugh Vandergraaf.

Lust, pride, conflict, raw ambition — how like a Sophoclean tragedy this has become: Hugh Vandergraaf plays self-blinded Oedipus, driven by the stinging lashes of the Furies to the fiery gates of Tartarus.

In great classical tradition, we begin with a prophetic curse. Though lacking in charm and poetry, the phrase "I'm going to get that pretentious son of a bitch" does resound with the blunt utility of a blacksmith's hammer. Dear Elizabeth, call me a predator, if you will, and a rapacious thug. But call me pretentious and it hurts. It's the lash of truth that cuts the deepest, and of course you have seen — through the protective skin of my studied lack of artifice — the sham and affectation. But in a manner you have been in my skin, haven't you, and have seen the corruption and decay.

Hear me, for this is my final speech to you, the jury, blunt and unrehearsed, without forensic fireworks or the rhythms of pretense to which your ears are so attuned. Let me have the floor; listen without too much shuffling and twitching, without that unblinking cold disdain that glittered in your eyes when set in my direction.

The very first time I saw you in a courtroom — when was that? the fall of 1995, some four-plus years ago — I felt a sudden whump, a lurch, as when a boat dips in the wake of a passing vessel. A clumsy simile, that, but a young woman who unabashedly reveals her secret passion for the sea might find it in her heart to forgive it.

What caused that pitch and flounder? Your confidence, your brashness, the breathless melody of words that flowed with so much ease and eloquence? How old were you then, twenty-four? A rising star, Venus ascendant from the east by way of . . . well, Coalsack, Idaho.

Venus, goddess of beauty, alluring flytrap. Ah, but you will accuse the master of the Wandering I of the crime of incorrectness should he dare speak of such delights as the sight of a slender, tawny-skinned blonde with saucy, mocking mouth and eyes as blue as the coral sea (permit this old salt the indulgence of extending his watery metaphor) who swam through my vision with the poise and grace and flow of a mermaid.

But I am growing discursive, yammering away like a shuffling fool in . . . what was that exotic land Nurse Ewanschuk spoke of? The State of Dementia. Our judge will soon be tugging open the curtain for the final act, so I will use this brief time with you to offer supplication.

I have loved and lusted; I have wanted too much, gorged myself at the banquet of ambition and pride; I have been thoughtless, reckless, even cruel. But all my dreams have not been shallow; I saw — and still see — a nation, an earth, of hope and joy and freedom. Give me that. I care.

Ah, but to what purpose, you ask. As the poet sings, "The worldly hope men set their hearts upon turns ashes and is gone. . . ."

Was it only a year ago last September that our tango of agony and despair began? I had intended to stick that conventioneering knuckle-dragger into the cage where he belonged, but you were so frowning and censorious that a contrary impulse seized me. This scolding bold young snip was not going to lay down the law for Hugh Vandergraaf. Or was she? . . .

The night continues cold and brittle. Above, the stars are shining like points of icicles; moon-flecks dance upon the black and surly ocean. A sudden southeast freshet bloats my sails, then snaps them back, and I must interrupt this sniveling eruditio to tack east toward Mutiny Bay.

You should have applied to me for your no-go zone — I would have given you a mile. . . .

"Who are you?" you demanded to know. "Who are you?"

Make yourself comfortable. Listen.

2 | Wednesday . . .

The weatherperson's prediction of morning rain discourages me from taking my twenty-four-speed to work; instead I walk. Besides, the climb is steep and I do not want to be sweaty when J.J. calls me into his office to lecture about my incivility of yesterday. I am dressed in a natty suit with calf-length skirt and a silk blouse with a soft tie. I'm even wearing a bra. What we have here is no ball-busting bitch but a responsible professional woman. I am going to look innocent when they come to get me.

Suddenly I have a niggling sense I am being watched or followed. This has been happening often of late: a warning bell goes off in my head. Usually when I turn there *is* someone behind me, though never a drooling monster; usually it's ordinary Joe Blow or Jane Doe, on their way to the office. But I still get spooked when that bell goes off, and (just in case) I always carry pepper spray.

And sure enough, when I duck into a Fourth Avenue cafetorium, I see a man pause outside, then quickly walk by, averting his eyes. Middle-aged and stout, an expression as if in pain, pouting lips, a furrowed frown. Right-wing crackpot, volunteer for the Christian Freemen of America, squad captain for Operation Finnegan.

Paranoia? I guess I do have a minor neurosis in that direction. (I also yield to the common superstitions – black cats and broken mirrors.)

But maybe the problem stems from caffeine addiction. Though I drank three cups at home, I take another fix in the coffee shop, and when I enter the office at nine-fifteen I am in a jangled state. I am greeted with a raised fist from my close and often outlandish pal, Franca Crabtree, but leery looks from other colleagues. They barely nod.

We are in one of the engorged phalluses, Fourth and Madison, floor thirty-three and part of thirty-four; we are bumping elbows in here, so we need to expand. I could use a little more space with all my conferences. Maybe Curtis Kaplan, unable to withstand being in the same office any longer, will leave and give me *his* space. Values instilled by my humble rural background still rebel somewhat at the opulent, self-satisfied air of these offices: rare species of wood, oak wainscoting, mahogany trim, plus tapestries, tropical plants, Georgian furniture. J.J. insists that when people are paying through the nose they want to know why.

My office is corridor left, past the extensive library where a few lawyers are huddled around old volumes of reports, seeking binding precedent. This profession is so servile to the past: retro-logic, our thought processes dictated by rulings from dark eras when witches were burned and slaves hanged for stealing silverware. But where else is there power? One works inside the system to change it – though I know many women and men who have been changed by it, their liberalism wilted, ideals misshaped.

Mattie Crooks, my secretary, occupies a desk just outside my office, at the rim of the secretarial pool. She's African-American, a drop-dead twenty-three-year-old with pierced nostrils and hair that looks like a scorched stubble field. I met her when we were organizing a write-in for Jesse Jackson and learned she needed a job; with Mattie at my side, I feel I am gifted with an extra brain.

"You're in court at ten," she reminds me. "Couple things for this afternoon: a spousal abuse and an arbitration from Microsoft, a supervisor with a case of the feelies. Saw you on the tube. You were smoking, honey. Take a slant at this."

I am on the front page of the morning paper, the *Post-Intelligencer*. I'm holding court in the hall after Vandergraaf's sentence: a finger raised defiantly, a sardonic tilt of the eyebrow, my wide mobile mouth working hard, denouncing the old boys' network. How flattering: I look as if I swallowed a peach pit. It's almost pornographic, too – my round, open mouth, the forward thrust of my pelvis.

"Junior is shitting green," Mattie says. "Watch out."

She has drawn open the blinds, and from this eyrie I can look over Puget Sound with its puffed white sails, its ferries, its toiling tugs and freighters. I love the sea and grasp whatever chances are afforded to boat with friends. Maybe one day I'll meet a man with an intellect who is attractive and charming and owns a sloop . . .

As I stare outside, harnessing my energy to tackle my untidy waiting desk, I become aware of a presence, and I know – as if from divination – that someone is standing at my doorway. I turn to see Curtis Kaplan, favoring me with a practiced wistful look.

"I managed to get next to myself last night," he says. "Wiped a few tears from my eyes. Hope that doesn't sound too unmanly for you."

"No, Curtis, it doesn't."

"Well, the sun still rises and the earth still spins around its axis. I guess I'd better get on with my life."

But he doesn't do that right away; he just waits, I assume, for me to allay his unhappiness, and I can't. I *like* Curtis, though I probably tease him too much. Well-mannered, never swears or makes sexist jokes, though a sense of humor would help endear him more to me.

"I accept full responsibility, by the way, for your out-burst at the courthouse. You wouldn't have gone over-board if I hadn't caused you all that turmoil."

"Thank you. It sounded that bad, did it?"

"Bad enough. Of course it was farcical, a suspended sentence. An insult as much to my sex as to yours. I don't blame you."

Junior Plum slides serpent-like into the room: J.J.'s son, Dwight Plum – everyone calls him Junior. He's the straw boss here, in charge of paper clips and time sheets, about fifty, fighting his weight, and he reminds you of a tall penguin, a big body on short legs, though he doesn't waddle but glides as if on in-line skates.

"Almost twenty after nine – have a rough night?" Junior watches everyone's clock, delights in seeing those billable hours mounting up. I have always felt that for some reason he holds some long-standing enmity toward me.

"Slept the sleep of the just."

"We have a trial coming up under Hugh Vandergraaf. A major fraud conspiracy. Major retainer."

"Plead them guilty to a lesser charge. Like rape. He'll pat them on the head and say boys will be boys."

"Hugh is understandably enraged." Hugh. It's as if they are pals. Had Junior been on the phone, truckling to him? "The fact is you read him entirely wrong, Liz. I've known him almost thirty years. He's very liberal and just happens to be a lenient sentencer. You'd better think about apologizing to him in open court."

"As much chance of that as a comet landing on your nose, Dwight."

"That was disgraceful, Liz, affects the entire firm. I believe J.J. would appreciate having a few words with you before we formally and publicly dissociate ourselves from your remarks."

Curtis, despite his avowal of responsibility, doesn't offer to take the heat. He merely says, "I think you should look at the factors, Dwight, it was an emotional moment. At certain times, Elizabeth can get . . . well, you know."

Junior nods sagely – a thought has struck: he can

salvage the good name of the firm. "Yes, of course, if we were to tell Hugh it was something, ah . . . now I'm not being sexist, Liz, but something biological, that time of the month, or —"

"Get a brain." I push past them, seething, and march out past Mattie's desk.

"Chill out, girl," she warns. She knows I can fly out of control; I am burdened with a notoriously short fuse that has more than once ignited in fireworks, and I have usually been the main casualty.

I can hear J.J. yelling from his office, though it is thirty yards away. I stop by the coffee room and my hand reaches out for my mug, but I draw back. More caffeine and I'll be climbing up his memorabilia-filled walls.

I have to admit I was terrified of God at first, back when he first hired me, a precocious nineteen-year-old seeking a summer job. He glanced over my pompous resumé, the big bullets on my first-year-law report card, the encomiums from my professors, and grunted, "What would you say are your worst faults?"

"I'm short, young, and female."

"Why do you want to be a trial lawyer?"

"I can't stand to lose."

"That's the stuff."

He took me under his wing, taught me how to fly solo. J.J. doesn't like faint hearts; he values initiative, independent thinking, and we're expected to find our own way (subject to Junior's minor course corrections), so I doubt he will land on me too hard. Plus, he prizes me for having won some critical skirmishes in the courtroom. And, frankly, I know he is fond of me — he has never had a daughter, or even grandchildren.

His door, as he likes to say, is always open, and there he is behind his desk, gaunt and bushy-browed, trim white beard, blaring into the speakerphone at a client.

"Lady, I don't care if they're *climbing* in through the window."

"They come out at night, when I'm undressing, Mr. Plum."

"Who let this crazy woman through?" he hollers, presumably to his secretary, super-organized Laurie. She looks flustered, takes over the line.

"I'm sorry, Mrs. Taylor, but I thought you said you were Mr. Plum's cousin." She motions me to go in.

"How do they get through?" he says, exasperated. "I get every cockamamie in the Pacific Northwest."

That becomes a problem when you're a name like J.J. Plum. Something like a hundred murder acquittals, many of the most celebrated trials of the last several decades, and two books written about him. He is seventy-four and still in harness, still knows how to work juries. He comes from ranching country, Lincoln County, west of Spokane; a good old farm boy in a string tie, that's his normal shtick – though there's a different look for a city jury. Shorter than his son, just under six feet, but much slimmer and smarter.

He waves me wearily to a chair beside a wall covered with framed newspaper headlines celebrating a fifty-year career. One can't blame the great J.J. for his little show of hubris.

"Coffee?"

"I'd better not."

"You off to court?"

"Yes, my injunction."

"Well, that's a good cause, you work on it." It appears he is not about to fire me. "I think you know you went a little too far."

"I said what had to be said. I used colorful, rhetorical language; that's what you tell us to do."

"Well, hell, so the judge dealt him a break, Liz. I've got less for worse. Got a serial rapist off once."

"I don't blame the lawyers, that's different; it's their job."

"Got the confession thrown out, went all the way to the Supreme Court. People versus McGrath, it's in all the reports." He seems about to go on a roll, but returns to matters at hand. "I think you should see Vandergraaf. You don't have to bow and scrape, just apologize for your choice of words."

"I won't do that, J.J. In my shoes, would you?"

He looks down at my feet. "Might be a struggle, but I could try." He enjoys his joke for a moment, then puts on a grave face. "Liz, Vandergraaf isn't the problem, the other judges are – they'll be aiming for you. Swat one horsefly, the others swarm and bite. Hate to see a career ruined over this."

I rise, stroll over to one of the framed news stories, read the headline aloud: "'Lawyer Jailed for Contempt, Claimed Judge Is Brainless.'"

"It wasn't that bad. No more brains than a prairie gopher, that's actually what I said."

"Back in 1955. Ruined your career?"

Though damaged on the witness stand, he grins, pleased that I have come up with a strong defense. "I was young then."

"I'm young now. And I can take it."

"Well, maybe you can. Maybe you can." He leans back in his chair, relaxing – deciding, I guess, it's not one of the great crises of humankind. "All right, if he gives you a bad time, tell him I'm handling it personally. I helped put him onto the bench; he owes me back dues. Still think you were unwise, Liz. You have to play the game more subtly sometimes. What the hell, you've got grit. I like that. Go give 'em shit."

Our talks usually end up this way: J.J. letting me twist him around my finger. He confided to a friend once that I brighten his day – and we relate on terms few others enjoy: he's an old cowpuncher and I'm a small-town girl from the Rockies.

Junior is still hanging around outside my office, expecting to see a completely shattered Liz Finnegan, but I swoop serenely by, blow Mattie a kiss, and pick up my briefcase and coat. Dwight glides behind me down the corridor.

"You'll be gracing us with your presence at this afternoon's meeting?"

"I'll try." I hate those office meetings.

"Good morning, good morning," I chirrup as I wend my way through the pro-lifers at the door to Judge Wong's court. They react as if they might catch an infection, and clear the way as I pass through the metal detector at the door.

The clerk beckons me, and bends to my ear: "Vandergraaf wants to see you in his court, Liz."

"Is he very ticked?"

"Big time," she says.

Judge Wong can't look me in the eye when he plumps onto his pillow, so I know it's a no go for the expanded no-go zone. Also, he wants to get his digs in over my besmirching a fellow judge, and when he delivers his ruling he almost implies I'm seeking to impose a totalitarian society on this great nation (conceived in liberty, whose founding fathers, etc., etc.). I should ask him to point out the clause in the Constitution that permits ghouls to surround a two-months'-pregnant fifteen-year-old and harshly condemn her to the eternal flames of hell.

My friends lead me out, a phalanx to protect me from the lifers, one of whom, a prim older woman, cannot seem to tear her eyes from me. She and her husband, the Kruegers – he's a Baptist minister from the

Bellingham area – appear at many of these functions. "May God take pity on you," she says as I move past her toward the door.

"Please let me pray for you," says Pastor Krueger, sardonically, I think.

We are in the corridor now, and I stop and turn to them. They are both in their late sixties, slight and short, almost at eye level with me, handsomely turned out, he in dark suit and clerical collar, she in an elegantly cut dress. They do not fit the mold – and perhaps I must admit to preconceptions – of howling holy rollers.

"And I'll pray for you, Mr. Krueger. I hope it is to the same God. Mine is loving and compassionate." I have broken my vow never to speak to these people. "Are you surprised that I believe? I do. I am a Christian."

I still go irregularly to church – usually during religious holidays or Coalsack weekends – though I'm half-hearted about it, perplexed by God, unsure why She allows fanatics to bomb clinics.

"Come on, let's go," says one of my friends, tugging my arm. But I tarry.

"I was also raised as a Baptist. Did you know that?"

"Then you must know that conception is God's greatest miracle," says Pastor Krueger, "an event of phenomenal beauty and mystery." He has a low, sonorous preacher's voice which I find disturbingly compelling. "Think of how lucky you are, Miss Finnegan, that among all the infinite possibilities of being, living or inanimate, you comprise a complex fusion of cells from which the Lord has molded a beautiful, breathing, thinking human being. He granted you a wondrous gift you would selfishly deny to others."

I would never have dreamed this tidy man would be capable of such calm, clear eloquence, giving a lie to my preconceptions of bigotry and spite. What do I say? Life is also for the living, for those who have a right to be unburdened by the unwanted? That answer seems without enough punch. I retreat to the old standby: "Would your God deny an abortion to a woman who was raped?"

"All life is precious. God does not discriminate."

"And if she was raped by a schizophrenic serial killer with AIDS, same answer, huh?"

"I would plead with the Almighty to answer my prayers for both her and the child. But if He puts us to tests, we must be strong enough to meet them. His ways are not ours to know."

And before I can come up with any brilliant riposte, I am dragged away, and after some subdued words to my companions, I break free and head down the stairs to Vandergraaf's court. I am unsettled by my contretemps with Pastor Krueger. *Among all the infinite possibilities . . .*

Harry Crake, a reporter from the *P-I*, catches up to me, and I rouse myself from my contemplative state.

"You going to appeal?"

"Naturally."

"I hear Vandergraaf wants to take a penalty shot at you."

"I'll be interested in what he has to say for himself."

"Watch it, he's unpredictable."

"It was an obscene sentence and he knows it."

"Don't let him knock that big fat chip off your shoulder."

Chip on my shoulder — that trivializes the causes I champion. But I suspect Harry Crake means well, though he impresses me as quite bleak and cynical. He is shaggy and unkempt, late thirty-something, with the haunted, unfulfilled look of many journalists; maybe they would rather be writing novels.

Harry is still with me upon arrival at room 746; within this sanctum, Vandergraaf is about to preside at a jury trial, a vehicular homicide. I am not sure how to handle him – he's particularly sharp for a judge, not just one of the warm bodies up there. And half my mind is still with Reverend Krueger and his complex fusion of cells.

"Do you know any good poop on this judge?" I think Crake is sufficiently on my side to ask him this.

"Kind of a renaissance guy, a real sportsman, dabbles in the arts, well-read, gourmet chef. A bachelor, and I don't know what he's waiting for: they're lined up around the block. No dirty laundry on the line. I haven't heard he cross-dresses or makes love to ostriches."

As I enter, a lawyer is questioning a prospective juror, asking about his attitudes to drink. Only a few seats in the jury box remain empty. I take a chair in the front, remembering to keep my legs uncrossed as Vandergraaf gives me a deep brooding study. He is so damned handsome with those piercing blue eyes, that wavy long hair. But I must boldly cross this eligible bachelor off the list of imagined partners for my occasional autoerotic fantasies.

"Ever had a drink and driven a car yourself, Mr. Jorgenson?" the lawyer asks a jury candidate.

The poorly thought-out question fetches the answer it deserves: "I don't drink."

"Counsel," says Vandergraaf, "would you like to take a short break? I have other business I'd like to attend to."

No lengthy recess, he's just putting matters on hold; this may not take long.

"Ms. Finnegan," he says, beckoning me forward.

I slowly glide to my feet, giving him my best bland innocent look, as if wondering what this could be all about.

"I had the pleasure, if you could call it that, of watching you on television last evening, Ms. Finnegan." Every syllable is impeccably pronounced, with occasional vibrato. The first time I heard him speak, a few years ago – we were sharing a counsel table – I shivered at the sound of those resonant tones. "I wonder if you would care to show cause why I should not cite you for contempt."

He gives me an icy stare. I toy with the idea of telling him I can't show cause because I have nothing but contempt for him. Punish me with a fine or imprisonment: I have determined that I am not going to mouth that tired nostrum, unfortunate-choice-of-words.

"I can't quite see that any contempt was committed in the face of the court, Your Honor, since I was in the hallway and you were in your chambers. What are the specifics of the complaint?" My tone suggests I am not about to lay prostrate at his feet.

He gives me a complete physical examination, several seconds, and it feels threatening, as if I am being undressed. I glance back – more reporters have arrived: the word is out that a maiden is to be sacrificed today to appease the King County Superior Court.

"First of all, Ms. Finnegan, my complaint has nothing to do with your expressed wish to have my head examined. Obviously, that was the overheated reaction of the immature zealot I take you to be. Your further medical advice regarding my brain was, I consider, of such an indecent and tasteless nature that I would be demeaning myself by attempting a response. Others of thinner skin who might rise to your bait would only be satisfying what seems a bottomless thirst for publicity."

I hope he doesn't think the blush rising up my cheeks is one of shame: they are hot with the glow of fury.

"It's the suggestion of gender bias that I will not tolerate."

The taunt about the old boys' club, that's what chafes. You can call a judge a bastard, but not a biased bastard.

"To suggest I would be influenced in my decision by the fact I happen to be male – your notion being, I take it, according to current feminist diktat, that all men are rapists and in a male hegemonistic society will always side with their own – to suggest that, Ms. Finnegan, is to commit the sin of blatant sexism. You, madam, are a female chauvinist pig."

Some nervous chuckles from behind me. He is trying to whip me raw in front of everyone, jurors, lawyers, reporters sitting around enjoying this flagellation in the public square. I look over at Harry Crake, who is sitting back with a sardonic grin. Chip on my shoulder? No, this involves a goddamn principle.

I try to control my voice: "Well, Your Honor, you're up there calling the shots and I'm down here taking them, and there's not much I can do about that, but I'd appreciate getting a word in edgewise. The sentence you passed yesterday was a message to society's have-nots that there's a double standard of justice available in our courts. And I'm not going to stand here and be insulted simply because I believe in the concept of equal justice for all."

Vandergraaf's face has reddened; the lines around his mouth are tight.

"Ms. Finnegan, may I suggest that this attitude that you put on of righteous feminist indignation is so callow and adolescent that I worry you are not of a maturity to be handling cases in our courts. Perhaps you need a long rest away from them to give you time to grow up."

"Your Honor, that's –"

He shouts, "I'm talking!"

I shout back, "I have a right to a defense!"

"You are an insolent little . . ." *Bitch*, he wants to say. He seems to have to steady himself. "Ms. Finnegan, I'm afraid I'm becoming quite bored with you. Let me just conclude with this: the garbage you uttered yesterday to the media and again today in open court reeks of a contempt you feel not for me but for our entire system of laws. But since I consider your comments to be so nonsensical and unprofessional as to be *beneath* my contempt, I will simply ask that you perform the inestimable courtesy of removing yourself from my sight."

I have reached boiling point and feel my lid about to blow. Say nothing more, Liz; button it, close it down tight. I barely manage to accede to these voices of reason, and turn on my heels and stalk from the courtroom.

I am in a sullen rage through the entire afternoon, half listening to my two new clients' accounts of sexist jibes at a Microsoft lab and domestic abuse at home. I, too, had endured an assault, a verbal rape. I tell myself: women like my clients have to live with abuse every day. But maybe self-pity is a more potent emotion than empathy; I can't contain my anger, and at one point catch myself flying off the handle at Mattie, then apologizing. In the privacy of my locked office, I fight back tears of resentment and exasperation.

I now realize Vandergraaf never planned to punish me for contempt: how could he do so without creating strife for himself by confirming he is indeed an antediluvian sexist bigot? No, he opted instead for a public humiliation, the revenge of power over the powerless.

At half-past four my brain is telling me, go home, go to bed early, sleep, get over it. But I must answer Junior's mid-week cattle call or my good name, I am sure, will be dragged across the boardroom carpet; Junior would be snide about my absence: poor thing, she must have gone home to rub ointment on her bruised ego.

I wander in a few minutes late, dragging my dark cloud with me. The boardroom is just off the library, a windowless space, an expensive de Kooning staring at us from a wall. We are only fifteen – some of the lawyers are out of the city; others can't be bothered with sitting around while Junior plays primary-school teacher. God himself rarely shows up at these sessions; he left the office early today.

My first destination is the fridge and bar near one end of the long polished table. I snap open a cold bottle of beer before sitting down to listen to Junior's litany of grief and rebuke.

"I see we've been keeping the Xerox corporation in the black again this month. I can't imagine the *Seattle Times* puts out as much paper as we do. I'd like to see those costs halved in the next month. Okay? Okay, Priscilla? Was that Toynbee's entire *Study of History* you were duplicating last week?"

"Just some deposition transcripts."

"Turn in your cellular phone," says one of the guys. This is the kind of comment one might think would inspire Junior to chide us for not taking these great affairs of state seriously. He ignores it. We are all constantly amazed at how such spears bounce off his rhinoceros hide.

"Let's make sure the client gets billed then, not J.J. Plum and Company." Junior reaches for some account folders. "Marcus, I couldn't help but notice, while we're dealing with corporate extravagance, that your last month's phone bill included twenty-three calls to a number in Austin, Texas."

"Aw, come on, that's where Cheryl is going to college."

"The calls averaged eighteen minutes."

"It's his *fiancée*, you cheapnik," someone says.

And so it goes, nickels and dimes and paper clips while we are bringing in fees of ten thousand, fifty thousand, a hundred thousand. Dwight Plum, unable to slither from under his father's omnipresent shadow, a flop when he tried to emulate him in court, has taken on an anal-retentive waste-management role with the firm.

Now Curtis Kaplan comes in, pours himself a stiff Scotch, and alights in a chair across from me. Oh, Lord, do I have to deal with him staring sympathetically at me, understanding my anger?

I return to the bar and open another beer – the first went down fast, did nothing – and lean against the wall staring at Junior's rump. Maybe I'll try to unbend tonight, go out with Nicholson to dinner. I need his caring ear, his healing sense of humor. The crap I took from Hugh Vandergraaf rankles more every time I think about it.

"Hansen, you're low this month. Five thousand in earned billings doesn't pay for the carpet cleaning."

"I have forty thousand in billables. What did you earn last month?"

Junior does not accept the challenge. "Let's go through the trial list. Gloria, is that malpractice suit settled yet?"

"No, and I'll need three experts at ten grand a head. Up front. It's a fifty-per-cent contingency."

"That's a whack of disbursements. Chances?"

"Sixty-forty."

"Settle it sixty-forty. Do we need three lawyers on that Bremerton Loans conspiracy next week? Oh, that reminds me, it's in front of Judge Vandergraaf, isn't it? Anyone been listening to the news on the radio? We have our beloved Ms. Elizabeth Finnegan being given a major dressing-down by His Honor this morning. What were some of the words used? Immature zealot, indecent, and highly unprofessional. My goodness, I didn't know she was capable of all that."

I am still at the bar, the unseen presence. He addresses me in the third person, not turning around: he doesn't see my raised finger. A few female comrades are making faces. "Stick it up your anal aperture, Junior," says Franca Crabtree, a practiced master of the unceremonious insult.

"Of course, a few words of conciliation might have averted this egregious but possibly well-deserved injury to her reputation. But no, she carried on about double standards of justice, practically called him a sexist bigot."

I knock back a big gulp of cold amber beer.

"We can only hope Vandergraaf doesn't take it out on the clients. I suggest those of you who will be counsel in that case firmly dissociate yourselves from her remarks at the outset of the trial. One might look at it cynically: he's liable to give each defendant thirty years to prove that on average he's a fair sentencer." He makes this labored little laugh, *heh-heh*. He wants us to know he's being funny.

"Junior, were you Vandergraaf's lover or something?" I ask.

"I'm with Liz on this," says Curtis. "It was the wrong message to send out, especially at a time when women are struggling for equality." He gives me a fist: solidarity. Franca, who thinks Curtis is a pro-female poseur, pretends to gag.

"I hope it isn't going to affect your client base," Junior says, finally pivoting around to me.

"Think of it as good advertising. My phone's ringing off the hook." But my affected jauntiness fails me, and I mutter bitterly, "I'm going to get that pretentious son of a bitch. One day, I'm going to get him."

"She does sound a little immature, doesn't she?" Junior says. *Heh-heh.*

"Are you using all the hot water, princess? This isn't the hot springs hotel."

I have been under the shower for twenty minutes. I felt terribly dirty for some reason: it's the reaction of someone brutally attacked. Three beers and a martini haven't deadened the pain.

"Save some for me. I'm not going anywhere with you while I smell like someone's discarded sock."

I turn off the shower, pull open the curtain, grab a towel.

"Stephane will be joining us, do you mind that?"

They probably had a date tonight. "Well, don't change any plans you made with him."

"Oh, yes, and leave you alone in your state of suicidal depression? Let's do Chinese, the Ho Ho."

Tying up my terrycloth robe, I proceed with him to the kitchen, bring out the vodka from the freezer. "I thought Stephane didn't want to be seen in public with you. Afraid somebody will think he's queer." Sometimes he and Stephane get together here, but usually in a small hotel they like: Dr. Stephane Vradjik is a scientist at a pharmaceutical company, with a wife, two teenaged children, and a housekeeper. Maxine Vradjik thinks he works late more often than he claims. I like Stephane but am unhappily complicit in this affair, and I wish he would make his decision before everything explodes around him.

"Nobody will notice Stephane. They will be seeing only the stunning young blonde who's had too much to drink."

"I'll try not to embarrass you." I tease the vodka with vermouth and pop in a baby onion. I sip.

"Wear the blue satin dress, princess. I want you to feel absolutely gorgeous."

You are what you wear, he says, which is nonsense. (Though it seems to work for him.) But I do like to dress up sometimes, wear makeup, show off. What is wrong with fantasy and play in ornamentation? Sure, appearance should not be an indicator of a person's value, and I'm no slave to the fashion-beauty complex, to the false needs of chauvinized women who go armed everywhere with eyebrow tweezers. I can fall back on a lazy excuse: I'm indoctrinated by Mother with her salon and her constant beauty tips.

The Ho Ho isn't far away, in Chinatown, the International District; the food is excellent, the décor rather bland except for Nick, who is dressed in one of his oddball combinations, alabaster and cherry. The dining areas are crowded for a weekday, but we have a table tucked into a corner of the main room. While we wait for Stephane, I bore Nick with yet another rehash of my dismal day.

"He gave me this look like he was stripping me naked. He's a wolf, I know the type."

"I've never seen anyone get under your skin so easily. Almost sounds as if you have . . . well, you know, a *thing* about this judge."

"I *don't* think so."

"I hate to use the word obsession, but . . ."

"Don't be ridiculous." I polish off my glass of Chardonnay. "Just the other day I was thinking: what a nice little me I am, I've never ever hated anyone. I'm *enjoying* hating him. It's actually a kick."

"I seem to recall, my pet, that you once said you had the hots for him."

"He has an attractive surface."

"Quite an intellect, I believe you said."

"He's an asshole."

"Dear me. She's in a dander. I think, princess, what you may need to do is go out and get laid."

I groan.

Dr. Vradjik wanders in, and he's wearing dark glasses, looking furtively about, checking to see if he knows anyone.

"Elizabeth," he says, "you seem perky enough.

Nicholson tells me you were the victim of a verbal mugging."

He kisses me on the cheek and slides into his seat: he is forty-seven, neatly bearded, a tall handsome man with expressive hands and a constantly tormented look in his eyes. He is Croatian-born but immigrated to England as a child, then settled in America after accepting a Stanford research fellowship.

Stephane had hired Nick to refurbish his office; on that first meeting curious looks were exchanged. Later Stephane came by to look at his canvases. I have not met his wife, Maxine, but she's apparently a forceful woman, quite striking.

"How're the kids?"

Nick is never comfortable when I ask about Stephane's family, but to do so is polite; he dearly loves them.

"Michael scored twenty-seven points last weekend in a game against Redmond High. Janice has her first boyfriend, an acne-faced lout who plays an electric guitar." He keeps looking about. "I don't like this place, too many people. Where's the waiter? I need a stiff one."

"And would you like it served straight up?" says Nick.

Stephane ignores the salacious *entendre* and brings out a pack of Lucky Strikes. He's an M.D., a health scientist, but nonetheless an addict.

Nick says, "You're squirming. What have you got, a case of palsy?"

Stephane lowers his voice. "I don't think they've noticed me, but there's a couple from my bridge club over there, far wall, by the bamboo plant. George and Francine Lindsey, and they're *very* cozy with my wife. Well, don't *stare* at them."

But we've been discovered. "Couple over there wants to buy drinks for your table," says the waiter.

"Oh, God," Stephane mutters. "A Chivas. Make it a double. Nicholson, why are you *smiling* at them?"

"Because they are coming toward our table."

Stephane has turned frantic. "You're visiting medical researchers. No, that won't work, they both have degrees in pharmacology. We're related somehow, we're . . . oh, my God, what am I going to do?"

Doubtless because I am a little drunk I perform an unrehearsed shtick rather than sitting properly and shutting up: I shuffle my chair closer to Stephane and reach over and take one of his hands, whispering into his ear, "Let's pretend we're secret lovers."

"George!" he says, hurriedly disengaging from me and rising. "Francine, how nice to see you."

They look uncertainly at me, hesitant now: they have stumbled onto a violation of the rules of bridge, someone reneging, playing out of turn.

"Just a little pause in the evening's labors," Stephane says. "I'm back to the lab in a few minutes. Oh, this is Elizabeth Finnegan, a lawyer. We've been going over a few things." He doesn't even attempt to introduce Nick.

Some stiff chit-chat follows about duplicate bridge, during which the Lindseys' eyes remain active, sizing up Nicholson and me, but mostly me, the tipsy fluffhead with whom Stephane is having *une aventure*. "We'll have to get together for a foursome," Francine says in an oddly suggestive way, still staring at me.

"For God's *sake*, Liz," Stephane says as they return to their table, "you were pawing me in front of them."

"I don't know if I did that right. Guess I thought they'd be more discreet about a straight affair. It's socially acceptable to have something going on the side, isn't it? They don't kick you out of the bridge club for that." Stephane is giving me a very dubious look. "Hey, I was protecting you from scandal . . . I mean, like worse scandal. I was . . . oh, let's talk about something else."

"Princess, I think you're snockered."

3 | Thursday . . .

Today the sun is out, a rare cameo appearance: I should duck the office, nurse my hangover on the bike paths, bring along a book, enjoy the views – Rainier is probably out today. But after the lacing-out I suffered yesterday, it might be thought cowardly of this female chauvinist pig not to pop into the office, so I buckle on my helmet and push and grunt up the hills toward those cold and ruthless downtown spires.

I don't know what got into me last night . . . aside from too much wine. Alcohol must have acted as a catalyst to my outrage over the public tweaking of my nose by Vandergraaf; the martinis and wine caused an apparently bizarre chemical reaction, I've been told. I don't remember.

Those bridge-club friends of Stephane's ate fast and left early, that I do know. Subsequently, I gave a bibulous demonstration of balancing spoons on my nose. We later investigated a couple of saloons, in one of which, if Nick is to be believed, I borrowed Stephane's dark glasses, put on a broad Russian accent, and convinced a table of tourists from Iowa I was the current Olympic figure-skating champion.

On such sporadic occasions when I forget my limits, I tend to enter a kind of fugue state. Events never get so out of hand that I go for midnight ocean swims or wake up in the wrong bed, but I do lose all sense of decorum. I embarrass my friends. I flirt with strangers. Memory cells do not function with oiled precision the morning after.

I find Mattie Crooks in my office sorting the morning mail. "There's some real wiggy stuff here." Letters, phone messages, faxes, e-mail printouts – mostly supportive, but interlarded with anonymous cowardly catcalls and threats: "Man-hating Lesbo whore"; "Lawyer bitch beware, HE is coming." Ah, yes, always interesting to see the astute minds of the opposition at work. But I cannot deny I feel stung, if not spooked, by these poison darts.

I think of that portly gent who seemed to be following me. "You will soon meet an interesting stranger" was the ominous foretelling of last night's fortune cookie.

Other letters are great. "Right on, Lawyer Liz." "You're the utmost." "A hug from all us femmes at Kirkland Electric." The support helps take the bite from my hangover.

To a note from Curtis are stapled two tickets to the Opera House on Sunday, front orchestra, Pacific Northwest Ballet, a production of *Firebird*. "Sorry I've been such a jerk. I was going to invite you, but take anyone you want." Thank you, Curtis, I may invite the stranger augured by the fortune cookie. His guilt-creation stratagems hit the mark; he knows I *love* ballet.

"And where do you think you're going today?" Mattie looks me over – my outdoors garb: jeans and my old Mariners jacket. I explain I have a big head; I need the fresh-air cure of a sunny September day. She sniffs at my breath, wrinkles her nose, slips me some breath mints.

"Forget it. I set three appointments this afternoon, and you have an eleven o'clock, a Beatrice Struthers."

"What about?"

"She wouldn't say."

In my experience, such reticence usually indicates a spousal-abuse case. Mattie knows not to ask such clients too many questions: they may be calling from home.

"Here comes the boss." Mattie leaves as J.J. strolls in, still in his coat, munching on a bagel with cream cheese.

"A dazzling day," he says, standing by the window.

He is looking out at the Olympics shining in the sun. "You should get out and enjoy it."

"I'm tempted."

"You're working too damn hard. It's not healthy. Take a week. Use my place on Kauai, it's empty."

"That's a very tempting offer." Clear my desk, clear my head. Cancel next week, frolic in the waves. Ready myself for those commission hearings: sperm banks, surrogate motherhood, new laws for new ways to overpopulate overburdened Mother Earth.

"When people start saying things like, 'I'm going to get that son of a bitch one day,' it tells me they need a holiday." Junior had ratted, of course. "No vendettas. Let's just wash it all out to sea. Okay?"

"Sure, J.J."

"I'll have Dwight arrange for a ticket. First class, get you started off right."

"Thanks, J.J. I'm sorry, I did let it get to me."

"*Non carborundum illegitimus*," he says. His favorite phrase: don't let the bastards grind you down.

I tell Mattie I'm off to Hawaii, to clear the week ahead, and I fly through my dictation, postponing some depositions, clearing as much as possible off my desk before my eleven o'clock. Ms. Struthers is late, and I begin to wonder if she has backed out – in spousal-abuse situations, many do. But finally Mattie sends her in.

I immediately have a powerful sensation that I have seen her before, though I can't recall the occasion. She's in her mid-forties, not much taller than I, though more rounded, light-brown hair, almost sandy, and worn short. Hazel eyes behind round spectacles. She has quite attractive features, though tinged by a sadness that I can also hear in her speech.

"Miss Finnegan, it's very nice to meet you finally." A kindly voice, but with an edge of anxiety. She looks around, at my busy desk, one of Nicholson's huge canvases behind it. "Nude Square Dancers," it's called, swirling naked figures. Maybe it is not abstract enough, and I wonder if she is offended.

When our hands meet, I feel an odd and unexpected energy flow. The suit she wears is *très bon ton*, of a color that perfectly matches her hair. I am puzzled as to why she is staring at me so intensely.

Now she strolls over to my framed law degree. For some reason, she smiles. Then she regards one of the family photos I keep on my desk: mother hugging me on graduation day, glowing with pride.

"My super long-time-single mom. I owe everything to her . . . well, my entire existence, of course."

"Your entire . . ." Ms. Struthers's words fade as she remains fixed on that photograph. Then she takes a deep breath and studies me again. "You're lucky." What does that mean?

I never deal with clients from behind the desk – it creates a distance, an inequality – so we settle around a glass-topped walnut table in the corner. She declines both coffee and juice, and seems reluctant to start, to tell me why she looks so troubled and pensive.

"I was there at that panel discussion last week. At Denny Hall."

That was at the University of Washington, a public debate about sexual abuse. And it's probably from there I remember her.

"I'm in second-year liberal arts. A late starter. The preferred phrase is mature student, but most of the young women who surround me are so modern they make me feel ancient."

She is forty-four, she tells me, and lives in Madison Park, an affluent area. Married happily for thirteen years to an aeronautics engineer at Boeing – clearly, I have assumed in error this is an abuse situation. No children.

"You'll probably find I'm rather old-fashioned, and

I am, really. Brought up in a religious home, loaded down with what you'll regard as a lot of conservative baggage. Pro-life Republican, worried about all the immigrants, that sort of thing. I'm not apologizing, that's the way I am. Or was. I'm changing. I guess being surrounded by a lot of young energy does that to you."

I nod. I am growing curious.

"So I'm starting over, seeing life differently. I . . . well . . ." She falters.

"What made you decide to go to college?"

"A sense that my life had not been lived. That I've lacked the courage to accept what it has to offer. That there's more. Anyway, I'm rambling. It's my second try for a college degree. I was in first year long ago, at seventeen, but I didn't continue because . . ."

"Yes?"

Her face is working; she is fighting a pain that seems to have been long with her. "I was perturbed, Miss Finnegan, when Judge Vandergraaf barely slapped the wrists of that . . . that rapist. And I was frankly steaming – you can ask my husband – when I heard how he chastised you in court."

"Good for you, Ms. Struthers."

"Beatrice, please. Even that 'Ms.' makes me uncomfortable, you can see how bad I am."

"You mustn't apologize. Elizabeth, though everyone calls me Liz."

"Elizabeth. That's such a lovely name. At that panel, you said seven of eight rapes go unreported, and they almost always involve a man whom you know."

"Or thought you knew."

"Yes. You mentioned a study – seventy-four per cent of women blame themselves. They encouraged him, or . . ."

"Or went into his room, or hitchhiked, or didn't cry for help." The reason for this interview is becoming apparent. I had argued at the panel that victims of acquaintance rape often suffer more grievously than those attacked by strangers. The assault is more personal, and because it is committed in circumstances of privacy and supposed safety the victim questions her judgment. Attacks by strangers, aside from being much rarer, are random and less personal and easier to recover from.

"I think I've been blaming myself for too many years. I was raped when I was seventeen, that's why . . . well, that's why I didn't finish college back then."

"That's terrible. I'm so sorry."

"It was early in 1971. Many years ago." Beatrice stares long and hard at me, as if working through some deep inner turmoil. Then she delivers herself of a great troubled sigh. "I was raped by Hugh Vandergraaf."

I'm quite breathless suddenly, my pulse jumping. I ask her to repeat this name, and it comes back the same. Vandergraaf.

"Excuse me." I buzz Mattie, tell her I am not to be interrupted by anything short of a six-point earthquake. I rise and fetch a micro-cassette recorder from a shelf. Miraculously, my hangover is fast disappearing.

"Do you mind? I'll make notes, but the tape will be a backup."

"I guess not." She seems unsure.

"Everything you say is absolutely privileged. I may not repeat it without your permission."

"Yes. I understand. I'm not sure what I want from you. I want advice, I suppose. I've discussed it only with my husband. Well, after it happened, I told my parents . . ."

Something gives way within her; she shudders and her eyes mist. I want to touch her, hold her hand, but she may not be one who takes well to intimate gestures.

"They didn't believe me . . ."

Her face creases with a pain that I feel as well. I wait until she composes herself, dabbing her eyes with a tissue.

"Can I get you anything? You're fine?" She nods. "Okay, let's go back to 1971. Let's go to the beginning."

"The beginning." She seems to become less tight, her smile more relaxed. "Those were terribly confusing times for me. I remember feeling in a daze: peace, love, life, laughter, the air filled with wild, improbable ideas. I was out of my element, I suppose. I'd lived an intensely cloistered life: no parties, no boyfriends, little in the way of joy. Father was – and still is – a man of strict rectitude. We played Bach cantatas at home, not the Beatles. Television and movies were works of the devil. Well, Elizabeth, you could hardly call me a typical child of the sixties."

She seems apologetic, as if expecting disapproval. But her voice is stronger now, a musical quality to it, a soft lilt.

"Enrolling at the University of Washington was about as rebellious as I got. I hadn't told Father I'd applied for a scholarship and we had a falling-out over it. He had wanted me to register at a church-run college in Kentucky. But I was a good student – probably because I was denied the usual teenage distractions – and the scholarship paid for everything: tuition, housing allowance, meals. It was a blessing. I saw university as a chance to break free, to escape from a confined past. As a concession to Father I agreed to stay at Rice Hall, which was a Baptist dorm for girls. I had no real idea what I wanted to major in. Something to do with words. Maybe history or literature – that's what I'm interested in now. Goodness, you'll think I'm terribly trivial, but I enjoy reading all those silly historical romance novels."

She looks embarrassed, as if the times have somehow made romance bourgeois and unfashionable. I feel a compulsion to reassure her: she does not have to feel so unhip, so desperately out of date. She is an intelligent person, and of a certain refinement – my mother might call her ladylike.

"Anyway, I joined the staff of the student newspaper, the *Daily*. That's where I first met Hugh Vandergraaf. He was a few years older, in his second year of law, assistant editor of the *Daily*; he wrote a lot of the editorials. I was just a . . . what do you call it? A gofer, compiled a column called 'Campus Notes,' something like that, did the odd assignment. Anyway, he . . . he was very attractive, still is, I suppose, and involved in all sorts of causes, student politics . . . Am I jumping around too much?"

"That's fine, you're doing great."

"He was a bit of a campus radical, he had this extremely long hair, and . . . well, he was very quick and intelligent, but he was shockingly profane at times. I remember one of his T-shirts: 'Get the f out of Vietnam.' I can't even say that word, isn't that ridiculous? Well, I can't deny that I noticed him. So different from my experience. Not that I had any previous dealings with boys. I guess I was the only virgin in Rice Hall. I almost felt like a freak."

She is blushing mercilessly. I like the unaffected way she rattles on when she relaxes.

"He was very bold, and started making . . . well, overtures. He leaned over my typewriter one time and said I was, quote, 'absolutely gorgeous,' which flustered as much as flattered me. He asked me out for dates a few times, but I think I was a little afraid of him. I'd been warned at home, of course, about all those dangerous long-haired hippies and their drugs and their free love and that sort of thing. I could just imagine bringing him home to meet my parents."

They must be quite the couple. As she carries on, I ponder an irony: I am far more politically attuned to the villain of this piece than to the victim. But I have met many others like the young Vandergraaf, radical posturers: scratch the surface and a festering machismo is revealed.

"Well, I went out with him just once . . . before it happened. That was on a Friday in late March. At the week's end the *Daily* staff used to get together for a few refreshments to wind down, and we were all sitting around and laughing, planning our April Fool's edition, and we had a staff photo taken for it. We ordered pizzas. And he asked me if I wanted to go out with him that night and I, well, I went with him — to a party on a schooner tied up at Union Bay — with some of his friends in the UW Yacht Club. He was fond of sailing."

Wouldn't you know, a man with a boat.

"And he was very attentive, quite nice, actually. We had a few drinks — just grape soda for me, I'm afraid — and he was being quite funny but very vocal; he carried on about the war and did an imitation of President Nixon. And, well, as we were standing at the railing, looking at the lights across the lake, he kissed me. My first kiss from a boy — I think I was just petrified. I pulled back rather quickly, and I think he got a stronger message than I intended. And that was it, and he drove me home — he had this old Volkswagen van with a peace symbol on it — and he didn't, you know, make any other efforts, or . . ."

She fizzles out. Her expression has taken on a sad dreaminess that speaks of a sorrow over what might have been. Handsome man, first kiss. I guess I understand.

"But all through the evening he was urging me to join him on a weekend sailing trip he and a couple of friends were planning. He said he had this lovely old boat that he kept up at Friday Harbor in the San Juan Islands. And I guess I decided, well, goodness, you're only young once. Break out. Live a little. And I said yes, I'd go. I just loved the idea of sailing; it seemed so freeing. Anyway, I wouldn't be alone with him."

They would be accompanied by Vandergraaf's chum

and his girlfriend: both UW students, both seniors. The man was a "tall, hearty, backslapping type" whom Vandergraaf kiddingly called Dumbo. His girlfriend was blonde and blunt – "brassy" is the word Beatrice uses – and sneeringly unfriendly to her, "putting on airs." She has lost all memory of their names, and hasn't seen them since that weekend.

On Saturday, an early-morning drive to Anacortes, the four of them in his VW van. At Friday Harbor they embarked on Vandergraaf's ketch, sailing northwest into Canadian waters, the Gulf Islands of British Columbia. I have biked some of those pretty islands – lots of Seattleites sail up that way.

"Well, our plan was to pull into a marina and have dinner, and so we berthed at a dock on this little island called Pender. I guess the Canadian customs office there was closed, but that didn't seem to faze Hugh, and he led us up to a ramshackle little resort with a bar and some kind of restaurant, and . . . I was having such a good time, and I actually did something very daring – you'll think I'm right out of some Elizabethan tragedy – but I had my first-ever alcoholic drink, and I remember thinking it was supposed to taste awful, but it was a vodka mixed with orange juice, and I couldn't really tell how much vodka was in it."

"You didn't order it."

"No. Hugh brought it from the bar."

Probably a double. "You felt its effects?"

"Heavens, yes. I felt quite strange afterwards."

"And was he making any advances?"

"Well, yes. Nothing too improper. A lot of touching. He pulled me onto his lap for a few minutes, and I felt his hand on my breast once, and of course I removed it. I think he got a little drunk. I was feeling giddy myself. I don't think I was overtly discouraging him, I'm afraid."

"Beatrice, you must stop blaming yourself."

"I'm learning not to."

"Yours was quite a natural reaction, I would think." Especially for the formerly cloistered Beatrice Struthers. I can just imagine her, seventeen, defying her sterile past, dreaming her dreams of romance, the freak of Rice Hall in her shameful state of purity.

"And there was a moon out, and the other couple decided to go for a walk, and I think Hugh picked up some beer, and he and I went back to the boat. And . . . that's where it happened."

The hard part. "That's fine. Don't be afraid to tell me."

"Well, basically, we started talking about his friends, whom I really didn't like – that sounds terrible, but it's true – and suddenly he just grabbed me and pulled me onto a bunk, and then his hands were all over me, in my blouse, under my dress, and . . . I didn't scream, I don't know why, but I tried to ward him off, and he kept coming at me, and . . . and he ripped my panties. And he raped me."

She is teary again, but holding up well enough. I think: what a traumatic first sexual experience. I ask her whether she was physically injured.

"Purple bruises. Both my thighs – he had his knees on them as he was . . . unzipping. My wrists, where he held me with his hands. And there was some blood, of course. From . . . you know."

"Yes."

"And a redness on my cheek, where he hit me."

"He struck you?"

"It was after I . . . well, I bit him."

"Where?"

"On the side of his neck. I pierced his skin; I could taste his blood." She shivers. "After he slapped me . . . he forced himself on me again."

"A second intercourse?"

"Yes."

This is becoming quite agonizing for her. "Why don't we take a little break. Can I buy you lunch?"

We both feel the need for fresh air, so we stroll to Pioneer Place Park, near my home. Despite the brightness of this warm September day, I find myself in a dark and turbulent mood. I am aghast. I would not have thought Vandergraaf capable of such violence. Beatrice's story has driven off my hangover; shock has replaced it.

At the busy triangle of cobblestones and trees that we call P.P. Park, I find no lightness in the sprightly scene of toe-tapping buskers and their equally engaging audiences, tourists with their knobby knees and plaid shorts and clicking cameras. Some panhandlers are working the rims of the crowds, others the outdoor tables of the restaurants.

I remember how Vandergraaf scolded me. I have a wild vision of marching into his court with a squad of cops. "You had farther to fall than most, Your Honor," I am saying as they haul him away. Oh, it all comes clear: there was a hidden personal agenda behind that soft sentence for Mr. Tyler J. Food Processor. Vandergraaf was finding himself not guilty.

Though I am overcome with empathy for Beatrice Struthers, I feel stymied. What course of action do I recommend? I'm not sure how I could bring Vandergraaf to court. There is a statute of limitations for rape: seven years.

Romio's, a pizza emporium, has a free table outside, and Beatrice, more relaxed now, purged of the worst of her trials of memory, says pizza sounds like fun. So we sit under the warming sun. I tell her I share an atelier near-by with an artist, Nicholson Jones, but that I'm actually a country girl, a long way from my roots.

"Coalsack, Idaho," she says.

"How do you know?"

"I've inquired about you. Watched your career in the press. I heard you were raised as a Baptist, which makes this easier for me."

I find it curious that she would be interested in my ho-hum past, but she plies me with personal questions, and as we eat I find myself buzzing away, logorrheic; my tongue won't stop flapping when I'm excited — it's my worst fault. I tell her about my dad's death, my home town, the scholarships that offered a means of escape, as hers did, but in my case from a different kind of bore-dom, small-town tedium.

In turn, she tells me she is an only child, too, and also comes from mountain country: Okanogan, upper Washington. Her parents have since moved close to the coast, the town of Lynden, near Bellingham, just below the Canadian border. She doesn't see them often any more.

"We're not estranged, though we don't share much these days."

Bellingham . . . who had I just met from that area? Pastor Krueger and his wife. Beatrice is Baptist, too; now I see the resemblance. "Krueger — is that your maiden name?"

She nods and doesn't look surprised. "Yes. I heard you had a few words with Father."

That ascetic, doleful preacher with his unexpected eloquence, his "phenomenal beauty and mystery" of conception. Had little Beatrice been dragged out to can-dlelight vigils, told to pray for the unborn?

They didn't believe me . . .

Her pizza slice only half eaten, Beatrice daintily

daubs her lips. "Well, Elizabeth, what do you think I should do?"

"About Vandergraaf? What do you want to do?"

"I want to be free of him."

Mattie must wonder at my grim look as I lead Beatrice Struthers past her desk. "Aloha," she says.

"I'm canceling Hawaii. And can you clear tomorrow?"

Her look says: what's going on? She picks up the phone.

Beatrice and I make ourselves comfortable again by the walnut table. I click on my recorder. "Feeling okay?"

"It actually feels good to release the past."

"I'm glad. Tell me what happened after he assaulted you."

Vandergraaf's lust apparently satiated, he pulled on his pants and casually went out on the deck with a beer. Beatrice assembled her clothes and belongings, fled the ketch, and ran up the dock. Vandergraaf, relieving himself off the side, called to her: "Hey, come back, what's the problem?" She is unsure if those were his exact words: they were to similar effect.

Ashore, she met the other couple coming down a path, but did not engage them, and she recalls the woman saying, "Looks like someone had a fight." Beatrice carried on to the marina office, but couldn't find anyone there. "So I spoke to a waitress from the bar who was outside talking to a friend. I think they were smoking marijuana."

The young woman – remembered only as tall and thin with long dark hair – led her to one of the staff cabins and briefly tended to her bruises with ice.

"Did you tell her you were raped?"

"I was in such a daze, but, yes, of course. I remember her saying something about there being no police on the island, and what did I want to do. I didn't know. I just . . . wanted to bathe. She seemed very confused, or stoned on marijuana. And she told me to stay there for the night. She had to go back to work."

Beatrice never asked for the woman's name. She showered, slept fitfully, then arose early in the morning while her roommate was still abed, and she simply started walking – the sailboat had already left the dock by then. A local woman picked her up and drove her to a ferry to Vancouver, where she found a bus to Seattle. She has only misty memories of this odyssey.

"In what way do you want to be free of him, Beatrice?"

"I want him to answer for what he did."

"In court?"

"Wherever he must answer."

But that rape is now statute-barred. Could he be reported to the Judicial Conduct Commission? No, that body deals only with misdeeds of judges committed while on the bench.

Her voice quavers. "He ruined my life. He denied me a career. I went back home, and I had a breakdown. I was sent to a rest home. I just now feel I'm recovering."

For twenty-seven years Beatrice Struthers has been struggling with her pain. She seems determined to right the wrong done to her – but what advice can I give? Even a civil suit in damages is precluded by the statute of limitations. Could I at least demand an official inquiry? They would hold it behind walls, a bunch of the old boys sitting around guffawing about how poor old Hugh let his dick do the talking.

Somehow I must help unlock Beatrice from the prison of her past, help her become whole again, heal her by making Vandergraaf atone for his crime. If he has any conscience, his cowardly act must still haunt him.

When I advise as to Beatrice's meager avenues of

redress, she listens calmly, though I sense disappointment. I tell her I am determined that appropriate people in high office will hear about this felony. I can only hope she has no illusions about the furor that may be stirred up by a twenty-seven-year-old accusation of rape.

"Did you discuss it with anyone afterward? Aside from your parents?"

"I don't really know. Maybe Gayle. Gayle Mitsuka, a Japanese girl . . ."

"Japanese?"

"Well, no, American, I'm sorry. She was the editor of the *Daily*. She's with some magazine now, I think."

Her name rings a bell; I have seen it in the masthead of a glossy to which Nick subscribes, a publication aimed at upwardly mobile home-and-gardeners.

"May I have your permission to talk to a few people about this?"

"Of course."

"How does your husband feel about it?"

"To be honest, Thomas is reluctant. He's a very private man. He finds this all very disturbing."

"Perhaps if I approached him . . ."

"I'd be grateful."

"And don't for one second blame yourself."

"I have stopped doing that."

After she leaves, I ponder. A private hearing, the facts hidden from the hot glare of TV cameras: no, justice must not only be done but seen . . . Wait a minute – this happened in Canada! Inner turmoil has muddied my thinking processes. Had I not recently read a news story about a Catholic bishop convicted up there of a thirty-year-old rape? And something about an ex-premier of Nova Scotia, too, facing a whole raft of decades-old sex charges.

I rush into Franca Crabtree's office: she'll know, she does a mishmash of domestic and immigration, but mostly criminal defense work. When I stammer out the saga of Beatrice Struthers her eyes light up. "Oh, baby, Hugh is up to his asshole in donkey-do."

I'm fond of Franca, though her scatological tongue often makes me cringe. My favorite office crony and co-conspirator is thirty-three, skinny as a pole, with red hair and gorgeous green eyes, and she has an odd ambivalence about the master sex. I think she suffers a slight case of misandry, but that doesn't stop her from chasing men, mostly losers. I suspect she sets them up to fail.

Franca's quick call to an attorney acquaintance in Vancouver confirms that Canada has enacted no statute of limitations for sexual assault. And of course rape is an extraditable offense. Franca promises to seal her lips until I have made a fuller inquiry.

That cocktail server who saw her bruises: I must somehow track her down. Gayle Mitsuka will be more easily found, at Pax Northwest Publications Ltd., where she is the editor of their *City Living Magazine*. Her receptionist puts me on hold, but not for long, and I am greeted breezily: "Mitsuka here, and you are Elizabeth Finnegan, the infamous lawyer? We were just talking about you."

I ask why and am told they see me as controversial, therefore newsworthy; she would like to run a piece about me. My ego can sustain a few more pounds of pressure, and I agree.

"I'd also like to talk to you off the record – about something that may seem rather bizarre."

"How intriguing. Does it involve anyone I know?"

"From a long time ago."

We make a date for lunch tomorrow.

When I return to my nest, I find Nick in the kitchen. The sweetie, he has been at the Pike Place Market: fresh jumbo shrimp, and he's doing a wine sauce. But I can tell he is in a down mood.

"You still wallowing in your silly little sulk?"

He drops the stir spoon, slaps his forehead, his typical gesture of despair. "I am in a veritable *abyss* of agony. Maxine Vradjik believes her husband is having an affair with a cheap floozy."

"Good God, you mean word is out? *Already?*"

"You may as well have rented a billboard. 'Stephane Vradjik is shtupping Elizabeth Finnegan.' It's already been around every bridge table in Bellevue, made several forays into the arts community, and I wouldn't doubt it's the feature item on *Seattle Tonight.* You have ruined not one relationship, but three: his and hers, his and mine, and yours and mine. I will not speak to you again. He called to say we have to cool it."

"Oh, God, I'm sorry."

"*Sorry?* Oh, the little princess is *sorry.* I am devoted to that man. My heart feels like it's been literally *ripped* from my rib cage."

"Oh, Nick, for God's sake, get it together. It'll pass over. I'll phone her, tell her it was just a joke."

"You'll do no such thing. Stephane has apparently explained it was a little fling and it's over."

"Yeah, right, she's convinced. Nick, that's the kind of lie men always come up with. This is getting ridiculous."

"More than ridiculous. I feel I'm playing a bit role in some squalid French farce. And how was *your* day?"

"I don't know if I can tell you."

The fiat against disclosure of clients' confidences, a commandment carved Moses-like into every lawyer's brain, has some ethically foggy escape clauses. How can you not tattle to the secretary who transcribes the client's words from tape? Other members of the firm are on a need-to-know basis only. Spouse or partner? Here the problem becomes dicey. Friends? Thou shalt not. Not even your best friend.

"Why can't you?"

"I'll set the table."

When we do not have guests, we like to eat at a window nook with a view north up Occidental Walkway, with its tridental globed streetlamps and neon window displays. The view is attractive: welcoming light spills onto paving bricks from galleries and restaurants restored from the days of honky-tonk bars, bawdy houses, and opium dens. In winter when the plane trees go bare we can see the plaza on Yesler with its totem poles.

Nick can tell I am bursting with news, but I use my mouth solely for the consumption of shrimp, while staring silently out at the street below. Heavy foot traffic: the Kingdome must be hosting an event.

"What's up, Liz?"

How to word this? "Let's say, for the sake of argument, there was a rape committed a long, long time ago. Say, 1971."

Nick was about seven years old then. Suddenly 1971 seems as ancient as the dawn of Athens. How does one prove an assault with such aged and weather-beaten evidence? What important details have been rubbed smooth and illegible by the sands of time?

"This is just an imaginary scenario, okay?"

"Uh-huh."

"Victim was a very sweet but square seventeen-year-old college frosh. The alleged perp was a hip twenty-two-year-old BMOC who would later go on to become a big-time local muck. Respected professional. He rapes her on a sailboat. The matter is never reported. Now she wants to make him pay for his crime."

Nick munches dolefully for a while, then says, "Maybe she should let sleeping dogs lie."

I glare at him. "Say that event almost destroyed her life. Say it caused her to have an emotional breakdown, and she never finished college."

"This imaginary person came to see you today?"

"And this wasn't b.s., she came to me with the straight goods."

"Who's the muck? Is this something very juicy, princess?"

The term of endearment hints that Nick has perked up. He loves scandal. I let my breath release, and fill my lungs anew. Ethics, shmethics, it will soon be all over town. "The Honorable Hugh Vandergraaf."

A jumbo shrimp may have lodged in Nick's throat; he chokes.

"*Entre nous*. Don't *whisper* a word. She was livid about how he treated me in court."

"Good God." He belts back half of his glass of Chardonnay, then studies me, frowning. "I hope, Liz, you don't see this poor woman as your tool for revenge."

"I *beg* your pardon. It's not that way at all."

"Liz, it's what everyone will say."

"I'm not the one making the complaint. I'm just a facilitator. That woman was *damaged* – physically, emotionally."

"I think you'd better do a reality check before you get too far into this. There's been controversy in the media. That's when the weird ones come out. Publicity seekers. Get your facts straight, dear; I'd hate to be the one to have to scrape the egg from your face."

"I've never met a woman more sincere."

"Anyway, the rules were a little different in 1971, that was before the age of total correctness."

"They weren't different!" I am feeling nettled at his laissez-faire attitude to something so fundamental. Is it that men just simply don't understand? She was debased, dehumanized. But the issue of gender imbalance is almost secondary; Vandergraaf is an abusive power-tripper and he is not morally fit to sit in judgment of his peers, especially his fellow rapists.

I am in the middle of a harangue along these lines when the phone intrudes, and Nick lunges to his feet, snares the portable unit from the kitchen wall. I assume he is hoping it's Stephane.

"Ah, she's here, yes. Who shall I say is calling?"

He blanches, covers the mouthpiece. "It's Maxine."

This is something I truly do not need in my life right now. "I'm not here."

"I said you were."

"Tell her . . . tell her I'll call her. . . . No, give me the damn phone." I'll just have to wing it. "Ms. Vradjik, how are you, this is Elizabeth Finnegan." I am businesslike and upbeat, and this seems to throw her off, because there's a pause.

When she speaks it is with a no-nonsense voice, though I can hear strain. "Miss Finnegan, I understand you're an attorney, so you know that I can name you in a divorce suit if this matter goes any further. I happen to have a wonderful family and I am going to protect them the only way I can. Stephane claims it's over between you and him, but I want to hear that directly from you."

I have been told she is a woman who takes no guff, a quality I normally find admirable.

"Ms. Vradjik, whatever you think might have been happening is not happening any more." What should I add: I'm sorry? I'm innocent. This is macabre.

"I'd really like to speak to you in person." Obviously, she wants to air it out.

"I'll phone you after the weekend, Ms. Vradjik. Maybe you should use the time to patch things up."

"I assume you have my number."

"I . . . well, yes, I do."

Given the circumstances, I feel I have handled matters with sufficient delicacy, but Nick again slaps his forehead. "'Use the weekend to patch things up.' Perfect. Just perfect."

"I *don't* want to meet with her. Now you get me out of this mess right now. Call Stephane tomorrow at his lab, and the two of you had better have a frank discussion."

Later, we watch a rented film, a comedy almost as ridiculous as the sitcom in which I've just inherited the starring role. But my mind wanders off: how do I grapple with the criminal past of Hugh Vandergraaf? Beatrice Struthers had a breakdown; persons suffering mental disorders often create elaborate fictions. Get your facts straight, Nick says. Yes, I must spend more time with Beatrice, satisfy myself she has not wandered off into a land of fantasy.

In my growing discomfort of doubt, I steal off to the phone and call her at home.

"I'm glad you called. Thomas would like to meet with you, and I thought this weekend you could come for lunch."

"I'd be pleased. I'm free all day Sunday." Then I realize that may sound spiritually incorrect. I apologize with a feeble joke: "I don't go to church as religiously as I should."

"We get back from services at eleven, so Sunday would be perfect."

She seems in a more relaxed humor. I tell her I have discovered that we can proceed with extradition and a rape charge in Canada, but we need witnesses.

Tomorrow I will play detective.

A freighter passes half a mile to port, and I hear its distant rumble. A blinking light above, an airplane's growl, and all again is silent but for the slurp of waves upon the bow and my halting unheard words of rue and self-reproach — a speech flung to the wind. The stars and the sea and the cold wintry night hear me. God's jury.

Did you ever think she had spoken false, your sweet Beatrice? Were there no whispers of doubt murmuring stop, reflect, who wins, who loses? But she was your revenge-wrapped gift from heaven and you couldn't wait to tear off the pretty ribbons to find inside the dagger that would strike down this sneering courtroom bully — now gratifyingly recreated as a subhuman monster. Had you known then what has suddenly exploded about you with such blinding light, would not hot tears have melted even a heart so ribbed with steel as yours? Where might have wound the paths we followed, the dreams we separately dared?

Ah, those nurtured dreams, those greedy goads of ambition. To carve a name upon the tablets of history, to change its course, to set our country's struggling sails into the wind, away from the shallows of inequity and civic decay. Judges make history; politicians wallow in it, thin reeds bent to the wayward gusts of reaction and corruption. But all bend to the highest court. True power, true dignity, reside in the dynamic exercise of the rule of law.

Dues have been collected, promises made. A career of craven adherence to the ideals (such as they are, banal and sapless) of the Democratic Party must receive its reward, a seat on the throne of the U.S. Court of Appeals. (This comes not from low-level hacks and drudges but from Senator Eddie Loovis himself.) But you know, my darling, don't you, that the seeds of cold ambition planted many years ago are now in fruit. Eddie hinted as much in open court — while describing me, in all his flatulent innocence, as "a citadel of probity and unwavering honor."

I observe that you are making a face, a moue of disgust, a pout of saucy disdain. Liberated women everywhere must march, raise banners, burn effigies of this swaggering cocksman on the steps of the Capitol. How puffed is the predator, you are thinking, forgetting for the moment the congenital pride and hauteur that have been bred into your own bones.

"You're on your way, Hugh. A little boost and you're at Everest's summit." This is Eddie Loovis after several single-malts from the hidden stills of Kirkcaldy, so one remains unsure if he spoke just whiskey-words or truly had the muscle to push me up to the airless altitudes of the U.S. Supreme Court. Perhaps. He's secure enough in his power to shoot for par after his fairway friend, the chief of state, has double-bogeyed the last green.

Had I bogeyed a few holes of my own in my youthful past? Any clanking skeletons that would return to haunt me? None, I assured him. Though I judiciously omitted to mention the f-worded T-shirt, I did not deny protesting the great American tragedy of this fading century. My brother died in that war. Bill Clinton ran from it. A generation earlier, my father shot down seven Zeros over Guadalcanal. My forebears fought in the war against slavery. Vandergraafs have perished for their country and killed for it.

But surely, Hugh, growing up in the sixties you had many opportunities to inhale marijuana. God, no, Eddie, not even tobacco. (This is mostly true. The thought of tar-coated lungs has always repelled me. Add to that distasteful memories of the thirty-dollar cigars my father stank of.)

Sexual indiscretions? Can't think of a single one, Eddie. Do you think that will hurt my chances?

The senior senator laughed and slapped my back and poured one for the road.

Hugh Hustle — did they really call me that?

4 | Friday . . .

Another splendid morning – it will not be spent in the clammy confines of J.J. Plum. A peek at the mirror has alerted me to the warning signs: an inching outward of the rump I've been perching on during a holiday-less summer. I am determined to make valiant struggle against my genes: I have seen how mother has begun to bulk up around the hips.

I put on shorts, throw my little Leica camera into a backpack, belt on my cellphone, and jump on my bicycle. Off I pedal, past the Kingdome into the I.D., the International District: Chinatown, Japantown, Little Saigon; noodle houses and community gardens, busts of dragons – and memories of tong wars and gambling dens, of race riots and shameful expulsions.

Maple leaves are tinged with gold; an autumn sharpness is in the air, and (as I put the dismal business with Stephane and Maxine Vradjik aside) I feel primed, eager for the hunt.

I wiggle through the traffic, clicking through the gears, powering my way up Capitol Hill – humpy Seattle boasts twelve such difficult rises: good for the butt. Suddenly, a premonition of doom: a black cat wanders across my path. I brake, turn, find another route that's not jinxed, then swoop down to Montlake Bridge, past Husky Stadium, and into the green campus sprawl and its maze of helter-skelter architecture.

The offices of the *Daily* in the Communications Building are busy with the youthful energy of idealistic students, desks crammed close together, political graffiti scrawled across the walls. But I am led into a quiet side room, where the bound back issues are kept.

Saturday, March 27, 1971 was the day of the rape, but I am seeking the staff photo Beatrice mentioned, in the April Fool's edition. That entire issue is a send-up: "Nixon Declares Peace"; "Phi Kappa Fumigated for Lice." The editorial-page masthead lists members of the "Daily Staph": Gayle Mitsuka, "idiot-in-chief"; Hugh Vandergraaf, "assistant idiot." Beatrice Krueger's name is listed under "proletarians." *Voilà*, here's the photo, spread over the bottom half of page five, a happy throng staring at the camera, glasses raised, pizza in evidence. "Porno ring uncovered," says the cutline.

Beatrice stands next to wild-haired Hugh, who is rudely looking down her blouse and grinning sophomorically. A fine pictorial memento for that Canadian jury: the campus hotshot captured in drooling glory the day before the rape. Beatrice is an exceptionally pretty young woman (again that sense of déjà vu), so innocent and winsome. The Japanese-American woman would be Gayle Mitsuka: spindly, wide eyes behind horn-rims, long black hair.

I leaf through the pages of several other editions, seeking Beatrice's byline, but to no avail. This must be the column she compiled, "Campus Notes": fencing club, play auditions, environmental committee, Campus Crusade for Christ. Here's an editorial with Vandergraaf's name below it: a tirade against Richard Nixon, full of pretentious words like "*weltschmertz*" and "grandiloquence." Pompous young radical at work.

I find him again pictured in the *Tyee*, the student yearbook, in a section devoted to the UW Yacht Club: 1970s student bourgeoisie. Vandergraaf, despite his left-radical pretensions, is obviously from a comfortable background. He's utterly cool and handsome in his turtleneck, though I see something in his light-hued eyes and lazy unaffected grin that unsettles me, and I don't know why. Several other snapshots of men – is one of them Vandergraaf's brash buddy, meanly referred to as Dumbo?

I spend some time at the copying machine, then wander outside and sprawl on the lawn and check with Mattie on my cell – no office catastrophes. Several more calls put me in touch with someone from the UW Yacht Club who tells me old membership records have been garbaged. Nothing is going to come easy.

That last fruitless task accomplished, I take a route north into Greek Row, the network of old frats and sorority houses, and look for Rice Hall, which I vaguely remember from my student days. I locate it on a quiet side street: a narrow three-story brick student residence, in Beatrice's time a dorm for good Baptist girls, but integrated now, as appears by the race-and-gender mix of young people outside on the lawn with their books. One of them tells me that an international student organization runs the building.

A few blocks farther north brings me to one of my favorite green retreats, Ravenna Park: fifty acres of wilderness and paths, a creek bisecting a deep ravine – second-growth rain forest, firs and cedars, ferns and salal and Oregon grape. I used to come out here for romantic walks with Marcel (the married French professor with whom I'd had a naughty affair of the heart – though I honestly earned those straight As). That was seven years ago. *Twenty*-seven years seems like eons.

If Vandergraaf denies guilt, as surely he will, his account will collide head-on with Beatrice's; as a judge he may be regarded as more credible. Is she strong enough to survive such a confrontation? I must not shirk the duty of advising her that she faces a stressful ordeal: the intrusive badgering media, the sarcastic thrusts of Vandergraaf's lawyers, a life exposed.

Maybe Vandergraaf can be caught in an obvious lie before he prepares himself to face a criminal charge. If I

were to confront him cleverly enough, play his game . . .
He's a womanizer; I remember how he stripped me
naked with his eyes. I felt a strange sensation. What? A
repulsion obviously, but something else, too, something
unwished for, unacceptable . . .

I stretch out on a rock above the purling creek,
wondering at the unease which has begun so frequently
to assail me. What ails this complex fusion of cells called
Elizabeth Finnegan? Is the source of this on-and-off-
again malaise merely loneliness? Does it stem from being
an only child? One uncle, no aunts, both sets of grand-
parents residing in the East: smiling strangers from
crowded cities who rarely visit Coalsack, disoriented in
the open spaces of Idaho.

A relationship might offer a cure: a warm body,
preferably male. Maybe I just need a hug. Why hasn't
someone opened a chain of hug shops, where one could
just go in and place an order?

The Virginia Inn on First Avenue, a hangout of the magazine crowd, is a dark but comfortable old saloon with
tables outside, and at one of them I find Gayle Mitsuka.
She is not as slight as in that old picture, and her hair
shows streaks of gray. I detect an edge of cynicism in her
smile, but it is relaxed, her grip firm.

I order a spritzer and we chat amiably about coincidence: I had called her only minutes after she'd uttered
my name to the assignment editor. I can tell immediately that I will like her; she is quite unpretentious.

"We'd like to do a photo spread — home, office,
courtroom — a cover story. Do you mind?"

"I'm flattered."

"Question: is she just a mouthy bitch or does she
sleep with her teddy bear? A freelancer sold us on it. A

male, he'll do a lighthearted view from the camp of the enemy. Warts and all, I have to warn you."

"No teddy bear, but I still have my old rag dolls."

"I'm sure you'll come off the page looking just fine." She lights a cigarette. "Bizarre, you said on the phone. It wouldn't have to do with your hassle with Hugh Vandergraaf?"

I am surprised. "Close enough. It's about him."

"I knew him from way back when. What have you got on him?"

I confirm that we're totally off the record, then show her the photocopy of the staff picture in the *Daily*.

"I look like a toothpick. Yeah, that's Hugh. We worked on the paper for two years together."

"So how well did you get to know him?"

She takes a deep pull on her cigarette, breathes out a fan of smoke. "He and I made out. Once. Frankly, I wasn't in the mood, and I'm not sure what really happened – he was incredibly pushy, and I just sort of caved in." Almost as an excuse: "He was a good-looking guy."

"And how was it?"

"Okay, I guess. I just couldn't get into it, and went along for the ride. But that's me. You'd hear talk in the ladies' room about him, how he was such an expert swordsman. I think he went through about every woman on the staff of the *Daily*. 'Hugh Hustle' we called him, collected female trophies the way you collect stamps."

"Do you remember the woman beside him?" Little Beatrice, his hand on her shoulder.

"Yes, Bea Krueger, she was a frosh. Very solemn and shy. Proper. I don't think she finished her year. She disappeared on us."

"Well, she has reappeared; I talked to her yesterday. Can I get right into it? This photograph was taken

March 26, 1971. She says Vandergraaf raped her the following night on a sailing trip."

"He . . . raped her?" Gayle seems taken aback. She squints through her cigarette smoke, quiet for a moment, frowning at the photo. "He made a lot of moves on her; she was cute. Yeah, I remember when this was taken. We had a party in the office. Hugh was circling her like a shark, though she wasn't exactly beating him off with an oar. Not sending out invitations – I think she was too shy for that – but they left together, and I recall thinking: another memorial cup on the shelf."

"He's still pretty magnetic. This is good, you have an excellent memory."

"Well, there's a reason that it stuck with me. Beatrice didn't return to the *Daily* office until a week or so later. And she had this stark, cheerless look in her eyes, and she didn't seem to want to talk to anyone. Hugh wasn't around at the time. But when she came in again a few days later he was hanging about – and he ignored her, it was like she didn't exist. She kept looking his way, and one time she disappeared into the washroom and I could hear her crying. And I was thinking: you bastard, you conned her into bed. I didn't assume rape, I'm not sure if that's his thing."

This all fits like an old worn shoe. Date rape. Self-blame. Male denial taking the form of rejection.

"Then I saw her two weeks later, during exams, just happened to bump into her on the grounds. And she was in an awful state. She wouldn't speak to me about what was bothering her, just said she wasn't completing and she was going home. I asked her, was it about Hugh? She nodded and turned and ran from me."

Doubts about my client linger no longer. Though Gayle Mitsuka's evidence isn't enough to retire on for life, she offers good corroboration and will definitely make a believable witness.

I ask if she knows anyone else who might help: former girlfriends, boaters, other staffers at the *Daily*.

"We had a staff reunion, actually, this summer."

"Oh, did Vandergraaf come?"

"No, so we talked about him."

And rather intimately. Gayle and several of her women friends, primed with high-potency punch, compared notes of their seductions by the swordsman. There was a pattern: liberal doses of what the crass call panty-remover, followed by cajoling and surrender. Though a tireless and unselfish lover (he was usually able to bring his partner to orgasm), he would politely discard each seducee after two or three dates, tossing them into his out-basket.

Gayle recalls only one relationship that lasted more than several weeks, but it ended suddenly and with apparent rancor in the spring of 1971. She was a business-administration student, Gayle recalls, but the name escapes her.

"But you know how rumors get twisted. A non-stop womanizer, yeah, but a rapist? Frankly I think it's the wrong profile. For her sake, I hope Beatrice didn't confuse seduction with rape. She was as innocent as they come – smart, but you know the type. She read all those trite Harlequin romances."

"Tell me more about this scuttlebutt."

Gayle seems to be doing battle with her conscience. Now she sighs. "Well, okay, this came out during the reunion – I was admonished not to breathe a word, so I'm not telling you this – but a name *was* mentioned." She points to one of the women in the staff photo: slight and dark-haired, an embarrassed smile, a round, cherubic prettiness. "Helen Collins. Now Mazur. Lives in Spokane. She was assistant ad manager. Didn't make it to the reunion, but I have her number somewhere." She looks up. "We have to shelve this, here's Harry."

My mind humming, I am slow to focus on the man coming toward us. Harry Crake, the reporter from the *P-I*, with his tousled hair and world-weary look.

He sits down with his pint. "Ms. Finnegan, I have been assigned to help satisfy your bottomless thirst for publicity."

I laugh. He mimics Vandergraaf well, his clipped crisp enunciation. This journalistic endeavor may offer some interesting side benefits. Harry is attractive in a craggy way.

"So tell me about yourself in twenty-five hundred words or less."

As the three of us huddle about the table, I find my tongue running amok – depicted here is our cover girl in one of her manic phases – and I cannot find the plug, yammering away about a life not fully lived. Harry makes irregular dry asides between ordering more drinks – he's something of a tippler. But it is cut-off time for me: too early in the day, and I have a meeting.

Before we part, Gayle promises to e-mail Helen Mazur's phone number – I will definitely try to talk to her this weekend. A second rape would be icing on the cake (a shameless way to put it), though maybe this time Vandergraaf is the victim – of baseless rumor. I don't know what mindless urges overcame him on that sailboat, but, to believe Gayle, he seems more Lothario than misogynist. Perhaps he simply suffers from an out-of-control libido. Or he could be one who constantly has to prove his manhood – to himself and maybe to the world.

I am only several minutes by foot from my meeting at the Abortion Rights Union, which is in Belltown by the Seattle Center, just south of our famous Space Noodle (I have never been up there: heights make me panic).

I am about two blocks from my destination when my warning bells sound and I again have that crawly feeling that I am not alone. It's a prickly sensation, my hairs standing up. I whirl about, and a man almost bumps into me: about thirty, slight of build, protruding eyes. Barney Google.

I duck into a coffee shop, and watch him carry on down the street – then he stops and stares in at me. When I catch his eye he looks quickly away, pretends to study something above him, maybe a sign. He's trying to look innocent, but it's those army boots and khaki pants that give him away. Head of the operations wing of White Citizens for a Free America. Target: Finnegan.

I remember I brought my Leica, but as I bring it from my bag he turns and walks quickly off; I snap only his backside. Next time, pal, the pepper spray.

But maybe he was just the municipal coffee-house inspector. I am beginning to mistrust my imagination – is it running riot, am I creating apparitions? This is Seattle. Safest city in America. Knock on wood.

The Abortion Rights Union is run from a set of cluttered offices above a bookstore in bohemian Belltown and the meeting is well attended – about twenty of us – because an SPD detective is to update us on the bombings.

While we wait for her, we nibble from a buffet table and catch up on personal news. Of course I am besieged with questions about my confrontation with Vandergraaf and I find it hard to discipline my free-range tongue, hinting at exciting developments to come.

Our guest finally arrives: Detective Ellen Oversmith, a large, stern woman in her early forties who leads the task force pursuing the bomber. She employs much law-enforcement jargon: "alleged perpetrator," "seeking to interrogate," "reliable informants," and can offer only vague reassurances: she is investigating leads, is unable "to fully particularize."

Her instructions about security precautions we have heard before: all clinics are now watched at night by armed guards. Later, over coffee, I consider telling her about my lurkers and followers but say nothing. I don't want her to think I am unstable with my paranoid imaginings.

As I enter my office I nearly bump into Junior Plum gliding from it. We perform a clumsy dance in an effort not to collide, two steps left, two steps right.

"Just stop moving, Dwight, and I'll squeeze past. Were you groping round my office?" I am forever suspicious about his snooping: Detective Plum, seeking evidence of waste and inefficiency.

"I just dropped off your ticket to Hawaii. I don't know how you always get around the old man."

"It's those womanly wiles. I'm not going, not yet. I'm canceling."

"Why? What are you up to, Liz?" He tracks me back into the office, watches me doff my backpack and bicycle gear.

"Interesting new case."

"For which you're doubtless well retained."

Money on the brain — it's a disease that afflicts our firm. Our referrals generally come with generous advance fees: that means we don't do enough pro bono work, and then usually only for the ink. This is wrong: we are well rewarded. What about the thousands of women who can't afford a pricey lawyer? Or the homeless? Smug Seattle doesn't boast about its six thousand impoverished vagrants.

"I can't see how clients can be very impressed by an attorney wearing jeans and a baseball jacket."

"Get with it; modern firms encourage casual dress. Tell me, Dwight, exactly how long have you known Hugh Vandergraaf?"

"We were in law school together. And I think we should consider that subject closed."

"What was he like back then?"

"He was bright, politically active, and had a compassion for the underdog. I'm proud to say we did a lot of civil-rights work together. We didn't make a great to-do about it like some Johnny-come-latelies I know."

And the great civil libertarian slides off on his little roller wheels.

"Your mother's on the machine," Mattie says.

The message: "Darling, I wonder if you'd call me tonight regarding a desperate life crisis." Oh-oh, what can she be up to? Not another man in her life. Also, a call from Maxine Vradjik: "We have to talk." Ouch, this is getting to be a pain in the derrière. Stephane will have to screw up his courage and speak openly with her before this imbroglio becomes something truly nasty. He has to come out; he can't keep hiding.

I check the computer: Gayle Mitsuka has transmitted Helen Mazur's phone number and address in Spokane. When I ring, I am treated to a recorded male voice, growling and curt. I leave all my numbers: office, home, and cell. I can only hope that if Ms. Mazur is a victim of an assault by Vandergraaf she will be bold enough to come forward.

Today's regular mail offers the odd semi-literate piece of travel advice to hot places. This one on lined paper makes me shudder: "When the next abortion factory blows up, I hope your in it." That's about the third note from this convivial pen pal: I recognize the penciled scrawl.

I think of the Kruegers from Lynden, Beatrice's parents. Do they condone this?

Here's something from a fan who asks if I'm married: a typed note and a snapshot of a musclebound lout posing in a bikini. Give me an emetic.

I find Curtis Kaplan in the library amid a jumble of books and papers: a brain-injury case that came in eons ago and is finally going to trial.

"I can't accept these."

I attempt to tender him the ballet tickets, but he merely sits back and folds his arms. "Why? Do you think there are strings attached? No way. It's a gift free and clear, no encumbrances. I thought you were crazy about ballet. But if you don't want to go, give them to Mattie."

He makes a studious show of returning to *Hodgins on Personal Injuries*.

Actually, I'm much relieved. I would have given an arm and a leg: when I had finally bestirred myself to buy tickets, all were sold. "Will you accept a check?"

He shakes his head, not looking up. "You really don't understand where I'm at, do you? I've accepted that it's over. It was great, and it's over. The gift is in acknowledgment of that. Sayonara, enjoy your life."

Nick is at his drawing board when I get home – he works unusual hours, sometimes through the night.

"The about-to-be-converted mansion of a rich and tasteless slob, a retired Alaska oil baron. He wants a fountain in the middle of his living room and a fucking aviary."

"You talk to Stephane yet?"

"Place has a library about the size of the Carnegie and he doesn't own a single book. He wants me to *stock* it. So people will think he can read."

"What did Stephane have to say?"

"Wants me to buy out an entire used bookstore."

"Nick, Maxine was trying to reach me at the office."

Nick's shoulders slump. "I'm sorry, pet, I haven't called him yet. I just couldn't."

"I'm *not* going to play this charade."

"It will blow over."

"Nick, I'm warning you: you and Stephane had better confront this."

The phone interrupts. It is Helen Mazur calling me back from Spokane, and I suddenly realize I don't quite know what to say to her: how do you dredge up such an ugly past event? So I tell her I am a lawyer and would like to see her in person about a matter from many years ago that indirectly involves a client . . . and I stall when I realize I am becoming long-winded and obtuse, and she says, "I'm sorry, what's this about?"

I explain as discreetly as I can, and when I mention Hugh Vandergraaf she is silent for a long moment. "I really don't think I can be of any help. I'm terribly busy now, I have supper on."

I plead with her to give me a minute to tell her why this is important, but she remains politely adamant: "I really can't talk." Then in a lower voice: "This isn't a very good time."

An unsympathetic husband lurks nearby. "What about some other time?"

"I'm really sorry, Miss Finnegan."

"Tomorrow?"

She sighs. "Yes, I'm free in the morning after ten."

Which probably means her husband will be away. I strongly sense timidity here, the dominated woman.

I sit for a moment and mentally arm myself for Mom's life crisis. She answers on the first ring.

"What's up?"

"I'm thinking of getting married."

I sit there and stare at one of Nicholson's framed oils: two human forms merging, two pulling away from each other. "Put a hold on it till I get there."

5 | Saturday . . .

Mom lives up in the Idaho panhandle, a three-hour drive from Spokane, so this family emergency works out for me in a way: take an early shuttle, pick up a rented car at the Spokane airport, drop in unannounced on Helen Mazur, plead my case, then head off to deal with God-knows-what in Coalsack.

A fear of flying is high on the list of Finnegan phobias, but my practice requires a lot of travel so I have had to come to grips with the concept of being trapped in an enclosed tube thirty thousand feet above the earth. My usual stratagem to help keep the plane aloft involves clutching the undersides of the arm rests. But the 737 lifts off gently into the rising sun, and soon I am soaring above the Cascades, their sun-bathed snowcaps shining brilliantly below me.

I try to read, to numb the mind with a cliché-ridden cant submitted to my commission hearings. "Birthright or Wrong," says the title. It barely distracts me. Those engines are making an ominous noise. Where is the nearest emergency exit, the supply of parachutes?

Mountains give way to forest, then plains, yellow and sere, then the flat interior, Kettle River, Coulee Lake – and soon the sprawl of Spokane rises alarmingly from below.

I will the aircraft into making a safe landing, then disembark with my fellow survivors and wobble to one of the rental booths. I am licensed but I've never owned a car, and though my dad was a mechanic I know nothing about them (I do know if you try to fix a flat, the jack can collapse and you can die). I take a weekend upgrade on a mid-size machine with new tires.

I am tentative about driving at first, but manage not

to miss the off-ramp on Interstate 90, which leads to Helen Mazur's address in one of the eastern suburbs. I am familiar with Spokane from my youth – its bright lights attracted many of us young moths from the country.

I proceed into a typical neighborhood *à la bourgeois*: sprawling ranch houses with camper vans in the driveways, all very WASP-like, none of those troublesome persons of color around to lower property values. The Mazur home is set back behind a lawn and flower beds, and the person weeding those beds, it appears, is Helen Mazur herself: a willowy woman as short as I, the size of female prey I assume Vandergraaf prefers.

The door of a two-car garage is open: her gardening tools are inside. Only one vehicle is within, a compact – it's after ten; the husband has presumably gone off in the family sedan. Ms. Mazur, in her garden grubs, looks flustered at having unexpected company, takes on a resigned look when I introduce myself. She has a slumping posture, a bowed spine, as if burdened by stress.

"I was on my way to see my mother in Idaho. I'm sorry I didn't warn you, but it came up suddenly. Those azaleas are gorgeous."

"What is it you want to know, Miss Finnegan?" Then she apologizes: "I'm rude. I just feel caught off guard. Please come in."

In the kitchen, waiting for the coffee, I do my best to soothe the tension I feel emanating from her, telling her something of myself, expressing interest in her home and family. Though it's a weekend, her husband, an accountant, is at the office doing year-ends. Only one of her three children still lives at home, and she is off studying for college exams. Bright student, future lawyer. You must be proud, I say.

We take our cups to the American-as-apple-pie living room – chintz, flowery fabrics, the TV set dominant, on the wall a framed letter of thanks from Senator Bob Dole.

I can see she is anxious that I get to the point of my visit, and I recount Beatrice's story, the details of which cause her to recoil. I ask if she remembers her.

. "Not well. She struck me as really innocent, maybe a little strange. I shouldn't judge. She seemed to disappear off the map of the earth. I wish I could help you – I just don't know anything about the matter."

It will be no easy task to breach this blockade. She is polite enough but very nervous. I show her the staff photo from the *Daily*. "Do you remember this occasion? March 26, 1971."

"Yes, I have a bound copy for that year."

"There's you. There's Hugh. There's Beatrice."

"It was such a long time ago."

Though her head may be swimming with memories, she seems disinclined to fish them out. She is silent, thoughtful, and I just let her be – she has guessed I am privy to inside information, knows I'm waiting her out.

"Yes, he was chasing her around. He pursued all the girls until he had his . . ." A struggle for words. "His satisfaction." She glances furtively at me, straightens the tablecloth, replaces the saucer.

I want to still those fidgety fingers. "Beatrice didn't finish her year. She was *so* innocent, never kissed by a boy. She had a terrible collapse afterwards, and this has haunted her all her life. She *must* do this, there's unresolved hurt and anger; she needs a purging of her sense of defilement, of being degraded. Ms. Mazur, isn't she entitled to that?"

"Excuse me." She covers her eyes with a napkin; they are suddenly wet. "I can't get involved, Miss Finnegan."

"Liz."

"My husband . . . he's not the kind of man who will understand."

"If you were raped, it's entirely between you and me. I give you my oath on that."

A deep breath. "He raped me in October of the next school term."

She releases her long-pent-up trauma, first slowly, then accelerating and with rising emotion. It is as if she has been gagging on blocked pain for all these years and is finally able to pour it out.

Like Beatrice, Helen had found Vandergraaf entirely too attractive. She went out with him three times: first a movie, at which she encountered a minor problem with his hands. A few days later, a game at Husky Stadium. Over drinks afterward, they engaged in a political argument (it is hard to picture this timid Young Republican defending her views) and it ruined the evening. He shouted at her, called her a crypto-fascist and "a Nixon nigger." He walked out on her that night, but on the following day, a Sunday, came by with his van, an apologetic look, and an offer of a drive in the country.

Though she accepted, resentment simmered: he wouldn't talk about their row. They found their way to Whidbey Island, where he parked by a lightly traveled woodland path. As they strolled, Helen began expressing hints that he might wish to explain his uncouth behavior of the previous evening. He became defensive; their quarrel re-erupted.

With unexpected suddenness, he stopped and kissed her hard on the mouth. When she pulled back, he seized her roughly by her buttocks, then began undoing her jeans. Confused, appalled, then terrified, she tried to back off, but fell. He pinned her, pulled off her panties, pried her legs apart, and forced his way into her.

As she completes this account, she is a river of tears. "It was horrible."

I can only imagine. Though I've heard many histories of rape, I have no true sense of the trauma, powerlessness and violation. "I'm sorry, I know it's so hard to talk about."

"But you know he . . . well, he withdrew before ejaculating, and he gave me a handkerchief, and . . . he seemed scared suddenly. Confused, a little emotional. He said, 'I hope I didn't rush things too much.'"

"*Rush* things? He didn't ask you not to report it?"

"No. He said I'd gotten him too 'hot.' I was dazed, out of breath, and I couldn't quite believe this had happened. I don't think I uttered a word the whole way back to town. He kept apologizing, saying he'd make it up to me. Can you imagine?"

"Barely. And you didn't report it."

"All I had were some scratches and bruises. I didn't want all the pain and grief; I didn't want to be a continuing victim. And I . . . I actually felt *ashamed*. Do you understand?"

"Of course I do." What a world we live in.

"These days — well, things are different, I guess. I wouldn't expect my daughter to react the same way. I did tell my girlfriend at the *Daily*. I had a little crying session with her the next night. She wanted me to press charges. I just couldn't."

"Vandergraaf has just rewarded another rapist with a suspended sentence. He shouldn't be sitting on the bench."

"I know — I read about it."

"You could make all the difference, Helen. I don't ask you to charge him, just take the stand for Beatrice."

"I can't, I just can't."

"Why? Is it your husband?"

She nods, biting her lip, very uncomfortable, head bowed, spine curved. "He just wouldn't stand for it, all the publicity, the snide jokes, the embarrassment he'd feel." *He'd* feel. "And his attitude will be . . . he'll think I asked for it. That's the way he is. He's old-fashioned, I suppose."

I have the picture. Reads *Hustler* on the toilet at his office. Thinks girls who don't put out are cock-teasers. I feel compassion for this unassuming middle-class woman: she is torn by fears of plunging her ordered life into disarray.

But as I am wondering how to settle those fears, her daughter, a student at Gonzaga, strides into the house, her arms full of books. She doesn't notice me at first.

"Ask me anything about the rule against perpetuities. Oh, sorry, we have a guest."

She is about twenty, and looks very like her mother in that old photograph.

"Hi, I'm Liz."

"Terry. I'm interrupting something." She is studying me with an unabashed curiosity, but recognition quickly dawns. "You're Elizabeth *Finnegan*. Hey, I saw you on TV. Giving that judge hell. Right on." I can see she is consumed with curiosity. "You okay, Mom?" Helen's eyes still show some red.

"Just perfect," she says with a false twitter and a big clenched smile. I see a person in incessant denial of inner disquiet. But if she has come this far, there is hope.

"All right if I desert you for dinner tonight, Mom? I've got a date." With that, Terry darts from the room.

"My little tornado," Helen says.

"Vibrant young woman." She seems not to have inherited her mother's timidity. "You're very close to her, aren't you?"

"Yes, the other two are boys. Not that . . . well, yes, Terry and I are close."

"I think you should talk to her about this."

I feel terrible because that brings another gush of tears. But she says, "Yes, all right, I will."

Coalsack is well off the main roads, on the eastern side of the panhandle, and fall arrives early up here in the Coeur d'Alene range, crisp and colorful, deciduous leaves ablaze in shades of yellow and red. In the distance, mountains capped by falls of fresh snow shoulder their way up into the sapphire sky. I realize I have missed the rugged starkness of Idaho, forgotten its beauty, my eyes dulled by the grayness of the coast, its washed-out hues.

I wasn't born here but near a little town in northern Washington with the endearing name of Twisp (over-anxious to get started, I scrambled from the womb in an emergency three-weeks'-premature home delivery), but my folks moved to northern Idaho when I was about a month old. So this is the land of my childhood, these mountains, these hillside farms, the great forests of cedar, pine, and fir. Sadly, I see they are being slowly decimated, more clear-cuts, wildlife habitats being lost. This is lumberjack country, pervaded by an attitude that noble battle is being waged against the wilderness.

A winding strip of asphalt leads me up to Coalsack: there is the Dairy Queen we used to haunt as teenagers; there's the roadside tavern in which I had my first illegal drink; there's the hay barn where my virginity was eagerly surrendered; there's the graveyard where my father lies buried. I endure a spasm of grief and loneliness that are still preserved in memory, and I turn off and alight and stroll to his stone and whisper words of love.

I can't remember my six-year-old trauma – it's an amnesic defense, the mind blocking the pain. The only memory I have recovered is that of Mother being tough, smiling through her tears. But what hidden damage do I retain? Those niggling neuroses, fear of flying, of dark spaces, anonymous stalkers on the street.

Now a turn past the lumbermill into town. Coalsack is split in two by a wide central street (poshly called Prosperity Avenue), along which are strung the main businesses: Idaho Savings, the Palace Hotel, the Elegant Cafe, Wong's Groceteria, and Ebenezer's Hardware, Tack and Feed. And smack in the middle of this throbbing nerve center of commerce is Salon Charlène (Mother's name is Charlene without the grave accent, but she thought it gave the sign class). She is squeezed between the Honest-Valu Emporium (we call it the local inconvenience store) and Peabody's Drugs, and one can enjoy the whole passing parade from behind her plate windows.

Our home is on one of the back streets, a timbered cottage on an acre and a half on the Coalsack River, but it's Saturday and Mother will be in the shop. She enjoys her work, chattering with her pals while she lops off their curls, and she has been at it for twenty years, ever since Dad's accident. She is mortgage-free at fifty-three and I still don't know how she managed that – no life insurance when Father died, a back-breaking loan to start her business, more loans to keep me in school. I owe her beyond measure for the abundant love she has given me.

Early Coalsack boosters – the town was founded in 1915 – had been over-optimistic during a short-lived mining boom, and designed Prosperity Avenue to be nearly as wide as the Champs-Élysées, so there is ample room to angle-park. We actually have a statue: the town founder, General Horace Millshaft, on a horse.

The same old grizzled crackers abound, folks who could adorn the pages of the *National Geographic*: the Unchanging Face of Rural America. Old Ebenezer James (though everyone calls him Scrooge) is outside his store having a jaw with the two slow-witted brothers (products of incest, it's rumored) who run the goat ranch down in the valley. Doc Fairbanks joins them, smoking one of his cheap cheroots.

Who among the rustics of Coalsack, Idaho, could Charlene Finnegan find to love? She has *taste*. I am going to be stern about this; I can just see her blowing her nest egg on some good-looking loser. Jake Bjorklund, she said. New guy in town, a mining promoter, a "dream machine." We shall see.

There are two older customers in Salon Charlène,

one waiting, one just finishing, my mother swiveling her in front of the mirror: it's Mrs. Hagerstrom, my grade-seven teacher. She sees me before Mom does.

"My goodness, is that my little Lizikins? Look at her, she's all grown up, a big-time city lawyer."

I give Mrs. Hagerstrom a peck and my mother a big hug – she has added a few ounces since I last saw her but is still what one might describe as petite: best fifty-three-year-old figure this side of the Missouri River. Men are constantly being smitten by her; she likes to charm them along. But until now she's been wise and choosy.

"Baby," she says, "you are looking *great*." She whips the sheet off Mrs. Hagerstrom, sending her shorn white locks fluttering to the floor. "Except the hair. Get up here, you've let it go." She turns to her waiting customer: "Marcia, I'll do you for free next week."

Mrs. Hagerstrom says, "Let's go, Marcia, let them be together. Liz, I just saw you in the newspaper. You must be so proud, Charlene. How did you bring such a brainy young lady into the world?"

Mother takes umbrage. "Why does everyone react as if it's some kind of accident I mothered a genius?"

Mrs. Hagerstrom leans to my ear and whispers, "I'm pro-choice, too."

"That's wonderful, Mrs. Hagerstrom."

Mother sees them out and hangs up the closed sign. I mount the chair and she does an inspection, making a face as she tugs at my hair. "What's this conditioner you've been using? Yech. We're doing a shampoo."

I give myself over to her tender mercies, and as I am being shampooed and shucked and shaped, we perform our competitive ritual of trying to out-talk each other: I carry on about my last few hectic days, she regales me with all the local gossip, neither of us ready yet to broach The Subject.

"Well, by the time she realized the guy gave her

crabs, her husband *and* her best girlfriend both became infested with the little itchy boogers, and you wouldn't believe the uproar. They'd been making out with each other, see? Your hair's so thin and stringy – you sure didn't get *that* from me." She has thick, luxuriant locks. "Well, I'm glad you put that judge in his place. They're all so corrupt. You remember old Judge Krummins? They got him for stealing from Maude Livingston's estate." She takes a breath. "How's your love life been, young lady? I hope you're not having one of those horrible affairs where you get all morose afterward."

"It's pretty barren. I have this bringdown from the office mooing around after me. What about *your* love life?"

"I feel just like a little girl."

"Mother, get serious. A mining promoter? I bet the guy's a crook."

"Jake's from Montana. He's got some ambitious plans. He's raising funds around here to reopen the silver mines because the price is booming."

"Mother, I'm sorry, I love you and I'm not going to let you make a mess of your life. What's he like?"

"A breath of fresh air. Oh, that's him."

She waves with dismaying eagerness and gaiety, and the man passing by the window waves back and winks: about mid-fifties, a drooping swindler's mustache on a crooked, handsome face.

"Okay, well, I'm going to suggest you put everything you own immediately into my name."

"Don't be silly. Jake is coming for dinner at six, and you're not to sit there cross-examining him."

"Oh, Mom, he's a heartbreaker. I can tell just by looking at him." I decide I will check for a criminal record.

"He reminds me of your father in a way."

"Dad wasn't a con artist."

"You'd be surprised."

"What do you mean?"

"He was a bit of a gambler."

"Oh, that." He was fined for running an illegal game, I'd been told, but in the catalogue of human sins, that is trifling.

"I'm saying nobody's perfect, and if Jake happens to be a little sharp around the edges I'm not going to complain. He's gorgeous."

"How far has this thing gone? Well, he's obviously seduced you, and now he's proposed. You didn't give him an answer, I hope."

"Not yet. I wanted your advice, but I see you're going to be all negative and unhelpful. I thought you'd at least keep an open mind. I can't keep waiting for Prince Charming or someone to show up. I'm frightened they're going to start calling me the old widow lady Finnegan. I've been alone for twenty years, and you should be more supportive."

I want to hold her, to give love and reassurance, but she has me imprisoned in the chair, scissors clicking away. I don't want this to turn into a spat – Mom and I have had a few of them, wails and screams that brought neighbors onto their porches. (We don't discuss abortion issues any more.) And, yes, it's unfair of me to try to deny her the comfort of love for her remaining years, but I will not have my hairdresser fleeced by a clip artist from Montana.

Eventually, she finishes my hair, and while she sweeps up I slip into her back office and scrunch by the phone. I should be able to find out what he's wanted for: Franca Crabtree has a close friend in the prosecutors' office who could run a trace. I get Franca on her cell and explain that one Jake Bjorklund is in the process of stealing my home town blind.

"Coalsack? What's to steal aside from your mother's heart? I think you're just jealous."

"Get the goods on him and call me back."

The shop swept out, the tools of her trade put away, Mom and I walk out arm in arm into the crisp fall day. I am determined to gently guide her through the hazards this liaison could pose. "I have to leave in the morning, so let's have fun. *Carpe diem.*"

"What's that, something you learned in bed with your French professor?" She still sounds miffed; I have handled matters poorly.

"Latin, Mom. Seize the day."

But I can't stop counseling her, and over coffee at the Elegant, I burden her ears with all the mining scams one hears about in the courts: salted claims, false paper, promises of 500-per-cent returns. He isn't like that at all, she says. Very worldly and easygoing. I sigh and drop the subject for now.

Anyway, we don't get much of a chance to be alone: people I had almost forgotten continue to descend on us, and after shopping, mother insists on dropping by at Mrs. Firke's garage sale.

And I get occupied there by Billy Hutton, who comes up behind me. "Hey, Lizzie, still looking deadly." He's a guy I went out with in my mid-teens, and we literally rolled in the hay. I remember thinking he was the most: two years older, a high-school athlete, a pitcher. First love. I haven't seen him in almost a decade, since he went off to pursue a sports career. I detect something sad and defeated about him, and it turns out he was recently cut by a minor-league team, and he's back here helping run his father's farm.

"Arm blew out. I had a few good years."

He still seems sexy, tall and rangy, a shock of black hair, and I am feeling stirrings and thinking: wouldn't it be fun to climb up into that hay loft with him one more time? Sneak out on Mom while she's cooking the dinner, a quickie for old time's sake, release some of the erotic tension.

As I am seeking the courage to ask him if he has plans for later, he waves over a young woman. "This is my wife, Carol," he says, and I feel very silly as I shake her hand.

At the house, Mom organizes for dinner and shoos me out like the family cat: "I don't want you getting me all depressed with your nittering and nagging. You meet him, then we'll talk."

"I'm sorry, Mom, maybe I'm being silly. I just want you to be careful, that's all."

I stroll through the old apple orchard to the river-bank. The water is fairly high for this time of year, and I can hear the distant roar of the falls. It was within its chilly pools in the dulcet days of summer that our hardy young Lizikins learned to swim. That is one phobia I do not suffer, the water.

Incredibly, the swing is still here, a worn strip of tire from dad's garage, ragged ropes suspending it from a gnarled willow tree. I remember him pushing me high into the air . . .

The sun is sliding into a gap in the western hills, and a wind has come up, cold from the north. I am too used to the soft Seattle air and I shiver. Seattle seems as distant as the galaxies, but I am not quite free of it: Beatrice Struthers and Hugh Vandergraaf haunt at the rims. Helen Mazur must somehow be persuaded to be stouter of heart. And maybe there are others, a trail of victims . . . What kind of hostile quirk does Hugh Hustle suffer from? The standard rapist profile is that of a man who sees women as threats if not mere objects; he turns to violence because he can't confront his own inadequacies. But Vandergraaf's record of promiscuity suggests he is more occupied with lust than hate.

I yearn to probe around the nuts and bolts and springs of his mind. I am obsessed, Nick claims. Surely not. I am merely curious to learn why a brilliant brain so misfunctions.

A car pulls up: sleek and shiny, an old Cadillac, the sort of carriage the Mafia parade in. Jake Bjorklund does not disembark immediately from this luxury liner, but pauses to comb his hair, inspecting himself in the rear-view mirror. I sense vanity. He is not like my father.

He grasps a bottle of wine and heads for the house with a confident, long-striding gait, disappearing from my view. I sneak through the orchard like a guerrilla fighter, moving from tree to tree en route to the living-room window. A peek reveals them moving together and holding hands. They kiss.

I will be proper and courteous. I will listen and observe. I will not cross-examine him.

I make a noisy entrance, giving them a moment to untangle, and when I stroll into the room he greets me with a dazzling array of teeth, which I doubt can be his, and a hearty salesperson's grip.

"Hey, you're damn near pretty as your Momma."

"Mother says you'd like to reopen some of our old silver mines. You must have got some good tests from them."

He does not confirm or deny. "Enough ore there to decorate every good-lookin' gal in the spud state with rings and necklaces. Matter of fact, I think we've come upon an old seam that was overlooked."

"How wonderful. And that's what the engineer's report said?"

Mother gives me an exasperated look as she hands me his wine bottle. "Put this to chill, and can you bring out the appetizers?"

A white Bordeaux; at least he didn't bring plonk. From the kitchen extension I sneak another call to Franca, who's been on the job but needs a description: about ten Jake Bjorklunds have been pulled from the computer.

I provide further particulars: "Six feet, dark, lady-killer looks, comes from Montana."

"See if you can con him into a set of prints."

For most of the evening, Mother stubbornly and inexhaustibly holds the floor, carrying on about every irrelevancy that comes to her mind, interrupting when I tell him I'll bet he's had an interesting life and asking what other projects he's been involved in, where has he traveled: the natural questions one would ask a new acquaintance.

When he is allowed to answer, he gives a wildly expansive but credible performance. "Been around the world so many times I can't figure out no more if I'm coming or going. Borneo, Russia, Timbuktu. Made a fortune, lost it twice. But the way I look at it, there's always another rainbow and another pot of gold." I wonder if he's using an alias.

Mom has served up fresh local trout, and Jake is adept at buttering up the cook: "Damn, this is better than the meal I had before my last hanging. Your mother cooks as good as she looks, don't she? Just can't believe she'd have a daughter that's her spitting image, I'd've guessed you were sisters."

Mom laps up this blarney. I fear she *knows* he is a bad guy and doesn't care. But he has a fustian charm ("Now you gals keep your hands soft and pretty and leave the dishes to me; I've scraped a lotta pots in my time"), and despite my apprehensions I begin to tolerate him. And when Mom finally decides to stop running interference, he reveals himself as quite gregarious and funny, puffing on a big cigar, telling stories on himself: ups and downs and debacles in his various mining adventures.

And I can see by the bright glow that emanates from Mother's eyes that she is completely enamored of him. And she does look younger. And very beautiful. If this is what love does to you, who am I to play the role of grinch? I will check out Mr. Bjorklund more closely, of course (his wine glass with his sticky fingerprints has disappeared, and may be found carefully wrapped in my overnight bag), but in the meantime I will permit her this divertissement. Sign no documents, I will tell her.

And the evening proceeds apace, Mom more relaxed now that she sees I am laughing at his jokes and not calling in the emergency response team. He may be a rascal but at least he is not boring, and unless he's a very good actor he seems much attracted to her.

Actually, I *am* a little jealous of her.

6 | Sunday . . .

After an early weary start to the Spokane airport – we were up past midnight – I switch on the car radio, and am dismayed by the forecast: storm winds. That is scary enough by itself, but now I find my flight to the coast has been delayed an hour for reasons vaguely explained, though I can see a maintenance crew outside fiddling with one of the wings. This inspires visions of loose bolts, fuel leaks, and exploding engines. Woman was not meant to fly.

After we board, the pilot broadcasts a hearty apology: a valve got stuck, we greased her up, and we're ready to roll. The man in the seat next to me says, "You always wonder if they're telling the truth," and I am about ready to pull out the vomit bag by the time the plane takes off.

And for added thrills, the Pacific front bucks and buffets the plane. The white puffs below begin to multiply and merge, and by the time we are over the Cascades I can see nothing but boiling cloud; Seattle is socked in, maybe Typhoon Zelda has hit. As we descend into this dark gray mass, I silently plead my case to God: I am so young, I have so much to do.

But again I live to tell the tale, and when wheels meet runway I pry my fingers loose from the armrests. In the Sea-Tac terminal, I wobble straight to a bar for a milk to settle my stomach. As I relax, my thoughts revert to Mother. I must admit to feeling some reassurance after that convivial evening with the expansive Jake Bjorklund. But I will not relent in my determination to peel back any layers of a shadowy past.

I trundle off in a taxi to Madison Park for my lunch date with Beatrice and Thomas Struthers. Once off the freeway ramp, we soon begin to roll past the fine homes of this district, shrouded in rain and gloom. Thomas Struthers must earn well as an aeronautics engineer. A private man, Beatrice said, deeply uncomfortable with the thought of a scandalous trial.

Here is their house, set well back, three stories, solid, heavily timbered, lots of room to roam for two people. I wonder if they tried to have children.

I dash from the driveway as Beatrice, who must have been waiting by a window, hurries toward me with an umbrella. She shelters me under it and actually gives me a hug, which I do not expect from her – maybe she is not as reserved and proper as I had thought.

As she escorts me into the house, she apologizes about the weather, almost implying it is her fault. "I'm sorry, we didn't expect this. You never know how one day will turn into the next." She is still in her church-going clothes, beige suit, a high collar.

The house is nicely enough appointed – not by Nicholson Jones standards, but tasteful, though just a little gloomy, the rooms almost too spacious. A library, so they must read. A large print of El Greco's Christ too somberly dominates a living-room wall. Other signs of firmly kept faith: the Lord's Prayer in a frame, an illustrated Bible with the tabletop books and magazines.

We are to dine in a parlor off the kitchen where a small table has been spread. Beatrice leaves to fetch Thomas – "he's down in his hobby shop" – while I peruse some photographs on the wall: marriage pictures, taken almost twenty years ago. Thomas is tall and thin and would be handsome if it weren't for the bulky nose. He looks older than Beatrice by about a decade. Already losing his hair.

And over here, austere and devout, Pastor Johann and Amy Krueger. He stares into the camera, directly at me, his mouth open as if shaping some rigorous silent accusation. *God granted you a wondrous gift you would self-ishly deny to others.*

Thomas has changed into casual clothes, and Beatrice must almost pull him into the room: I can see he is very shy. A mumbled greeting, negligible eye contact, and he doesn't know what to do with his hands, which he uses to tug at his collar. He does not have much hair on top now – he is close to sixty. I can tell he is anxious: here's the radical lady lawyer who is about to turn his life upside down, dragging his wife into the quicksand of the courtroom.

Beatrice spoons out seafood chowder, and Thomas says a brief grace before we reach for our spoons. He is ill-adept at small talk, and listens dispassionately while Beatrice chats about her classes at UW. Her world is opening up: literature assignments include Joyce and Hemingway, tame by today's standards but rather raw material for Pastor Krueger's daughter. "It makes me absolutely blush, some of it; I guess I'm just too old-fashioned." Always apologizing. I wonder if she, like Helen Mazur, felt ashamed after being violated.

I ask Beatrice to fill in some gaps in her life. She had been so emotionally wounded by her rape that she entered a rest home, the Faith Baptist Hospice in Everett. After a stay of a few months, she was deemed well enough to take on light domestic work in the interior, providing home care for an elderly couple. A relapse sent her briefly back to the hospice.

She spent the next year with her parents, helping with church chores, teaching Sunday school; then Pastor Krueger found her a part-time clerical job in Olympia, the office of missionary and social services of his conservative branch of the Baptist Church. While at this future-less job she undertook missionary training, then spent four years in Angola and Bolivia before returning to answer in person a written proposal of marriage from Thomas Struthers, with whom she had carried on a correspondence since missionary school.

Clearly, Beatrice needs Thomas's support for her coming ordeal, and I try to bring him out, asking questions about his work, but he is laconic in response: he is conducting a project involving air pockets and wind tunnels. I try bantering with him, saying I hope he's not the guy who designed the sticking valve that held up my flight today. I barely get a smile. He picks at his salad – he'd rather be in his hobby shop.

Finally I tell them about Helen Mazur, though I withhold her name. Beatrice looks shocked, but I also read something of triumph in her face, a sense she knows she is right in what she is doing, and that this episode confirms it.

Thomas says, "How can that man be allowed to judge others?"

My spirits are quickened by his reaction. I ask, "How do you feel about it all?"

"I guess I wish it would go away." He makes what for him is a speech: "Miss Finnegan, I love my wife. I don't want to see her hurt. I'm only a few years from retirement and I'd hoped we would spend it in seclusion and peace."

"I think she needs closure on this, Mr. Struthers, if she is to enjoy those years in peace."

He finally looks directly at me. "You asked how I felt about it, and that's it. Darned unhappy about it. But let me tell you something else: I will stand by her every inch of the way. How long will it take for the case to get to trial?"

Beatrice takes his hand. It's a teary-sweet scene in the parlor off the kitchen, a couple in love exchanging shy smiles. I decide this gentleman has jam.

"I think we're talking quite a few months. There'll

have to be an extradition hearing, and I don't know how fast the courts move in Canada."

"So what do we do now?" Beatrice asks.

I tell her I'd like her to join me in a visit to a prosecutor in British Columbia.

The weather is still foul; Beatrice insists on driving me home in her Mercedes sedan. She opts for a scenic detour, along Lake Washington, which is black and sullen under the dense sky. The heaviness in the air seems to create a pensive mood.

"The other woman who was raped, was that long ago, too?"

"The same year. You will know her, I think. Gayle Mitsuka put me on to her. Oh, by the way, she said you and Vandergraaf were at the *Daily* office some days later. Did he say anything to you?"

"I don't even remember being there. I was in a terrible emotional state."

It is as if she was amnesic: when she attempted to return to classes, a thick fog settled in, broken by brief glimpses of clarity (shaking herself awake in a lecture room, feeling sick on a dormitory toilet). More clearly recalled was her explosion after she retreated to her parents' home. She accused them of being uncaring. An unchaste daughter: to them, that was the tragedy.

"You told me that before he raped you a second time you bit him on the neck — where, exactly?"

"Low, near the collarbone. The right side, I think."

"Was there blood on the bedding?"

"There must have been. It was on my clothes."

"I need to clarify one other thing — I assumed he ejaculated within you. The other woman said he didn't."

"I don't know. Maybe partly. I was sticky all over." She is, of course, blushing.

The subject is too bleak and awkward to dwell upon, and we fall silent. When I glance at Beatrice I see she is staring sadly at the vast urban lake separating Seattle from the Eastside – a few hardy obsessives are out there in their boats. To brighten the mood, I tell her about my visit to Coalsack, my overprotective concerns about Mother. She laughs.

"She sounds like a wonderful person. You're so lucky." She is thinking about her own parents, her rigid theocratic upbringing, because she says, "Father and Mother are both devastated that I'm doing this. I went up to see them yesterday. They don't want to believe I was raped. Twenty-seven years later they still don't want to believe."

"Did you tell them who your lawyer is?"

"Oh, yes, and they gave me an earful about you. They feel you're putting me up to it; I should get a second opinion. I told them they should talk to you. They'd find out what a wonderful person you are."

I am not sure why she would express such strong feelings about me; howsoever, I'm beginning to reciprocate them. J.J. would have us abide by a firm rule: don't get too close to your clients. But to me that is baloney. I do my best work for people I care for.

Having got to know Beatrice more fully, I'd like to speak to her parents again, that prim, elegant Mrs. Krueger, her tidy husband with his sonorous voice.

We double-park near the Washington Shoe Building, and Beatrice declines my offer of a hot chocolate in the loft, though I can tell she is curious about how I live. But I pause before stepping out of the car – I've noticed a man in a sodden raincoat and a baseball cap standing near my doorway. It's the same guy whose picture I took the other day: a vacant, trance-like stare, Barney Google eyes.

I'm startled when Beatrice says, "I know that man. I'm not sure from where."

"Wait here." But as I gain the sidewalk he looks my way, then quickly marches off, almost a jog. I return to Beatrice's window. "In church, maybe – is that where you saw him?"

"Maybe. Elizabeth –"

"I'm fine. Don't worry. Whoever he is, he's a coward. I'll call. Drive safely."

Of course I am not as buoyant as I pretend: the Washington Militia has my address. I unlock the street door, brave my way up the dark staircase, and quickly enter our atelier. I am going to reinforce our locks. I am not going to let them do this to me.

Home lacks the comforting presence of Nicholson Jones. His note is stuck on the fridge: he's meeting with that Alaska oilman. He had better not be late – I am escorting him to the ballet, courtesy of Curtis Kaplan.

As my tub fills, I wander about, disrobing, checking my closet for an outfit with the right flair for tonight; I play the answering machine. Curtis: "I just want you to enjoy the hell out of yourself." Making me pay the price. My biographer, Harry Crake, also calls but leaves no message; he'll phone back. The final message is from Mom. "Well, what did you think of him?" We hadn't had a chance to dissect the evening with Jake. In turn, I get her machine. "He's nice, Mom. Real charmer. Just go slow and easy for now, though, okay?"

I turn off the taps and ease myself into my hot, scented bath, and for a moment lie still, listening to the rain rattling the panes of glass, to the creaks and moans of our old building. I am overcome again by that feeling of being a stranger in a strange land, *une âme perdue*, a lost soul. It's oppressive. It causes another bout of anxiety. I wish I knew its source.

Washed and scrubbed, my hair blown dry, I pad aimlessly about in my robe and slippers, looking for something to distract me from this sudden mysterious state of inner dissatisfaction. A welcome ring from the phone, and it's Harry Crake.

"I thought we might start off by getting to know each other better. Say, over dinner."

A kind of date? I might enjoy that. "Where do you have in mind?"

"How about my place?"

Sounds dangerous. "Sure. When?"

"Tomorrow?"

I teach at Seattle U. all Monday afternoon, a strenuous day. But what day isn't? "It's a done deal. Oh, say, your paper did a long interview with Hugh Vandergraaf some time back. Do you think I could get a copy?"

"No problem. What's up?"

"Just doing a little digging. So how do I find you?"

He gives me directions: a houseboat on Lake Union. I don't think I will mind being better acquainted with Harry Crake. Spirits are raised, the gremlins are creeping off to their cold, dark dens.

As I am trying on an outfit – I'm thinking formal, my little hip-hugging tuxedo suit – Nick finally arrives, stomping into my room, venting, histrionic.

"I told that flatulent Alaska gas-bag I'm through. I will not play a part in the gutting of that fine old house. A sunken hot tub in the indoor garden was the last straw. I have my standards. Give me a drink."

I hand him his martini. "We're just having a quick salad and sandwich. We've only got an hour. Get dressed."

"You're *not* wearing that. It's the most utterly unfeminine thing. I want to see legs. Wear something short and shocking or I will not go with you."

"I am not putting myself on show."

I pursue him to his bedroom, where he starts

shuffling through his own clothes. "Then *I* will go formal." In the manner of a butterfly: he draws from his closet a maroon jacket, chartreuse pants.

"Well, I guess by now you've had that long heart-to-heart with Stephane."

"One finds it simply impossible to go to a ballet straight." He finds his stash of marijuana in a drawer, begins rolling up a joint.

"Oh, God, you didn't call him."

"Princess, it's the weekend. I can't very well phone his *house*. Anyway, I'll see him tonight. He and Maxine go to all these things."

"You didn't tell me *that* – I'm not going."

"Their seats are lower balcony, you won't see them. I'll slip out during intermission and try to catch him in the drink lineup." That smacks of truly awkward planning. Why do I have a sense Nick is not taking this seriously enough?

"Toke?"

"No, thanks, I'm having enough trouble with reality as it is." I get reefer madness. Nick likes the potent strains: after one suck I become inoperative.

As he puffs away, I tell him about the character who was hanging around the building. His response is, well, it's a busy neighborhood, there are always people hanging around.

"In the rain?"

"Now, pet, let's not be seeing apparitions everywhere, it puts such a damper on things."

I am actually becoming high by standing near him, so I escape to my own room. I am suddenly tempted toward the risqué: the tight black microskirt and stilettos, and maybe a hot-red lipstick. The backsliding feminist *femme fatale*.

When Nick emerges from the shower and sees me adding the final touch, a gold anklet, he applauds. "An ankle chain, perfect: she's a prisoner of love. The ladies will gasp and the gentlemen drool with envy. Why, they wonder, is this long-stemmed rose being wasted on that flamingly obvious fairy?"

When he is loaded on his favorite brand – home-grown Yakima Whack – Nick becomes poetic in a brain-garbled way.

"How many hearts will she capture tonight, how many men will toss sleepless abed, haunted by this vision of Elizabethan Finneganic elegance? I will not be able to beat them off. But they'll be doing that themselves, won't they, pet?"

I do an entrechat, my hands clasped above my head. My mood has done a quick change; I am ready for the evening.

"Tonight, will she meet her knight in shining armor bright? I worry about you, princess. I think you need someone to love."

"You'll have to do."

"Is she waiting for Mr. Perfect?" And he dances off to get dressed, singing, "Some day my prince will come." The nuances are suggestive.

Though I find Stravinsky too discordant for my uneducated ears, the music is vibrant and inspires spectacular dance. I wonder where Curtis came upon such good seats, half a dozen rows from the front. I shouldn't feel guilty – probably a gift from a client.

Nick is wholly engrossed: he actually mumbled something non-disparaging about the 1910s set and seems taken with the primo ballerino. Lost in dance and music, I feel myself spinning free from my other whirling world.

Intermission intrudes; I will remain attached to this seat through its thirty minutes. Maxine Vradjik is some-where in this hall.

"Come," Nick says. "Let us circulate among the denizens of upper society."

"I thought you were going to track Stephane down."

He takes my hand and pulls me to my feet. "You're being wasted here, a flower unseen in the wilderness."

Common sense tells me to stay, but I ought not to become a kind of phantom of the ballet because other persons mucked up, and I head out to the mezzanine lounge with him.

While he joins a drink line, I take up a station, by the railing, which offers an extended view, but not of Stephane or Maxine. Many dress shirts are in evidence, local business barons, a few of them morose, brought here by wives bejeweled, *en grande toilette*. As Nick promised, I find myself the target of numerous eyes. Those who know me – and several lawyer acquaintances are here – will have grist for the office gossip mill: did you check out the feminist in hooker drag? I try to convince myself my outfit makes a subtle, humorous statement.

I recognize a politician or two, the mayor, two state legislators, some senior partners of Davis, Wright, Tremaine, one of the biggest firms in town. There's William Christiansen, the libel-law expert. Justice Laura Towney, from the State Supreme Court. Joe Bigelow, from my own office, who does tax hearings. He salutes me with his drink.

And there, walking stiffly side by side, come the Vradjiks. She is a tall woman, and most attractive in her ankle-length dress, a green match for her emeralds. I slip behind a broad back, wait for a few seconds, but I can't help taking a peek. Stephane is paying for drinks. Maxine has disappeared from view. I start sidling toward Nick, to warn him, but she suddenly walks across my path, and I brake. She stops and turns. She stares. She approaches.

"You're Elizabeth Finnegan, aren't you?"

"I'm afraid so." I suppose she has seen pictures of me.

"How are you enjoying it so far?"

I assume she means the ballet. Maybe something else. "It's quite beautiful."

She takes a quick, full measure of me. "Yes. I can see why he'd be attracted. I've heard about your women's-rights work. Is this what the liberated female wears these days? I must be out of touch."

"Ms. Vradjik, would it be all right if I phoned you tomorrow? This isn't a good place to talk."

"I take it breaking up someone's marriage doesn't offend any of the principles you hold."

I start to walk away, but she follows in hot pursuit. "No, please, Elizabeth, there are some questions I want to ask."

"Not here."

"Just *stop* avoiding me." Her voice has raised, and others are turning toward us. I slow down and sigh, and face her. This is awful.

"Ms. Vradjik, I'm afraid there's been a mistake. I am not seeing your husband. I have never gone to bed with him. If he told you that, he lied."

"He won't make love to me any more. He doesn't even try. When do you do it? When he claims he's working in the lab?"

"This is *enough*, okay?" Ears everywhere are tuning in. Come in, Nick, where are you? We have an emergency. I want to blurt out the truth: Stephane is gay; he's in love with another man. But Maxine becomes even louder, and suddenly seems to go unglued, her eyes wild and hot.

"You're nothing but a whore, a cheap slut!"

Shocked faces swim by, Justice Towney, Joe Bigelow; this will be all around the office, all around town. Rushing toward us now are Stephane and Nick, but I keep marching, my face as red as a fall tomato.

I sit through the rest of the ballet in a state of black dismay. If this *danse macabre* really happened, if it wasn't a waking nightmare, I am the laughingstock of the Pacific Northwest.

My fury at Nick is so total that I cannot find words to express it, even in the soundproof privacy of our home. Recoiling from my malevolent silent stare, he begs forgiveness, promises curative action. Now, a headache, pliers twisting at my brain, and I'm holding myself tight for fear I will disassemble and fly off in all directions.

"Princess, please, I just didn't find a chance to *deal* with Stephane. He took her home immediately. I'll go over there tomorrow and straighten it out, I promise on my deathbed."

I stalk off to the washroom and gulp down a couple of aspirins, then climb into what seems my own deathbed, demons swirling in the darkness with their whispered maledictions.

As Mattie Crooks hands me an offering from the morning mail, she sticks her finger in her open mouth as if trying to gag. I pick up the envelope by the edge, like a soiled tissue. "How would you feel if you got sucked up a vacuum tube to die, you whooring conkubine of Satan." My pro-life pen pal. This time his note is in ink, and there are a couple of smudges.

I stick it carefully back into its envelope. "Please take this to Ellen Oversmith at police headquarters. Handle with care." I hand her, as well, the roll of film with the picture I took of Barney Google's behind. "Suspect number one."

"Freak city. Jeez, Liz, you look like shit. Is this getting to you?"

"Something is. Whole big fiasco last night. Tell you after I shoot up."

Uproarious laughter is coming from the coffee lounge, and I know why as soon as I enter: my comrades fall silent, and Joe Bigelow suddenly glances at his watch, drains his cup, and dashes off. Junior Plum wears an infuriating smile, but the others look embarrassed.

"Goddamnit, Junior, wipe that obscene grin off your face, you look like a sick cat. No, it's not true, none of it, I didn't . . . He's *gay*, for Christ's sake. Oh, never mind, it's too garbled. Just don't go around spreading false rumors, Junior, or I'll haul you into court for slander."

Curtis Kaplan is here, too, looking at me with reproach, as if he thinks I'm bluffing, or covering up. Even Franca Crabtree is regarding me with a big arched eyebrow.

"Is J.J. in yet?" I ask. "I have to talk to him." The time has arrived to let the boss in on a real scandal, Vandergraaf, prepare him for the uproar.

"I don't think he'll be in today," Junior says. "He's not feeling well. This incident, of course, isn't exactly the medicine he needs to buck him up. Were any judges present?"

"Yes, along with the entire *cream* of Seattle society. It was the worst night of my life. Anything in the papers?"

"No," says Junior. "Praise be to Allah. I'd like to see a report about this messy business on my desk by noon."

"No, Junior, I'm not going to feed your masturbation fantasies."

I take a long gulp of coffee, feel its surge of energy. I take a refill back to my desk, turn my back for a moment on a loaded in-basket, and stare out into the gloom. I hear the door close behind me. Curtis hovers somewhere near.

"Thanks for the tickets. Made my weekend."

"I'm there for you if it helps. That woman must have, uh, lost her balance. The jealousy thing. There's one guy in my Saturday group who actually had to be hospitalized when his wife had an affair, he got so sick."

He's at my side now. He puts his arm around my shoulders. "Is there anything I can do? I told you I'll always be there for you as a friend. I mean it."

Maybe I am not listening to my inner ear, but I am seduced by his bromidic words of comfort and let my body snuggle into his. I feel him tremble, and momentarily fear he will assume wrong and make something serious of this, but he merely pats my shoulder, then releases me, and administers a rather skilled massage between my shoulder blades. Maybe he has conquered his infantile infatuation.

Curtis knows Nicholson, so when I tell him about

how this comedy of errors came about, he's quick to understand, and he persuades me to join him in a chuckle over it. He continues his gentle massage.

"Look, maybe I can talk to this Mrs. Vradjik for you. My trial is off, their last offer is ballpark, so I've got some time. Let me mediate."

That seems a good idea. Nick has failed me. The truth has to come out. Let the chips fall where they may.

"That's what friends are for."

"Thanks, Curtis."

Mattie's main task this morning is detective work: the dredging up a critical and hopefully alive witness to Beatrice's twenty-seven-year-old bruises — that long-haired female waiter from Pender Island — and also to locate the other couple from the sailing trip. If she finds the task too consuming, we'll use our staff investigator.

While she is on the phone, I sit and gather my strength. I will do this. I will make contact with the enemy.

After his bailiff gives him my message, the Honorable Hugh Hustle rather promptly calls me back. He is guarded, over-polite: "Yes, Ms. Finnegan, what can I do for you?"

"I thought we might have a private chat, Your Honor."

A pause. He is wondering if the female chauvinist pig seeks to make amends.

"I should think that can be arranged. When would you like to meet?"

"Would tomorrow be a good time?"

"I'll be waiting for a jury. Feel free to come by about late morning."

Still cautious, but friendlier. I see him placing the phone back on the cradle, musing, perhaps thinking about the possibilities, running his fingers through his long, cascading hair. Yes, I will beard the lion in his den.

Mattie on the speaker: "There's a couple to see you. Reception told them you only take appointments, but . . . it's Beatrice Struthers's parents: Johann and Amy Krueger."

I go swiftly to the waiting room. Reverend Krueger stands; he wears a suit formal enough for a funeral, his wife just as austere, in navy blue – it is as if they have just walked out of a Victorian melodrama.

Pastor Krueger bows, a European mannerism. "I apologize if this creates an inconvenience."

"Not at all. I'm pleased to see you both." They hesitate when I extend my hand, but take it. He has a tight grip, but Amy's is soft and tentative. She is cautious, out of her element, but carefully absorbing everything, like someone strolling through a wildlife park. Her eyes widen as we pass by Mattie at her desk. Here is something satanically exotic: a frizzy-topped African American with nose rings.

They sit. I ask if they would like coffee or tea or juice. They decline. Johann Krueger clears his throat.

"Mrs. Krueger and I are quite ill at ease being here. Frankly, your office might be the last place in all of creation that we would wish to visit." The big voice that emanates from this little man rises in sermon-like pitch. "But we are brought together despite a seemingly unbridgeable gap in our understanding of the word of God and your defiance of the wondrous miracle that is the process of human procreation –"

Amy Krueger softly interrupts. "Please, dear, don't."

He continues in a less wrathful tone: "Beatrice said you would be willing to talk about this very difficult matter."

"Mr. Krueger, I'd like to know why you object to what she's doing."

Johann looks at Amy. She studies her hands.

"Miss Finnegan, I cannot allow myself to believe you are an uncaring person. I cannot accept that you see this shameful business only in terms of political profit or as an opportunity to bolster your career —"

"Johann," says his wife. He wants to rail; Amy may have a different agenda.

"Yes. Very well. As I say, if you care for Beatrice, please be warned that what you are doing will only bring harsher tragedy to her life. Our daughter has not been blessed with great emotional stability. She was in a depressed state for many years. We, ah, consigned her to a place for help, in fact." He breaks eye contact. "May I assume she told you she twice attempted suicide that same year?"

I am a little shocked, but maybe I shouldn't be. She had undergone incredible trauma.

"Mr. Krueger, doesn't your sense of morality rebel at the idea of someone like Judge Vandergraaf sitting in judgment over others? Don't tell me he will be judged himself, because that doesn't undo his harm. He raped your daughter."

A long silence, then he says, "Did he, indeed? And you know this for a fact."

"I expect one of the reasons Beatrice is doing this is to convince you it really happened."

I want to give them a tongue-lashing: What solace were *you* offering? What support? You greeted her with callous disbelief and you still stubbornly hold to it. You're the ones who sent her over the edge. *Consigned* her to a place for help — likely fundamentalist brainwashing.

"How can you not believe your own daughter? How could you not feel shame?"

But Johann remains composed. "For one thing, Miss Finnegan, she did not tell us of this . . . strange business until nearly three weeks later. We had her undress and there were no signs of injury. She has always indulged in fantasies, lives in a world –"

Amy once again restrains him, her hand on his arm.

Johann's voice becomes muted. "Please understand, we love our daughter: she is a precious gift. We cannot bear to see her wounded."

I rise and turn to the window, not wanting them to see how anger and sorrow have brought me so close to tears – such a chasm separates me from these people. *We love our daughter.* Do they, really?

"I had never dreamed I would find myself asking anything of you, Miss Finnegan. Except that which I would ask of anyone, to search their soul and seek the word of Jesus. But now I beg of you: save her from the agony she will suffer."

I still cannot look at them, and stare into the desolate gloom of this cloud-darkened day, the leaden waters of the sound.

"Mr. and Mrs. Krueger, I am going to ask you a question. Please be absolutely truthful with me."

All I hear is shuffling.

"Do you know who bombed the abortion clinics?"

"I think we should go," Johann says.

I whirl and face them; he is rising. "It's a simple question. Why can't you answer it?"

Amy Krueger grasps Johann's hand, directing him back to his seat.

"We do not support that kind of action," she says.

I move close to her, bending so I can look directly into her eyes. "Of course you don't. But you have some idea who's behind it, don't you?"

Another look passes between them, more telling than speech.

"Who throws firebombs on the Holy Day? Search *your* hearts."

"Johann has spoken against it," she says softly.

I turn to him. "To whom? Does he attend your church?" The man lounging outside my apartment building in the rain: Beatrice was sure she had seen him before.

"By what right do you ask me to betray those who have sought my counsel, Miss Finnegan, however misguided they may be?"

"It's not just one man," Amy begins, "I think there's a group —"

And now it's Johann's turn to censor her. "That's quite enough, dear. We shall be going now." They both stand.

"Whoa, hold on. What group?"

"Mrs. Krueger was merely speculating," says Johann.

At the door, Amy Krueger abruptly turns and looks pleadingly at me. "Please help us."

Help *us*? Why are they so desperate? "My task is to help Beatrice. This group — would you be willing to talk to the police?"

But Johann is at the door, tugging at Amy, who hesitates, then dutifully walks out behind her husband.

A group . . . they know who the bombers are: it was written on their faces in billboard letters. I dictate a memo, recording this conversation while it is fresh: a group of men, that means at least three, probably members of Reverend Krueger's flock — the True Gospel Baptist Chapel in Lynden is his bailiwick.

Then I call Detective Ellen Oversmith and fill her in. Go up to Lynden, I urge, visit the Kruegers, lean on them gently if you have to. This could be the break we've long sought.

I phone Mother, and we have an animated conversation about Jake Bjorklund. I try not to douse her moonstruck dreams, and again I counsel caution. "Don't jump into anything just yet, okay?" I don't tell her I'm waiting for the results of my inquiries as to whether Jake has a criminal c.v.

I spend the rest of the morning preparing notes for this afternoon's lecture at our inner-city college, Seattle U. It's a Catholic institution but liberal, and the Seattle Office for Women's Rights sponsors my adult extension class, oriented to embattled homemakers. Inspired by my contretemps with Maxine Vradjik, I will talk to them today about the legal consequences of marriage breakdown.

By afternoon, the rain has slackened to a drizzle, and I take to the streets by foot, a stretch of ten blocks up to the campus atop First Hill. My route takes me through Freeway Park, along pedestrian bridges over I-5, that ugly scar across the city's midsection, and while I am walking among the flower beds and waterfalls above the screaming canyon I again sense a presence. I am being followed.

I do not turn, but stroll toward an alcove above the freeway and fumble in my bag for the pepper spray. But this is a very unsafe place. I am trapped. Who would hear my screams above the waterfall and traffic roar? Raped, mutilated, my naked body flung onto the path of an eighteen-wheeler . . . But no one passes by. I peek out. No one there.

Get a grip.

Feeling foolish, I shake my head to rid it of its capricious pixies, then toil up to Broadway and Madison, to the cramped campus, and into the Patricia Wismer Building.

Though I am still recovering from a bad night, I surprise myself by being reasonably eloquent and rather funny, and I soon have my attentive audience of thirty involved in a relaxed free-for-all. They are eager to learn how to put a hold on the bank account of the ungrateful adulterer for whom they've slaved in kitchen and bed after working all day at office or plant or store. Many of these women have been through bad relationships and have examples of their own to relate.

I feel complimented by the groans that greet my announcement that I have arranged for a substitute for three months starting in January. Those commission hearings will take me to Washington, Detroit, Houston, Los Angeles. Though I dread the long flights, I will enjoy a lull from my taxing Seattle practice: wedged in among twenty other counsel, I will be lucky to slip a few words in. The job will be easy digging, as they say in Coalsack.

Lecture over, I call a taxi – I must rush home to dress for my dinner date with Harry Crake. I am wondering: should I arm myself with a prophylactic device? That seems too bold and presumptuous.

The hundreds of floating homes on the south shore of bustling Lake Union comprise a community in which streets are canals and sidewalks are cedar boards. Many of the new structures are tony; decades ago, most were cozy bohemian hideaways. Harry Crake's place appears to be one of the originals: funky, single-story, shake roof, about as unkempt as Harry. He greets me on the floating dock, smelling of whiskey.

Inside is a low-ceilinged central area, a bed unmade in a narrow room just off it. In the kitchen, a small table is laid out, wine glasses on it. Atop the stove, a steaming pot.

"Bouillabaisse, specialty of the house." A slight slurring; I can see he is working on a bottle of Jack Daniel's. "Here's that interview we did on Vandergraaf." He hands me an envelope. "You've got something on him?"

"I can't talk yet. Stay tuned."

What Harry's tuned into is a football game, his eyes drifting over to a small set in the corner, the sound turned low but audible. "Finds a hole up the middle, and, oh, he's stuffed." "He's not getting up, Dan." What a graceless sport, three-hundred-pound tubs crawling over each other.

"Green Bay and Dallas," he says, maybe expecting me to appreciate the momentous nature of the match. I have never been able to make head or tail of this game.

I peer closely at some snapshots arranged about his desk. A smiling woman, vaguely Asian. A tow-haired boy of twelve or so.

"My wife and son. I get him alternate weekends."

"Oh, I'm sorry. Is this a recent break-up?"

"Last May. Twice a month plus two weeks in summer – that's all the goddamn judge gave me. Along with a license to tap me dry. I have a secret for you, Liz. The legal system sucks."

"You've been through the family-court mill."

"I've been through the mill, all right."

This subject seems to put him on a slow burn: there is a corrosive quality to him now. Feeling discomfort, I fall into nervous chatter, but probably err in choosing as my topic that lively session today at Seattle U. about a wife's rights in marriage. He says, "Yeah, what about a husband's rights? Who teaches that?"

"Well, it's the same. Rights are equal."

"That's why she gets the house and I get to rent a crummy houseboat. That's why she gets custody."

"What caused the break-up?"

"Sheer incompatibility. I loved her. She hated me. So we didn't fit. *I'm* the victim of mental cruelty, but *she* wins the separation. Guess I had the wrong lawyer."

"But you're still married? It was just a court-ordered separation?"

"Yeah, and I'm going to appeal it. Do you mind if we talk about it a little bit?"

"Um, well, sure."

And all through dinner – to the obscene background

noise of players going up the middle and into the end zone – I hear about his separation proceedings and the many insults and wrongs he was subjected to. The old song: he's a victim of male-bashing, discriminated against by the system, economically enslaved by his parasitic wife, deprived of visitation, his son brainwashed against him by a selfish absentee mother who refuses to give up her career in real estate.

I try to lead him away from this self-pitying history, gently guiding the conversation to the subject I assumed we were to talk about: me. Though he asks a few questions about my career, he remains gloomy and dispirited, and eventually switches me off in favor of the tube. "Clock ticking. Swing pass to Smith in the slot – and, oh, did he get clotheslined." "Let's look at that injury again, Al." Let's not. But Harry seems to find morose pleasure watching the replay.

So much for the romantic evening: I misread this blood-sports fan. My worst fears are confirmed when he turns off the set and starts hauling out bulky legal files: family court orders, lawyers' letters, transcripts. I am to pay for dinner with legal advice.

And of course I am trapped into doing so: he is to author a feature article in *City Living Magazine*. I do feel sympathy for him: he should have more access to his son, of whom he is obviously fond. But I am beginning to see why this marriage didn't work.

As intoxicated as he becomes, he makes no first-down pass attempts, and I'm definitely not in a mood to catch any. Anyway, he probably wants his wife back: in unguarded moments he speaks caringly of her.

He asks a few more questions about me, scrawls a few notes, and tells me he now has a "sense" of me. By ten o'clock I'm smothering yawns. I apologize, tell him I had a long day after a rough night, and we agree to finish this so-called interview another day.

"So you don't think I should appeal," he says, escorting me back out to the dock.

"Move it out of the courts. You both belong in a counselor's office."

"We tried."

"Make some changes, Harry. Try again."

"Like what changes?"

He stumbles over a plank, nearly falls into Lake Union.

"Like stop drinking."

It is midnight when – after ensuring the doorstep of the Washington Shoe Building is free of lurkers – I alight from a cab. Though the staircase light has burnt out, I manage the climb to the loft with a minimum of paranoia. I am hoping Nick is still awake so I can hear his latest excuses about *l'affaire* Vradjik, but I can hear him snoring in his bedroom.

On an easel in his studio, a newly started work: two people reaching out for each other, but there is fear in their faces. I take my research paper to bed with me, "Birthright or Wrong." It puts me to sleep.

I dream of couples coming together and splitting apart like amoebas.

The inquiring moon sends shimmering reflections from the sea and from the snow-thick beaches of Whidbey Island as we speed on newly sprouted wings of Zephyrus, past Useless Bay, Mutiny Bay, toward Mystery Bay and Deception Pass — how aptly named, these coves and inlets of our ghostly northwest coast. The Wandering I *dips through a foam-flecked sea, jib, mainsail, and mizzen taut and straining, the stays singing a shrill lament.*

But I sing boldly back: accept what is; the moving finger writes, and having writ, moves on. The uncensored history of Vandergraaf is done, complete; the bad cannot be bowdlerized to suit the stern correctors of word and deed who march in triumphant victory through the streets of our brave new world. I am me, unsanitized, culturally inconvenienced, the same assistant idiot of the porno ring who stared down Beatrice Krueger's blouse. Forgive me as I am — or cast me out with the useless refuse of your past; I care not.

But know this: I am forever in your skin as you are in mine. There is a cellular consciousness we share in brain and gut and muscle, a vigor, a drive, a commitment to risk, an aptitude for a life lived hard. From each of our hearts flows a social conscience, too, though I hear you scoff. The rapacious predator really flatters himself.

Very well, have it your way. I have compromised an expendable slice of my soul — but only in the knowledge that great objectives cannot be attained without small sacrifices of honor. (Cut the liberal crap, Eddie ordered, a congressional hearing is coming. You've matured, you're realistic, hard-headed like your father). If I have lately seemed to falter and appease, understand that I am also older and softer by a generation. In my time, I fought as hard, shouted as loud, petitioned, marched, condemned.

121

Unmask that angry young revolutionary. Seek beneath the strut and smugness and you will find a naked, frightened survivor of the refugee camps we call military bases. In Okinawa or Panama or Lubbock, Texas, the same oppressive stench of duty and firm belief, of faith in America, in her supremacy. The stifling schools, the spiritless streets and playgrounds . . . the saluting obsequious lieutenants, the bed-hopping generals, the alcoholic wives who knew their place and silently suffered.

And you're speculating, yep, that fits, seen it before. Adulterous abusive father, a mother who hides the vodka behind the cans of noodle soup. Ineffective parenting, inadequate role models.

She finally left him — and me, as I was in my adolescence. Why did I blame her, not him? But I felt rejected, cast untimely from her bosom . . . anyway, she had always disapproved of me, the recalcitrant child, the pouting little rebel who didn't fit within the family mold. She favored Jerome, of course, the hero, the firstborn who inherited my father's warrior mantle. And though I loved Jerome, I held for her only resentment and antipathy. So what was going on? Perhaps your estimable Dr. Boorstein should listen to this; she is a clever woman, I am told, and might light a path for you through my mental smog.

Mother died many years ago, spiteful, lonely, rejected more by me than I by her — I was not at her funeral, and even before her passing I had expelled her from my mind. Does that sound cruel? It is impossible to convey an image of the immeasurable gulf that divided us.

My father's life was almost as tragic. You can't knife your way up through the ranks without cost to your sense of self-worth. Unless you're a psychopath.

In all those early years I had no friends but one — my brother. Jerome was braver than I, reckless, with an insatiable appetite for life. Betrayed by that warped sense of obligation trained into firstborn sons — and thoughtlessly encouraged by our mother — he enlisted. And he paid the price. When the phone call came I fled to my bedroom — home was Tacoma by then, McChord Air Force Base. I couldn't cry. I listened over and over to an LP I bought that day. Dylan. The times they are a-changin'. Only a pawn in their game. When my father called it music for chickenhearted ninnies, I spun the album against his wall of medals, and marched back to college shouting Ho-Ho-Ho Chi Minh.

When he died I shed no tears. But I finally cried for my brother.

Upon your visit to my chambers did you see his picture on the wall? Jerome, my hero . . .

I was pleased that you'd come, by the way, and was not inflated with any sense of victory. What I said I meant: I admired your spunk. Did I leave enough for a tip? In the rapture of the moment, I can't remember.

What time is it? How far to journey's end? Never mind. For this brief dark span of time I am where I must be, alone under brittle stars and pulling moon, upon the swelling bosom of the sea. . . . Tomorrow comes too soon, but when the cold grip of night gives way to our ultimate day of destiny I shall be there to meet it. I am ready; I am eager; the wind is at my back.

8 | Tuesday . . .

As I tank up at my neighborhood Starbucks, I spread out the clipping Harry gave me, written shortly after Vandergraaf's election in 1996. The heading is in quotation marks: "For the People not the State." But which people? A photo of the new judge in his robe, smiling, leaning back, feet on desk. It says: hey, I'm not one of your stuffy old farts.

The article is replete with advertisements for his fair-mindedness, couched in a cautious, almost pandering turn of phrase. "'I believe the individual must always precede the state, which exists only to serve its masters' democratic wishes.' Though of liberal bent he is quick to affirm that politics must remain outside the courtroom. 'I see my role as a dispassionate arbiter between proponents of opposite but often deeply felt belief.'" He fears he will not satisfy everyone; judges never do. However fair, they are damned for being wrong by half the litigants they face, while burdened by fear of error and injustice, and so on.

As to matters personal, the story is skimpy. Born February 1949, which makes him forty-nine: twenty-two in 1971. Two years in the Peace Corps. Former senior partner in an aggressive mid-sized firm, several benchmark trials involving civil rights. Sadly, he says, he has never enjoyed the comforts of marriage: "'I am unfairly accused of being single-minded, too wedded to my work,' he said with a laugh." He lives up in Ballard in an "unpretentious" waterfront bungalow.

Interesting: a prominent Democrat, former chair of the party's state committee, a major backroom broker. A truncated political career, though: a run for Congress several years ago. "Thankfully, I was mugged by the electorate. I think they showed good taste." A genial self-deprecating touch: no bloated delusions of grandeur here. I recall having skimmed this article a few years ago, deeming that it depicted a likable man.

Oddly, I did not know him well when he was in practice, though we were both engaged in civil-liberties causes. We shared a courtroom for half a day here and there. He was always affable, even charming. In my innocence I failed to translate the message from those probing eyes. They were saying: I'm game if you are.

I had fantasies over him. How sick.

Old New York Dutch, the article says. His father a deceased air-force general, a Second World War hero who, after retiring from the service, joined the board of the Typhon Corporation, a munitions giant. A military father, an arms dealer, is that what warped Hugh? Was his self-professed liberalism a way of sticking it to an unloving father? He also recently lost his mother. His only sibling, a brother, died in Vietnam. I sense a sadness – he was "much attached" to him.

How does he spend his spare time? Reading, reading, reading: a devotee of classic literature. Recreation? "Keeping fit is one of my healthier obsessions. Running, tennis, old boys' baseball, skiing in the winter." He has a small chalet up by Mount Baker, near the Canadian border. "But my happiest moments, my most precious, are spent upon the sea. I love its freedom, its lonely splendor." He owns a thirty-five-foot ketch.

One day I'll have a boat like that . . .

I gulp down my coffee, head uptown. A pleasant day at last: ocean breezes, fluffs of cotton dappling a deep blue sky.

Junior, almost predictably, is standing guard as I exit the elevator. The human time clock: I am late punching in.

"Eleven hours and zero-nine minutes. How good of you to finally grace us with your presence." He waves the morning paper. "It's in the gossips." He reads: "'The ballet was just as entertaining between acts, when a society matron used some choice words to accuse a well-known feminist lawyer of doing a *pas de deux* with her husband.'"

"I'm beyond caring, Dwight. Is J.J. in today?"

"He has a bad flu."

"There's something very important I'd like to talk to him about."

Junior tracks after me to Mattie's desk; she is on the phone. "Then you should talk to me."

I don't intend to offend his delicate ears with sordid tales about his old pal. He will find out soon enough.

"If it's something that important, then I should know." Hovering over the desk, he picks up a transcript of my interview with Beatrice. I snatch it from his fingers.

"Junior, I'll mind my business; please do likewise. Is J.J. seeing visitors? How about this evening?"

Junior rolls off on his ball-bearing legs. "I'll call him."

Mattie puts the phone down. "That resort up on Pender Island? They say it burned down about twenty years ago; it's been rebuilt, but they lost all the employment records. So far, no luck with Hugh's boating buddy either, Mr. Dumbo."

"Okay, hon, keep at it. Look, has that big oaf been snooping around here a lot?"

"You want me to hide the file?"

"Yes, and please wipe everything from the hard drive. Make about three backups first, give one to me and hide the others."

"Check."

"Also, can you find out who prosecutes cases up on this Pender Island and make an appointment for tomorrow? Just tell them it's about a rape complaint involving a prominent person. That should pique their interest."

The day's mail includes a pious screed awash with Bible citations, but nothing else has arrived from the zealots today; maybe they've reached the end of their attention span. An invitation to address the Women's Executive Club. More briefs to read for the commission on reproduction. No calls from Helen Mazur in Spokane. Has her free-spirited daughter, Terry, yet persuaded her to do the brave thing? If you were raped, I told Helen, it's entirely between you and me. I may have erred in granting such a wide undertaking.

"Here's the print you wanted."

For what it's worth: the retreating rear end of the commander of the Washington Militia – or whomever.

I pop into Franca's office. "Were they able to run those fingerprints on Jake Bjorklund?"

"One piddly piss-ass bounced check, a hundred-dollar fine and restitution. He beat another charge, insider trading."

I don't know what my reaction is. Some disappointment, a sense of affirmation, but relief that he is not on any most-wanted list. I suppose he's just a fiddler with half-baked dreams. For now, I'll avoid playing matchbreaker; Mom's happiness is all that matters.

"Got to run. I have a heavy date with Hugh Hustle."

"Don't get him too riled up. I'm in court with him Friday, the Bremerton Loans thing. He may be a prick, but he's a defense-minded prick."

"How do you think I should handle him?"

"Keep your legs closed. He's so cute, though. I'd be tempted."

"Franca, you're disgusting."

"Oh, *you've* thought about it."

"Yeah, right, constantly." That's history.

Lawyers are moping outside Vandergraaf's court with the strained expressions of those who wait for juries. The defendant is pacing in the corridor – he's in trouble: .09, a missed stop sign, and someone killed in the other car.

The courtroom is empty but for Vandergraaf's tiny, pretty bailiff, who nods somewhat sourly and points me toward his chambers door. It's open, and I can hear him talking in precise, clipped consonants.

He is in his shirtsleeves, dictating an opinion into a recorder, quoting from a casebook, unaware of me at his doorway. I must assume he is a hard-working judge – between tennis and sailing and all his reading, reading, reading. Reluctantly, I have to admire him for his vigorous life, his ethic of *mens sana in corpore sano*. He looks in excellent shape – outwardly, that is. Who knows what resides within?

Walls that are not filled with books display various framed degrees and certificates and a photo of a smiling, confident young man in uniform. His brother? No bemedalled father up beside him. There is a kind of intellectual untidiness about his space, books lying open, piled on chairs.

Now he starts chewing the end of a pencil. It is something I do regularly; Nicholson finds it disgusting.

I knock. He starts, looks up, then rises like a gentleman: a lady is coming in.

But he doesn't offer his hand – there are matters that remain unforgiven. My first task will be to unruffle his feathers. Do I feel badly about the subterfuge I am about to enter into? Mildly underhanded, yes, but for the greater good.

I am directed to a deep padded chair beside his desk, close to him, four feet away. I sink into it, too low, uncomfortable: my skirt rides up and I'm forced to keep my knees tight.

"Is that sad-faced man out there guilty or innocent?"

"Innocent. It was a lapse of judgment. But the jury will convict. I'm aiming at around three or four years. Do you approve of that, or would you have something to say to the media about it?"

"All right, judge, I'm sorry. I walked out into a sea of microphones and said the first thing that came to my head. On reflection, I wouldn't have said this was an illustration of gender bias, the old boys' club. You're too much your own person."

"Ah, is this Finnegan's wake? Somehow you do not strike me as a person who wears sackcloth comfortably." His eyes flicker to my knees. I pull down my skirt, self-conscious. "Did J.J. force you into this?"

"It's a free-will gesture, Your Honor. Well, Dwight, his son, was goading me. Real admirer of yours."

He smiles. There is a change in him, a confiding tone: "My one-man fan club at law school. While some might have considered Dwight a bit of a nosepicker I found him abrasively charming."

"He's not at all like his father, is he? Someone must have slipped him the wrong genes."

"No, he's adopted." My eyes widen with surprise. "It's not much talked about. J.J. keeps his family secrets."

"I had no idea."

"Then it's our secret."

He is leaning forward now, and I feel my body stiffen and clench, resisting, defending against a disquieting pull; I remind myself he is an obsessive philanderer who objectifies women.

"Actually, I just met another old friend of yours from college days. Gayle Mitsuka."

"Ah, yes, Gayle. We worked on the *Daily* together. I wrote churlish editorials: my angry-young-man phase. How is she?"

"Full of pep. She wants to do a story on me for her magazine. To satisfy my thirst for publicity."

His face creases handsomely as he laughs. "That smarted, didn't it? I could see I got your Irish up. To confess, I admired your spunk. You *are* Irish?"

"The Ulster kind. Potato-famine immigrants. You go

back a few generations before that, I guess. Early Dutch settlers. I read a piece in the paper about you."

"They floated over in their wooden shoes, no doubt. Well, Elizabeth — I don't offend if I use your first name?"

"Of course not."

"This jury will be out for some time, so would you be interested in lunch?"

I worry: am I involved in an ethics problem? By agreeing, am I engaging in entrapment?

"If the canons of feminism proscribe the acceptance of offers from gentlemen, I will allow you to pay for your own meal."

"Lunch sounds like a pleasant idea." I will maintain a wary politesse.

I maneuver sideways from my low chair while he puts on his suit jacket. No tie. A curl of chest hair where the top two shirt buttons aren't done up.

"I know an interesting little place on Capitol Hill. If you like Greek."

"I do."

Now he is staring at my midriff. But I realize he's interested in the cellphone strapped to my belt. He writes down the number and fetches his bailiff. "Call me if the jury seems to be getting close."

The bailiff, whose name I think is Juanita, a slim Hispanic woman, takes the note, darts a quick, appraising glance at me. "Enjoy your lunch," she says, and her words seem almost sardonic.

We could call a taxi, but Vandergraaf prefers to take his top-of-the-line Land Cruiser, a step up from the old vw van. He also owns, he says, a classic Alfa Romeo, but the Toyota handles better on the steep road up to his chalet at Baker.

"Do you ski?" he asks.

"Since I was three."

I am now to be invited to his chalet. But the offer is not forthcoming; I'm a little surprised at that.

The Bacchus Restaurant is on a quiet, shaded street and is dark and snug: a wine-cellar atmosphere with murals that look more Czarist Russian than Greek. I decide I can't handle more than a salad. Hugh insists on wine with his kefthnethes, asks if I'll join him in a drink. I don't demur, and he orders a superior California Chardonnay – without asking what I might prefer.

I have no difficulty steering him to the topic of boating, and he tells me jocularly he has "oft plied the ocean blue" in a classic wooden ketch he inherited from his father. Its name (so apt a play on words): the *Wandering I*. Can it be the same boat on which Beatrice was raped? I assume so – a ketch is not that common a sailing craft.

"I over-boldly set out for Fiji once, but gave up at Hawaii." I tell him I have an unrealized passion for the sea. (What an unsubtle thing to say: it's almost as if *I'm* doing the flirting here.) Again I am expecting a come-on, but he doesn't offer to show me the ropes.

Handle this right. It is now or never and he is disarmed. A blatant lie could be just as telling as the truth, and I shall be the witness to it at his trial. The police, with their prior warnings, would be greeted with stony silence while a battery of lawyers speed to the scene.

"Here's a memento from your past I came across." I show him the old photo from the UW student paper. "That's Gayle. That's you."

He chuckles over it. "Where did you find *this*? 'Porno ring uncovered.' I'm totally embarrassed."

"April Fool's issue."

"Oh, I remember, our annual attempt at sophomoric humor. The assistant idiot. I do look like quite the idiot, staring down at that girl that way."

"Do you remember her at all?"

"Damned if I do. I don't think I can remember half these people."

"Gayle said you went out with this young woman that night."

"Really? She's rather attractive; I showed exceptional taste. I don't think I was into long relationships back then. Girls kept crossing me off their list."

"Beatrice Krueger. You don't remember going sailing with her the next day? Up in Canada?"

"I'm afraid not." He is suddenly suspicious. "Why is this important?"

"She told me you raped her."

"She . . ." His face turns pale, but there are flecks of red on his cheeks. "If this is a joke, it shows an exceptional *lack* of taste."

"It's no joke. She's a client. She intends to lay charges tomorrow."

There is now a savage darkness in his face. "Do I assume you advised her to do so?"

"Yes, of course."

"Do I also assume I'm being blackmailed?"

"Absolutely not. This isn't about money."

"You snake." He slides his chair back, sweeps out his wallet, fishes out some bills. "You vile little bitch." He rises and hurls the money on the table.

"You don't even remember her."

"You, young lady, are about to be disbarred."

And he flies off in an extreme huff. I sit there in contemplation, picking at my olives and feta cheese. Then I take another glass of wine and pen some notes about his amazing lack of memory while my own is fresh.

I return to the office to find Junior hovering about Mattie's desk, but he scurries off when he spots me.

"Gag me," says Mattie. "He asked to see what you've been working on. I told him you had the file."

The news will break soon enough: Mattie has set up a meeting tomorrow in Victoria, the B.C. capital, with one of the head prosecutors there, one Benjamin Mulholland. Seats are reserved for Beatrice and me on the *Victoria Clipper*. The trip is two hours by catamaran.

"He'll see you about four, after he's out of court. He has this real bitchy English accent. Love it."

Franca, who has been in family court, skips in to ask about my meeting with Vandergraaf, and I treat her to the entire story.

"So he didn't make any passes?"

"Not really."

"Not that you didn't invite any." A twittering voice: "Oh, I'd love to learn how to sail."

She manages to make me feel sleazy.

What else must be done before tomorrow? Helen Mazur in Spokane . . . I'll call her after the rape complaint has been filed. That might encourage her to step forward, to stand up to her imperious partner. She never once mentioned his name, always as "my husband," but the directory has him as Wilkie S. Mazur, Certified Public Accountant.

I will also visit the crime scene on Pender Island, which I have never set foot on, though I have bicycled on several of its neighbors. The Tourism B.C. Web site hadn't told me much: two islands connected by a bridge, farms, parks, trails, a couple of resort marinas. The one I intend to visit, on South Pender, is called Bedwell Harbour.

Two clients with their tales of abuse this afternoon: oft-told stories, men taking out their inadequacies on weaker others. I have trouble concentrating; I am still seeing Hugh's face, that look of enraged betrayal. The episode has strung me out. I'm sapped mentally: Maxine Vradjik, Hugh Vandergraaf, stalkers at my heels.

Curtis has left me a message, so I roam down the hall to his office, which is on the opposite side of the building: a view of Lake Washington and the Cascades. On a clear day, as this is, you can see the great white breast of Rainier to the south, Mount Baker far to the north. There it is, gleaming in the sun, cone-like. Hugh Hustle's hill. His red-faced rage at lunch still causes a slight wobbling sensation in the knees — I cannot deny my apprehension at taking on this pillar of the courts.

As Curtis looks up from the book he's reading, I say, "You don't seem to have much on your plate today."

"I've put it aside to volunteer for my favorite charity."

"Which is?" I glance down at his book. *The Art of Understanding Women*.

"You. I've talked on the phone with Maxine Vradjik. We're meeting for drinks this afternoon. In about forty-five minutes, in fact. I'm about to do a little crisis intervention."

I lie down on his couch. "What are you going to tell her?"

"I've talked to Nicholson; I have persuaded him the time has arrived for plain talk. I'm going to tell Maxine you were covering up for Stephane, and that he's involved in a same-sex relationship. Nick says they both test negative for HIV, so I'll at least be able to ease that concern."

"How did she sound on the phone?"

"Troubled, but willing to talk. I think she feels badly about the public spectacle. Junior showed me that nasty little item in the *Times*."

"Oh, God, he's been showing it to everybody."

"You look zonked. What have you been up to?"

"Where do I start? Give me one of those back massages."

He perches beside me and starts gently working along my spine. "We do this in group. Not only feels good, but lowers some of those rigid interpersonal barriers we create."

He's adept, finds all the tight muscles. You have to give Curtis credit; he tries so hard. Relaxing under his healing touch, I give him an overview of the Queen versus Vandergraaf, just the highlights, the unprivileged information. He doesn't say a word through this, and I ask him why.

"I'm thinking."

I sense doubt. And I am picking up another kind of vibration: someone else is among us. I look up. Vandergraaf's fan, the nosepicking adopted son of J.J. Plum, is standing just inside the doorway with a majestic scowl.

"Okay, Finnegan, I know what you're up to."

I am not sure what he means. Does he think he has barged in on an act of gross indecency? Then I realize he is in a very distraught state. His hand shakes as he thrusts a notice at me for tomorrow's weekly office meeting.

"You'll find yourself high on the agenda. The theme will be teamwork. Skulking about like a Gestapo spy, hiding files from the office manager, indulging in secret inquisitions of a respected member of the judiciary: these are not signs that you feel you belong." So obviously Vandergraaf has already phoned him. "Is that what you want to talk to J.J. about? I can give you his reaction. You are to call a halt to this jihad or you're out of this firm!"

He is shouting; they can probably hear it in the secretarial pool.

"Get a grip, old buddy," Curtis says. "You'll rupture something. Grab a chair."

But Junior waddles in circles, flapping his hands like flightless wings.

"He never touched that woman in his life. Rape? Hugh used to turn them away from his doorstep; he got all he wanted for free. It's bullshit and you know it. Oh, yes, you were going to get that – may I quote you – son of a bitch, even if you had to hire some floozy actress to cry rape after almost three decades."

"You are full of sour *prunes*! She came to me; she's a very proper Christian woman, and she wants to heal, she wants to scour a blemish from her past."

"Why wasn't I *informed*?"

"Because you'd just prattle away to him. I wanted to catch him unawares today."

"That is the lowest possible trick. Who do you think you are?"

"A lawyer who does a service requested by a client."

"I want to see that file on my desk in five minutes."

"You'll see nothing! I'm not having you censor my practice. What's this love-object thing you have with Vandergraaf?"

Junior stops his pacing, and though I have shouted him down, his eyes are still malevolently on me. "J.J. expects you for six o'clock cocktails. I trust you will be prepared to seek guidance from him." And the nosepicker skates off.

"I don't know, Liz." Curtis has a solemn look. "Do you want to get yourself into this?"

"You heard Junior: 'He never touched that woman in his life.' Vandergraaf told him an absolute lie. You're a witness."

Curtis has to rush off for his personal interaction with Maxine Vradjik, so we don't debate his misgivings. He'll call me this evening.

I dial out to Salon Charlène in Coalsack, feeling a need to connect with Mother. She is in high spirits: Jake is taking her out to Variety Night at the school auditorium. I don't dare mention my sneak peek at his minor past misdeeds and resist the temptation to ask if he has yet opened any silver mines. She is still mulling over his proposal. Her new-found sense of caution reassures me, and our bright, brisk chat serves as an antidote to the tension I have felt since my encounter with Vandergraaf.

I connect with Beatrice at home, just back from the campus, and arrange to meet her tomorrow at Pier 69. "How are your classes – been able to study?"

"Oh, yes, I'm what they call a wonk."

"Good for you. How are your parents?"

"Determined to be miserable."

"They came to see me."

"Yes, I was peeved at them for that."

"I think they know who's behind the clinic bombings."

"I wouldn't be surprised."

She is moving so far beyond them; I sense a growing strength in her.

It's an exhausting climb by bicycle up Queen Anne Hill, a desirable neighborhood north of Seattle Center. It was *the* better district about a century ago, but now some of the mansions have been converted to apartments. But J.J. lives in a grand home on West Highland Drive with terra cotta facing, four rambling stories.

Panting, walking my bike the last hundred yards, I attain the pinnacle, and catch not only my breath but a stunning view of Puget Sound and the Olympics, the sun descending toward their peaks with promises of awesome silent fireworks. I lean my bicycle against the garage, remove my helmet, shake out my hair, and march bravely up the stairs.

J.J. has been long widowed, but it's said he sleeps with his housekeeper, Vladmira, a buxom Russian immigrant of uncertain years. She kisses me on the mouth, then slaps me heartily on the back. She is quite outgoing.

"Always I like to see you. You are beauty for this old house. The czar waits you in drawing room. Why they say drawing room? Nobody draws."

I am led through a doorway; J.J. and Dwight are taking a glass of sherry, standing by the bay windows and staring silently out over the docks of busy Elliott Bay. J.J. is in his dressing gown, and seems well enough, though he has a tissue at the ready for his nose. Junior has the smug look of the school tattletale.

"Just a little head cold," J.J. says. "Though I was feeling a lot better before this Vandergraaf business was dumped on me. I thought I told you to go to Hawaii."

"Junior, I'd like to talk to J.J. alone. You'll only get into another flap."

Before Dwight can protest, J.J. tells him to keep Vladmira company in the kitchen, then pours me a sherry. "Sit. That's the most comfortable chair." It's a lounger, and I lean back on it. "I know one version: Hugh Vandergraaf is being hung up to dry by a vindictive young lawyer. What's the other?"

I lay it out, chapter and verse, starting with Beatrice showing up shyly at my office last week, ending with Vandergraaf storming from the restaurant about five hours ago. I also tell him of my trip to Spokane, my interview with Helen Mazur.

J.J. interrupts between nose-wipes only to clarify details. He paces, then stands at the window with his back to me. I wish he would sit down; he doesn't look in top form. I can see past him, stippled clouds daubed with pink. "Beautiful," he says, and I don't know whether he means the sunset or what I've just told him.

"It's a creaky old vehicle, isn't it?" he says finally, turning to me. "Maybe not time-limited in Canada, but still: twenty-seven years of collecting mold, dust, and rust. Minor damage, as these things go. Bruises they can't prove. Woman with a sad history of emotional difficulties. Reluctant witness in Spokane with weak evidence of doubtful admissibility. If it falls apart — or if he's found not guilty, as likely he will — you'll be elbow-deep in cow flop."

"Why? I'm just a facilitator."

"Because they'll say you were obsessed with the destruction of Hugh Vandergraaf. You will be seen as the petty, politically correct feminist whose act of vengeance backfired."

I am gaping at him in astonishment: how can he not see how tawdry and base these events were? "Candidates for the bench are rejected if they smoked *marijuana* in college, for God's sake. This guy is a mini-serial rapist. It's *not* a matter of my being *prideful*."

"But you are prideful. You are *damned* prideful. It's by far your worst quality, Elizabeth. You take slights too much to heart; it results in poor judgment. You're like a dog with a stolen bone, skulking about, doing the Canadian government's gumshoe work – and probably not well. They're going to be damned resentful."

"I can't believe I'm hearing *you*, J.J. Plum, talking like this. You hate corrupt judges. I have to tell you that Beatrice Struthers intends to have her day in court."

"Then both of you will be destroyed."

With that calm augury of disaster, he sits in an armchair. I am utterly dismayed. I had not expected J.J. would do this to me. Maybe they're *all* in it, the old boys' club, J.J., Curtis, Nicholson, too.

"Do you have any control over her?"

"Well, influence, but . . ."

"Liz, if you keep the lid on, it's to your vast advantage. Vandergraaf will be in hock to you. Hell, you'll *own* him. What sweeter revenge than to have him not only forever indebted but in cringing fear of you. That fear parlays into favors from the other rabbits up there."

"I couldn't look myself in the face if I backed off now. I couldn't practice law."

"And you might not be able to. Vandergraaf is capable of carrying out his threat to disbar you."

"Not if he's convicted." This makes me *so* sad – I

have a vast respect for J.J. Remain unruffled, I tell myself, reason with him. "I bow to your experience right down to my toes, J.J., but I don't agree it's a weak case. Beatrice is a very believable witness, and Helen Mazur is admissible as proof of similar fact."

J.J. responds to my calm defiance with some petulance. "You have to look at your future with the firm, Elizabeth." He mumbles this into his Kleenex, uncomfortable, as if the words were rehearsed for him.

But his muffled threat provokes me, and I tilt up to a straight sit, vainly trying to suppress my dismayed reaction. "Is that what Dwight wants? Well, he doesn't like me, I'm sorry. He doesn't handle bluntness well. You do. I'm going to see the Canadian authorities tomorrow. We're laying charges. And if you want to fire me for that, do it."

J.J. shakes his head. "No. Wouldn't do that." He seems listless, defeated. *What the hell, you've got grit.* That is what he said when we last talked. *Go give 'em shit.* Some kind of change is coming over the old man. He's losing his own grit.

I say softly, "I'm sorry we have to disagree."

"Well," he drawls, "disagreement is what makes us lawyers a living. Liz, I can't back you up on this. I'm not going to be galloping in on a white charger and plucking you from the lynch mob you're going to face. Your skin. Good luck."

I am being peremptorily dismissed, and feel offended. But I swallow the gall I feel. "I'm sorry, J.J., it's the way I am. Rest up. Eat lots of borscht."

Vladmira grabs me as I head for the door. "We love you stay for dinner."

"Oh, I can't do that." How awkward that would be. I make a dozen excuses, I'm on a bicycle, my life is in turmoil.

Junior pursues me outside, perhaps to ensure I mount my bike. "Hawaii doesn't sound so bad after all, does it? I take it the old man renewed the offer of his condo? But please come back. We don't want you leaving the firm, Liz. You're a big part of it."

"Tell Hugh *he'll* be taking a holiday. Remind him to pack a toothbrush." I strap on my helmet. "Oh, look, it's a glorious sunset."

I sail off into the hot flames of the dying sun.

As I dismount by my building, I think: how wonderful, a lurker is here to greet me. I pull out my camera and step closer. This is a new one, a bedraggled young man bundled in an overcoat several sizes too large. "Spare change for a cuppa coffee?" He smells of booze.

"You *need* a coffee." I give him a dollar, then ascend glumly to the fourth floor, still feeling the sting of J.J.'s censure, a slap in the face, an abandonment of principle.

But other crises are unfolding. I find Nicholson in his room dressing in a flurry.

"Going out?"

"I just got a call from Stephane. He's in great pain."

"The disease was only going to get worse, Nick. The operation was necessary."

"He's afraid he's never going to see his kids again."

"Why? He's a good father."

"You know *why*."

"Oh, the courts aren't that old-fashioned. I'm sure he'll be permitted shared custody. I'll get Franca to act for him. Has Curtis called in yet?"

"No, and Maxine is nowhere to be found and she hasn't even phoned. He thinks she's with her lawyer. He's at home alone with the kids. I have to go to him."

I take his arm and pull him like a stubborn donkey into the living room and shove him into an easy chair. "You stay here. You'll only make things worse."

He pouts. "I want my martini."

"That's better. We do nothing until we hear from Curtis."

I change into my robe, kick my underwear toward the hamper. I'm played out, ready for early bed, but I'm also hungry. Nicholson has done absolutely nothing in the kitchen, including last night's dishes, so I put some water on and open an uninspired bag of spaghetti. I return to him with the martinis. He gulps his back. "Another."

I give him mine. "There's leftover sauce in the fridge. Water's set to boil. Clean the dishes while you're at it. I'm jumping in the tub. If Curtis calls, bring me the phone."

Curtis has forgotten how to use it? He met Maxine for drinks at three-thirty, and now it is a quarter of eight. She hasn't killed the messenger; the police would have called.

I climb into the tub, turn the faucets on, feel the water creep up my sides, feel my toes and nipples tingling. An unwelcome image intrudes, an apparition: tall with searing blue eyes and silver-blond hair. I sink into my bath in self-disgust. From what subterranean recesses of my mind did *he* come from?

Nicholson walks in, hands me the phone. "It's Curtis."

I pull myself together. "Curtis, what took you? It's after eight. What happened?"

His voice sounds haunted: "I just got home. I'm emotionally exhausted. I just can't describe . . . She was beautiful, Liz. Very strong woman. We had a drink at Pier 70. It turned into dinner; she didn't want to leave. We got into some incredible sharing. And then we went for a walk by the waterfront park, and – did you see that sunset? It was like a message from God."

Nick asks, "What's he saying? Did she hit the wall when he told her?"

I hold up a hand to silence him while Curtis burbles away breathlessly.

"And then we kept walking to the end of the park,

talking non-stop all the way. Mostly me. I really opened up to her; I don't know what got into me. My dysfunctional marriage, my loneliness, my search for . . . well, inner meaning. The stuff I know you laugh about. She was sharp; she spotted my problem right away. I'm too reactive, too sensitive. We're going to meet again tomorrow; she's a woman of style, so I think the Hunt Club at the Sorrento. We have so much in common; both play some bridge and like the same movies. Did you know she's a Woody Allen fan? I thought I was the only one left who doesn't find him passé."

"What about Stephane, Curtis? What is she going to do?"

"Oh, well, she'll work it out with him, don't worry. I think she's doing that now. She's more together than you think. And she was just appalled about how she treated you. In a way, it was a relief for her to know; she's been physically lonely. She was wondering if she was unattractive. I told her, no way —"

"What is going *on*?" Nick is agitated, straining his ears to the phone, trying to catch some of this bizarre outpouring.

"Just a sec." I cover the mouthpiece. "It's bad," I tell him.

Nick slaps his forehead. "How bad?"

"Curtis has gone bonkers over her." Back to the phone: "Sorry."

"Anyway, we just sat on a log sharing our feelings — it was very intense, and we held hands, and we started crying again — until the stars came out and it got a little cold, so we went back to our cars — and . . . well, what can I say?"

"It turned out all right."

"I mean, what a perceptive woman. She knows exactly where I'm at."

Eyes open and the demons of sleep flee. A blanket is on the floor, the sheets are crumpled at my feet, and a pillow has been wrestled from its slip. I recall how Hugh Vandergraaf intruded himself into my thoughts last night as I was in the tub, and feel queasy inside.

I rise and don my robe. The sounds outside are of an awakening city. It is the last day of September, a gray morning, its light falling softly on a shelf where the rag dolls I collected as a child stare at me with their button eyes, their false, stitched-on smiles. Where do I find the strength to face this day? I am still suffering the shock of J.J.'s defection to the old boys' camp. I don't seem to have a single male ally. When a brother is attacked is the first primal male instinct to grab one's testicles and run?

While Nick slumbers on, I crank up for the day, gulping down my coffee, feeling its electric jolt, arming myself to invade the border: cellphone, camera, a change of outfits in a suit bag and something casual in a backpack for a planned side trip to Canada's Gulf Islands.

Before making my way to the ferry, I drop into the office, and I am no sooner at my desk than Franca Crabtree slips in, locking the door to ensure privacy from the peregrinations of Dwight Plum.

Word is on the street, she tells me. "The boys uptown are deep in session; they're hoping to rescue Hugh's hanging decorations."

As if on cue, the King County prosecutor, Percy Schoenenberg, is on the line. I have had several sessions with this glad-hander, pressing women's safety concerns. In a falsely chirruping voice he asks me if my hectic schedule might have a little hole in it this morning.

It's nine-thirty; the ferry leaves at eleven. "Can we do a rain check on that, Percy?"

"Well, look, it's . . . urgent. Actually, we have the attorney-general's special assistant here, Stan Grogan. What about right now? Do you think you could drop around the courthouse?"

They have sent in the head of the rescue team: Stanfield Grogan, the attorney-general's spin doctor. Maybe I should ascertain what they are up to. Could it be they will be urging Vandergraaf to resign in exchange for our not proceeding? However unlikely that would be, no harm is done by listening. I tell him I'll drop by.

"It's the boys uptown," I inform Franca.

"Tell them to get fucked and lay back and enjoy."

It is rush hour at the courthouse, and instead of waiting until the end of time for an elevator, I walk up to Percy's office, where he and Grogan descend on me like hungry buzzards. Percy Schoenenberg is fifty, red and robust, loud checked suit, ready-to-wear smile. Smaller, wiry, wearing pinstripes, is the man who lost to him in the 1996 Democratic primary: Stanfield W. Grogan, now a bureaucrat. The burning issue before the voters was who would be tougher on crime. We're about to see.

Percy takes my left elbow with one hand, my right shoulder with the other, and ushers me to a chair, winking and cooing. The office is grand but in disarray, more resembling a rumpus room, a TV in the corner, crumpled balls of paper beneath a wastebasket hoop. A huge framed photo, sunrise over Rainier, a print of Percy shaking hands with our ever-smiling president.

Grogan is about Percy's age, probably brighter, certainly more suave and dapper. Conservative Democrat whom I've not had much luck lobbying.

"Any word, Mr. Grogan?"

"About what exactly?" His smile disintegrates; he is caught off guard.

"The additional women's shelters you promised."

I can tell he can't remember any promise – that is because he never actually made one. But he recovers with a lie. "We were planning an announcement, as a matter of fact."

"Oh, good. And the increased funding?"

"We're seriously looking at it, Elizabeth. *Very* seriously."

This sudden generosity takes me aback. Anything you want, Elizabeth. The moon.

Grogan delicately brushes off a chair before sitting on it. Both these men are close to Vandergraaf's age, contemporaries. Were they, like Dwight Plum, his college buddies? Political cronies, anyway: Vandergraaf was state chair for the Democrats.

"Well, you've been making quite a name for yourself, Elizabeth," Grogan says.

"What a future," says Percy. "You're a registered Democrat, right, Liz? By golly, I look at you, and I think: State Legislature, Congress, or – well, with just the right boost there'd be no stopping you."

I can be president if I agree not to push on with this frivolous exercise.

"You gentlemen are very flattering, but I think we should get to the point. What's on your minds?"

Grogan's smile reappears. "Well, it's this strange allegation against Hugh Vandergraaf. Elizabeth, you can't deny it, he's one of the brightest stars on our bench. And just between friends – I know you won't repeat it – he's being tapped by some of Bill Clinton's boys for the U.S.

Court of Appeals. You know where that stepping stone leads. He'd be one of the great Supreme Court liberals of the next century, a Cardozo, hell, a Holmes. Minority rights, affirmative-action programs, women's right to choose: he has an agenda for all that stuff."

That stuff. "So what's your problem?"

"Well, we wanted to hear from you in confidence, because we were, ah, curious as to what you really make of this business. We don't know much about the Krueger woman." He looks at some notes. "Struthers now. Apparently had some major mental disorder. Quite respectable, though, I gather."

"A minister's daughter."

"Yes." Grogan clears his throat. "Would you say she'd been a little overprotected? Naive, perhaps?"

"We were all naive once, Mr. Grogan."

"Stan, please – even my enemies call me Stan."

"Even *I* call him Stan." Percy emits a chuckle with the hollowest of rings.

"Might we infer that at seventeen she was perhaps more, ah, sexually unworldly than most?"

"I'm sorry, I don't know what you're driving at." I turn to Percy. "Have you already talked to Judge Vandergraaf?"

Looks are quickly, anxiously exchanged. "I think we can be blunt, Liz," says Percy. "Yes, we took a full state-ment from him last night. He . . . volunteered, didn't waste a minute, came right in after he'd talked to you."

"With or without a lawyer?"

"All by his lonesome. Nothing to hide, that was the sense I had."

"It's a weird kettle of fish, isn't it, Elizabeth?" Grogan says. "Do you think religious guilt comes into play? Denial? A refusal to accept what happened in an unguarded moment with a young man she, ah, had quite a thing about?"

I feel ire begin to stew within me; this is sexual chauvinism in the extreme.

"Is that what he told you? That she consented?"

"We understand he's willing to take a polygraph."

"Oh, boy. Well, fortunately you two won't be on the jury. I have to push off. I have a boat to catch."

But Grogan motions me to stay in my chair. "We just want to know if you had any concerns, Elizabeth. Any advice for us. Any other way you might suggest we deal with this. Any . . ." He stalls.

"Offers?"

"Well, let's say that has crossed a few minds." Percy takes the ball now; they are tossing it back and forth like something hot to the touch. "Hugh has a lawyer now. We can sit down with him, try to work something out, a token payment for her perceived injury, a quiet nondisclosure settlement. I take it you haven't done anything precipitous like go to the press, or —"

"What's he willing to pay?"

"Well, Liz, we haven't broached the matter with him yet, really not our business." Percy shrugs. "Something to offset your fees perhaps, or . . ." He has the habit of throwing in that useless conjunction at the end of incomplete sentences. "Idea is to avoid embarrassing the courts, or causing people to distrust the system, or . . . Make everybody happy."

I rise. "I'm embarrassed for *you.*"

Grogan pursues me to the door, voice tight, aplomb lost: "I think you and your client, who I hope is not as gullible as obviously you think a Canadian jury will be, had better take a couple of days to think this over. It's ancient history, Elizabeth. If a judge's career is destroyed all over some spiteful notion of yours to seek revenge —"

I turn to confront them. "In the last election both of

you ran all over the place promising integrity and being incredibly severe on crime. You'll have a chance to prove just how zealous you are by co-operating with the Canadian authorities. It's been a pleasure."

Finding a taxi in this town in wet weather is as uncertain as winning the Lotto, but the old waterfront streetcar substitutes well, so I jump aboard and rattle off to Pier 69, where the *Victoria Clipper* is loading.

Beatrice is waiting for me in the departure lounge, smiling to herself, reading a Salinger novel, a class assignment. She rises to greet me, gives me a squeeze.

"You seem in a pretty good mood," I say.

"I've made my peace with what I have to do. How do you feel?"

"Nervous. I'm not sure what to expect." My spirits have picked up, though, after watching the old boys squirm this morning. *They* are nervous. I wish I could stay on a level plane: I hate these quick dips and rises.

"Well, now, *you* relax. I'm the one who'll be in the dentist's chair."

"And you're going to be drilled. Just be as forthcoming with the prosecutor as you were with me."

"I'll do my very best."

Her toughness and resolution constantly surprise me.

The *Victoria Clipper* slides away from Pier 69, easing through the boat traffic on Elliott Bay; now engines thrust and the jetfoil powers north, up the sound. This is definitely the preferred way to fly, just inches off the water. We are in the upper lounge by the window, through which I watch the silver towers of Seattle wane, then disappear into the autumn gloom.

Hugh was on his way to the U.S. Supreme Court, was he? Wait till Bill Clinton's *boys* hear about his student days. Though when I pause to reflect, maybe this president feels some empathy.

My cellphone rings: Harry Crake. "Where are you? I hear you're doing an end around – there are rumors flying all over."

What the hell is an end around? "I am sitting beside a woman of sterling character who is about to charge Hugh Vandergraaf with rape."

A loud exclamation. He entreats me for more; I promise him the facts will quickly come to light. "You'll be the first to know, Harry."

Beatrice and I talk awhile about the coming interview, then I riffle through some of my commission briefs. "Uncontrolled Birth." "Sperm for Sale – Who's Baby Is It Anyway?" The three months of hearings will probably stretch to four. I am looking forward to them: the warm weather in L.A. and the Southwest will keep the winter blahs at bay.

Soon we are sweeping past Whidbey Island and out the inlet, into the open waters of Juan de Fuca Strait. I spend some time preparing Beatrice for the questions that may be asked of her, and soon the landmass of Vancouver Island approaches. Victoria is at the southern tip of the island, a quaint city that cashes in on its Englishness for the tourist trade.

Disembarking, we breeze through customs, head for the cab line, and are quickly by the postcard inner harbor with its stately graceful Parliament Building and the castle-turreted Empress Hotel.

According to the directory in the nearby government building, Mr. Benjamin Mulholland is regional Crown counsel, which presumably puts him near the top of the prosecutorial totem pole. Beatrice takes up her book while I am led into a large square office redolent with flowers in planters and hanging baskets: it's an English garden. Sliding doors lead to a solarium offering further proof of Mulholland's obsessive hobby: a jungle of flowers and ferns.

He pauses from slopping about with a watering can, gives me a long appraisal, then says in a cultivated voice: "Miss Finnegan, how delightful. And how can I possibly assist you?" I had imagined urbane and svelte, but he looks vastly out of shape, sloppy mustache, ample bay window, rumpled sports jacket with old-fashioned leather elbow patches, silk tie with some kind of school emblem on it. He doesn't wipe his hands and his grip is wet.

Setting down his watering can, he ushers me to a seat, and I hand him my capsule one-page summary of the rape complaint and a folder containing the interview transcripts. Everything but Helen Mazur; I'm keeping my promise to her.

He reads the summary, squinting at it, frowning. "Intriguing. Dear, oh, dear."

Then he stands, making a series of pained faces as he picks dry leaves from a vine.

"I heard you described," he says. "The Seattle suffragette, someone called you. I rather had a vision of some pinch-faced ultra-feminist. Political correctness, and all that. I must say, you don't fit the image."

Who is this, chair of the local chapter of the old boys' club? I am suddenly on guard: has word flashed across the border? He does not seem all that surprised by what I've laid before him.

"We're here to swear a complaint, Mr. Mulholland."

"Yes, fascinating. Truly." His eyes on me, a smile that seems more of a wince.

"Mrs. Struthers is prepared to sign an affidavit."

Mulholland looks at his watch: just after four. "Yes, we shall have to deal with that, of course. Need to talk it over with some of the boys from the RCMP. I say, you wouldn't mind staying overnight in one of our fine hostelries? No rush, what? After . . . what is it, twenty-seven years? You might like to toddle up to the Empress for tea; I'm sure they're still serving it. Lovely old lady, that hotel. I think I can get you a rate there; let's stop by my secretary's desk."

As he maneuvers me to the door he places his hand on my waist. I want to slap it.

"We do have the right to prefer this charge, Mr. Mulholland?"

"Yes, quite. Swear an information. Perfect right to do so, law of the land. Otherwise, I'd be in deep trouble with the members of the fair sex, wouldn't I? Quite the fad, these days, bringing up these old rape complaints. Women's prerogative, of course, in this age of correctness. Tawdry business, however, though I must say a bit of a hot potato."

I say, old sport, rather.

"Shall we say tomorrow, dear, about noonish?"

"Noonish is fine."

In terms of his regard for women, this unctuous gentleman seems to have popped out of the wrong century. But I tell Beatrice, as we wait outside for a taxi, that I'm sure our mission will be rewarded – however reluctantly. I ask her if she wants to join me on the early-evening ferry to Pender Island.

"I'd only get upset. I wouldn't be in good form tomorrow."

So I help her check in at the Empress: a rambling chateau surrounded by manicured lawn and sumptuous flower gardens. I change into jeans in her room, leave my suit bag there, then continue by cab to the Gulf Islands ferry terminal, which is a considerable distance up the Saanich Peninsula. As the meter clicks, my turbaned driver wears a smile that intimates I've made his day.

I find myself on a sleek new ferry for the forty-minute hop to the Gulf Islands, and we traverse an inner sea dotted with lush green isles and islets rising from rocky shorelines. North Pender Island, fast approaching, seems hardly deserted – houses command many positions by the deeply indented shore. Like other islands I have visited near the border, this one promises some gentle attractions.

We pull into a small ferry slip bordered with luxuriant madrona trees and stately Douglas firs atop rocky walls. I step ashore, breathe in the sweet autumn-evening air, and watch the vehicles climb up the hill.

Then I find myself standing alone in silence at the dock. I hadn't much thought about how I was going to get from one place to another. How do I make my way to Bedwell Resort? Did I expect a bus service?

But there is a relaxed easiness about these Gulf Islands, and I should have no problems hitchhiking – and there is still enough light. I sling on my backpack and trudge up the hill. A sourpuss ignores my thumb, a woman in a van shrugs and points to a side road which she enters, but a couple of minutes later an old pickup heaves to and a gnarled pipe-smoking rustic in coveralls beckons me in.

"Where you headed, young lady?" he says in a lazy rumbling voice.

"Bedwell Harbour."

"I can only get you a short ways – it's quite a piece down the other end. Why would you want to go there? Bunch of fancy condos and big Yankee yachts. Ain't right, all these city people with their big ideas coming over and changing everything."

And he launches into a monologue about protecting the island from "those damned lying developers and greedy timber-cutters." He points out some sad-looking clear-cuts.

I reassure him I'm a firm conservationist, and explain I'm from a small town myself. He frowns when I tell him I'm a lawyer, but his eyes light up when he hears I'm probing into the past of a big-city judge. Soon, he swings off onto a driveway and parks by an old frame house. He steps out, leaving the engine running.

"You take this here truck, and go on your way. The wife and I are staying home by the fire tonight. Just bring it by in the morning."

"Well, I –"

"Clutch may be failing, just make sure you push it right down. Follow the signs, hang a left where the road forks, or you'll get lost in a goddamn subdivision."

I am not allowed even the pleasure of asking his name and barely manage to thank him before he kicks his boots off and steps into his house. Obviously, folks here – when not dealing with damned lying developers – are much like those of Coalsack, easygoing and trusting.

But I am less than trusting of this truck, and before maneuvering it onto the road, I check the tires; they seem not too worn, and I pray I will not be called upon to change a flat. I simply would not be able to; my father's death will always haunt me. But we had an old Chevrolet pickup at home that I regularly drove and, once under way, I find this truck handles well enough, despite its grunts and wheezes. I am soon chugging up and down the wooded hills of North Pender. Newly swathed fields, misty in the twilight, deer feeding among the Herefords. An urban intrusion: a modest mall with teenaged hangabouts. More hills, hang a left, a school, a timbered one-lane bridge that takes me onto South Pender, a long winding road by shoreline and farms, and a steep dip down to Bedwell: a lovely bay, its still waters glowing mauve under the dying sun.

It is about a two-star, I would guess, a main building with rental units, several new condos. I stroll by a public lounge near the water and I listen to the waves lick at the shore and to muffled laughter from the bar. About a dozen pleasure boats are tied up at floating wharves which feather out from the main dock. Beatrice Krueger was raped somewhere out there. I evoke Vandergraaf pissing off the side of his sailboat, asking, "Hey, what's the problem?"

What *is* the problem, Hugh?

Behind the main building, a cabin, probably for staff, maybe the same one in which Beatrice stayed the night. Where is her stoned host now, the server from the bar? Like many former members of the soft-drug culture, she is likely living a middle-class existence somewhere, her children raised properly, told to resist drugs.

The pub is light and cheery, with a broad view of the bay; but only a few tables are occupied, mostly by boaters, I assume, city-dwellers. But the two women and four men quaffing pints of beer in the corner appear to be locals: especially the graybeard and the ponytail with their worn jackets and floppy boots. As I slide onto a bar stool, they turn in unison, staring at me as if I'm a Martian, and the men start preening, tucking in stomachs, finger-combing hair.

The bartender tells me I have my choice of rooms: the season is almost over. Her boss is away, so she will give me a key and I can sign in tomorrow morning. Then she says in a warning voice: "Local Romeo approaching. Don't worry, he's actually very harmless and sweet."

It's the ponytail, a craggy-faced fellow of forty-plus with a broad smile and eyes that twinkle. He climbs up beside me, toting his not-quite-empty pint. "Another one of them, darlin'." Then he turns to me, offering his hand. "Stash. That's what they call me." He is struggling to hide that paunch: such an endearing exercise in male vanity.

I say, "Hi."

"I wish."

"I'm Liz."

"You on one of them big boats out there?"

"*I* wish."

"Sitting here all alone, I figured you might be one of the casualties. You get a lot of Sunday sailors can't handle the confined space, eh. If the boat don't go on the rocks, the marriage does."

"No, I'm not a boater. I'm a lawyer, actually." I lower my voice, confiding: "I'm here investigating a serious crime."

From his expression, this might be the most exciting news ever to reach Pender Island. He inches closer. "What sort of crime? Maybe I can help."

I pay for his beer, order another half for myself. "You been on the island a long time, Stash?"

"I guess. Since I was two weeks old, eh." He's proud of his island pedigree, tells me he's been the main party-hardy guy here since he got kicked out of high school. Works as a carpenter when he works.

"This happened a long time ago." And I give him enough rough facts to whet his curiosity. "The suspect is now a judge."

"Yeah? Right on."

Would he remember any of the staff from 1971, in particular a certain skinny pot-smoker, long dark hair?

"I'd've been seventeen, eh, but I used to sneak in here." He calls to one of his friends: "Woody, over here."

Woody joins us, an amiable stout in an Expos cap.

"This is my new real good friend, Liz. She's over

here looking for some old pecker tracks." I laugh. I like Stash's droll disarming grin.

After I fill Woody in, the two of them bounce names back and forth, peeling back the years to 1971.

"Not Marie, that had to be later, '75, just before the fire."

"Carol Handy? She useta do a lotta reef."

"Naw, she was too short."

"What about that dame with the big set, Roxie or Doxy or something?"

"No, she said skinny, eh."

They carry on in that manner, animated, seeming to forget I'm here.

"What about – I'm thinkin' of that real wired chick had some hassles with the horsemen. Weird name. Talia?"

"Thalia. Let's see, '71. Didn't she get busted for dealing that year? I bet that's the one."

"Yeah, wonder what ever happened to her?"

"Did a year in Willingdon, I think."

That is all they can bring to surface, but a good beginning. Though police records might show a Thalia, I shudder at the thought of a witness with a record.

"Kinda slow in here," says Stash. "There's some music happening at the bar at Browning. What do you think, eh, Liz? Wanna head out?"

The offer tempts. Hang around with the locals, dance, flirt, sooth those flutters of tension I have been feeling. And these guys seem absolutely harmless. Stash is attractive in a rough-hewn way, but hardly my type. I will take a night off from my quest and lightly sample the social life of Pender Island.

At the sound of my alarm, I awaken with a roaring head. Outside my window are beach and boats, a breeze-speckled bay, green islands, white clouds. This view persuades me I am not in a loft of the Washington Shoe Building, but I am unsure where I am or how I found my way here. A chapter of my life is missing.

My confusion continues for several minutes, but just as I am wondering whether I should panic, last night comes barreling back: I am on a funky Canadian island, following a trail of pecker tracks. What brings about this amnesia? More evidence of a brain overwrought, its synapses fraying. Too much adrenaline. Too much booze.

I am to pay the price today. They are breaking up the pavement and laying sewer pipes in my head. All my tension of recent days must have ignited in a blowout, and I fear I didn't retain much reserve last night. The second time I've been looped in the last ten days, and again events are shrouded. I hardly ever party so hardy. A martini, on average, a night. Hungover, amnesiac, mind-scattered: someone, please, consign me to a place for help.

I am amazed that I had enough forethought to set the alarm last night. Eight o'clock. I must make the nine-thirty ferry. I drag myself to the bathroom to do what repairs I can.

Look at those red eyes. I was of clear mind for our three hours in the Browning pub – my reflexes sharp enough to beat Stash a few times at pool, though I suspect he wasn't trying hard. From bar to after-party: hosted by a woman with an immense capacity for the homemade wine she insisted on sharing too abundantly. I think I became too boisterous. Men had to be peeled off here and there – with help from Stash; I remember him helping untwine the arm of at least one persistent suitor. The local Romeo turned out to be Mr. Chivalry. He attended on me like an old-fashioned butler with food, drink, and uproarious island stories, and made no advances. He would stare at me when he thought I wasn't noticing, the heartwrenching look of a beagle begging for food.

Yes, that's how I arrived back here: Stash practically had to carry me to my borrowed truck, and he did the driving. Though as drunk as I, he possessed excellent local knowledge. "I could drive this route blind, eh." Somewhere we pulled over for a while and talked, and nestled a bit. I remember expecting matters to go further, but . . . Or did they go further? But no sticky evidence in the bed, no sign of recent male presence. I wonder how he found his way home.

I shower, perform simple but essential cosmetic repair, then dress. Though I cannot bear the thought of breakfast, coffee seems a precondition to getting through the day. I can only hope the restaurant is open.

I notice I had forgotten to lock the door; when I try to push it open, it budges only two feet. I slip through the gap, and there, lying on my stoop, gently snoring, is my loyal beagle, Stash – he looks chilled, though from somewhere he has found a blanket. I bend and gently rouse him.

He mumbles an apology, the terms of which are muffled and unclear, and shakes his head at my offer of a ride. I pull him to his feet and steer him into the room, and with a gentle shove propel him onto the bed.

After settling my account over coffee, I make my way to my borrowed truck, sloppily parked on a gravel lot. The winding ride makes me dizzy, but I persevere to my benefactor's driveway and house. He is outside feeding yard chickens.

"I can call a taxi from here," I say.

"That's a good one." Laughing, he climbs in beside me as I slide over. He honks to scatter the chickens from our path. As we head out I try to rasp some thick-tongued words of thanks, but he seems quite bored with my gratitude.

"Heard you had a rootin'-tootin' time here on Pender."

"And I'm paying the price." Oh, God, this whole island must be talking about the debauched Seattle lawyer.

"Hope you nail that there wife-murdering Supreme Court judge."

I am in too much pain to take in any scenery either on the ferry or the taxi to Victoria. Aspirin dulls the sharpest edges, but my head still feels like a clanging gong. I must find some way to avoid smelling like a wino when I rejoin Beatrice. I dare not tell her of my behavior last night – she'll think I'm a libertine.

There will be no more stress-induced weak moments. As soon as this rape complaint is formally made I can let the Canadian Crown take over. I will escape to Hanalie Beach on Kauai for a couple of weeks and catch up on my reading. I'll hold Beatrice's hand when she needs me, but she'll be in the care of the Royal Canadian Mounted, who always get their man, a legend I trust is well-earned.

Beatrice doesn't answer my call from the house phone at the Empress Hotel, and the clerk says she has left no message. Nor is she in any of the restaurants. Eleven-thirty, and we have a meeting with Mulholland in half an hour. And I am anxious to shower and change from these wine-stained jeans. Maybe Beatrice forgot I had left my dress in her room, went for a walk and a shop, and decided to meet me at the prosecutor's office.

Mulholland will just have to deal with a woman wearing yesterday's unwashed denims. In one of the restrooms, I brush my hair, apply more camouflage to those tar pits beneath my eyes, redden my lips, and remind myself to pick up Clorets. I leave my backpack with the concierge and head out along the waterfront.

Worry nags me. Why hadn't Beatrice left me a note? A macabre scenario: Vandergraaf's minions have whisked her away, her body will be found floating in Victoria harbor. I think: maybe I'm a target, too. And suddenly I am feeling very anxious, and as I near Mulholland's building I hear those warning bells.

I walk on, trying to deny the impulse to turn. I wish I understood this illogical phenomenon. I am on a safe city street in broad daylight; I *know* I'm not about to be attacked. I have preached this gospel many times: statistically, women are comparatively safe with strangers; over 90 per cent of rapes involve acquaintances. Yet when I endure this strange feeling, I can't convince myself of my own argument.

The door I seek is just ahead, but now I hear fast footsteps behind me and I quicken my pace and fumble in my bag for the pepper spray. Then I look over my shoulder: my pursuer is Harry Crake, trotting to catch up to me.

"Been waiting for you to show up. I want this story." Harry turns to a press photographer standing by the front door. "It's okay, Luke, I found her."

"*How* did you find me, Harry?"

"Made a few calls. Our guy at the capitol says the A.-G.'s office is in crisis and their first-string tackle has flown up here."

"Stanfield *Grogan*?"

He nods. I wish I had a clear head; this is not coming together for me.

"So what's happening with this rape charge?"

"You're about to find out." I feel a mounting concern. What are these agents of the state up to? And where's Beatrice?

I ask him if other media are on to this.

"Yeah, I called the local paper to string for us in case I couldn't make it. Probably all over the joint by now."

He's right. Outside the prosecution offices, a woman with a tape recorder and a man with a camera, a CHEK-TV logo on it. Another reporter walks from the office and briefs us. "Mulholland is apparently in some kind of meeting. Can't interrupt him."

When the receptionist in turn tries to stall me, I push past and march down the corridor to her boss's office.

When I walk in I observe, from between the potted ferns, this scene: Beatrice is seated primly on a chair being interviewed by a man who couldn't look more like a police officer if he had a badge tattooed on his forehead, cold gray eyes, gray temples, military cut: senior RCMP brass. A junior officer is operating the tape machine, a lanky bespectacled nerd with an Adam's apple as big and active as a yo-yo. Mulholland is wandering about picking yellow leaves from his ficus trees.

"Will someone have the courtesy to tell me what is going on?"

"Ah, here she is at last," says Mulholland. "Moved matters ahead. Hole opened up this morning. Inspector Clough here fetched Mrs. Struthers from the hotel; we didn't know where to look for you."

Beatrice appears puzzled. "I thought this was arranged," she says softly.

"Perhaps a little misunderstanding," says Mulholland. "Not a problem. We're getting on famously."

He introduces RCMP Inspector Clough: "Rather an expert at this sort of thing."

I'm sure. His fellow investigator, who is staring at me in an odd, astonished way, doesn't rate an introduction.

"And of course you know Mr. Grogan."

I whirl: Stanfield W. Grogan is trying to look invisible, half hidden by a potted dieffenbachia. "I've had the pleasure," he says serenely.

"But this is none of his business, Mr. Mulholland."

"Come, come, we must be courteous to our American friends, hands across the border and all that. Can't extradite without their help. And he has access to some information we lack."

"I wonder if I might speak to my client alone for a few minutes."

"I'm afraid that makes for a spot of difficulty. Interrupts the flow. You wouldn't coach her, I quite know that, but we've reached the climax now. As it were. Actually we're having a little chat about the aftermath. Of course, you appreciate you're here at our pleasure. Lawyers aren't normally invited to these private little parlays." A wet smile. "It's not as if *she's* under investigation, is it now?"

Then why does it seem that way? Grogan's presence at this *cercle privé* galls me no end, and I'm infuriated by the peremptory way this interview was organized, but there is no sense riling the Canadian Crown — they have no choice but to lay the charge. So I accept Mulholland's offer of a chair, apologize for having seemed rude, and let Inspector Clough carry on.

"And your parents sent you where?"

"It was a place of care in Everett, the Faith Hospice. Run by the church. My father's church."

"And you were there for several months?"

"Off and on. I spent some time with a retired couple in the Okanogan area, looking after them. Then I guess I had . . . some more emotional problems. I returned to the hospice and stayed until about February."

"So you were almost an entire *year* in recovery?" This is Mulholland.

"Longer. I was very depressed."

Clough continues, "And suicidal."

They have done homework; that wasn't in her statement. I offer Beatrice a weak smile that doesn't offer much encouragement. She knows I do not like the direction this is taking. The gangly cop working the tape machine still can't keep his eyes off me. What's *his* problem?

"Perhaps suicidal," Beatrice says. "I believe I took some pills at the hospice."

"From your medication?"

She nods.

"I will kindly ask you to answer. This has to be recorded."

"I was told so. I don't really remember."

"Do you recall what drugs you were on?"

"No."

"And you slashed your wrists another time?"

This scene has been lifted directly from the Spanish Inquisition. I feel fury mount.

"They said the cuts were superficial; I don't know. Those times remain quite hazy."

"Ah, very cloudy, would say?" Mulholland again.

"Very."

"Excuse me," says Grogan, and he whispers something to Mulholland.

"Just to take a step back," says Mulholland, "you had something to drink the night of this unfortunate business?"

Unfortunate business. He's smiling, but I can read his disbelief.

"Yes."

"Her first-ever taste of alcohol," I chime in. "Vandergraaf ordered it."

The inspector, coldly: "Would you mind if we heard it from Mrs. Struthers? Was it a strong drink?"

"Yes, I suppose. Vodka with orange juice."

"And you felt its effects."

"Very much so."

"He was being friendly? Solicitous?"

Beatrice glances at me again. She's not slow; she knows her words do not fall on fertile ears. "I should tell you quite bluntly that I found him attractive."

Mulholland interjects, "Physically."

"But I definitely wasn't inviting him to rape me."

"Oh, goodness, no. I take it, however, you had some experience with matters of . . . shall we say, of a sexual . . ."

Mulholland's question lingers, incomplete and menacing.

"None. I'd never performed the sex act."

"But you had the, ah, usual fantasies, as it were?"

I jump up. "This is grotesque. We're here to swear out a complaint, and you're probing into her nonexistent sexual history. Vandergraaf will hire his own lawyers, okay?"

Mulholland, with his saccharine smile: "Just elucidating, just elucidating."

Several more questions, then another huddle between Grogan and Mulholland, who then says: "Bully for you, Mrs. Struthers, you've been of invaluable help. Now I wonder if you'd mind too awfully much leaving us with your counsel for a few minutes?"

What a vile charade. I usher Beatrice out and return to them, and I feel my fuse burning fast, racing to explosion.

"Okay, what's going on? We are here to lay a charge."

"Of course, my dear. Terribly expensive enterprise, however, what with the extradition, witnesses from afar. Burden to the taxpayer in this day of budget cutbacks. In a way, it's really not our problem, is it? Foreigners, nonresidents. I don't think they ever cleared customs, so in a way it didn't legally *happen* in Canada."

"Mr. Mulholland, I'm not green. I almost hate to tell you this, but I once wrote a thirty-page brief on international territorial jurisdiction."

An embarrassed chuckle. "Yes, well, perhaps, but you see the problem. *Very* difficult case. Absolute wet dream for any clever defense counsel. Rather risking her health with this, don't you think? Which is precarious at best. And with a judge's reputation on the line . . . well, surely you can talk to your client, and –"

But I cut him off and turn to Grogan. "Nice try. There are some reporters out there wondering what you're up to."

Grogan turns white; obviously he didn't know. Looks are exchanged. Inspector Clough turns to his aide, who clambers up – to a full height of six and a half feet – and goes out to check, almost knocking over a chair in his haste.

Grogan brushes nervously at his cuff. "Calling in the press – you disappoint me, Elizabeth."

"I didn't call them. They tracked you here."

"If you say, but surely it's obvious, Elizabeth. Alcohol, infatuation, ignorance of the facts of life, a pious woman ashamed at having permitted herself to engage in the physical act of love, becoming demented, recreating it as rape. I'm sorry, but her account is just too unlikely. I know Hugh Vandergraaf. It's just not in him."

"No, he's a good Democrat."

"Nonsense. If you think there's something political . . . I suggest you sit down with her and *explain* the facts of life."

I feel one of my terrible explosions coming. Stay in control, for God's sake, Liz, don't let the plug pop loose. "We'd like to swear that information, Mr. Mulholland."

"Yes, of course, simple matter for your client to do that. But I'm afraid we . . ."

He looks at Grogan, as if seeking permission. Grogan

purses his lips, working at this, weighing the political implications. Then he nods, as if giving Mulholland assent.

"In this country, Miss Finnegan, we have something called a stay of proceedings. Prosecutorial discretion, that sort of thing. Puts a complete halt to it. Sends the whole thing balls-up. Last over, as we say."

"You wouldn't *dare*!"

"Can't see any way around it, really. Simply not a winnable case. So I'm afraid it's exactly what we'll do."

"I wonder if you gentlemen would excuse me while I go out for some fresh air." I swivel toward the door, but turn again to face them. Here it comes: I'm going to blow my top, and I know it, and I can't stop it, and to hell with it. "You chauvinist assholes!"

I fly out to the waiting room, drag Beatrice up from a chair, and sweep out, bumping hard into the tall, gawky cop as he's coming in. He puts out an arm to prevent me from tripping over his big feet and stutters an apology.

Now our way is blocked by microphones, notepads, cameras – the numbers of press have tripled, and women and men are frantically firing questions.

"You want a quote? Okay, well, let's see if I can think of some generous way to describe what my client and I have just been subjected to . . . how about: a disgusting exhibition of supine Canadian colonial mentality organized by a misogynist cabal of empty-headed morons desperately protecting their shriveled male egos. And if any one of these fatuous, preening, bureaucratic bastards wants to sue me for slander, they're welcome to do it, I'd love it, because . . . because . . ."

My tongue staggers to a stop: a sharp splinter of an idea has just stuck in my mind, and if I can just wiggle it loose and study it . . . yes, there may be another way to drag Hugh Vandergraaf into a courtroom.

"Because what?" says Harry Crake, daring me.

I am seething, I'm hungover, and maybe I'm not

thinking, but I can't back away. I am going to do it, I am going to throw down the gauntlet.

"Because I am telling you they are hiding a felon from the law; they are protecting a . . . a dangerous sexual predator, a rapacious thug." Immediately I know I have overreached, but the tempest in me clouds reason and won't stop whirling. "That individual's name is Hugh Vandergraaf and he is a judge of the Superior Court of the State of Washington." I indicate Beatrice. "He violated this woman, he raped her, and I want the entire world to know she's also the victim of an international conspiracy to suppress the truth."

Mulholland and Inspector Clough are out here now, at the edge of the scrum, and the prosecutor is snidely critiquing my bravura performance. When I catch the phrases "hissy fit" and "hysterical female," I stretch an arm to him, grab him by his school tie and yank him toward me.

"You priggish gutless toady, I'll show you a hissy fit!"

An arm is around me, firmly restraining me, and I release Mulholland, who retreats in a fluster to the wall. The inspector tries to herd us to the elevators, but I continue my press conference, answering their questions about the rape: time, date, location, torn panties, purple bruises, blood, a bite mark on her assailant's neck.

"How do you spell Vandergraaf?" a reporter asks.

11 | Friday . . .

Over a leisurely mid-morning Colombian-select cappuccino, Nick and I spread the dailies upon a table we have appropriated at the Yesler Way Starbucks.

"Oh, my," he says. "He's darling."

Harry Crake had found an old picture of Vandergraaf in the UW yearbook, and it is on the front page: young, turtlenecked charmer smiling right at us from the deck of a sailboat. A more recent rendering, set in his chambers, shows him sorrowful, or at least contemplative. Just one picture of me, though, taken over Mulholland's shoulder as I grab him by his silk appendage. My eyes are blazing blue stars, my mouth open in a roundly voweled epithet. That pompous office gardener, doing Grogan's dirty work.

"I think you should take a little holiday, princess. It's going to be coming down deep shit around here for a while."

"Let the shit rain."

The *Times* also has an interesting front page: they managed to scoop a very good print of that 1971 April Fool's edition photo: "Porno ring uncovered." Hugh Hustle leaning over the freak of Rice Hall, straining for a glimpse of breast. In addition to the main story, there is a political sidebar discussing Grogan's hurried visit to Victoria, his Democratic ties with Vandergraaf. Good stuff.

I arrived home too late last night to catch the imbroglio on the set, but the story must have been beamed across the continent because I took phone calls from L.A. to Boston. The Seattle Women's Law Center is planning a protest and co-ordinating a march.

"I'm heading up to the office. I want to see Junior's face."

"Hawaii. You mentioned Hawaii. Maybe you need a rest."

"I'm not tired. Or do you want me out so Stephane can move in? Is that settled?"

"Very unsettled. He's staying in the Roosevelt for now. Kids are with the woman wronged. Princess, are you absolutely sure you're in control of your thought processes? This character could sue your panties off."

"That'd be a change. He usually rips them off. I *want* him to sue. It's the only way I can drag him into a court of law." I tell myself that challenging him to seek damages for slander is akin to sacrificing one's body for the cause. If I do nothing else, at least I will raise consciousness.

"You *sound* lucid. It's not some rare form of . . . you know, mad cow disease or something?"

I dare not deny – especially to myself – that I was not only in an almost uncontrollable temper but damn hungover, so maybe I wasn't too lucid. I try to reassure myself it doesn't matter; I said it and it's true and I'm glad.

As I head up the hill to my building, Mom reaches me on my cell.

"Why are you so skinny all of a sudden? I had to check the horizontal to see if it was set right. I'm sure it's the stress that made you do it. Toiling like a slave for that Mr. Plum twenty hours a day and all your good causes on top. I think you better hustle your ass back here and breathe some fresh mountain air. There's all those pollutants in Seattle, and who knows what they do to your brain."

"Good God, Mom, I'm fine. I know exactly what I'm doing. I exploded a little, okay, but that was for the cameras." This is a fib, but I don't want her worrying. "How's it going with Jake?"

"I'm in a horrible tizzy. Clarissa – at Ringcrafters? –

she told me he bought a diamond. He's taking me for dinner tonight at Fung's Palace."

She is seeking filial consent. I astound myself by silencing all inner doubt and blithely saying, "Go for it, Mom."

But it is she who is now cautious. "I'm going to give him a big maybe. I think we should try living together for a while."

"Oh, won't *you* be the scandal of Coalsack."

"I'll love every minute of it."

I am comforted by my mother's prudence, but when I arrive at the office I am accused myself of lacking such quality. Friends are concerned that I have become unhinged: here's the raving lunatic who was carrying on about international conspiracies. Even Mattie gives me a dubious look.

I ask her, "Is J.J. back in the office?"

"Came in this morning."

"How's he taking it?"

"He sounded pretty ratty. Says you're digging your own grave."

"Oh, Christ. Junior?"

"Berserk. Needs a straitjacket worse than you."

Franca Crabtree slips in and puts a hand to my head to check my temperature. But she is more supportive, and of course surmises right away what I am doing. She is worried, though: this could backfire. "He's got deep pockets, he's not going to get some shithouse lawyer. Defamation – it'll probably be Bill Christiansen."

"Yeah, but he can't get away with just suing me; he has to go after the media, too. Think CBS or NBC or the Hearst chain aren't going to get the best legal eagles in the whole damn country? It's a winner, anyway." I say that with seeming hearty assurance: it probably sounds like bluster. If the worst happens, the office has defamation insurance – though I could be stuck with a huge deductible.

"And if he doesn't sue?" Franca asks.

"Then it's like an admission of guilt. The Canadians would have to act. Aren't you supposed to be in court? That Bremerton Loans conspiracy in front of . . . I can barely say his name."

"Put over to Monday. The rapacious thug is meeting with his lawyers. I heard there's some kind of press conference planned."

Junior finally pokes his head in. "You've *ruined* him."

"All I've done, Junior, is slap his face and challenge him to a duel. Let him clear his name if he can. You can be his second."

"Oh, do you really think he'll rise to your scurrilous taunts?" He rolls in and almost surrounds me. Red eyes. Breath-freshener. He must have taken it hard: how protective he is of his demigod. "No, he will not. Nor will he descend to your level to wallow in your mud."

"Well, he's got to do something, doesn't he?"

"He'll rise above it. He'll laugh it off. More garbage spewed from the mouth of the feminist zealot, he'll say. You *are* beneath his contempt." He finally backs off, out of breath after having said his piece.

"Liz, you are a bad, bad girl," says Franca. "Take her out to the woodshed, Dwight, it's the only way they learn."

"Do I take it you are a part of this conspiracy, Franca? But perhaps I'm leaping to a hasty conclusion: you are no doubt here to minister to the patient. Does she know she suffered a severe breakdown? Some people just can't handle the stress, I suppose. By the way, Elizabeth, I think the old man wishes a few words."

Mattie interrupts on the speakerphone: "We have a hostile on the line."

I'm snappish: "Please, Mattie, you know the routine. Tell him I'm with clients."

"You know I would, girl, but it's a certain party from Spokane." This is in code: she knows Junior is here.

"It's a personal call, Dwight."

As Franca, picking up the cue, leads Junior out, he takes one more petulant shot: "He had a chance to go all the way, to the country's top court. What could you be *thinking*?"

A hostile on the line. This won't be Helen, more likely her husband. And it is: Wilkie S. Mazur.

"Listen, young lady, you keep your nose out of our private affairs or I'll personally flatten it."

"Mr. Mazur —"

"I know you were here; I've heard all about it. We had a family discussion this morning, and you will not — repeat, not — involve Helen in a slimy effort to nail some poor bastard on a rape charge."

"Mr. Mazur, stop, listen to me —"

"You'll stay out of our lives or by God I'll break your meddling neck."

"You've just committed a criminal offense, Mr. Mazur."

But he just talks over me with the same ice-cold virulence. "I want you to listen very carefully. You are never to come here again. You are not to phone Helen or to have any contact with her whatsoever."

"Let *her* tell me that."

And then her voice comes on the line. "Miss Finnegan, I've decided not to interfere."

"Interfere? Helen, please be your own person!"

"I'm sorry, the matter is closed. Goodbye." End of conversation; she hangs up.

I am beside myself; I bang my fists on my desk in fury. No one is here, thank God, to see these tears of anger and frustration. Guy needs a frontal lobotomy. What did he do, give her a couple of blows to the face? Somehow, I will circumvent this number-crunching sexist dictator. Terry, her daughter, may be the means of access.

God has summoned this sinner. Might as well get it over with. I straighten my shoulders and make my way down the hall, where J.J. is standing beside his open door, talking to his secretary.

"I have no comment. Keep telling them that till their ears get sore of hearing it." His nose is still red, his eyes watery, but he's over the worst of his dreadful cold. "Good morning, Elizabeth." Very formal: this is not good.

After leading me in, he plumps onto his big swivel chair, then put his glasses on to study me. I don't sit, just lean toward him over a highback chair, trying to look bright-eyed and certain of my objective, though I'm disheartened now: Helen's subjugation to her husband has put me in a funk.

"The press has this notion that I'm somehow responsible for you. They want to know what I'm going to do *about* you. Well, I guess I'll just tell them I'm not a censor. As far as I'm concerned, the First Amendment is holy writ. I've never told anyone in this firm what to think or what to say or how to say it, and I'm proud of that. If you go too far it's your rump on the line, and I'm just going to hang around and watch it swivel in the wind." He is reacting with unusual severity.

"You know me, J.J., I say what's on my mind. Especially if it's true."

"In case you think I'm as dumb as a fencepost, no, I don't assume you unthinkingly blurted out those unappetizing sound bites. I believe you thought about it. Maybe for only for a second and a half, but you reckoned to draw him into the bullring with you. Have you any idea what you're up against? For instance, bankruptcy?"

"The first defense to slander is the truth."

"And the truth is on your side? This woman suffered a total emotional breakdown; why are you so damn bullheaded sure she was raped? Consider the possibilities: amnesia and a repressed memory reconstructed to satisfy the demands of Christian guilt. I'd acquit him on what you've got, so will any jury. And how do you know she's not out-and-out lying to your face?"

"You don't know her. I believe her with all my heart." But I am feeling my confidence start to melt around the edges. J.J. is persuasive, his powerful voice vibrant but pitched low.

"I've been suckered by too many clients to buy their goods straight off the shelf. I remember one, Meir, had me going right until he gloated he was wrongly acquitted of murder. That was in 1963, Salt Lake City . . . never mind. You're quick on the uptake, Elizabeth, but brains don't come ready-packaged with wisdom: you don't have the years, you don't have the experience."

I slide into my chair, overcome with woe. This is worse than I had expected.

"A predator, that's one of the phrases you used. One act of rape doesn't prove a man has a propensity for it. Where's your proof?"

"Helen Mazur. I think."

"You *think*?"

"Little problem with the head of the family Gestapo."

"Yes, and if she doesn't come through, your claims of Vandergraaf being a sexist predator are pretty damn thin gruel."

"*Sexual* predator."

"*And* rapacious thug. My God, woman, do you realize that even if a jury were to believe Mrs. Struthers, you're still hugely liable for those not-so-carelessly tossed asides? Where's your client's proof? What witnesses do you have? What corroboration?"

"I'll find that woman who took her in, the waiter at the bar."

"Don't bet the farm on it."

I'm exasperated. "What would you have me do, J.J.? I said my piece and if he sues he sues."

He hunches forward, staring at me in a totally

dumbfounded way. I don't think he's acting, although you can never tell with J.J.

"Have you looked at the consequences? If he wins, your career is shattered, in ruins. You will be disbarred as a lawyer, discredited as a person, *and* because jurors will assume we have defamation insurance, the award will be crushing."

I say weakly, "But we do have insurance."

"I'm afraid not." A peeved note in his voice: "I have just spoken to Dwight about that."

I feel somewhat faint.

"You'll have to carry the bag alone, Liz, and after it's over you won't be able to pull a nickel from your pocket for the bubble-gum machine. He's going to claim malicious defamation, young lady, and he has enough evidence of malice against you to sink a battleship. And it's malice that gets him the big jury award, the multi-million-dollar jackpot."

"Dwight doesn't think he'll sue." My confidence is so wilted now that I'm praying he won't.

"Yes, and Dwight believes in fairies. If Hugh Vandergraaf doesn't take action he will not be able to sit on the bench with honor. He has no choice but to take you to court or resign."

"So you think I should grovel at his feet for his mercy and forgiveness."

"I'd like you to permit me to speak with him."

"And tell him what? I flew apart at the seams? I've gone off to lie on a psychiatrist's couch?"

His voice now takes on a weariness. "Let me try to spread some foam on the flames, Elizabeth. Do me that favor." His cold has sapped him, and I have a sense he has not much strength left for this trying day. I know he cares for me, though he is not the kind of person to show it, and it dismays me that I have caused him so much pain.

Yet I feel a fire of stubbornness igniting deep inside

my gut. How could I live with myself if I back down, what price surrender if I go through life compromised and defeated, if I can no longer look myself in the face — or any abused woman, any victim of rape?

"Nobody ever died from eating a few words," he says softly.

"I would. I'd choke to death on them. I can't, J.J. I can't apologize for something that is a matter of deep principle. I'd self-destruct."

"You're your own worst enemy, Liz."

He is about to say something more, write me off, banish me to some Siberia reserved for the prideful and the perverse, but now Junior comes charging in clutching a portable radio. "Sorry, but you'll want to hear this. Hugh Vandergraaf has resigned."

I sit up. My ears aren't working? I thought he said "resigned." A tinny voice from his radio: ". . . told reporters his client is putting his reputation on the line and expects to be fully vindicated by the electorate in the November elections."

Of course, that's what he'd do. I sag hopelessly back onto the chair.

"Repeat," says the announcer, "Judge Hugh Vandergraaf, subject of allegations of a twenty-seven-year-old sexual assault, has announced he is resigning from the King County Superior Court but will seek re-election this November. His lawyer, William Christiansen, has filed suit in that court against Seattle attorney Elizabeth Finnegan, claiming eight million dollars in damages for malicious defamation."

"Well," I say, feigning cheer, "I guess he's fallen into my trap."

"Congratulations," says J.J. "Shut that damn thing off." He turns his back to me, swivels to the window, and stares out at the clouds gathering to the west.

Wind and sails hold firm as a dawning light begins to tint the eastern sky. Our day of reckoning is about to burst on us in all its fearful glory, a day when reputation must be revived or die.

"Reputation, reputation," grieved ill-fated Cassio, "I have lost my reputation, the immortal part of me." How intact remains my immortal part, Ms. Finnegan? Oh, you have scraped away some flesh, but such wounds might heal in time. All but one — and dare you boast of that?

Ah, Elizabeth, were those imputations slung from reckless passion or had you hoped to prod me stumbling blindly from my lair, to taunt me, bait me, strip me bare before the world?

I suppose you were insulted by that Laurel and Hardy routine in Schoenenberg's office. No problem, they told me. They were going to fix it right up. Scrappy little thing, but she's out of her league.

What choice had I but to respond — like a man, as it were — to your glove-swipe across my face?

I sensed your puzzlement while we waited at the chessboard for one or other to push a pawn. My intended game was queen's gambit declined. You were to think: how calm must be the grandmaster of the Wandering I to maintain such spurning silence for fourteen months and fourteen days. Why did I sit there like a lump, you ask, while the storm clouds loomed darkly overhead?

The pathetic truth: I had hoped this war of wills would fizzle out, give like smoke into the sky, the fortifications of reputation left standing, singed a little, maybe, but holding up against the raking enfilade of scandal. And so I bunkered down and waited in aloof anticipation of your offering of remorse. None came. Bullied by my counsel to make and give discovery, I demurred — why give the hitwoman bullets for her empty gun?

It was generous of Dwight to do so on his own — don't you

think? – with his "He got all he wanted for free." Of course I knew I had to swallow that, the handyman, the campus cocksman of the class of '71.

Ah, fair Elizabeth, those days remain such a blur of fury and anguish. I was flailing away in an indiscriminate rage at the world, pouring forth scorn and vitriol, grabbing onto whatever lifelines were thrown me: a pair of reaching arms or upturned lips, a breast upon which to cast my tears of lost fraternal love.

They never found his body. His bullet-riddled bones may still be scattered bleached upon the banks of the River Kan. It was two days before the Christmas of 1970. He was caught in crossfire, survivors said. But we weren't sure. We waited, we waited.

How long did it take me to recover? A year? Longer? That I passed my exams seems a miracle. I sought surcease in sex. Each carnal interlude was a narcotic hit of escape from hell, and when it wore off I needed more, and there was always more, sportive women eager for my bed, bearing their gifts of lotus and nepenthe.

I was grabbing for life. I was frightened. I was ignorant. My mother had never taught me how to love – how does one find it, feel it, grasp it? As if it were corporeal, soulless, made of flesh. Too late comes understanding. Too late, a wasted revelation.

What did I know of women? What does any twenty-two-year-old? Yes, I used them in a way your consciousness so implacably abjures. And I am not without regret or self-reproach. I do not need a mass demonstration beneath my window to wake me from some long-unliberated sleep. I am there, your comrade, arm in arm.

You're wrinkling your nose. How patronizing. But I say take the helm, command this leaky ship of state, nurse pillaged overpopulated earth to health again. We give it all to you, our legacy of poverty and war, of bigotry and greed, pollution and decay. Lock us from your bedrooms, give us lists of simple mindless chores, do not let us play with knives and guns and chainsaws.

But these words are cheap and hollow, and repentance comes too late. You did not forgive, and why should you have?

But you itched to peer inside. All those bold looks of bewilderment flung my way spoke of a more than passing interest in the forces that misshaped this blighted soul. Or was I merely regarded with the amiable interest of one strolling through the zoo and pausing at the hyena cage? Though a cruder canine analogy comes to mind: two circling dogs, sniffing at each other, seeking the scented messages of where we've been and who we are.

Who are you? you asked.

Now we know . . .

And all your tears and mine can never wash the truth away.

No matter. I am not deterred in my resolve; I am confident of my course as I speed toward the belly of Juan de Fuca on a beam reach to the open sea. The sky pales and stars begin to fade. Dawn blushes coyly before the rising naked sun. . . . Thus begins judgment day.

PART TWO

December 1999

A good name is better than precious ointment.

– ECCLESIASTES 7:1

12 |

Junior hasn't been able to corral too many of us cattle for the weekly office meeting: some of the lawyers are boycotting him until he pries open the purse for the office Christmas party ten days hence, an extravaganza at a five-star restaurant. J.J. wouldn't be so miserly — but he is not in circulation: he's recovering from a heart attack suffered four months ago. I have been blamed, of course: I caused the strain to his heart.

I sit at the butt end of the long table, opposite Junior, so I can stare at him. It is quite amazing how the nosepicker won't look at me any more, as if he feels guilty about something. For instance, his strenuous non-support, during the last fourteen months, of the defendant in the looming trial of Vandergraaf versus Finnegan. Or perhaps he merely feels chagrined that one of his most notorious cost-cutting measures, dispensing with expensive libel insurance, has come home to roost — at least for me.

"I count a dozen loyalists," Junior says. "Are we waiting for others or do I take it the empty chairs denote a widespread industrial unrest is afoot within the ranks of our merry little band?"

"Stop being such a cheapnik," someone says.

"I'm afraid our budget for frivolous activities has been exhausted this year. That drunken brawl which some of you would prefer to call the annual summer barbecue emptied the piggy bank. Those who wish to celebrate the season will just have to ante up from their own pockets. J.J. Plum and Company is not running a charity for well-to-do lawyers."

"We've booked an entire restaurant, Junior."

"Yes, at Canlis, for almost a hundred dollars a plate, champagne extra – let's say a minimum six thousand. I could buy a trip around the world with that."

"Stop in Iraq, don't hurry back," Franca says under her breath.

"Shall we look over some of last week's little extravagances? The bill of 3,982 dollars and thirty-seven cents to refurbish your office, Alex, came in exactly 1,982 dollars and thirty-seven cents over projections. How can that be? Did we go for the gold-plated desk this time? Did we manage to find an original Cézanne for the wall?"

"No, Dwight, we bought from the Goodwill. Two thousand dollars doesn't buy jack-shit."

I suspect I go to these meeting because I have developed a morbid fascination with the way Junior finds such masochistic enjoyment from being belittled. He invariably comes up smiling. Paddle me harder, I so love it. I wonder if he's an aficionado of bondage, though he probably can't find anyone kinky enough; divorced once, he has never managed to sustain a relationship.

Curtis Kaplan, as usual, joins us late, dragging his way to a chair. He was feeling jaunty when I finally returned from those commission hearings (the three months had extended to five, then seven, then eight, finally ending this August). Now he is back to examining his emotional entrails. I don't think his relationship with Maxine Vradjik is too serene. Also causing him distress is a forthcoming trial: he represents a paraplegic boy.

Stephane's coming-out party this post-Thanksgiving weekend is close upon my twenty-eighth birthday, and the events will be joined: Nicholson has been planning it for months, and I think he intends to propose to Stephane afterward. Stephane finds the loft too "grotty" and he has bought a waterfront place on Mercer Island. I must now find a new roommate, someone who won't mind sharing quarters with a bankrupt former lawyer. She said pessimistically. But I must not permit myself such disheartening thoughts. Think positive. I can win. I will win. I must win.

"Is your case going to last all of two weeks, Curtis? Those disbursements are killing us. Surely you'd think they'd settle."

"It's going at least as far as the courthouse steps. Their last offer came in at only four mil. Poor kid, only twelve years old."

"Yes, of course, that's what the courts are for, fair compensation. What's our slice of pie, the standard twenty points?"

"Seventeen and a half."

"That low? It's like leaving money to mold in the ground, Kaplan."

"Buys a lot of Christmas cheer at Canlis," someone says.

"Okay, my friends, here's what we'll do: Kaplan brings that settlement in, J.J. Plum and Co. will ante up."

And we will all celebrate Christmas thanks to the fact some poor boy has become a lifetime paraplegic. All this office avarice is making my stomach clench, and I know a drink won't relax it, but I need one nonetheless: an eggnog to celebrate the season. If I do not put on some weight I will look like one of those starving models in *Vogue*. Being sued for eight million dollars tends to put one off one's food.

I join Derek Philpott at the bar where he is making himself some tea. He is our libel specialist, and has helped me out with the pleadings, but I am not using him for the trial. He is too . . . polite may be the word. A negotiator. A conciliator. I want a counsel with some starch. Which is why I have retained the infamous Elizabeth Finnegan. (What a howl of disbelief and protest greeted *that* announcement around here.

Unheard-of! She's off her rocker! Lawyer who acts for herself has a fool for a client!)

Of course when I made that announcement, I was expecting Vandergraaf would be suing the media, too, and facing a battery of top libel lawyers. But he has deliberately ignored the press, and now is one on one with lonely, stubborn, willful Liz, too proud to beg for help.

"I thought you'd be preparing," Derek says. "You're only a few days away."

"I'll be ready."

"You don't seem very concerned."

I am hiding it well. "What have I to lose?"

"It could get well into the millions. You can't predict a jury."

"Blood from a stone." I had a nest egg of fifty thousand dollars, mostly in mutual funds and savings bonds. It was deposited to Mother's account to repay those extra loans we had discovered she'd made to me. If I declare bankruptcy I can always find a job tree-planting.

"You can mitigate your damages, Liz. You know he has Supreme Court ambitions – they can be salvaged by an unequivocal apology. And he's well-to-do; he may be willing to take a smaller chunk if the apology is big-hearted enough."

"Up his backside is where I'll apologize."

I am pessimistic, though. They are convinced my case is shabby and are reeking of overconfidence, casually proceeding without depositions or interrogatories – no discovery of my case at all; it is most odd. The entire Seattle legal community is wondering why.

I suspect they simply decided a favorable outcome is assured; after all, Vandergraaf was acquitted last year by the biggest jury of all, the electorate. He won back his judgeship with a three-to-one plurality, proudly trumpeting his passing grade on a lie-detector test. He played the victim; the public didn't know all the facts . . .

Do *I* know all the facts? Who are their witnesses? Mine are a paltry few: Beatrice Struthers, Gayle Mitsuka, and I am still holding out hope for Helen Mazur. Tomorrow, I will be talking again to Terry, her daughter, with whom I've already had a few surreptitious meetings in Spokane.

Vandergraaf's lawyers will obviously claim Beatrice had consensual intercourse, then argue that because she suffered a breakdown she cannot be trusted to be mentally stable and reliable. To counter that, I will present a psychiatrist, Dr. Ann Boorstein, who works with abused women. She will testify Beatrice suffered a depressive reaction, an opinion based partly on subpoenaed patient records of the Faith Hospice, where Beatrice was incarcerated in 1971. I can't find the registered nurse who worked there, and the attending physician is long deceased.

As for the one key witness I would give my left ovary to locate, the server at the Bedwell bar, the search has come to naught. Thalia Loralee Pfeiffer is her full name, according to the ex-manager at the Bedwell Resort. I have almost given up hope of finding her and I don't know how reliable she would be in any event: her sheet shows two convictions for drug-trafficking.

I have also reached an impasse in my efforts to locate the couple with Vandergraaf and Beatrice on the sailing trip to Pender Island. We spent weeks contacting hundreds of former students at UW, but came up clueless. I worry that Vandergraaf may spring them on me – but what can they say? They didn't witness the assault. They went for a walk. They saw Beatrice leaving the dock, upset. How can they explain her failure to return to the boat or the bite mark on Hugh's neck?

I am grasping at straws, however; if Beatrice doesn't do well on the stand I am doomed. I try to tell myself: *che sarà sarà.*

Junior is droning on about our plans to take over the

entire thirty-fourth floor next year: heavy capital expenses, don't expect last year's Christmas bonuses. Groans.

But he is not being his usual entertaining self, and it's late and I have other things to do. And I can't get this eggnog into my shrunken stomach. Curtis catches my eye as I am about to leave, rises to join me, but Junior won't let me escape without his goodbye dig.

"Ah, before you deplete our diminishing numbers, Elizabeth, do you have any proposals on how to further embarrass the firm? Or were you quoted correctly in that waiting-room glossy which featured your smiling face on the cover?"

"What quote?"

"When you regaled your interviewer about the characters in the office? About these people, your *colleagues*. About the office manager being, quote, a delightful windbag?"

"Sorry, that kind of slipped out. The delightful part."

Harry Crake was finally able to dry out long enough to write the piece, which only recently appeared, well timed for my jury trial. I am presented as breezy but down-to-earth, though I think Harry is disgruntled at me: my advice that he seek counseling didn't work, nor did AA, and he and his wife are back in court, a custody tug-of-war.

"Not much wonder that she gets sued for slander." Dwight is complaining to an almost empty room; people are filing out, giving me winks. I receive much quiet support from the firm. Not J.J., though — my many visits to his bedside have gained me nary a whispered word of encouragement, and he avoids the subject. The heart attack was not serious, thank God, but enough to keep him home.

Curtis still cannot break his annoying habit of trying to steer me forward with his hand on my elbow. "Can we go out for a drink? I need to talk."

"Curtis, I have a million things on my desk." It is a swamp: almost a year out of the office at those reproduction hearings, three months catching up on the backlog – when I returned, files were piled several feet. A two-hundred-page brief for the Planned Parenthood Association is yet unfinished.

Curtis follows me into my office, where Mattie is tidying up. "Can I bring a friend Saturday night?" she asks.

"Of course. Bring the entire band." She is having a fling with the second coming of Jimi Hendrix, a local blues guitarist. "You and Maxine will show up, Curtis?"

"I think she'd feel uncomfortable."

"It's *my* party, too. I'd feel badly." My birthday is actually the seventh, the Tuesday coming. I'll be observing it in court; Hugh Vandergraaf will not be offering gifts. "Give me a sec or two. I'll meet you at the Oly, okay?"

Curtis slopes forlornly off. I suspect he is one of those persons destined for unhappiness – or it is the road he seems to choose.

Mattie hands me an opened letter. "Passionate love note."

Yet another Captain Hornblower at the tiller; this one is about to leave for Acapulco and needs one more crewmember for his complement of two. He dares enclose his photograph: sweat-stained undershirt, muscles in place of brains. How I wish I had never confided to Harry Crake I have a passion for the sea. *She despairs of finding Mr. Right.* "*I think I scare them away.*" *Her dreamboat, she says, is about sixty feet long with a mast.* I must have had too much wine.

I *am* beginning to despair. I count just two brief dalliances in the last year. One was a long-haired set designer from Pasadena whom I met while I was trying to collect myself on Kauai after the slander suit was launched. That affair culminated in one hot non-stop night, then he flew back to Hollywood for a shoot. The other was a Ph.D. in biology, one of the commission witnesses in Houston. He didn't know *that* much about biology, especially female anatomy. I would have flunked him.

Since then, I have dated a few times and been more than subtly importuned, but I am a victim of my own high standards. It's not just that I need a body to share; that is there, but I'd settle for some closeness, some intense affection. I am tempted to return to Pender Island and look up that protective guard dog, Stash, and share a blanket this time.

Into my backpack goes the file: Superior Court Cause 98-2-01620-1, Vandergraaf versus Me – it goes home with the defendant every day. Mattie and I have almost had to work in code to keep the office quisling from poking his nose into it. We are constantly deleting material from the computer because we're sure Junior sneaks into my office at night.

Final pre-trial conference on Friday, Judge Mavis M. Luckwell presiding. She has been brought up especially for the case from Eastern Washington, the Tri-Cities. A judge's judge, they say, which sits well with me: a judge is being judged. She seemed to take a path down the middle at the last pre-trial, though she castigated Vandergraaf's lawyer for requesting depositions after the cutoff: our rules strictly forbid last-minute pre-trial examinations of opposing witnesses. Christiansen has Beatrice's affidavit, anyway, courtesy of the Victorian English gardener.

Mulholland's grimacing face graces my wall now: Harry Crake gave me the print. I am grabbing Mulholland's tie, and the tall, ungainly Mountie has his arm curled around my waist, trying to separate us.

How I would love to see their expressions if Vandergraaf loses. *When* he loses, damn it. During my lonely hopeful hours of preparing for this trial, I have often fantasized: there skulks the plaintiff from Judge Luckwell's court, a sheepish smile of resignation on his face. Then it is back to Canada for this dumb blonde. They marched in Seattle, Tacoma, Vancouver, and the pressure forced the B.C. attorney-general to announce he may prosecute the rape complaint – though he will await the outcome of the slander trial.

No lurkers dog my heels as I head up the block and a half to the Olympic Hotel. I haven't heard those warning bells since I started therapy with Ann Boorstein. She says it is a learned sense of defensive watchfulness: women pick up clues, a strategy of survival loosely referred to as women's intuition. I was probably imagining I was being followed. Ann says I'm not paranoid, but I do have an overactive imagination, and there is nothing wrong with that. I am seeing her for my ups and downs: my anger, more particularly. I must learn not to fly out of control.

It has been all quiet on the abortion front – no more bombings since Detective Ellen Oversmith had a long, serious chat with the Kruegers. They would not own up to knowing the perpetrators, Johann becoming indignant and righteous. But I suspect he spread the word.

Curtis greets me in the lobby of the Oly, a grand inn spruced up by the Four Seasons chain, and suggests Shuckers, the oyster bar. "I'm famished. Maxine doesn't cook for me."

"Why should she?"

They have been nesting for six months at her place: the house near Alki Beach was part of the settlement. The children are with her, and Curtis seems to be bonding with them.

I decide to snack, too – Nicholson is out tonight preparing for his opening – and order some beer and oysters, raw Olympias: I hope I can manage to slide them down to my stomach.

"I don't know how to say this. It's really not something

I wanted to bring up in group. But – you won't laugh, will you? – maybe I need a woman's perspective . . ."

"Don't feel awkward."

"I don't, ah, meet her needs. In bed. I mean, I'm sure I score about median in terms of a healthy sexual drive, but I think she's in the top percentile."

For some reason, this tale of carnal woe causes my own tide of anguish to ebb. I cannot hide a smile.

"I guess you find this uproarious."

"No, Curtis, not really, but I don't think it's the end of the civilized world. You've been under stress. I know your trial is weighing on you."

He pauses until the server lays out our plates of ice-imbedded oysters, then leans forward. "It's got so bad I'm afraid to come home and face her. She wants to do it as soon as I walk in. I mean, she, you know, *grabs* at me. By the, you know . . . And I can't do *anything*."

I attempt to hold a stern and serious expression, but can't. "Sounds like spousal abuse to me."

Curtis takes umbrage. "Oh, I'm sure if gender were reversed, you'd be totally sympathetic and on your high horse about it, but when a man is the victim it's just one of life's little jokes."

"Curtis, I'm sorry, I can see it's concerning you. Eat your oysters, they're supposed to be an aphrodisiac."

"Old wives' tale."

"Why do we never hear of old husbands' tales?"

Curtis looks aggrieved, though I'm only joking to cheer him up. "Please, Liz, I'm trying to get my head together over this. I mean, at some level I feel as if I'm not – horrible expression – not a real man. I can't help it, I've been socialized by the mythos about potency and virility. And now it's compounded by performance anxiety."

"Well, maybe you're on a sexual down cycle."

"There's worse. She . . . well, she has this, um, vulgar mouth. When we do get into it, she vocalizes. Some people do that, I know, but I find it — how do I say? — not very romantic."

"Puts you off your stroke."

"If you wish to express it so coarsely."

"What does she say?"

"Elizabeth, don't . . . Well, all right, to satisfy your prurient interest." He looks down at his plate, his ears blazing. "'Pump it into me, baby. Give it to me, honey, hard . . .'"

He breaks off as our young server freezes in the act of reaching for our empty beers. She says in a hoarse voice, "Excuse me, would you folks like another?"

"We'd better cut him off." I think I've entered one of my manic phases — I have been soaring and plummeting like a flimsy kite in capricious winds since Vandergraaf served his summons. But Ann Boorstein says life is a roller coaster: ride it; have fun with your neuroses.

"How mortifying," Curtis says as the server leaves. He struggles with me for the bill she hurriedly dropped on the table. "No, I'm paying. You'll need all your spare change." Like almost everyone else on planet earth, he takes a dim view of my chances against Vandergraaf. "Sorry, I shouldn't be so self-concerned when you've got the fight of your life on your hands. It's selfish of me."

"Don't worry, Curtis. If I lose, I'll quit the practice anyway because the law will have been proven an ass."

"Well, that sort of brings up another thing. She wants me to try different, ah, methods. Like . . . how do I put this — going into the wrong place."

I am about to down a last slimy oyster, but return it to my plate.

Fourth Avenue is bright and busy, the shops open late for Christmas traffic. It is the last such celebration of the twentieth century; a millennium is over: buy, buy, buy to show your love of Jesus. At the Bon, I wander among the counters. Mom, Nicholson, Mattie: what gifts might they need or enjoy?

Down the street, at Nordy's, I pay extravagantly for a Giorgio Armani outfit for Mother suitable for the wedding — it is set for New Year's Day and I'm footing the entire reception. (My attitude is: spend it all; Vandergraaf won't get a brown Abe.)

I have made several forays to Coalsack, pleased each time to find Mother's live-in relationship with Jake Bjorklund still happy and tranquil. He is not the worst scalawag who could have come down the pike, and I've always found something admirable about people who are full of dreams. No silver has been dug from those mines, of course, but he has devised a scheme to finance a hot springs resort nearby. He is so enamored of Mom (and her down-home cooking) that I'm sure he won't be taking any sudden leaves.

I escorted Beatrice to Coalsack for Labor Day, though she went reluctantly, and there was an awkwardness between her and Mother. Jake, too, noticed they seemed to keep a polite distance from one another, and strove to keep us entertained with his yarns.

The galleries are busy in Pioneer Square: tomorrow is locally known as First Thursday, and artists and dealers are setting up their new displays. It is a ritual: first Thursday of the month, galleries and craft shops hold openings simultaneously; art lovers come from far and wide to browse. Nick has a show nearby at the Davidson, and as I stop at the window I can see him within, fussing and fretting, adjusting one of his canvases of moving figures. Pacing outside is Stephane Vradjik, chaining Lucky Strikes.

"He won't let me help." He mimics: "'I don't try to interfere when you're isolating a new DNA molecule.'"

"How did it go today?" His divorce and custody are being handled by Franca Crabtree; they were in mediation again today over the two teenagers.

"I've had to settle for weekends plus a month in summer."

"They'll soon be grown."

This isn't what he wants to hear. "*She* gets custody. *She's* living in sin with that little shit from your office. Why is my crime greater? Michael even *testified* he wouldn't mind living with me. Why does some simpering self-adulating fool get to be their father figure?"

Such acrimony is normally not part of his nature. "Want to come up? Maybe you need a drink."

"No, I'm dragging Nicholson out kicking and screaming to an art film from Canada, of all places, that he might just *try* to enjoy. Nicholson is so low-brow. I suppose he's invited all his beatnik friends for this beastly Saturday-night outing. I wish he hadn't trumpeted it as some kind of rite of passage. Coming out – I feel like going back in."

Despite the grumbles, I know there's deep affection between these men. They will grow old together.

The Washington Shoe Building is lit and cheery. A couple of low-rent galleries on the bottom floors are being dressed up and there is activity on the staircase, a couple of neighbor friends hauling down a heavy sculpture.

In the loft, I sip my ritual martini as I peel off my clothes and run the tub. Look at that skinny wretch in the mirror: adopt this starving child. *Anorexia nervosa.* I did manage to ingest most of those aphrodisiac oysters, and hopefully I'll add some seasonal cushioning.

I cannot tell if it is abstinence, oysters, or my carnal conversation with Curtis that has filled me with such sexual yearning. No man is an island, said John Donne. Well, no woman is, either. God, I need a lover.

I close my eyes and dream . . .

13 | Thursday . . .

The view from my office window is blinding: sunlight reflecting from a vast pillow of fog below, towers rising from it like castles in the sky. No sign of Puget Sound, but the Olympics are out, their peaks showy and bright. The NPR weatherperson calls this an inversion: fog has blanketed the sound, but the sky is clear above.

Ten o'clock, and the offices are nearly empty; a mere scattering of lawyers and support staff have managed to find their way downtown. Mattie has yet to show, though Junior is here, seeking someone to replace the missing receptionist.

When I turn to my work-filled desk, I'm caught off guard: a short, pretty woman is standing just outside my door. I have met her. Where?

"I'm sorry, I didn't see anyone at the front desk."

Hugh Vandergraaf's former bailiff, Juanita Calvo, that is her name. Mexican-born, I think, but with only the faintest trace of accent. Not quite five feet, slim and dark.

"That's all right, everyone's late. Have a seat; I'll get you some coffee."

As I attend to this task I ponder whether this woman comes as friend or foe. She was tense during our brief meeting in Vandergraaf's chambers: she had seemed possessive of him, hostile to me. But she is no longer employed in the court system; I heard she had problems managing her work.

"Careful, that's hot, we warm the cups." I lay them on the walnut table and sit next to her. "I hope the fog will clear, don't you? Though it's pleasant in a way, makes everything seem so languid and mysterious. Well, it's nice to see you again, Juanita. How are you?"

"Not too well. I can't get a job."

"Oh, I'm sorry. What happened to your old one?"

"I couldn't handle it any more. I wasn't comfortable in those courts."

I pick up an edge of bitterness. "Was there something more to it than that?"

She looks away, playing with her hair: black and straight, a perfect part down the middle. "I worked two years for Judge Vandergraaf. I couldn't stay with him any longer after that."

Curiosity swells like a balloon. "After what, Juanita?"

"Beatrice Struthers was not the only one."

What have we here? The pulse quickens.

"First, I want to know – can I sue him?"

"That depends on what he did to you."

"For all my lost wages, and damages for injury and to my future prospects. Special damages, or punitive, or whatever it's called."

She sounds as if she's ordering from a menu. I might be prepared to pump her hopes up, but, however curious, I am cautious about one who seems so mercenary.

"What happened exactly between you and him?"

"He raped me."

I put this conversation briefly on hold, calling Mattie, asking her to intercept all calls.

"Sorry. He raped you?"

"Yeah, two times. I didn't do anything about it, because I . . . well, I liked him. And later I found out he was also seeing another lady."

"Just a minute. You said he raped you *twice*?"

"That's exactly what he did. On our first night, he took me out for drinks and he got me in such a state I didn't know what I was doing, and I don't remember a thing until I woke up in bed with him. If I don't remember, that's rape, isn't it?"

"What about the other time?"

"He came to my apartment at midnight and we had sex there."

"Did you consent?"

"He's the boss, what am I supposed to do? He actually fooled me into thinking I was the only one."

The story unfolds slowly and, to my ears, painfully. Between the lines, her tale is this: seduced, deluded into a false belief her affections were being returned, Juanita Calvo quit her job upon learning another woman had been lurking in the wings. The wound festers the more because she can't find new employment. Remedy is being sought through a lawyer known not to be overly fond of the judge.

The alcohol-aided seduction occurred this spring: dinner, several drinks, and she awoke in his bed after coitus. The other episode took place, oddly, on the night after the Court of Appeals raised Tyler J. Henderson's rape sentence to three years. Vandergraaf was upset; she invited him to come by her apartment. Late that evening he showed up tipsy (but with flowers and a bottle of wine) and "did it to me" again. She also fellated him at his request, but her efforts failed to return him to his previous manly state. He fell asleep and stayed the night.

Then Hugh callously traded her in for the other woman.

"Mrs. Yvonne Fairhurst. She's a society lady, and she's married." A fact which seems to add to the affront. "I overheard them talking on the phone."

"I see. Do you know of any others?"

"Oh, there were lots. He took different women out sailing."

"How do you know all this?"

"My phone was sometimes off the hook."

Where does our busy future justice of the U.S. Supreme Court find the time to employ himself with so many women? Seducing his bailiff: there's profit to be made if I can pry that out of him on the stand. But I dare not call Juanita as a witness; a jury of even the most enlightened will consider her understanding of rape stretched.

I spend another hour tape-recording her, offering considered assurances as to her rights of redress. Though her case for assault may be weak, she has a harassment claim – she was certainly in a disempowered position with Vandergraaf, so any consent was colored.

As Juanita is about to leave, she asks, "What do you think this is worth?"

"Let me think about that."

A harassment suit on the eve of the trial: would that be playing by Queensberry rules? A rational part of my brain warns me not to be too precipitate: Judge Luckwell might get the perfectly correct idea I'm seeking to influence the jury; she could turn them against me. J.J. has often told me I must learn to restrain myself; I am too impetuous.

I will assign Mattie to check out Mrs. Yvonne Fairhurst, society matron. I wonder if her husband knows?

Junior rolls in unannounced, clutching some of Mike Gustafson's time sheets. Mike is our full-time investigator, a retired police captain who dislikes judges and despises rapists; he has been sworn to secrecy.

"This kind of leaped out at me." Dwight is referring to the notation "Re: Finnegan:" eighty non-billable hours of Mike's fruitless pursuit of the missing number-one witness.

"Yes, he's running a few errands." Thank God I removed all references to Thalia Pfeiffer's name.

"Are we assuming the firm is bankrolling your defense? I think not. You demonstrate an utter . . . who is this Thalia Pfeiffer he's looking for?"

I am betrayed; Junior must have put splints under Gustafson's nails. "Just a witness. Thought she might be able to add something."

"Can't find the waitress, can you?" An infuriating smug smile. "Latterly, a merchant of misery, I'm given to understand. You must be quite desperate if you're having Gustafson spend half his working hours trying to locate a narcotics trafficker."

If the plaintiff's legal team had any thoughts of backing down, they'll turn to vapor when Junior reports in. Down I slide, back into the pit.

"Oh, by the way, be prepared for a deduction in your monthly draw."

"That's really small, Junior. I'm going to speak to J.J. about it."

"I man the desk at which the buck stops until he's up and about. And that won't occur until late next week. I told him it's risky, but he insists on going to work. I would imagine you feel terribly contrite about the pressures you've put on his heart." He is about to leave, but pauses. "I think you're in for the shock of your life next week. Good luck — you'll need it."

What shock? His words unnerve me, especially because I suspect he's privy to the plaintiff's secrets.

But he doesn't elaborate, and wheels around to the door, mumbling: "Shameful. Ugly business, this libel. Tarnishes the good name of J.J. Plum and Company."

I call after him, "Thanks for standing behind me, Dwight."

I wait until he is out of sight, then stride unhappily down to Mike Gustafson's office. He looks hangdog as he tells me Junior threatened to give him the gate if he didn't squeal.

The good news: Mike has a lead on Thalia Loralee Pfeiffer, though a sketchy one. He thinks she's in Panama. I don't have to guess what she's doing there.

"The tip came from a deep throat in the DEA." Mike was in the SPD for forty years and has connections with all the agencies. He definitely looks the part of a retired lawman: meaty, a doughnut belly. "Cocaine. It's a Canadian show, but the Mounties ain't interested in talking to me. Got downright abusive."

"It's a start: she's somewhere in Panama. I hope you didn't tell *that* to Junior."

"No, I said I reached a dead end." He will keep at it.

Terry Mazur told me she'd call after her mid-term evidence exam today, and she is on schedule.

"How did it go?"

"Creamed it."

I have offered her a summer job with the firm: we are always looking for bright prospects. Was her mother ever as spirited as her? As a college student, Helen had been gutsy enough to stand up to Vandergraaf in political argument. Housebroken now, so servile.

"And how's everything at home?"

"Fairly tentative. We don't talk about it. Dad would go ballistic if he found out I'm acting as go-between."

"How ballistic?"

"He'd disown me. Maybe leave her. That's numero uno, her big concern."

How does such an effervescent young woman spring from the seed of such a cold-hearted bully? As may be expected, Terry has often been in conflict with him, though she stands up better than her mother. Wilkie Mazur is controlling, yes, but I pick up no hints of physical abuse at home. Terry's feelings for her father are ambivalent: he is a good provider with a strong work ethic, ambitious for his children.

"I hate to say this, Terry, but, honestly, what kind of marriage can your parents have if it comes apart because she performs a citizen's duty?"

"I know, but she looks at it, like, how many forty-eight-year-old women ever find another husband? The thing about Dad, with all his other qualities, he earns majorly, he's generous, and he doesn't screw around. I don't, you know, not care for him." A catch in her voice.

I find it hard to understand the dynamics of this family. Her two brothers are young business successes. It's as if Wilkie Mazur drew all the strength from his wife and had it transferred to the children.

"Have you tried to talk to him?"

"Well, with Dad, it's . . . you don't bring up the topic of rape. It's not that he's into, you know, all women really want to be raped and at heart they really like it or bullshit like that. But I guess he has this attitude where women sometimes invite it. He thinks Mom will be accused of that. He doesn't want scandal. He's . . . just a very conservative guy. Especially gender-wise."

"Is there no way of bringing Helen around?"

"I hate to say, but I don't think so. She feels awful. She started crying the last time we tried to talk."

"Well, I'm sorry, but she'll feel a whole lot better about herself if she stands up to your father on an issue of principle. Terry, I need her testimony — and so does she; it will help her heal. I have to get her out of Spokane."

"She won't come."

"Well, I'm serving a subpoena on her tomorrow. I gave my undertaking not to use her as a witness and I must honor that, but I want her here so I can talk to her alone."

Terry sighs. "Maybe if she got a subpoena she'd relent, she'd have an excuse. I'll keep trying."

As the day wanes the fog thickens, rolling into the lower streets near Ann Boorstein's building. I have a four-o'clock therapy appointment with her. I have also asked her to draft an assessment of Vandergraaf; she may have some ideas about how to expose the furtive sociopath within. *I hope I didn't rush things too much*, he had said to Helen Mazur. She had got him "too hot."

As I grope through the haze, I feel a sudden chill, and across the street I make out someone standing, staring at me. Why isn't he moving? Man in a fog – a stalker? Then I realize he is merely having a smoke outside his office building. I thought I was cured of such baseless fears. I *am* cured. Mind over paranoia, that's what Ann says. You're not crazy if you think you are.

Ann's heritage building is on First, old but spruced up, art deco and terra cotta. Her office is on the twentieth floor, overlooking the Alaskan Way Viaduct and the ferry terminal – not that we can see them today.

"Want a juice or anything?" she says as she leads me into her homey office and plunks me into an overstuffed chair.

"Just a coffee, I guess."

"The hell you'll have a coffee." She fetches orange juice from her fridge. "Have you cut down at all, or are you still pouring that stuff down your gullet? Still a little wasted is what you look. But better."

Though Ann comes from East Side Manhattan, she's an earth-mother type, wholly unpretentious, never applies makeup, and dresses with a casual unconcern for style. She is fifty, practiced general medicine for fifteen years before doing her postgrad, and she is forever counseling me to improve my physical health. Overconsumption of coffee is unhealthy, of course, but junkies don't have very good ears.

"I'm cutting down. I'll try to quit when the trial's over."

"Don't do me such a favor. And you should eat. I worry about nutritional deficiency. Getting enough exercise?"

"Walk every day. I'm going to try a little cross-country

skiing this winter. I'll get back onto a fitness regime when the pressure's off."

"You still optimistic?"

"Well, you know I get these ups and downs. I suppose I feel a fatalism beneath it all. One thing *really* disturbing me is I still can't keep Hugh Vandergraaf from intruding on my, um, daydreams."

"You mean when you masturbate."

I color. "Yes. Sick movie. I just ring the curtain down and get depressed."

What pulls me so perversely to him? I am bewildered by such thoughts, spooked by whispered hints from deep within that I knew him from a life before, that we were bonded once, lovers reincarnated. But this is occult claptrap, too bizarre even to discuss with Ann.

"You don't have rape fantasies, though?"

"No. Never."

"I get besieged with those. Rhett Butler hauling Scarlett O'Hara upstairs for a little bodice-ripping copulation. Liz, we're all fascinated by evil at some level. Even attracted to it. Evil ain't boring. It's not a big deal, but you should work on it."

"So what's your take on Vandergraaf? He's incredibly promiscuous." I tell her about how he used Juanita, the affair with Yvonne Fairhurst.

She settles into her couch. "The literature calls it a wolf complex. Two basic types: there's the sheep in wolf's clothing, a milquetoast with either a nagging fear of impotency or doubts about his heterosexuality. This is the kind of guy who has to prove over and over he's a *schtarker*, a man."

"Somehow that doesn't fit the image."

"So more likely he's into a power trip. Discards a woman prematurely in the narcissistic belief he's conquered her, then it's on to the next one. I don't have to tell you, Western society has always eroticized male power. He may even think Beatrice consented – after all, how can any woman *really* resist his charms?"

"He's far more intelligent than that."

"Even good minds are capable of self-deception, Liz."

So ego-deluded that he passed a lie-detector test? Thankfully, polygraphy is regarded as erratic pseudo-science, inadmissible in court.

I ask if she needs to see Beatrice again.

"We're having lunch on Sunday. I looked at those records you got from that black hole of Calcutta they stuck her in. 'Dementia,' 'morbid delusions': nineteenth-century phrases for something they know nothing about. The woman running the hospice was barely out of nurses' training. One visiting doctor, not a single psychologist. Treatment basically consisted of drugs and prayer. I'll prepare a critique for you. Okay, anything else been on your mind besides this all-consuming trial?"

"I had that creeping feeling again today, imagining I was being watched – first time in months. Maybe there's too much rape in my head."

"Hear any bells?"

"No, but sometimes I think I'm a total neurotic."

"Who can you trust who isn't? But you're a whole treatise, Liz, so many phobic uncertainties, yet such a powerful self-will."

We've talked about this often. The confidence (sometimes just short of arrogance, I suppose, though Ann kindly refrains from using that word) comes, we're sure, from a stable childhood filled with love, enhanced by a gift of superior intelligence. She said pretentiously. The driving will is an attribute of the prematurely born. The fears and superstitions derive from the wrenching early loss of my father. Maybe his death explains my fits of anger, too, but I also inherited from him my rebel spirit.

"You haven't had any more episodes with alcohol, have you?"

Like my unrestrained evening on Pender Island, she means. I have told her that when I drink too much, it is as if a wild, uninhibited pixie inhabits me.

"No. I'm not a good drinker. I *hate* not remembering afterward. Believe me, it's not going to happen again."

"Moderation is good, but I don't think alcohol is a real problem for you. Something else . . ." She muses. "Do you still get that sense of being a little empty and lost out in the big, wide world?"

"Sometimes. When I stop moving long enough."

"Maybe that's why you keep moving. We need to know why that bothers you. Who am I? What am I doing here? Those are the big questions we should all be asking."

"I guess I feel I should be more centered."

"Yeah, but exploring the edge of the unknown is a lot more productive."

I smile. I suppose I should be gratified that she lets me be my imperfect mixed-up self.

Mist pours ghost-like through the streets of Pioneer Square, swirling among the clutching fingers of trees, settling over the huddled and the homeless. But on First Thursday, the more fortunate are also here, art lovers and collectors. Other distinguished guests include a pillow-bellied Santa Claus collecting for Goodwill and two uniformed officers bicycling the cobbled mall on Occidental: pickpockets proliferate on First Thursday; thick wallets abound. Here is the Davidson, a sizable crowd inside already. There is Nick, flighty and excited, guiding several possible patrons around.

And already a few red stickers have appeared on his works. I steal inside, sidle up behind him, listen to his art talk: "What I'm trying to do here is express our universal despair within the frantic thema of the dance"; "We are all denying our truths, this says, living out our pretenses"; "These figures on a playground represent a childhood we deny ourselves in the incessant contemplation of our own mortality." He might be stoned.

I lean forward, whisper into the back of his ear: "Bullshit."

He turns, grinning. "And this incredibly beautiful woman is a symbol of the utter futility of being." To the others: "Excuse me. Wander about. Oh, and feel free to join me for a glass later."

He points me toward the back room, where wine is kept for the anointed few – moneyed buyers and friends of the artist.

"Microsoft millionaires, I think. Sold my 'Four Figures Competing for a Bar Stool' for almost two grand, and one of them is sniffing at the nun giving head to the priest."

"Is that what they're doing? I thought that was called 'Nun Praying While Priests Dance.'"

"In actuality, it's an expression of the imponderability of God's gift of immaculate contraception. Red grape or white? I think Chardonnay for the shining princess."

"Nick, I can smell the cannabis on your breath."

"I get nervous when I'm stoned."

"You mean, when you're nervous, you get stoned."

"However you want it." He clinks my glass. "Here's to fine arts and rich farts. Go find Stephane, he's wandering about in the fog like a spaniel who's lost her puppies. Very Edgar Allan Poe-ish out there, excellent night for murder."

"Nicholson!"

He emits a haunted-house cackle.

"Don't *do* that."

"How did it go at the couch doctor's? Did we get our head shrunk back to size?"

"I actually think I'm progressing."

Am I? Strolling along Occidental in the patchy mist, unsettled by Nick's macabre sense of humor, I see his humanoid creations floating like wraiths over bricks and cobbles: staring silent ghouls. I shake my head to scatter the false images that seek to confuse me. That thin man in the shadows by the Gold Rush Museum: he is probably waiting for a friend. (Have I seen him somewhere before, a stalker? How unlikely.)

Oh, my God, Hugh Vandergraaf is walking from a gallery just down the street. Suit and coat, all alone, looking rather friendless. He hasn't noticed me and I don't want him to. I'll be seeing him soon enough; tomorrow is the final pre-trial. I abandon my search for Stephane, head quickly toward my building. But I slow my pace. Why should I be afraid of him? He is here as a buyer.

I have read that Vandergraaf is an art connoisseur. (And of Louis XVI–revival furniture. And a devotee of classical music. My researches have yet to determine which composers he favors, but he's a patron of the Seattle Symphony. How does he find time? When does he sleep? Why do I care?)

Now, for the first time in months, I hear bogus chimes pealing false tales. I laugh at myself; these are jingle bells, and they are coming from that Santa Claus down the street.

But just as I am ten steps from my door, I hear a hissing voice behind me, and a stab of fear bolts up my spine.

"Burn in the fiery torment, you baby-killing hellhag!"

I am frozen in terror, unable to answer simple mental commands: to flee, to scream, to turn to look at him.

A horrifying evocation of my own bloody murder knots my intestines.

I know he is advancing; his voice is rising, harsh and venomous. "Dyke. Whore. Concubine of Satan."

I race for my door, my rubbery fingers fumbling into my bag: find that pepper spray. But all my bones are knit tight with fear, and he is so close I can smell the heavy staleness of his breath.

And now he grabs my arm, swings me about, shoves an object in my face – not a weapon, a book, the Bible.

Here comes someone running hard, shouting, and I think: there's a gang of them.

"Get your putrid hands off her!"

I lurch to the side as my attacker hits the wall, propelled there by a push. He collapses, his forehead scraped and raw from where it struck, his protruding eyes bulging from the pressure of the shiny black shoe that sits atop his neck, the knee upon his back.

I slide slowly down the wall myself, staring at a polished shoe, my dazed eyes now travelling slowly up to Hugh Vandergraaf's face, long, disheveled hair, burning brilliant eyes.

"Are you all right?"

"Okay, I think."

"Hallelujah," the man on the ground squeaks. "Sing out in praise of Jesus."

"If you pull this kind of stunt again, you'll be singing in the boys' choir." He drags the man to his feet, twisting his arm behind his back. I struggle up, too, dazed.

All manner of thoughts are tumbling through my head, but the one that sticks the hardest is this: how absurd – Hugh Vandergraaf appearing out of the blue, my savior. Of all the hundreds of people milling around Pioneer Square, why him? Had he spotted me in this mist, followed me?

And this welcome realization comes: I am not delusional. The confused Bible-thumper is my old friend,
Barney Google.

"I only talked to her," he says. "I have my God-given
right of free speech."

By now a crowd has assembled, mostly neighbors
from upstairs who heard the ruckus, plus the two police
who were on bike patrol. After listening to my scarcely
coherent account, one of them handcuffs the protesting
fanatic, cautions him that he is being charged with
assault, and calls a wagon.

The other officer flings open a notepad, and as she
conducts interviews, Stephane Vradjik wiggles his way
through the crowd, looking harried and confused.

"I'm a doctor, let me through. Is anyone hurt?
Elizabeth, my God, what have you done?"

I explain I am the innocent party and tell him to
check in with Nick, and then I wait for a quiet moment
to express some carefully worded phrases of gratitude to
my unlikely rescuer. But he doesn't wait for thanks,
turns, begins to walk away.

I catch up, try to match his long strides. "Sincerely,
I want to thank you, Judge. I feel incredibly awkward."
At what? At sharing the oddity of this moment with a
man who is trying to sue my face off for calling him a
sexual predator?

"I grappled with a first instinct, which was to watch
him take a go at you with that Bible." An ironic smile,
but eyes that are not fierce with the antagonism he must
feel for me: they are like sad, distant stars. His hair is
slightly shorter these days, not quite collar-length, and
with more salt-and-pepper flavor. He may have added a
pound or two, but still looks fit.

"It was unexpectedly kind. So odd that you happened to be ... Well, what *were* you doing near my door?"

"That is *your* door? I was on my way up to a gallery

inside. Adieu, Ms. Finnegan, I shall see you tomorrow." But he stops walking, inspects me ruefully.

"Elizabeth, I wonder if you really appreciate what you're getting into. I don't want to see you walking blindly into a maelstrom that will destroy you and your entire career. Nor do I want to put Mrs. Struthers through the calvary of pitiless cross-examination. Whatever you think of me, however you are determined to revile me, you have left me with no choice."

"You have a choice."

"God, you make me want to weep at such a squandering of talent." His rich baritone shivers with emotion: "Damn it, you're a forceful, brilliant, and committed young woman. You could have done many great deeds for many important causes, most of which you dare not dispute I share with you. But to waste your career and reputation on a spiteful vendetta merely because a judge spanked you and sent you to your room — it's so puny, so demeaning, so senseless, so tragic." He walks away.

I stand there listening to the perfect, clipped echoes of his speech fade under the eerie boom of distant foghorns.

14 | Friday . . .

As I stop en route to the courthouse to gas up at a Seattle's Best Coffee filling station, Detective Ellen Oversmith rings me on my cell.

"The individual you met last night is one Carson Wilkes."

"Does he have a record?"

"Do you remember that Muslim temple in Bellevue that was razed a few years ago? He was arrested on suspicion, but we were unable to link him to it. We believe he is implicated in the abortion bombings, but he's not co-operative. He talks, but does not make sense. He may be psychotic, so we're having a medical team look at him. Meantime, we'll need you to sign a statement."

"I'm sure he's the one who wrote a lot of those notes to me, Ellen. 'Concubine of Satan,' that's what he called me last night – it was in one of the letters I gave you."

"Yes, it's his writing. He will be incarcerated for quite a while."

"Thanks for the reassurance, but there's more squirrel food running around out there."

The elevator door opens to reveal Hugh Vandergraaf standing alone in the middle of the ninth-floor rotunda. A slight nod of acknowledgment, a shrug from me. Of the millions of people who live in metro Seattle, who emerged from the fog last evening but this man who is ubiquitously present in my mind. Some implausible trick of fate? Had he been anyone else, I would have kissed him.

My thoughts about him remain in turmoil. He spoke so convincingly last night. If I am wrong, I have done a terrible deed. But how *could* I be wrong? Has Beatrice lied to me? Has Helen? How improbable.

Another elevator disgorges Bill Christiansen; he confers with his client as they follow me to 941, the room Judge Luckwell is using.

The curtain opens Monday, and I still cannot understand why they so urgently moved to expedite the trial, then let the time for discovery of our case slip by. Bill Christiansen could have held pre-trial examinations of me, of Beatrice, and unearthed everything we know. I suspect he was waiting for me to make the first move, to seek discovery from *his* client. But I waited him out; now we're both cut off. Sure, I would like to have had a prior whirl at Vandergraaf, but I was hoping to fortify Helen Mazur's spine and spring her at them.

And what if, as Junior has implied, he is keeping an eight-million-dollar secret from *me*? What could that be? Their pleadings give nothing away: intercourse is denied, and in the alternative (as if you can have it both ways) the aforesaid Beatrice Krueger consented.

Bill asks the bailiff to inform the judge that we'll join her presently, then draws me aside. "You don't mind if Hugh comes along?"

"If he has nothing else to do," I say archly.

He gives me a look of rebuke. Bill is not much over fifty, reedy, immaculate, always appears as if he just walked out of a barbershop. He is not someone a casting director would choose to play a top trial lawyer, though Bill might find a role as a funeral director: expensively cut black suit, soft confiding voice, formal demeanor. That will fool the unwary opponent – he can suddenly turn and bite. Though ingenious and cunning, he is not without honor.

"I heard you and Hugh had an impromptu meeting last night."

"Yes, he was quite brave."

"But you didn't kiss and make up."

"That is absolutely insulting, Bill. This isn't a lovers' quarrel."

"*Mea culpa*. Elizabeth, this trial can be avoided. Hugh doesn't want to nail you to the cross; we're prepared to accept something you can finance. Both of us know a jury could easily come up with some astronomical figure that could never be paid and that would leave you entirely bereft. There's no point in that."

"What's the offer?"

"We'll go down to one million dollars, plus a full public and unreserved apology, and then he wants to put this behind him without seeking your disbarment."

"A million . . . May as well ask for a billion, I don't have that kind of money; I'll *never* have it."

"Twenty years at fifty-thousand per, no interest. You must make twice that a year. If you don't, you soon will. Think of it as an expensive bar fee – you'll still be able to practice."

"Forget it. And he can *eat* his apology. I couldn't live with the self-betrayal."

"Elizabeth, understand this: there'll be no quarter given. I know you just might be able to prove Hugh hasn't lived an impeccably moral life, and that may be awkward for him. Particularly because of . . ." He leaves the thought unsaid. "Let's just say there are embarrassing aspects to this case and that's why we're offering this solution. Not that we think our case is difficult: there can be no question that he didn't rape that woman. He'll take his lumps, but the consequences for you will be devastating."

"Worse if every time I'm at the mirror I look at a cowering hypocrite. I think we should see the judge."

"I think *you* should see a senior lawyer. J.J. Plum comes to mind."

I ignore this paternalism. A million dollars – that's unthinkable, absurd. I would be the rest of my life strapped to the wheel paying it off. I am wondering what particular awkward matter has prompted the offer, as laughably ungenerous as it is. The sordid business about seducing Juanita Calvo, his bailiff?

We file into chambers, Hugh Vandergraaf so close behind me I can smell his aftershave. I really do not like the idea of his being here, but I don't want Bill thinking his presence will rattle me.

Mavis Luckwell is wiping her spectacles, squinting out the window as if trying to discern shapes in the fog, but she turns as we enter and takes an appraising look at Hugh. I have to assume they've met at some judges' conference or other, but I have no sense of any closeness between them.

Luckwell normally sits in the town of Kennewick, near Walla Walla, on the Columbia River. She is quite young for a senior judge, mid-forties, unpartnered, career-driven, reputed to be a rock-ribbed Republican. Physically, you would have to say she's over-endowed, though she keeps everything cinched tight, including her hair, which is in a chignon. She would be more attractive if she'd loosen those stern lines in her face. I worry she may be one of those professional women who feel forced to prove they're as tough as men.

"Please sit down, everyone. I hope this fog won't be penetrating the courtroom next week. Are we all agreed on what the issues are?"

"They couldn't be clearer," says Christiansen. "Miss Finnegan's entire speech to the press of last year is restated in our pleadings. 'Sexual predator,' 'rapacious thug'; I believe those were some of the phrases used."

I flash a look at Vandergraaf, who is impassive. "And a detailed account of a violent rape," I add.

"For the record," Bill says, "I reiterate my concern that we have been denied the right of discovery." I don't know why he is making such an extravagant issue of this.

He has my client's entire statement; I have nothing from Vandergraaf.

"I reiterate my ruling. You know the practice of this court. You were two days late in requesting discovery. *After* you moved for an expedited trial, I might add. Frankly, I am surprised at both of you. No timely discovery, no motions *in limine* as to issues of law or fact. I have never seen a case of this gravity dealt with in what *seems* such a lackadaisical way, so I must assume there is method in your madness. My sense is that each of you are seeking to hide some salient evidence. I don't mind being kept in the dark, but I must warn you I will deal abruptly and severely with any matters that do not come properly before the court."

She gives each of us a reproving look, then glances at Vandergraaf. She must be curious about him, this scholarly, handsome man with the intense, blue, unblinking eyes.

Now she turns to me.

"I also believe it is very foolhardy of you, Ms. Finnegan, to come to trial unrepresented. It speaks of an arrogance, as if you consider there's no one more qualified to call upon. I hope you are able to hide that from the jury."

"I'll live with my decision, Your Honor."

"The rules permit the parties to ask reasonable questions of prospective jurors. They will be reasonable or they will go unanswered. I shall deny any challenges that are gender-based and can only hope we'll achieve an equality of the sexes. Ten days remains everyone's best estimate? This had better be over by Christmas, that's all I can say."

We agree to do our best.

"Any exhibits not in issue that we can stipulate? Or any agreed facts? I see no heads bobbing. Well, I have to suppose you know what you're doing. Maybe you folks up in King County manage things differently. This is an extremely sad business. I assume there's no humanly possible way to avert this trial."

Bill looks at me. I maintain a stony silence. "It appears not," he says.

"Ten o'clock on Monday, then."

I make my way uptown through the hidden silent streets, listening to the mournful grunts of foghorns in the harbor. Headlights probe the gloom, unseen cars crawling through the sludge-like atmosphere. A sound of brakes, a crunch of metal, a curse: a driver unable to see the traffic lights.

Though it is almost noon, many desks are vacant in the office, the staff still dribbling in, comparing horror stories of their blind odysseys to the inner city. But again outside my window a bright and brittle sunlight bathes the cotton fields below.

In the lounge, I entertain Franca with last evening's tale from the crypt and the irony of a rapist's *beau geste*.

"He just happened to be there?"

"Gallery-hopping. He's a connoisseur."

"Yeah, of what, female flesh? You sure he hasn't been following you?"

"Why would he do that?"

"Maybe he's infatuated with you."

"I hardly think so."

"Yeah, that's kind of dubious." We smile at the concept.

Curtis Kaplan strolls in, looking pleased with himself. "Think we have settlement. Insurer's head office has found another five hundred thousand. The firm has to spring for the banquet."

"I'm sure knowing that will make your client ecstatic," I say. "How does he show it, with a lift of the eyebrow?"

"Liz, don't. Believe me, this has been extremely painful."

"What a depraved profession," says Franca. "Just a broken arm? Aw, gee, that's too bad. Oh, a broken back and a shattered pelvis, too? That's excellent, much better." She flips a wave and leaves.

"Sorry, Liz, but we won't make it to your birthday. Maxine has agreed to join me in a couples workshop this weekend. A retreat out in Snoqualmie: body work, hot tub, the whole bit. The group facilitator is supposed to be one of the best in the business, certified rolfer, lovely man, reeks of compassion, they say. Specializes in sexually overenergized people – is nymphomania still a permitted word these days? Anyway, that's what we'll be working at."

"That sounds kind of demanding. Sure you're up to it?"

"You let me worry about it. I'm a pro at these things. I'll help Max deal with her problem, naturally; I'm really just going along for the ride."

"Well . . . happy rolfing."

Mattie is in my office, sorting out the mail. The hate letters have dwindled to a trickle, but that magazine piece continues to inspire a few semi-literate catcalls. I like this one: "Dear Lawyer Elizabeth Finigan, whats your fee to suck my toes."

"Do I quote him the usual hourly rate?" She hands me a memo. "Got the poop on Yvonne Fairhurst." The woman who stole Hugh Hustle from his former bailiff. High society, indeed: she lives up on millionaire's row on Capitol Hill, wife of the chair of several boards. A society-page photo: low-cut gown, theatrical display of bodice, expensive teeth. She is beautiful, of course, probably older than she looks: a closeup might show the tucks and lifts. The cuckolded husband glowers at the camera: paunchy in a tux.

Should I drop a bomb in court? That could backfire. But maybe I should let her know the cat is out of the bag: word will get back to Hugh that I'm hot on his amorous track; he'll be fretful on the stand. This affair may have prompted that derisory offer of settlement.

When I call Ms. Fairhurst's number I am told by her maid that Madam is away for the day. I leave my numbers.

Mattie tells me Wilkie Mazur called. "I won't repeat what he said."

"Don't be so bashful."

"He used a five-letter word starting with B and ending with itch." A predictable reaction to the subpoena served on his wife. "Oh, and Reverend Krueger phoned; he wouldn't say what it's about."

Usually these calls have to do with his concern about his beloved daughter's welfare. He need not worry: she is unwavering and unflappable, and, in an almost surreal way, eager for the battle.

No answer at the Krueger household; I tell his machine I will be tied up all day and will call this evening: I want no interruptions when Beatrice comes in for her courtroom rehearsal.

Beatrice wiggles out of her backpack, which is heavy, full of books. She hugs me, pecks me on the cheek, and we nest ourselves around the walnut table.

"I heard you had an incident, Liz."

"I'll tell you all about it."

As I do, she cringes, then laughs at the absurdity of it, applauds. She is definitely not the same person who shyly introduced herself to me a year ago September. Not only is she more outgoing, she has shed a dozen years, and now looks like a regular college student in boots and jeans, wool sweater with a badge: a clenched fist holding a flower, the campus women's movement. We shared much time on bicycles this summer, and I joined her and Thomas on a few church outings, even attending services with them. It's the Bea-and-Liz show now, we have become quite close. We don't agree on abortion, but that is our only disagreement.

I apprise her of current developments; then, to ward off any nasty surprises next week, I look searchingly at her and say, "Bea, I hate to ask you this. But you *have* told me everything?"

I am disquieted that it takes her so long to answer. And I don't take much comfort when she does: "No, not everything."

"I beg your pardon? Amplify that."

"It's nothing, dear. Nothing that affects the case. I don't know why I even mentioned it . . . Heavens, what am I going on about? I've just taken a mid-term exam and handed in my last paper. Liz, I think I achieved an excellent grade on Modern American Lit."

Why does she change the subject? What is she hiding from me? Clearly, she feels awkward about the matter, because she cannot hide her blush.

"Dr. Carstairs is letting me take my mid-term after the holidays. She's so wonderful − and she makes me laugh. Such a turn of phrase. The penocentric society, the primacy of sperm."

Dr. May Goddard Carstairs. She was my guru in my student days, still is. I pulled strings to register Beatrice for "Sources of Gender Inequality," calling May at home to entreat her. She said she would be delighted to have Ms. Struthers.

A concern much weighs on me: what could be too embarrassing to share with her friend and lawyer? But I decide not to press her immediately; that would make her overanxious. I explain I am about to take her through a cross-examination. I am William Christiansen and she is on the stand in front of a packed court. I ask every unsettling question I can think of, forcing her to recount the assault in the kind of muckraking detail which unfeeling counsel often solicit. We perform this dress rehearsal for three hours, and she is quick and articulate throughout, stands up well enough through the weak part of our case: her internment, her suicidal depression.

At the end I ask her, "Ms. Struthers, have you told this jury everything? Is there anything you wish to add?"

"Those are the gruesome details, Mr. Christiansen." She smiles but drops her eyes.

"Tell me, Bea."

"Why did I bother to say anything? It's forgotten, and it really doesn't change anything."

My pleas are met with such blushing reluctance that I speculate the matter may involve a young girl's indiscretion. But I won't let it go.

"*Please*, Beatrice."

She bites her lip, looks around as if for rescue, then lowers her head.

"I have a bit of a criminal past. I was once fired for theft."

The unfolding story is so innocent that I'm almost taken aback at her hesitation to tell it. While in part-time employment in Olympia at Baptist Missionary and Social Services – some years after the rape – she had pilfered some office supplies and documents, had been caught out and dismissed. No charges were laid.

"That's *hardly* the crime of the century, Bea. It's not as if you have a record."

"It was a sin, though, wasn't it?"

I try not to laugh at her discomfiture. "Heck, I got caught trying to filch a Hallowe'en mask once from Peabody's Drugs. He that is without sin, let him cast the first stone."

She corrects the citation. "'Let him first cast a stone at her.'" A wan smile.

"You have to tell me things like that, Bea. You have no idea what they may try to dredge up against you."

"I'm sorry."

"Stop being *sorry.*"

Winter's early twilight has me staring pensively from my office window at a violet sky that is turning mauve as the sun slides behind the Olympic peninsula. Lights blink on in the spires rising from the fog; the streets below are still lost in the thick murk.

Beatrice left a few minutes ago, cheerful again, determined to do her best. But I am becoming melancholic — perhaps the doleful scene outside, of darkening day, has put me in this mood. And I am still perturbed by her withholding of information, however trivial.

Troubling questions nag at me: has she also tried to deny — or unconsciously reshaped — important events? Was the shame of being the victim of a seduction too much for her chaste conscience to bear? Is the pain of misremembered rape more easily endured?

How ghastly if that turns out to be so. I shall have grievously wronged Hugh Vandergraaf, ruined forever an innocent man's chances for high judicial office. But I must not allow myself to be harried by such doubts: they dishonor my client and weaken my resolve. After all, it is *I* who am being sued; my career is at no lesser risk than Vandergraaf's. Sometimes I feel as if we are two people without brakes, hurtling to some terrible destiny. Maybe one of us will escape unscarred, maybe neither.

"There's a twink in the waiting room," Mattie says from behind me.

"Tell the twink I'm closing up shop." I begin packing my files away.

"I told him you're tied up until the next millennium, but he won't go away. He's been waiting for three hours. He looks harmless, real shy. All he'll say is that he's from Canada and it's important."

I start when he's ushered in: I *know* this person. A towering six-foot-six and gangly, wire-rim glasses, a straw-colored thatch that badly needs a comb, an over-exertive Adam's apple.

"We were never introduced, and I suppose you don't remember me anyway."

But of course I do: it's the ungainly officer who was at that inquisition in Canada. He says he's Sergeant Nathaniel Duff of RCMP External I, whatever that is. I remember him giving me continual, curious appraisal in Victoria.

"How could I forget?" I lead him to the framed print on my wall: here's Sergeant Duff with his arm around my waist, trying to protect Mulholland from, quote, the hysterical female.

Duff breaks into a wonky grin: it is oddly sweet. "I still get a chuckle over that. He wanted me to charge you with assault. I told him to get a life, preferably one with a sense of humor."

"Oh, good, you're not here to arrest me."

"No, ma'am, I'm definitely not. In fact, I'm not here at all." He has an odd musical twang: Atlantic Canada, I think. "I haven't driven down from Vancouver, I've never been in your office, and I'm not the one who gave you Thalia Pfeiffer's phone number and address."

I look at him with astonishment. "Do sit down."

He is all legs and arms as he folds himself into an armchair.

"How do you know I'm looking for her?"

"A Mr. Mike Gustafson was trying to work over some of our people in narcotics. A query went down the line and it led to you. And that gave me an excuse to come calling."

"Any time, Sergeant Duff." Both my spirits and

pulse have quickened. How has he managed to unearth Thalia Pfeiffer?

Here comes that grin again, boyish and bashful: hard to tell how old he is, maybe thirty-five.

"You look a little thinner." He picks up one of my mangled pencils and passes it to me. "This your protein supplement?" He peers at me over his glasses with a kind but reproving expression. "I guess it gets tense when you take on the world."

"It hasn't exactly been a Saturday night on the town."

"Let's see if I can lighten your load." Slowly, so I can write it down, he recites from memory a telephone number and a street address in a restored section of Panama City called San Felipe. Then, warning me again this did not come from his lips, he explains that the RCMP and DEA are working on a joint sting. "Thalia is a minor player; it's her employers they're after, several Colombian gentlemen with Seattle connections and bad tempers. I think you want her out of there before the takedown."

"Why are you doing this?"

"Because you've been dealt a crooked hand. Maybe also for some reasons that aren't obvious."

"Like what?"

He rises. "I have to go, Miss Finnegan. It's a three-hour drive."

"No point rushing at rush hour. Let me buy you a drink."

He is a foot and three inches taller than I and must bend as he squints at the photograph once more. "Sorry I latched onto you like that; I used to be an amateur hockey referee. I didn't mean to be rough."

For some reason, I burst out laughing – partly because of the way his face contorts into droll expressions, partly as a response to something mischievous and clever in his eyes. But mostly because of buoyant renewed hope: Thalia Pfeiffer is alive and well in Panama City.

"I can't think of anything I'd rather do than have a drink with you. But not tonight. I couldn't handle it."

What does he mean by that? But quickly he leaves, nearly colliding with the open door. Two left feet.

Though the offices have emptied, Mattie — protectively — has stayed behind.

"What do you mean, a twink? He's a doll. Let's dial this number."

A woman answers in Spanish, and I am in immediate trouble. Mattie, who took three years of college Spanish, takes over.

"It's some kind of maid or housekeeper. *La dueña* won't be home till late, *muy tarde*."

"Explain I'm a lawyer and I want to help Thalia and in return I need her help. Tell her it's *very* important, and Thalia can call collect any hour of the night."

Will she remember Beatrice after all this time? Can she leave Panama fast? A criminal record — will they even let her in the country? All I can do is cross my fingers and hope.

I arrive home in time to help Nicholson lug up one last twelve-pack of champagne.

"Who's sponsoring this party, Bill Gates? How many people have you invited, anyway?"

"In attendance will be about forty assorted faggots and artists, plus your paltry two dozen bra-burners. I hope you invited your mother and her rough-hewn beau."

"They're coming."

I should have invited Nathaniel Duff. So bashful and maladroit, but I sense a bright mind, and he performed a noble act in coming to me.

"Oh, it will be quite the gala ball. We'll put those millennium parties to shame. Help me blow up some balloons."

"In a sec."

Johann Krueger turns his music down to answer my call. Handel's *Messiah*, I think.

"Amy and I were wondering if there might be a chance of having a few words with you this weekend."

"Is it important, Reverend Krueger? I am terribly rushed."

"It's about the trial next week. I, ah, well, it appears that both Amy and I have been subpoenaed."

"Jesus . . . sorry. By Judge Vandergraaf's lawyer? Well, obviously, because it wasn't me. Yes, definitely I'll talk with you."

He would like to meet tomorrow, Saturday, in the afternoon. I will be home preparing for our party; I give him the address.

Johann's revelation truly nettles me. How dare they tender Beatrice's own parents as witnesses. But Christiansen would not subpoena them out of the blue; they must have given statements . . .

Now it dawns: William Christiansen didn't seek discovery because he hoped to keep the Kruegers hidden, then to pop them out of a cake in the middle of the trial. They are key to his strategy of showing Beatrice suffered a mental illness complete with fanciful delusions. They had greeted with utter incredulity their only daughter's report of a rape. How will a jury react to that?

Silently fuming, I answer a summons from the phone, hoping it is Thalia Pfeiffer: no, it's Yvonne Fairhurst. I didn't expect her to call, and barely conceal my surprise. She is curious, she says, as to what this could be all about.

I hesitate, take the plunge. "Someone mentioned you as we were discussing Judge Vandergraaf."

She does not pretend to be ignorant of the current hot topic of the salons of Seattle. "I have nothing to do with your nasty libel action."

"Ms. Fairhurst, you may be brought into it — I'm not sure if that can be avoided. I thought it fair to give you advance notice, but I hope Judge Vandergraaf warned you of the possibility."

"He did *not*. We haven't talked to each other for months. Look, we have to meet. This is not good."

"When can we meet?"

"As soon as possible."

I suggest breakfast tomorrow at the OK Hotel Cafe, a locally famous bistro a few blocks away, near the water.

"If you're sure it's not too public," she says.

"I doubt that anyone you know would go there."

I might offer not to bring up her name — if she offers some quid pro quo. However mean-spirited that may seem, the practice of law can be brutish when one is a candidate for insolvency.

An inflated balloon escapes from Nick, flies farting toward my writing table, and falls spent and limp onto the floor beside me. Something symbolic about it all.

15 | Saturday . . .

The telephone jangles by my ear and I am roused from a disturbing dream: I was in flight, slogging through snow. Two a.m., says the digital clock.

Panama is calling. "Yes, I'll pay the charges."

"Well, halloo there." A frantic energized voice. "Am I connected to Elizabeth Finnegan? What's the emergency, honey? Man, I *need* a lawyer."

She sounds speedy. Cocaine. "Good morning, Thalia – but it must be almost dawn there."

"Yeah, I just got home. I had to party with all these wired assholes, they wouldn't stop."

"Okay, don't say anything, just listen." I can't tell her a drug bust is about to occur; the lines may be tapped. But I do explain, with some careful emphasis, that it would be advantageous for her to leave Panama immediately for Seattle, indeed that it would be very rewarding if she caught the next flight. "It's about a girl who was raped in 1971 on South Pender Island, when you were working at the Bedwell resort."

"Just get me out of here; I'll say whatever you want."

I feel a flood of relief. "I'll make arrangements."

Sleep does not reclaim me for hours. I find myself propped on my pillows staring out into the misty gloom of Jackson Street, listening to a melody of foghorns and distant sirens, unable to still the tremors of anticipation, the fires of renewed hope. But I am also bothered by that interrupted dream, trying to remember it.

I was dressed for a ball. I was wandering lost through snowy fields. Or was I on skis? A man was tracking me, gaining – I knew him but could not place him. I heard bells, felt danger.

But these memories are indecipherable fragments, and when I close my eyes, sleep brings an altered, more benign reverie: I am a child on a swing and someone is gently pushing me, and I hope it is my father.

Yesterday's mist has been supplanted by the cold clarity of one of those brittle December days the north wind exports from Canada, a high arctic air mass. A lazy morning sun, barely inching above the southeastern horizon, makes no effort to keep the puddles from freezing.

Bundled up, I negotiate the slippery sidewalks leading to the docks, proceed under the roaring Alaskan Way Viaduct, and duck into the OK, which, with its adjoining gallery, is popular with the young-and-artistic crowd. A folk musician with an acoustic guitar is playing quiet breakfast riffs.

I have no trouble recognizing Yvonne Fairhurst at her corner table. Three strands of gold, angora sweater, dark glasses. I pick up a coffee at the bar, join her. She isn't interested in talking about the weather, moves directly to the subject of Vandergraaf.

"How did you find out?" she asks.

"Another woman."

A cynical smile. "Which of the great multitudes?"

She has long auburn hair, patrician features, no fat. A down-home quality about her – and maybe the angora sweater – hints she wasn't born to the upper classes.

"We told no one. We met where nobody knew us."

"I assume it must have recently ended. How long did it go on?"

"It was a . . . little summer interlude. Look, Elizabeth – can I call you that? – I'm going to beg you with my whole goddamned heart not to do this to me. It's not just me: Randolph and I have kids, they're still in school, all three of them. Randolph's a good man, a good father, stable, solid – I care for him. I wanted an adventure, that was all."

This comes out in a rush, frank, up-front; I had not expected such forthrightness. She removes her glasses, wipes wetness from the corners of her eyes.

Though feeling her distress, I must make my case. "If I lose in court, I will be bankrupted and probably disbarred for life. More importantly, Yvonne, this is about justice, about the right of women to feel safe."

"What good will it do to mention my name? I have nothing to do with something that happened a quarter of a century ago."

"It's not that simple. I am also accused of calling him a sexual predator. I intend to ask him about his obsession with seduction. If he evades, I may have to get specific."

After we place our orders, omelets for each of us, Yvonne sits bowed, biting her lip.

"Maybe we can work something out," I say softly. "Will you be candid with me? Woman to woman?"

"If it's off the record. And if you *promise* to keep me out of this."

I have been burned before – the promise to Helen Mazur has come back to haunt. "Okay," I say with a sigh, "I promise. How did you meet?"

I can see she has decided to gamble on me, and she relaxes and relates this history: she had known Vandergraaf for several years through intersecting social circles, but it wasn't until last spring, as he and the Fairhursts were sharing the head table at a Symphony Society fund-raiser, that the flirting turned bold. After dinner, Viennese waltzes from the Seattle Symphony string section. Randolph didn't like to dance. She swept onto the floor with Hugh. He mentioned his chalet at Mount Baker. She liked to ski. Her husband would be in Zurich over the weekend, a banking trip.

They did little skiing during that first get-together,

and she found their lovemaking so enjoyable that, when weeks went by without contact from him, she took the initiative. During the summer they met twice at a motel, twice more at the Fairhursts' condominium on the Oregon coast, and once at Hugh's home, a gentrified bungalow in Ballard.

When I ask about the sex, she is forthright. "It was great. He pushed all my buttons. But then . . . I'm afraid it started getting . . ." She is searching for a word. "Uncomfortable."

Ultimately, their encounters began to take on a dull routine: quick, entering before she was ready, a lack of tenderness. She cannot explain this change in him, though I suspect the master of the one-night stand must have decided the woman had been sufficiently conquered, and he wanted out.

"And I began to think . . . well, of course he had started this action against you, and I'd believed like everyone else he'd been terribly libeled, but then . . . for some reason I started wondering. Anyway, I decided to stop living dangerously. That was my summer romance."

We fill in a few gaps, and again she demands and receives assurance I will not disclose her name. After we part, I trudge to the waterfront, Alaskan Way, a long flat run for weekend joggers who are out today in force, bundled, spuming clouds of breath. On the water, ferries crisscross a choppy sound and the wind is chill.

I ponder how to use the disclosures from Yvonne Fairhurst yet keep my promise. Vandergraaf's lovemaking had become uninspired, perhaps hasty, but hardly aggressive – he is an adulterer, but so what? More cogent: he betrayed a man with whom he had become friendly.

On my cell, I call Mattie at her apartment and ask if she has made arrangements with the travel agent.

"Yes, and Thalia's *very* eager to come up. I think she knows something's just about to land on her. Anyway, her tickets are at the United counter in Panama for an overnight flight via LAX. She'll be in Sea-Tac by about two p.m. tomorrow. I had to put it on your VISA."

I'd be a lost lamb without Mattie.

Now what to do about the Kruegers? If what I suspect is true, that they have been co-operating with the plaintiff, I might forget all I have learned in anger therapy.

My door opens to a merry, seasonal scene: Nicholson and three friends are bustling about the kitchen, attacking a pile of pumpkins: a post-Thanksgiving sale at the market. They are slicing them, mashing them up for pies and tarts, an assembly line to the oven.

They are well into the wine, chattering in their acerbic, world-weary way about the straight world and its arcane rules and rigid mores. But Nick's voice is strained, a frantic edge to it, and when he sees me walk in, he drops his masher and puts his mouth to my ear.

"Thank God you're back. They've been here half an hour, the good pastor and his wife. It's just too unbearable, American Gothic in the living room."

I hang up my jacket, take a deep breath, and launch myself toward our open living area, into which loud chatter carries from the kitchen, much of it too explicit for my guests, I fear. Johann and Amy are perched like hens on the edges of their chairs beneath a net filled with balloons. I picture myself playfully releasing the net, watching the balloons cascade over their heads.

"Sorry I kept you waiting."

"We didn't realize you were having a function," Johann says. He is huddled into himself: his hands are in his lap – he dares not touch anything, that's how one contracts HIV. They haven't even removed their coats.

"My twenty-eighth birthday." Keep it simple.

"We both offer our deepest congratulations." Boldly

he speaks for his wife, but she says nothing, a wincing smile. She appears pale.

"You met Nicholson?"

"Yes." No further comment.

"Let me make some tea."

"Please don't trouble. We'll be on our way directly after our chat, since, ah, we have some shopping to do."

I slide into a chair. "I think I met one of your parishioners the other night. Called me a baby-killing whore."

"I regret that," Johann says. "We know about it. He's not well."

"Yes, and how well are his friends, the other bombers? Do you care enough for their health to turn them in?" I cannot help but be curt with him, even though he is Bea's father.

"I'm afraid that's not what we're here to discuss."

"Johann, if you stubbornly insist on protecting these people, how are you going to live with yourself if they maim or kill someone?"

"May we talk about the subpoenas?" He cannot seem to look at me.

I sigh. "Okay. I take it you've given a statement to the plaintiff's lawyer because otherwise he wouldn't dare call you."

"We didn't know we would be asked to come to court. They assured us it wasn't necessary."

"Obviously they weren't very forthright. When were these statements taken?"

"Ah, good question: some months ago . . . last winter, I believe."

"*Last winter?* Why haven't you told me this before?" I am astounded – they didn't even tell Beatrice. Again I am met with stone-cold silence. "Do you have copies?"

"Regrettably, no."

Johann is eyeing one of Nick's canvases, "Dance of the Naked Sailors." He looks away.

"Well, what did you tell them?"

"The truth, of course. As we imparted it to you."

"Did you tell them you didn't believe her?"

"We felt bound to do so, Miss Finnegan."

"And all about her breakdown?"

"Yes, her suicide attempts."

"Which were probably her way of trying to reach you, and you just . . ." I lower my voice; I must try to keep my temper. "Never mind. Why have you come here to tell me this?" Finally, some feelings of shame? At the eleventh hour, they wish to repent, to stand by their daughter?

"It has been suggested there may be ways to resolve this dispute, through, ah, some form of settlement."

"Who suggested? Mr. Christiansen?"

"We're here of our own accord, Miss Finnegan."

This smacks of blackmail. Miss Finnegan, if you would be so kind as to pay through the nose, we won't have to crucify our daughter. Remember the anger lessons, Liz — be rational, think things through. "Is there anything you told Mr. Christiansen that I might not know?"

"Yes, well, we did mention a sorry episode during her work history. I think you know that after her health improved she worked in Olympia for our missionary office. Has Beatrice told you she was fired there for theft?"

I maintain a bland expression. "Theft of what?"

"Office supplies. Some records went missing, too, though she said they'd been misplaced. When she couldn't produce them she was let go. It's a minor thing, perhaps, but when Mr. Christiansen asked me if there'd ever been instances of dishonesty, I just couldn't lie."

With concern out of proportion to her misdemeanor, Beatrice had confessed to me she had taken a stapler, some boxes of stationery. Petty theft and mislaid papers — how heavily guilt weighs upon the honest heart. "What else did you tell them?"

"Naturally, he wanted to know if there had been other occasions when she had not been truthful, in addition, as he put it, to the matter of the alleged rape. Well, of course, there were more than a few falsehoods uttered, particularly in her teen years, usually to do with persons she was unwise to associate with, certain evenings unaccounted for, a secret friendship with a young man, that sort of thing."

"I see. If that friendship was so secret, how did you discover it?"

"Careful parents tend to know these things. At any rate, we couldn't say she never lied to us."

Why are they so determined to malign their child and weaken her testimony? Why so adamant she lied about the rape? Clearly, a blind and prideful stubbornness afflicts Johann, and in refusing to admit error he compounds it.

"*Exactly* when did you first talk to Judge Vandergraaf's lawyer?"

"It comes to mind that would be about a year ago."

My ears hear evasiveness. My eyes observe the body language, the guilty shifting. I turn to Amy.

"When did you and your husband first talk to the other side?"

She cannot look at me. Probably she has been warned to be silent.

"We talked to a prosecutor first, I believe," she says, dropping her eyes.

"Would that be back in late September of last year?"

"I believe so," says Johann.

Upon learning of the rape complaint, this couple had hurried off to the county prosecutor's office – that is why Beatrice's interrogators in Victoria knew there had been suicide attempts. I am unable to control my fury and I rise, my voice tight and hoarse.

"You volunteered your concerns to the King County prosecutor, is that it? You tried to sabotage your own daughter." I shout, "You bitter, heartless man!"

They both turn white, and seem to be growing small in front of me, shrinking from my wrath, their faces torn with what I hope is pain.

I cannot bear to face them any longer. "Excuse me, I'm very upset. Please leave."

Johann stands, helps Amy to her feet – she is shaken and unsteady. His face is riven with taut lines and his voice has lost its resonance: "Do you think we do not care for Beatrice? We seek only to rescue her."

But he catches his breath, and as I follow them out, his voice grows more full and orotund. "Yes, to rescue her. From the evil you espouse. We see what you have done to Beatrice. You have wreaked terrible changes, you have corrupted her. You have served as the hand-maiden of the Antichrist in his evil work to debase and blight her soul. Because you have entranced her with ideas that are subversive of the Word, she no longer walks on the pathway of God but on the twisted road to damnation!"

The thunder does not abate until I have marched them to the kitchen, to the front door, where Johann pauses, surveying the pumpkin crew, four astonished gay men standing stock-still, pillars of salt.

"Filth and degradation," says Johann, pulling Amy through the doorway. She sends me a haunted look, as if beseeching me, then they head down the stairs.

"I think I've had too much to drink," says Nicholson. "I could have sworn Grumpy the dwarf just did a guest spot in the kitchen. Princess, stop standing there in such a sour pout, give this the satanic taste test."

I take a bite of a tart. "It's okay. Maybe needs some cinnamon."

He hands me a glass of wine, strokes my hair, hugs me, and his ministrations do soothe my ill temper. I shall not let those miserable people ruin my day. The next time I see them will be in court. The handmaiden of the Antichrist will be ready for them.

Mother and her beau arrive in the late afternoon after all day on a bus, looking bushed but peppy enough. While Nicholson takes Jake on a guided tour — it's his first visit to the loft — I attend to Mother's needs, organizing a shower, helping with her toilette in the spare room.

"By the way, Mom, why didn't you fly?"

She had been a pour of words till now: her wedding plans, the latest hot items from the boudoirs of Coalsack. But it is a nervous chatter. I inherited that trait from her; I am a gushing stream of consciousness when I'm anxious, so I sense she bears unwelcome news.

"Well, Lizzie, we're putting every cent into something." She says this too brightly.

"What do you mean?"

"Jake will explain everything to you; it's too complicated. Oh, do you like this dress? God, I hope I can squeeze into it."

Skimpy, too revealing. "Very sexy. Mom, what's going on?"

"Jake has stumbled onto something, it's all very hush-hush, and you can't say a word to anybody. When you have a few moments, draw him aside. He'll explain it better."

I become impatient with this stonewalling. I have visions of her life's savings fluttering out the window on little wings.

"We brought you a present." She reaches into her bag, pulls out a scroll-like object, gift-wrapped. The card reads, "To my million-dollar baby. Happy twenty-eighth!"

Mom zips up the dress. She does fill it out, but there is no overflow. I can only hope to look as attractive at fifty-four. "You got it, flaunt it," she says, spiraling in front of the mirror.

I open my present. It's a stock certificate. Thirty thousand shares of Nipigon International Goldfields Ltd.

"Now, those shares are in my name like I think you wanted, but they're really yours. All those mutual funds you transferred – well, we reinvested them for you."

"Mother, I had nearly fifty thousand dollars put away." All my savings.

"They're going to be worth twenty times that in a week."

I bolt out of the room like my heels are on fire. Nick is in the kitchen with his friends, but Jake Bjorklund is nowhere in sight.

"Ah, yes, Jake," says Nick. "Well-traveled fellow. Did you know he lived for a year with the pygmies of –"

"Where *is* he?"

"Took a walk around the block. Said he didn't want to stink up the place with his cigar."

He is in a taxi to the airport. He has flown the coop with all our hard-earned eggs. I grab my jacket and race down the stairs to the sidewalk.

No sign of him on Jackson Street or on the mall. I slip around the corner, toward the Kingdome. It is dusk, freezing again, and as I round the corner I almost perform a pratfall on the ice. But now I catch a whiff of cigar smoke. There he is, leaning against a storefront door, staring thoughtfully at the Kingdome.

"Biggest concrete roof in the world. Looks a little like a big orange-juice squeezer, don't it?"

"What is this bullshit about a company called Nipigon Goldfields?"

"Well, now, that happens to be a little operation

started as a hole in the wall, now on its way to being worth several billion dollars. I'm on the inside track. Had to board the train before it left the station."

"Well, you're not taking me for this ride. Who's ever heard of this company? Is it listed?"

"Nasdaq Exchange. Canadian outfit." His voice drops. "Point-seven-five per cent ore, that's what the assay report is going to say. When it's released next week."

"Oh, no, you don't. Jake, if you have some insider information, you know that's against the law, and so is gambling with other people's money."

He draws the cigar from his mouth, taps a long ash from it. "Them thirty thousand shares of yours, and another fifty we got for ourselves, we bought 'em three days ago at a buck and a half, and now they're up to one-eighty. That's only on rumors. I got the real jack from an old trusted comrade just back from Sumatra, geologist I once rescued from a tribe of heathens on the upper Congo back in '79 –"

"Jake, stop. Just tell me what you've got me into."

"Fifteen hundred hectares of buried treasure. The Indonesian government's been looked after in the usual way, so Nipigon's got its development permit and they're ready to dig. Figure I might build a palace for your mom about half the size of that building out there."

He blows a couple of smoke rings, and winks at me. I don't know what to say. Is he full of the usual wind or really on to something? I believe *half* his stories. But he seems so cocky and convinced this time. And do I really *care* if I profit from the bending of capitalism's rules for the rich?

"Let me mull it over for a couple of days. We can always sell those shares, right?"

"Well, now, Liz, I wouldn't be too hasty; they're gonna grow like a snowball rolling downhill at spring melt. You just trust the golden touch of Jake Bjorklund. Always wanted to marry a beautiful rich lady, and that's what I aim to do."

I want to remonstrate further, but my anger wilts. He is such an endearing gas-bag. I will check this company's prospectus tomorrow. I hope Mom did not put a big mortgage on the house.

I take Jake's arm and we stroll back home. I am not going to break into a sweat over the matter: if the stock starts slipping, I'll tell Mother we have to sell.

Our party mix of gays, artists, lawyers, and feminists does not quite gel at first, everyone in this liberal milieu tentative, perhaps concerned about seeming politically correct, even to the point of avoiding lawyer jokes.

Gregarious Jake saves the party, his tales growing more grandiose with every drink. An audience listens rapt at his feet, traveling his world: darkest Africa, Tibet, the steppes of Russia. Meanwhile, Mother strolls about inviting people to the wedding: I can imagine the reaction in Coalsack to the arrival of half the homosexual community of Pioneer Square.

I have a critical date tomorrow with Thalia Pfeiffer so I dip only into the nonalcoholic punchbowl. I try not to let the stress of my trial show, and rebound from guest to guest with a cheerfulness that I hope does not seem feigned.

Nicholson, however, becomes screamingly drunk, loudly foul of mouth, embarrassing Stephane with an indecent speech and a toast welcoming him to the fairy kingdom. Stephane would rather be watching a film from Albania. In truth, he'd rather be with his two teenagers: he has them for the weekend. Michael, seventeen, and Janice, fifteen, are bright and mellow beyond their years, and they're not afraid to pop in early, before skipping off to a rock concert. Stephane sat down with them last year. Though he talked to them of divorce and inner repair, he emphasized that his deepest concern was for their happiness. They truly love him.

Franca brings a date but Beatrice arrives husband-less, a good idea, I think: shy, straight Thomas would be ill-at-ease. He has watched his wife's metamorphosis more with awe than concern, I've observed, but he has a good heart and seems content to let her flower in fields of her own choosing. He has his hobby shop.

Bea spends a lot of time with her professor, May Carstairs, who honors me by showing up. But I am per-mitted few opportunities to talk to her; she is continual-ly surrounded.

Mattie arrives late with her new flame, the blues guitarist. Their softly exchanged glances hint of strong shared feelings. Mattie and her musician, Charlene and Jake, Nicholson and Stephane: everyone has somebody.

Almost everyone.

I think of that tall Mountie, Sergeant Duff. A nerd, I thought. How wrong I was. An ungainly Ichabod Crane, yet rather attractive – his face has interesting crooks and angles, especially when he smiles.

Recovering from a brief spasm of loneliness, I deter-mine I shall enjoy this party, and I put on some old Stones music, and soon everyone is on their feet. Me, too. I dance with Nick, Franca, Stephane, everybody. I dance wildly, barely controlled, a whirling dervish, a trance of escape. And all night I am free of Hugh Vandergraaf's sad, dark eyes, though I am not sure why they have begun to haunt me so.

The moon dims; the stars spark out. I had the night, and now it flees from me. How little time is left to speak of life and love and loss before my journey's end. If I miss a scene or two of this distended drama of my past, feel free to pencil in the ignoble bits and gaps. Vain, verbose, improvident — jot those down. A man of ample means not showily displayed. A rebuilt bungalow in homely Ballard, though on the water's edge. A glassed-in case of first editions, an art collection bought at whim, for whatever reasons pleased me.

On an occasional First Thursday you will see me in your neighborhood, ever alert for bargains and the chance to save a maiden in distress — but pardon the expression: if I am to patronize, I should at least avoid cliché.

"That is your *door?" I said. As if I didn't know. Your address was in our files. I'd seen you in your loft — if only in a magazine — grinning like a leprechaun from behind a shelf of Raggedy Anns and Andys.*

Not coincidence but purpose — one then obscure to me — propelled me to your doorstep. I had glimpsed you from across a street, then followed you as you cock-walked off home. You slowed, you cast a glance behind, but I was hidden in the misted darkness. I don't know what thoughts churned through my mind when that sorry little man leaped at you — I simply reacted. I was confounded later by the fact I felt the remotest concern.

But what was it I felt toward you? Something obsessive? If not, certainly a bleak admiration for the impertinent feminist zealot who spurns the counsel of cooler heads, who marches into court alone to wage hopeless cause against impending ruin.

Or was it just antipathy and rage I felt? Having grown up with a limited vocabulary of the kinder emotions, I wasn't sure. Had I confused hatred with something else with which I had no experience? They say hate is twinned with love, and both can be as dangerous. But cancel love. It visits, it delights, it flees, and only pain is left: isn't that the way of it?

Yet I suffered such a thirst to know the sublime passion those of my generation sang of: love, love, love, it makes the world go round. Damn it, where was my paltry sip of it? Where did one order it? Who bottled that stuff? Was there a sizzle, an aftertaste when the glass was drained? I must have assumed it would show up one day, unexpected, unsolicited like junk mail through the slot. If one were to sleep with enough women, surely it had to happen. It was a matter of statistics.

Though my father holds the record . . .

Ah-ha! cries the shrink in you, clearly the subject was overcoming feelings of inadequacy by taking on the characteristics of his unloving father, identifying with him, competing in an effort to prove himself the better man.

Who could compete? The general's carnal excesses were the talk of every canteen and mess from Riyadh to Tacoma. But his were the convenient conquests of service slatterns and Filipina whores; I sought those who challenged, women rejoicing in their liberation, demanding more of me than I of them. I hear you fiercely shouting your objection. Innocent lovely Beatrice, fragile downtrodden Helen Mazur: dare you add those to your cold statistics?

You are out of order, Ms. Finnegan. This is my speech, my day in court, my hopeless search for love.

Did it all come too easily for love to grow? Dwight was right: there never seemed a shortage of demand, and yet my emptiness of heart remained. In my final year I petered out, and fled shamefully, in an impotence self-imposed, into a hermetic private world.

I found more happiness in that. And as the years passed I found a kind of abstract love in the retrogressive logic of the discipline we share, the spirited clash of minds in combat. With success came ambition, with more ambition, more success. And we know where that has taken me. . . .

Not that I forever remained in purdah. I partook of the odd careless fling as occasion offered, conjoined even in the sin of adultery, though rarely with the wives of friends. I once attempted what might be termed a relationship: does five months suffice?

Then — only in the last year — it started up again. A descent into the flesh. Depressed, befuddled with fear and whiskey, I gave myself to all who offered, heedless of consequences. My bailiff (how did you stumble onto her?); the ravenous Yvonne Fairhurst, another affair you appear to know too much about. Incongruously, this sudden regression seems associated with you, the flailing response of one who has just been pushed into the shark pool. I'm grabbing again. I'm reaching out. Help me.

This is how I handle stress. Some drink to excess, some overeat, some go fucking crazy.

So commit yourself, Vandergraaf.

Shall I admit I wandered past your open window as you partied into the night last Saturday? "Everybody Needs Somebody to Love." Damn it, that's my music, my generation, my life, my empty life. Don't take it all from me.

The wind has shifted and I must pull in the sheets and come about. Behind the Cascades, a mauve sky turns to gold; to the west, the snows of Olympus are pierced by the lances of Apollo. The jurors are awakening from their slumber, dazed and doubting: who speaks true, who bears false witness?

I am on a dock, naked and in flight, now trapped, and hands are reaching from the sea, my warning bells tolling mercilessly . . . No, again it's the phone. Who calls at a quarter after six? Such ominous dreams – this impending trial is too much with me.

I finally find my phone hidden under a pile of clothes I had set aside to wash. It's Detective Ellen Oversmith: an unusually brittle edge to the voice of this grave unwitty woman. I am still sluggish, much spent from my night of dance, and find it hard to piece her words together: "thought you should be apprised," "another incident, similar m.o.," "two individuals injured, one in serious condition with burns."

Brain cells start to activate. I ask her to begin again, slowly. Not a clinic this time, but the offices of the Abortion Rights Union in Belltown. And not exactly the union offices, either – a second-floor apartment beside it, a gasoline bomb mistakenly thrown at the wrong window of the building.

I dress hurriedly, cradling the phone in the crook of my neck. "Who was hurt?"

"African-American woman, age twenty-three, five months' pregnant, and I'm afraid she miscarried. Her three-year-old son has burns to his face and torso. Serious but stable."

The Molotov cocktail was flung from the street; it glanced off a ledge, exploding outside a bedroom, shattering the window, spraying the outer walls and an interior portion of the room with burning gasoline. The woman managed to smother flames on her child's crib and carry him out onto a back fire escape. Firefighters arrived in time to extinguish the blaze before any structural damage occurred.

"When did this happen? Did anyone see it?"

"About oh-two-thirty. The incendiary device was projected up there by a slightly built Caucasian male who had stepped out of a red older-model Ford full-size pickup truck. Another male was driving, heavy build, older. An insomniac gentleman observed the perpetrators from a stairwell. An in-state license, but he didn't get the number. We've exhausted any immediate leads, but we think it's some sort of revenge action. Anonymous male person called 911 yesterday with a message about freeing Carson Wilkes or there would be, quote, retribution."

"Retribution . . ." Big word. Cribbed from a sermon? "Can you pick me up?"

It is a two-hour drive to the town of Lynden, a hotbed of pious dogmatism (some years back, in a well-publicized blow against degeneracy, the town council passed a law banning dancing). This trip is going to jam up an overbooked Sunday: Thalia will be phoning my office as soon as she arrives; also flying in later today is a reluctant Helen Mazur, subpoenaed against her will. I am putting her in the Vintage Park, where she'll be pampered, perhaps freed from the strictures imposed by her husband.

The morning is still young as our unmarked cruiser purrs by the obsessively neat yards and homes of pretty Lynden. Ellen and I are looking for the True Gospel Baptist Chapel, east of town: the Kruegers live next door.

I intend to do some of God's good business there: to urge that Johann and Amy Krueger share in the pursuit of a holier cause than fanning the flames of hatred. If they are righteous in more than word they must atone for this sin. Those flames almost consumed an innocent child and a single mother who lost her fetus. The boy will live, we're assured, but his physical and emotional scars will survive, too, a testament to the evil that is preached here.

There by a wandering creek stands the church, a large immodest structure, stained glass, blue aluminum siding, a tall spire, its cross decked out with incandescent light bulbs. Beside it, in matching blue, a split-level residence behind a flat treeless lawn surrounded by a clipped hedge.

As we pull into the driveway a curtain parts: austere Pastor Krueger — already in Sunday suit and clerical collar — stares gravely at us. At the door he bows ever so slightly and silently beckons us in.

"Johann, I think you know Detective Ellen Oversmith. She'd like to have a few words with you and your wife."

"Of course. We heard about it on the radio." He shakes his head sadly.

We are led to a living room that is almost uncomfortably clean: plastic covers on lampshades, slipcovers on the sofa, Jesus framed in pious pain above the fireplace. But there's a wall of books: Beatrice told me he reads voraciously. A desk with papers spread upon it: Johann has been preparing today's sermon.

"That woman lost a baby five months in utero, Johann." I walk to the window, look out over the still creek; it is icing under a bright, cold sky. "There's a certain irony about that, isn't there?"

"I am deeply distressed."

If true, it is hard to tell. He is without expression, though his face looks more pinched and sallow than usual.

He offers coffee and returns to the kitchen. We settle into chairs, and from an open doorway I pick up a low conversation between him and Amy. When he returns with a tray, his face seems set with even harder lines.

Johann asks about the victims. Ellen says they are

lucky to be alive. "Do you know anyone in possession of an older red Ford pickup truck, sir?"

He doesn't respond for a moment, stands quietly at the window, his hands behind his back. "I have prayed for that woman and her son and the child who was in her womb. Beyond that, I regret to say I can be of little assistance."

"Johann," I say, "I do believe you know who was in that truck."

"How can that be? I was not there."

His discomfort is palpable. He cannot look at either of us directly, and is stiffly holding his cup and saucer.

"How can you pray for those people while you protect the men who nearly murdered them? Have you asked God about the justice of that?"

"What passes between the Deity and me is not yours to know," he says sharply. "You are most impertinent."

"Are you willing to answer my question, sir?" says Ellen. "Do you know anything about that truck?"

"We live in a rural area. There are many trucks, of course —"

I speak impatiently: "Oh, stop evading, Johann. You can be forced to testify on an oath to God: would you dare defy Him in doing so?"

"I will seek counsel from Him, Elizabeth, not from someone who defies His teachings."

Ellen may feel out of her element here, and is content to let me carry on. "If we're to get into a religious debate, let's talk about the morality of a murderous act, and of those who condone it by their silence."

"I do not *condone* it." He says this in a pulpit voice, large and plangent. Then, lower and strained: "As I say, I will seek guidance on these matters. I also have a duty of silence to those who have come to me in confidence. Now, if you do not mind, there are matters that beg my attention —"

But he is interrupted by a small, still voice from the doorway: Amy Krueger, standing with a dishtowel. "No, Johann, it isn't right."

"Stay out of this, my dear."

She speaks sharply: "Johann! I am sick of this! Do the right thing. This time, do it."

This time? What other errors of faith have been committed by this man of strict unblemished virtue? He has paled; he has been spoken to in fierce terms by the only one of God's creatures he seems afraid to defy. His cup rattles in its saucer as he nervously places it on a bureau, his head bowed, his lips moving silently.

When he raises his eyes they are damp and swollen. He looks at Ellen, then his wife, then directly at me. "There is a terrible despair in my heart. How they have misconstrued the word of God. It's not my fault. I spoke only of His anger at the sins that are counseled at that place of evil. They took it upon themselves to seek retribution. They were wrong." And he repeats, "It's not my fault."

It is as if he is seeking absolution from me; I offer him none. He has poisoned ears with his calls to the simple-minded to do the shameful work he calls God's justice.

He sighs deeply, then leads us from the house.

We follow his car up a narrow road into the hills east of the lake, then along a bumpy dirt road to a weather-beaten farmhouse. *Voilà*: behind a shed is revealed a red Ford pickup.

"I should have ordered backup," Ellen says. "I hope we're not in some trouble here."

Knock on wood, because trouble is what we are in. A stout middle-aged man has emerged from the front door holding a rifle. A younger, smaller man follows him out, carrying a shotgun. Ellen is on her radio, calling all cars, ready to accelerate out of here.

"Keep down!" she says. She removes her service revolver.

But Johann is out of his vehicle, calmly walking toward them. The rifle is raised, though not pointed. A sharp order from Johann – and the weapon is lowered.

Johann has reached them now. I cannot hear what they are saying, but the two men go to their knees, and he joins them. They remain there for several minutes, then Johann picks up their guns and leads the two men to our car.

"Cover me," says Ellen.

"*What?*"

I have never held a firearm in my life, but here I am with a trembling two-handed grip on a Smith and Wesson, pointing it God-knows-where as Ellen gets out, walks over to them, and handcuffs them together. They do not resist.

And this tense time draws quickly to a close. It all seems a dream, and when I return the gun to Ellen I want to pinch myself to prove I am really here, in front of this hillbilly house with a cop, a preacher, and two sad-looking wretches who seem more confused than danger-ous. Not exactly the cocky soldiers of the radical right I had expected. Were either of them among my stalkers-on-the-street? Maybe, but I am too frazzled to be certain.

Johann turns to me, his face wet with pain and grief. I feel great pity for this troubled man, who, from some deep hidden level, fascinates me. How I wish I under-stood him.

Distantly comes a siren.

After a couple of hours of interviews and paperwork, I race from police headquarters to my office. No message from Thalia Pfeiffer, though it's nearly three o'clock and a call to United Airlines tells me her flight has long since landed at Sea-Tac. I fuss and fiddle, chew at a pencil.

When she finally calls, I sigh with relief. "Where are you?"

"Actually, I'm in the local slammer."

"You're joking."

"I wish it was that funny."

I share that wish.

The interview room in which I am to meet Thalia is depressingly ugly and bare of all furniture but a table and metal chairs. The DEA has charged her with importing the six ounces of cocaine they found in the lining of her suitcase. I am quietly seething.

But Thalia enters smiling, wiggling her fingers in a wave. I presume she's wearing the clothes in which she was arrested, jeans and a T-shirt with a mola design. She is a graying hippie, forty-eight, five-ten, thin, lines of dissipation.

"Took a chance and blew it," she says, shaking my hand.

"You should have known your name was on the computer. Where are your brains?"

"Must've left them behind. Anyway, maybe I can make a deal. Narcs said they ain't interested in mules and they want me to roll over."

"What's that mean?"

"Finger the supplier and my connections up here, and I get off light, maybe two years. They're all vicious fuckers, anyway, them guys, said they'd blow me away if I didn't do this job. I wouldn't've been the first. Had to get out of that weird scene, I was feeling trapped. Look, I don't have any bread, but if you wanna, like, represent me, I'll help you cook this character's ass you're suing."

"He's suing me."

"Okay, whatever."

Not much in the way of higher intelligence here. Smiling, shrugging, nonchalant. "I don't do criminal work, but I have a friend in the office who is sharp."

"Okay, if you get me an ace who can scale them down to maybe a deuce or something like that, I'll be an unbelievable witness for you."

Unbelievable is exactly what I fear: Christiansen will have a field day. I can well imagine the disgusted faces on my jury.

"What am I supposed to remember?"

"Just tell me in your own words, and I'm going to record this if you don't mind." I dig into my briefcase for my compact tape recorder.

"Well, like, I guess it was summer – no, spring. And I was kind of basically working for tips in that joint and what I could make off moving a little weed. Sort of hiding out there on that dopey little island, staying away from some bad people in Vancouver. So I remember me and this guy was doing a spliff outside the bar when this girl comes up to us and, like, she's really unzipped, eh, crying, shaking, carrying on like that."

"Who was the other guy?"

"Haven't the faintest, some local yokel. Anyway, so it turns out she'd been raped by this turkey."

"She told you that."

"She said, 'Please help me. I've been raped.' Or attacked, assaulted, I'm not sure. And I took her up to my cabin and, yeah, it looked like it really happened, 'cause there was these bruises on her thighs and arms, and I think her neck. And some blood on her clothes, like he cut her up or something. I saw her panties were ripped because I helped her undress. I got her into the shower, gave her a bed. I figured later we'd maybe go and report it, but I had to get back to work, and when I woke up the next morning she was gone."

Her version accords remarkably well with that of Beatrice; I am impressed and very relieved.

"So I just, you know, figured she'd decided to write it off like just another bad night. I had a few of those; you gotta just lay back and hope."

"Did she describe the man who raped her?"

"Her boyfriend."

"That's what she called him?"

"Well, it looked that way. So I didn't think it was, like, *that* serious. Banged her on his boat, I guess, and when I went back around ten o'clock and looked through the window there was this sailboat motoring off, which I thought was pretty weird, late in the evening, and what an asshole to run away like that. Good-looking guy, actually, not one of the droids who used to sail into there."

"You saw him?"

"Oh, yeah, earlier, when they was in there eating and drinking it up. That's where I first saw the girl, and she was kind of snuggling up to this arrogant dude with long hair. Sat on his lap; he was doing some heavy squeezing."

I show her the April Fool's photo from the UW *Daily*. "Recognize anyone here?"

"Man, that was a long time ago." But she points to Beatrice. "Hey, I think that's her. And maybe this guy beside her."

I speak into the tape machine: "The witness has identified, unaided, Hugh Vandergraaf."

What this woman lacks in cerebral skills her memory compensates for. I put her though a harsh cross-examination, and – given that time blurs the most acute of memories – she passes my tests with surprising ease. She is specific about the little but important details, even the clothing Bea was wearing: slacks and a sweatshirt with the emblem and name of Rice Hall. I write out a statement and she signs it. I am optimistic now, even jubilant: she is as close to an eyewitness as one ever finds in a rape case. And I can put those nattering fears to rest that Beatrice has fantasized falsely, that Hugh is an innocent victim of a reckless and spiteful crusade.

From the temporary human storage facility which is the depressing downtown jail, Thalia is to be taken tomorrow to the federal courthouse for arraignment, and once I am outside I call Franca, explain the situation, and ask her to tend with care to our new client's needs.

Then I call Bea's machine – she is seeing Dr. Boorstein today – and exuberantly announce the news. Now if only Helen Mazur can come through.

The Vintage Park is in the heart of downtown, an old hostelry with a lavish facelift, expensive details, complimentary estate wine around the lobby fireplace. The desk clerk confirms that Helen Mazur has checked in – but, to my dismay, not alone.

Her husband answers the house phone. "Is this Elizabeth Finnegan?"

"Yes, it is."

"The two-faced lady who promised my wife she wouldn't be forced to go to court?"

"Mr. Mazur, I would like to speak to Helen."

A woman comes on the line, but it's not Helen. "My name is Lorna Beale, Miss Finnegan; I'm an attorney. Can we have a few words in the lobby?"

This is about to turn into a bad movie. I was soaring after talking to Thalia, but the sudden intervention of a lawyer takes the wind from my kite.

In a few minutes Lorna Beale walks in: fortyish, oiled with Olay, overdressed in a chi-chi suit with silk blouse. Her card informs me she is with one of the larger Spokane firms.

She leans toward me with a friendly smile. "Isn't this such an interesting case? The issues are *so* central to women's concerns."

"I'm glad you feel that way."

"I'm not one to get my name in the headlines, but I can count a few quiet victories. Nothing to make me arrogant."

I guess she assumes *I* am, but at least she mouths the appropriate political sentiments. "Lorna, it sounds as if we can do business. If I can manage just half an hour alone with Helen —"

A raised hand: a stop sign. "Elizabeth, I *wish* it was possible." A resigned shrug. "This is very sad for me, but her instructions are absolutely clear. And you did undertake not to drag that poor woman into this."

"*Poor* woman?"

"Well, she's rather subjugated, isn't she? Wilkie's a regular throwback to the dark ages." Now she draws even closer, staring at me intently. "This is just between us; it's terribly privileged but I want to save you a *great* deal of embarrassment. You see, it turns out she's quite disorganized about what actually happened way back when on Whidbey Island with Judge Vandergraaf."

My last dregs of wine descend into an empty clenched stomach. I can tell she is about to utter a huge lie. Anger management: pause, reflect, seek the other person's point of view.

"I'm afraid that despite what she told you earlier, she now concedes she didn't truly resist him. There was a little rough-and-tumble in the bushes, maybe, but when I asked her to be absolutely honest with me, she was forced to admit she went along with it. Let's face it, Elizabeth, here was a handsome young man — who she knew had a reputation among the ladies — leading her into the woods, and of course no one's going to believe she didn't know what was going on. . . ."

"How dare you invent these lies for her."

She sits bolt upright. "Those are *her* words. In the presence of her husband and me."

"Oh, I'll bet *he* was there."

Lorna Beale's smile wanes and flickers, then returns with renewed false vigor as she glances at her watch. "I have a flight back, so I'll make this brief. You gave my client a formal undertaking not to force her into a courtroom against her wishes. If you break that undertaking I will have something to say both to the court and the bar discipline committee."

You hypocritical, calculating . . . Harness the anger, Ann says, put all that energy to better use. I am firm but calm: "I'm released from that promise. I told her if she was raped it's between her and me. Now you say she wasn't. So I intend to call her to the witness stand."

The smile holds, frigid. "Do you *really* want to take that chance? If you shoot yourself in the head . . . well, be my guest. In the meantime, my client is under instructions not to speak to you for any reason. Or to anyone else about the case."

I rise. "Her subpoena is returnable tomorrow. I'll see her in court. You can tell the gentleman who retained you that he's welcome to stick around at his own expense. Have a nice flight back."

I leave for the office with a sour taste in my mouth. I am not going to allow that unctuous counterfeit feminist to keep Helen locked in her cage of fear: I will fly her daughter out here, and maybe Gayle Mitsuka can locate some old school-friends to beseech her to stand proudly. I am still ahead of the game: I have Thalia Pfeiffer.

In the library, I organize myself for tomorrow, but my head is swimming with images from this frantic day. I slept only four hours last night; the wells of energy have dried.

Between waves of fatigue come those old feelings of being disoriented, lost in the wide ocean of a loneliness

I cannot understand. What am I doing here in this desolate time and space? What forces have compelled our foolhardy Jeanne d'Arc to a point of her life where twelve American citizens are about to decide whether she be saint or witch?

And what the hell does Elizabeth Finnegan (who ever she is) think she's trying to prove by being her own lawyer at her own inquisition? Headstrong, rash, even flaky: I've heard those words whispered around office and courthouse. Arrogant, too. Last night Franca urged me to let her join me at counsel table: she would put everything aside. I couldn't explain my need to make this journey alone because I don't understand it myself. For some reason, I am too covetous to share this trial: it is my life, an obsession, a personal rite of passage.

As I reflect, as I go deep within my heart, my motives clarify: I realize that if I cannot successfully defend my own true words, the validity of which rings so keenly for me, I am not fit to be a lawyer. Nor would I want to be, not if the system is capable of such grotesque error. And I can do it. I am not J.J. Plum, but I have skills. I have won almost every case I've fought. I can do this. Repeat after me. I can do this.

I go home to leftover pumpkin pie and an early bed.

17 | Monday . . .

I am met in the office by greetings and smiles: my "bravery" in helping collar those anti-abortionists has won much mention in the morning paper. Three men have been charged in connection with a series of arsons, the article says. That must mean they managed to implicate Carson Wilkes, the man who struck me with the Bible. I feel pleased about my contribution.

From Junior, a surprising reaction: "Hear, hear. Good going. This is how we prove to the prejudiced public that lawyers take on a social responsibility; they aren't merely thoughtless money-grubbing parasites."

Such unexpected affability only feeds my suspicions, especially since I detect a strained quality in it.

"Well, thanks, Dwight. How's J.J.? Is he coming in to work?"

"He said he's preparing for re-entry this week. He told me to, ah, wish you luck."

Those words are pleasant to my ears.

Franca left a note: she is off to federal court to represent Thalia Pfeiffer and will return with a signed affidavit.

Rain pelts my office window, a cold pour that may yet turn to snow. I must remember to have my ski harness fixed before I bus to Idaho for the holidays. I hope I can look forward to a few days of sun on Coalsack Hill, the rope-tow slope where I learned to ski.

Mattie has taken several messages, nothing urgent, mostly friends and clients, well-wishers. I tell her to do her best to keep my practice in suspended animation for the next two weeks, stall any appointments. I want only one matter on my mind, Superior Court Cause 98-2-01620-1, Finnegan versus the heir designate to the U.S. Supreme Court.

On the ninth floor, a milling throng: media, women's-movement friends (warned to avoid impudent demonstrations of support), sensation-seekers, the usual devotees of live drama, the mostly retired courtroom aficionados who race for the front rows at notorious trials.

Voices descend to a hush – ominous? – as I tote my heavy briefcase by these curious faces. I smile for them. I have found a vital witness at the last minute; I am ready; I am confident. And I'm *not* going to give up on Helen Mazur.

"Witnesses report here," reads a sign on a door near the courtroom. The room is empty but for the Mazurs, both seated, she in her usual slouch. Wilkie is a tightly wound man, thin-lipped, red of face, slightly overweight.

"Good morning, Helen. Mr. Mazur, I'm pleased to meet you."

He refuses my hand, folds his arms. "This is an absolute *outrage*."

"May I speak to you alone, Helen?"

"Just *tell* her."

"I can't talk to you." Nor look at me. She speaks so faintly and looks so sad I want to comfort her, and I am deeply troubled by the agony I am causing her. Her mate is like a gob of matted gum in the hair – how can I rid myself of him?

"All right, let's sit on this for a few days. I probably won't need you until Friday at the earliest, but I'm afraid the subpoena requires you to stay in town. There is an interesting exhibit of Salish art at the Burke Museum,

Mr. Mazur." I don't want them waiting outside the courtroom – too many enemy spies.

"I am not at the moment interested in Indian art, *Ms.* Finnegan. This is damned annoying. I coach a bantam hockey team. We practice every third night."

"That's very civic-minded, Mr. Mazur." I pause at the door. I address Helen, but my words are also for Wilkie. "Helen, where's that feisty young woman who stood up to Vandergraaf as he was spouting all his propaganda and calling you a fascist? Sure, you love your husband. Love, honor, and obey, right? Well, that last imperative is now wildly out of fashion. You have to be true to your heart. Please believe in yourself."

I depart. Did I notice the slightest straightening of that bowed spine? Wilkie instructs a boys' hockey team, he has an accounting business to tend to – I cannot imagine he will stay all week. Knock on wood.

I take a deep breath before entering 941, one of our larger courtrooms; it is ornamented with abstract canvases, loaners from the county arts commission, splashes of color against the drabness of windowless walls. The opposition troops are arrayed at one of two large adjoining counsel tables: Vandergraaf, Christiansen, and a young woman lawyer. Much outnumbered, I may benefit from that grand American trait called siding with the underdog.

Beatrice is here, seated by her husband, stalwart Thomas. Harry Crake, on the sidelines, gives me a sloppy grin – he has probably braced himself for the day with an ounce or two of corn whiskey. He is no doubt pleased that Judge Luckwell has banned the cameras of the opposition, the visual media. ("This is a solemn inquiry, not a peep show.")

I confer a few moments with the Struthers, then cast a cautious glance at Vandergraaf, who is in earnest consultation with his lawyers. He favors me with a look that would scorch a rock. Is he wishing he hadn't started this?

Or even that he had lived life differently? Sorry, Hugh, but here we are, locked in the law's unholy embrace.

"All rise."

Mavis M. Luckwell walks smartly to the bench, sits, nods, waits for the case to be announced, and says, "If we're all ready, let's select a jury."

The two dozen candidates sent down from the jury co-ordinator's office comprise a fair demographic cross-section of greater Seattle, though there are not as many young persons as I would like. Older folk, of course, tend to be more conservative, are more likely to align themselves with authority figures – like judges – and less inclined to accept that no means no when uttered by a seventeen-year-old woman to a desirable man. I am not likely to achieve a majority female jury so I'll have to be picky about the men: examine them carefully for redness of neck, says Ann Boorstein. Family men are what I want, fathers of daughters.

She drafted a profile for jurors most likely to side with me: "Young, honest, fearless, somewhat distrustful of the system. Remember to make eye contact. Anyone who can't smile, avoid like the plague. Don't be afraid of intelligence. You prefer the upright and the God-fearing as long as their minds aren't closed; they'll more easily identify with Beatrice, less with the campus rake with his get-the-fuck-out-of-Vietnam T-shirt."

Jury selection is possibly the most critical part of a trial. In civil suits, counsel are constrained as to the number of prospective jurors they may excuse: three is the limit. So there must be give and take: Bill and I will somehow have to find twelve finalists and a couple of alternates who don't offend either of us.

Judge Luckwell briefly explains to the panel that slander is spoken defamation, as opposed to written libel, then squints through her glasses and reads a short summary of complaint and answer. She asks each candidate in turn whether the publicity has predisposed her or him to a verdict. One professional-looking woman thinks about that question, then says, "To be absolutely honest, I would be biased." She is excused. Damn.

As Bill Christiansen and I begin our questioning of these conscripts of the justice system, I notice Mavis Luckwell casting looks at Hugh with an air of puzzlement. Join the club. He once catches her staring, and she quickly looks away. He is deadpan, impossible to read.

The first juror to be sworn is a stevedore, which may seem the wrong kind of occupation, but he has a sensitive expression, laugh-lines, a thoughtful way of answering questions. Two children, wife teaches Sunday school. The next to be selected is a male electronics engineer with A.T.&T.'s wireless division, quick intelligent eyes that do not waver from mine, stable marriage, two daughters in high school.

The next person is the grinch who stole Christmas; he regards me with an accusatory petulance – I am responsible for all his woes in life. Humorless, shifty of eye, he seems too eager to serve his country. "I like to keep an open mind," he says, but I read male anger. Despite my efforts, he is seated: I shall save one of my three challenges for him.

We seat several women, then two middle-aged family men and a hip-looking young Southeast-Asian American who sells rebuilt computers from his home and seems to hold progressive views.

By noon break, we have exhausted our allotted challenges. One seat remains empty; we also need two alternates. I decline an offer from friends for lunch. I prefer to be alone during trials, to concentrate my thoughts; besides, I am too strung-out to eat. So I pull up my coat collar to brave a solitary walk in the cold rain.

I choose a route to the Pike Place Market, and find it, as always, bustling, even in bad weather. I pick up a

Wall Street Journal from the newsstand and check the Nasdaq listings. Nipigon is a bullet: up forty-five cents. I have examined its prospectus and all seems in order. I'll keep faith in Jake and stay on the train.

Upon my return journey, my way is briefly impeded by a figure who emerges from around a corner: Hugh Vandergraaf in a long Dr. Zhivago coat, on his own lone winter promenade.

"Into each life some rain must fall," he says, and steps over a puddle to allow me to pass. I rummage in my head for an appropriate response, another line from Longfellow, but can only force a stiff smile.

As I carry on down the street, I feel, if not rattled, quite ill-at-ease. I am not sure what effect he has on me; it is uncomfortably compelling, unnatural. I am concerned as well that he seems too calm, too pleasant, too urbane. A worry afflicts me that I will hardly have him at my mercy on the stand. Do I have the skills to take him on? How would J.J. do it? Make scrambled eggs of him, that's what he would do. I fear I'll serve up a less palatable breakfast.

Franca is waiting for me in 941. She hands over Thalia Pfeiffer's affidavit, sworn and signed.

"She hasn't got brain one. She going to be any fucking help?"

"Oh, God, yes. She almost clinches my case."

"If she's telling the truth."

"Why would she lie?"

"I don't know. . . . There's something just a little too devious about her. Can't help thinking she has the facts down too pat about a rape way back in '71. Maybe I'm out to lunch, but she was awfully anxious to co-operate, to come up here."

"She thought the police were about to pounce."

"That's what she claims. I'm sure she's okay – I'm sort of being devil's advocate here."

Thalia *was* almost too willing to aid me. More worrying is that her help may be seen as a payoff for our putting together a deal with the DEA. Also, I am starting to wonder if Sergeant Nathaniel Duff was using me to bring her up here, which would be most devious of *him*. Have I been too trusting? I would like to phone him, but that might not be wise – he came to me in secrecy.

"Thalia's been so eager to put out for the feds I got bail down to fifty grand. Know someone who wants to put it up?"

"High-risk investment. We'll just leave her where she is."

"Make sure they don't try to connect you with the dope trade, Liz – you brought her up here."

"They wouldn't stoop to that. Would they?"

"Never trust a cornered dog."

She is right. Be ready for anything.

The first ballot pulled from the box this afternoon brings up a robust African-American woman: Shayne Wells, thirty-three, a nurse. Two daughters, churchgoer. When Bill asks her if she has any negative feelings about lawyers or judges, she says, "Well, they never did me any harm. So far." That prompts general laughter. But behind her easygoing manner may there be found a smoldering antipathy to authority? Inescapable, all my black sisters tell me, given their experiences with prejudice.

She is seated; now we have a gender-balanced twelve, six and six, all sworn to well and truly try and true verdict give. Ten must agree on that verdict. I am in their hands.

After the alternates are chosen, we break to allow the jury to settle in. Bill has indicated that after opening speeches he will call character evidence: a coat of whitewash is to be applied to his client. The flip side of this strategy: it puts Vandergraaf's character squarely in issue and widens my target.

Bill draws me aside to ask if he can dispense with some minor witnesses.

"Give me your list, I'll look them over."

"No, my offer holds: I'll show you mine if you show me yours."

We are interrupted by two of his staff lugging in a thirty-inch television and smaller sets for the judge and the audience. We are about to see the hysterical female in action in Victoria, B.C.

"Do we really need to call anyone from the TV crews to prove the videos?" he asks.

"I'll stipulate, but what do you mean, videos, plural?"

"There's the one of you up in Canada, of course. But we thought we'd start off with your remarks outside Hugh's court after the Henderson rape sentence."

"Proving what?"

"Malice. Tends to enhance damages."

I suppose my call for the castration of Vandergraaf's brain might qualify as proof I harbored a prior grudge. Again, there is a trade-off: the jury will know of the compassion Vandergraaf feels for rapists.

Still, I should force the judge to decide the issue, test the waters, so while the jury is out I argue that righteous indignation does not qualify as malice. Mavis Luckwell listens patiently, then simply says, "Overruled."

"One more brief matter," Bill says. "I see Mrs. Struthers is in court. As a probable witness, she should be excluded."

I argue vigorously against that: the case is really about her; she stands in the shoes of the defendant; I need her here for constant consultation.

"I'm against you, Mr. Christiansen," Mavis says. "Bring in the jury."

Mr. Grier, the electronics engineer, is in the lead, a

likely choice for foreperson. Think about your two teenaged daughters, Mr. Grier.

Bill Christiansen opens with a lucid outline of his case: the defendant's allegations – "prompted by a deep-seated malice against my client" – would be met with firm denial of "each and every spiteful accusation."

I rise. "Your Honor, this is simply not a proper opening. Mr. Christiansen is arguing his case."

"Sustained," says Judge Luckwell.

Bill reigns himself in, but still carries on forcefully, resolute and serious: there is nothing to be made light of here, ladies and gentlemen. The jury is attentive, impressed by a passion in his voice that does not seem staged. His speech is short: he doesn't give away any secrets he may hold or name his witnesses.

I am even briefer. "I am accused of uttering words which I have undertaken to prove are true. You'll hear the other side first, and I have no doubt you will listen and observe carefully. All I ask is that you keep fair and open minds until my turn comes. You've all heard there are two sides to every story? There will definitely be two sides to this one, and your duty will be to decide who speaks truly, who does not. And to those who may be uneasy about the trial extending into Christmas, I will do my best to ensure you are with your families then. By shutting up now."

They all smile, some chuckle. Judge Luckwell, too, might harbor gratefulness behind her sober exterior.

We move directly to a showing of the videos; the jurors watch without much expression. But occasionally one or other of them peeks at me or Vandergraaf, more intensely as the second tape is played, my outburst outside Mulholland's office. What passes through their minds? Is that young woman one of those shrill feminists you hear about? Rapacious thug, did she say? That handsome gray-haired judge? Look at her all alone there, friendless, must be marginally obsessive.

Bill's first witness is Judge Owen Bristow, whom I know only by reputation, a portly, tough old bird retired earlier this year from the Washington Court of Appeals. This is a different role for him, an ordinary witness, stripped of authority, and he seems uncomfortable.

I snatch up a sharpened pencil; we are under way.

"How long have you known Judge Vandergraaf?"

"For twenty-five years. He was hired by our firm as a student."

"While still in law school?"

"Yes, one year to go."

"And what was he like then?"

"A few rough edges." A wry smile. "We smoothed them out."

"And he remained how long?"

"After ten years he went out on his own."

And during those ten years, he proved himself "capable beyond expectation," showed "diligence and dedication," impressed by being "utterly honorable in all his dealings."

And did he gain a reputation for honesty and integrity? Quite so. Never had a complaint. Had he ever betrayed signs of a violent temper? Not unless that embraces being forceful in argument. How did he relate to women generally or in the office? With appropriate courtesy and propriety.

Since their professional ways parted, they have seen each other only irregularly, but Judge Bristow followed his acolyte's career. Impressive history of taking on civil-rights cases, often without fee. Eloquent and often dynamic in his appearances before Bristow at trial or on appeal.

Vandergraaf glances at me: how am I taking this? I acknowledge him with a smile. I'm cool, Hugh; butter doesn't melt. I'm chewing on my pencil only because I like the taste of wood.

Normally it is poor practice to cross-examine character witnesses: you only make the halo shine brighter, J.J. says. But a brief line of questioning seems in order.

"Judge Bristow, before you retired this year from the Court of Appeals, did the case of People versus Tyler J. Henderson come before it?"

He screws up his face.

I help him. "A rape case. Appeal against Judge Vandergraaf's sentence of community service and five years' probation."

"Yes. I wasn't on the panel that heard it, but I remember it being discussed."

"And you know the appeal court held the sentence to be excessively lenient and raised it to three years' imprisonment."

"I believe so, yes."

Next up is a former chair of the state bar association, who is cloyingly effusive: "A remarkable man with potential to become one of our most renowned jurists."

I object. "This isn't evidence of reputation, it's a personal opinion. Evidence Rule 405."

"Sustained."

I am jolted that Vandergraaf is able to produce, as his next witness, Senator Edwin Loovis, who flew in from D.C. to be here with us today. He is a major rainmaker, golfs with the president. A sparkling future is ahead for Vandergraaf, he says; the eyes of Washington are upon this "citadel of probity and unwavering honor."

I content myself with a couple of questions to establish Vandergraaf is his long-time political crony. But I am discomfited: Loovis has weight.

Bill finally produces a woman, Susan Marks, a buxom young lawyer from Redmond who helped run Vandergraaf's election campaign last year. We hear of his overwhelming mandate "despite all the accusations that were made about him."

It was a hostile campaign, she claims (though the candidate we backed was in fact relatively gracious throughout). Vandergraaf won "handsomely," three to one.

Bill asks, "During the campaign did he take a position on women's issues?"

"Absolutely. Complete equality."

"And do you consider yourself a feminist, Ms. Marks?"

"Oh, very much so."

"And during all your dealings with him, has he ever made any advances of a sexual nature?"

"To me?"

"Well, yes, or to anyone?"

"Not the slightest."

Do I pick up a wistfulness in her smile? The jury will learn he prefers them slightly trimmer, not as generously full-figured. I cannot think of a single question I would want to ask her: she is dangerous, a devotee.

Now comes a former client from Vandergraaf's days as a do-gooder, an exceptional witness for him: he had saved her family from penury, successfully suing a loan shark for return of their life's savings. Again, I object: improper evidence of reputation. Again, I'm sustained, but a juror gives me a reproving look: I am trying to obstruct the truth about this selfless soul of charity.

I am cringing as the clock ticks off to half-past four. End of day one of this popularity contest: the plaintiff is quickly filling his dance card.

I wilt further under the oppression of the despairing attitude of Harry Crake, who joins me in the elevator. "You better start moving the ball down the field. He sounds like Jesus Christ."

"Harry, anyone with Vandergraaf's connections can find half a dozen people who owe him favors to stand up and say he's God's gift to the galaxy."

"What does Senator Loovis owe him? Hugh's handlers seem goddamn confident to me. They have some trick plays up their sleeve; I can smell it."

"Armpit odor." Or maybe it's his stale whiskey. I am forced to share his cloud as he walks me to my building: they're winning over the jury, they've got the crowd on their side. He offers a pitying look as he parts from me.

His pessimism is contagious – Mattie sees it in my face.

"Bad start?"

"Had to sit there and listen to a bunch of sucks. Did the number-cruncher check out?"

She knows I mean Wilkie Mazur, and shakes her head. Also, she has had no luck reaching their daughter in Spokane – she is in the middle of exams. Damn, this is so frustrating.

I feel a sudden loss of energy. Coffee. I need coffee.

In the lounge, I tell everyone who wants to enjoy this afternoon's farce to watch it on the news. Curtis Kaplan, who seems to have come away from his couples workshop hale and enthusiastic, marches sprightly with me to my office, trying to jump my battery with bromidic analogy: a trial is like life, a hilly road, one day you're struggling uphill, the next you're coasting. He exudes a better energy than the bad-weather forecaster who walked me to the office, but there is an eerie edge to his optimism. He doesn't sound like Curtis Kaplan.

"It's a catharsis for you, this trial, isn't it? A cleansing of the soul. And I see something primal in your hunger, your need to win. Something orgasmic, orgiastic."

"Orgiastic? Are you on some kind of drug?"

An odd, sly, self-satisfied look. Had they rolfed his brain at Snoqualmie?

"So how'd it go?" I ask.

"The workshop?"

"No, your cranial lobotomy."

"Great. Just great. Incredible body work, good vibes, a lot of letting go. And we all did a little sex-change operation."

"Oh, good, you've become a woman."

"Just kidding. What happened is Arnie, the facilitator – he's this lovely mensch, by the way – asked the males to reverse roles, be the acceptors, not the initiators or aggressors in sexual play."

"I thought that's how you and Maxine were doing it anyway."

"Okay, I have to buy into that. But now I can accept it as a legitimate means of playing out my fantasies."

What does that mean? The mensch, the guru facilitator, has tuned him to a different frequency, a post-hypnotic trance. "Curtis, I sense a new phase."

"There are no phases. There is only deepening of understanding. I'm quoting Arnie. We, ah, did something out of the usual, Max and I."

"Do I want to hear this?"

"We played bridge." I'm confused. Bridge? "Maxine brought along two close friends, a couple from her duplicate club – you know that Max has international points? She's a fanatic – and so we . . . made a foursome." He leans to me, winks in a way I find almost repulsive. "After a couple of rubbers, we . . . swapped partners. If you get my point."

"You rolfed somebody's wife?" Shy, introspective, clean-minded Curtis Kaplan: too bizarre. Dummy at bridge – new meaning is given to the expression.

"But listen. Later, in our own cozy log cabin, Max and I did it. Enjoyed sex with each other. No, blunter: we fucked – Arnie isn't into sexual euphemism, he made us each say 'fuck' fifty times." He moves close, intense, sharing. "And, Liz, it was the best we've ever had. The best . . . fuck."

"Curtis, you went in there reasonably normal and you've come out kinky."

He takes affront. "You're really old-fashioned, do you know that? Beneath the skin of thoroughly modern Lizzie hides a squeamish Victorian prig. Well, let me tell you, Max and I expect to be playing a little *more* bridge with George and Francine. They're a stellar couple, sensitive, very bright. They have *Ph.D.s.*"

"They're pharmacologists."

"How did you know *that*?"

I stay late at the office, tackling my desk, preparing for tomorrow, and arrive home in time for a quick martini before dinner. Nicholson and Stephane, who has joined us, let me rave on about all the treacle that was dished out in court today. It has done in my appetite; I can barely touch Nick's ham and yams.

I ask Stephane how his weekend with the kids went.

"Despite the interruption of that sordid formal *outing*, I managed some time with them. These are important years, critical, their adolescence. We spent all Sunday at a craft fair looking for something suitable for their mother. No one will ever say I've tried to turn them against her. How did she survive her idiotic workshop with my sub?"

I wonder if I should tell him. But surely he has a right to know, and in a weak moment I will eventually blurt it out to Nick anyway.

"You remember that couple from your bridge club who spotted us at the Ho Ho Seafood? You introduced them to us. Pharmacologists, you said."

"George and Francine Lindsey. What about them?"

"Well, Maxine brought them along to the workshop to let the inner child free, or whatever they do."

"How that surprises me. Two stuffier and more unimaginative drones I cannot imagine."

"I don't *think* so. I guess you never really got to know them. They swing."

"On what children's playground?"

Nick cocks a sardonic eyebrow. "She means they exchange partners, darling. I assume Kaplan had a go at Francine while George boffed your wife."

"That's exactly what happened."

Stephane shoves back his chair, startled, looking as if a wasp stung him on the behind. "I hope *not* in the same bed. This is scandalous. Sheer depravity. How am I going to explain this to Michael and Janice?"

"Maybe you shouldn't," Nick says.

"*Maxine* did that? I want to throw up. Did your Mr. Kaplan say she enjoyed it?"

"Sort of," I mumble glumly. I have opened up a can of writhing worms.

"What indescribably scummy behavior. *Wonderful* example for the children. I'm picking them up right now." He rises abruptly, looks for his coat.

"Whoa, just a minute." I move between him and the coat rack. "Worst thing you could do; she'd get a court order, full custody. Talk to your lawyer. I'll phone Franca right now." I dial her at home.

Still steaming, he talks to her, then listens, I hope getting an earful of sobering second thought.

Nick says, "You and your big mouth, princess."

The source of all my woes. Why can't I master the simple technique of closing it?

18 | Tuesday . . .

Harry Crake, perhaps regretting his bleakness of yesterday, extends me a word of encouragement before we get under way. You're right, coach, time to get the ball out of my end of the zone. A sold-out stadium today. The court smells slightly rancid from the many wet bodies: we almost had to swim through the dense rain to find our way here.

Bill Christiansen won't tell me who is next up to bat: we are continuing our stubborn standoff. But when Judge Luckwell, impatient with our games, asks Bill how many more character witnesses he has, he says, "We have pared them down to one."

I turn to Beatrice, who is sitting behind me, front row, and she gives me a hidden thumbs-up. She looks almost too respectable: long fawn skirt, white blouse, no campus feminist badges. I can sense her strength; its aura seems to surround her like a shield.

"Mr. Randolph Fairhurst," Bill announces.

The jury must wonder why my mouth is hanging open as I watch this balding older gentleman walk confidently up the aisle. The plaintiff is calling a man whose wife he bedded several times.

"You are the chairman of the board of Fairhurst Pacific Enterprises Ltd.?"

He is. And also president or chair of its several major corporate satellites. Honorary head of this or that charity, president of the Seattle Symphony Society.

"And do you know Hugh Vandergraaf?"

"I've known him for a number of years, particularly as a director of the Symphony Society."

"He gives of his time?"

"Eagerly and freely. Chairman of the fund-raising committee."

"And do you know of his reputation for honesty and integrity?"

If I hear that phrase once more I am going to chuck my double-latte breakfast.

"Utterly trustworthy."

I feel I am dying here, felled by my own weapon, a careless promise I made. Two persons in this courtroom know something the cuckold doesn't, and I can't do anything about it. J.J., help me, whisper in my ear, tell me what to do. What was my undertaking to Yvonne Fairhurst? Not to involve her. I need time to think this over, no time to do that. These thoughts bounce so noisily around my head I am distracted from Fairhurst, who is carrying on about Hugh being "a gentleman of the old school, particularly when it comes to the ladies. Sought permission once to ask my wife to dance." He finds this droll, a low laugh.

"Your witness," says Bill.

The last line Fairhurst tossed in affords an opening; maybe I can wedge it wider.

"Mr. Fairhurst, he asked *your* permission to dance with your wife?"

"Frankly, it was a relief. I'm not very good on my toes."

I smile with effort. I fear the jury likes him.

"I think I saw you and your wife on the society pages. Yvonne, yes? She's a very attractive woman."

"Thank you."

Thank you? "And did Mrs. Fairhurst dance with him?"

"A couple of times, I believe."

"Prior to that all three of you were seated at a head table – this was last spring, wasn't it? – a five-hundred-a-plate soiree for the symphony?"

He looks at me oddly: how would I know all this? "I believe so."

"And Yvonne danced with him, talked to him, enjoyed his company?"

"I didn't pay much attention."

I look at Vandergraaf – he is chewing on *his* pencil. I can tell it wasn't his idea to subpoena Randolph Fairhurst. He probably thought it would look odd if he vetoed this magnanimous gesture.

"And I believe you had to leave on a business trip that took you out of town the next weekend."

"I can't be sure; I make many trips."

"Your records would tell you that, wouldn't they? I believe it was a trip to Zurich."

He gives me the strangest of looks, a mix of concern and suspicion, then fumbles in a pocket, produces a miniature electronic daybook, and punches in some figures. "You're right."

"Your wife didn't go with you?"

"No, she never does."

I could ask him if she likes to ski. I could ask about the condo on the Oregon coast. I don't. I thank him. I climb off my tightrope and sit.

Fairhurst is still frowning at me. Now he looks from Bill to the judge but avoids Vandergraaf, who is not looking at him anyway.

"You're excused," says the judge. "Thank you. Next witness, Mr. Christiansen?"

"Pardon me a moment, Your Honor."

Bill sidles up to me as Fairhurst leaves.

"That was as sleazy a piece of work as I've ever seen in a courtroom. I'm shocked at the innuendo, and I'm confident the jury is, too."

"Well, Bill, maybe your client hasn't told you about all his charitable contributions."

The intensity of my look tells him I am not putting him on. He turns to Vandergraaf, who is seemingly unconcerned, giving study to one of the abstract paintings.

But I am concerned that I am not making eye contact with the jurors. Maybe they think I *was* sleazy. It *could* look that way. This may have backfired.

"Do you have another witness, Mr. Christiansen?" Gentle sarcasm is Judge Luckwell's preferred tool for goading counsel along.

Bill returns to his table. "I wonder, Mrs. Struthers, if you would care to take the stand?" Caught totally by surprise, I drop my pencil to the floor. I turn to look at Beatrice: she is hesitant to rise, seeking my permission. I nod. We must not seem ruffled, but I'm sure my smile looks waxen. Why would Bill call her as part of his own case? To catch us unprepared? To soften a later blow? No, obviously he wants to prove she fell apart, point the jury in that direction immediately.

He is smiling, knows I'm rattled. "I take it, Your Honor, that I shall be entitled to cross-examine her as an adverse witness."

I rise, stilling slight knee tremors. "I don't agree. He's calling her as his own witness, apparently to support his case."

"Let's put our heads together," says the judge, and we join her in a sidebar by the steps to the bench. The issue is critical: if Bea is declared adverse, Bill has full license to ask leading or hostile questions.

"Elizabeth said she stands in the shoes of the defendant. I agree."

"So do I," says the judge.

"Could we take a recess, Your Honor?" I ask. I hope for a chance to give Beatrice a last-minute pep talk.

"I'd rather we get on with it, Ms. Finnegan."

No wriggle-room. I return to my table. I don't let the jury see my crossed fingers.

Beatrice takes the oath with what thankfully seems calm confidence. I pray she will maintain that state. She is not afraid; she has said so many times.

"Mrs. Struthers, I want to ask you about some emotional difficulties you had in late 1971 after your relationship ended with the plaintiff."

I sputter: "*Relationship?* That's hardly the word."

"Rephrase, Mr. Christiansen."

"Thank you, Your Honor." Implying the judge has done him a favor. "Let's get into that, then. You were a first-year liberal-arts student. Hugh Vandergraaf was a second-year law student. You both worked on the student newspaper that year and became friendly."

"Friendly. I suppose so. Casually."

That's right, look directly at him, Bea. Don't turn to me. The jury will read any silent appeals for help.

"You dated?"

"Not at all. He asked me out several times. I finally agreed. Once." That word is calmly emphasized.

"I think it's fair to suggest there was a bit of flirting going on."

"It was very one-sided, Mr. Christiansen."

"Oh, really? Yet on a Friday in late March you gladly accepted his invitation to attend a party on a schooner tied up at Union Bay."

"With some trepidation, actually. I didn't know him that well. I knew he had a reputation with the young women on campus."

Nicely slipped in, though Bill does not seem fazed. "Mrs. Struthers, what would you say if I told you that you were seen kissing him at that party?"

He has a witness with the memory of an elephant, so I have to assume it is Dumbo, the loudmouthed college senior who was on the ketch with Vandergraaf. Maybe the brassy girlfriend, too.

"He kissed *me*. I didn't respond. Well, I did, I pulled back; I was startled."

"And yet you agreed to accompany him on a sailing trip the very next day."

"Yes, but not alone. We were with another couple."

"Not to beat around the bush, Mrs. Struthers, you were powerfully attracted to him to the point of infatuation."

"I found him . . . very interesting. Different. Attractive, yes."

She sounds far too tentative, and I fear the jury, not knowing of her strict religious background, her shyness, might think she is overly coy. Maybe they have the sense she did indeed suffer from that cruel disease of the heart, infatuation. Yet to know Beatrice is to know a woman of virtue. She would never have succumbed.

"You desired him, didn't you?" A quick thrust, his voice raised.

"I'm not sure what you mean." Oh, God, too evasive.

"Isn't it true, Mrs. Struthers, that during that entire boat trip you were in a state of physical desire for young Vandergraaf?"

And for the first time, her eyes meet mine, but go quickly back to Bill.

"I'm not sure," Beatrice says softly. "I'm not sure if I even knew what desire was. I would never have let myself go that far, Mr. Christiansen. I know that absolutely."

"Very well, we'll have a chance later to explore what went on during that sailing trip, perhaps when Ms. Finnegan calls you. But now what I'm interested in — and I hope you'll not think me unkind — is the fact that you suffered a major mental collapse in that spring of 1971."

"Yes, but how major it was, I don't know."

"You were institutionalized."

"I was placed in a care setting, yes."

"For almost a year."

"Not the full time. I was released for a while to do some volunteer care with a Christian couple my father knew."

"And you suffered long periods of anxiety and amnesia as well." Bill is keeping his voice low, just solicitous enough not to offend the jury. He is very professional, I have to admire him.

"That's quite true."

"And there were suicide attempts?"

"Yes. Twice, I'm told. I can't remember either of them."

"How strange. Mrs. Struthers, if I were to suggest to you that your difficult time was brought on by a feeling of rejection, what would you say?"

She pauses a while, thinking. Why? Just say it: her difficult time was brought on by a feeling of being raped.

"Partly."

"Oh?"

"I felt rejected by my parents. They didn't believe that I was raped."

That's very quick of her. Get it out now, before Pastor Krueger bellows it to the jury.

"Did you not feel romantically rejected? By a law student by the name of Hugh Vandergraaf?"

"Mr. Christiansen, if he's the same law student who raped me, the answer is no."

Firm and indignant. Bill seems taken aback by her toughness. Was he expecting a pious milksop?

"As I say, we'll have a chance to debate that allegation later," Bill says, showing signs of brittleness. "For now, what I'm interested in is this, ah, care setting you mentioned."

"Let's take the morning break first," says Judge Luckwell, who has been regularly studying Vandergraaf over her glasses, often frowning. One would think that would make him nervous, but he is not afraid to meet her eyes occasionally.

It is unwise to talk to a witness under cross-examination – jurors resent last-minute coaching – so I simply telegraph a wink and a smile to tell Beatrice she is holding up well. But I am unpleasantly impressed with Bill's work: he is setting up his central argument that she was unstable, that she fantasized the rape. And I am afraid the jury has begun to take to him: his poise, his politeness, his failure to fit the public's stereotype of the sneering mouthpiece.

Here comes Harry Crake with some discouraging words; I am to be told to start kicking the football. I avoid him, call headquarters, chat with Mattie about various office leftovers. Vandergraaf is in the corridor, a couple of female spectators engaging him in sprightly conversation, giggling. He has groupies.

For the balance of the morning, Bill contents himself with bringing out as many details of Bea's illness and slow recovery as she can remember. He makes a point of her faulty memory, probing for minutiae which he knows aren't there. Ultimately, she will be compared with Vandergraaf, whose recall will be keener, every detail retained as to how she seduced him in the starboard bunk. And how will he explain her hurried departure from the boat?

The hospice, a small building in a reposeful park-like setting, was located near Everett, south of Bellingham, and was run by the Conservative Baptist Congregation. She remembers no one from the staff but the visiting physician and young nurse. For a few weeks she was confined to her bed, though as her recovery continued she was permitted on the grounds. From time to time her parents would take her away, weekends, church affairs. She can't remember many details of those, either, or anything of significance during the several months of volunteer home care she performed that year. But should she be expected to remember events so trivial?

Bill has taken control of the witness; he is calm, crisp, incisive. Does the jury see her vagueness as due to trauma or do they suspect she deliberately refuses to admit to the inconvenient, such as the true reason for her suicide tries, the true source of her turmoil: her unrequited love for Vandergraaf? Her ambiguity is damning, at variance with her more specific recollections prior to the boating weekend.

After an hour of Bill's gentle nudging of Beatrice, we break for lunch. Again, I decline offers of noontime company: I would only depress my friends.

Outside, Seattle's famous drizzle relentlessly continues. I stop at Bakeman's, try to do battle with a bowl of soup, then take a vigorous hike to Belltown, expecting at every corner to turn and find Vandergraaf graciously smiling, offering a cape for the puddle.

Resuming his cross-examination, Bill continues to fall over himself to be polite. "I understand," he will say, or, "Yes, I appreciate that." The soothing tone of the doctor whose patient can't admit to her own disease. Beatrice is wearing down under this barrage of civility, becoming short in response, testy: "Can't remember," "Sorry," and – the worst – "Anything could have happened," that coming in response to his query as to whether she threw a bowl of porridge at the nurse in the hospice. Bill must have tracked this woman down.

He skirts around the rape, except to imply it was either imagined, made up, or misremembered, then returns to an earlier theme. "Mrs. Struthers, you went on that weekend cruise expecting him to make romantic overtures to you, didn't you?"

"No, I expected to be treated with courtesy."

"You wanted him to make advances."

"I'm afraid I wasn't ready for anything like that."

"A handsome young gentleman, an inviting weekend of sailing among bucolic islands: did that scenario not suggest romance to you?"

"Romance . . ." She falters. "Romance isn't what I remember, Mr. Christiansen."

"You didn't go to the police afterward?"

"No, but I spoke to a waitress. You know about that."

"So you claim, but you haven't see her since, have you?"

Beatrice makes the mistake of looking at me but recovers with a disarming shrug. "No, I haven't." Which is true. But there is that blush, as if she considers she has spoken falsely.

Bill doesn't seem to notice our silent exchange. "In fact, you didn't report a rape to anyone for three weeks, and then to your parents, isn't that so?"

"I was ashamed. It's hard to explain."

"Yet you remained in college until then, and you continued your work at the *Daily*, correct?"

Sad but true, though Gayle Mitsuka told me she was like a zombie, and tears were shed in the women's room. I can only hope the jury senses the deep turmoil she was in.

"I really didn't know what I was going through, Mr. Christiansen, a lot of confusion and depression. I was carrying on like some robotic creature."

"You kept returning to the newspaper office in the hope of seeing Hugh Vandergraaf again, didn't you?" Bill's voice has lowered ominously, and I almost feel a denseness in the air, a calm before the storm.

"I never wanted to see him again." I wonder if that is too widely put: I presume she wanted to confront him, but Bea's motives for going back to the student newspaper office remain inscrutable to her.

Bill retrieves a note from one of his files. "Then why did you write him this?"

I rise too abruptly; the jury knows I am caught by surprise. "Would you do me the pleasure, Mr. Christiansen, of showing me that?"

He returns a tongue-in-cheek look; beside him,

Vandergraaf is enjoying my vain attempt to conceal anxiety.

The photocopy handed to me is typewritten, but sorrowfully I recognize her signature. One sentence: "I don't understand why you won't speak to me."

I try not to let my shoulders sag; I tell myself it's not so bad. But it is.

"The fact is you placed this note in Hugh Vandergraaf's typewriter some ten days following your alleged rape. Do you agree?"

Beatrice studies the original, looking entirely too dejected. "I don't know. I might have. I can see myself wanting some explanation –"

"Please just answer the question."

"I don't recall the note."

"Yes. It's painful to remember matters better forgotten, isn't it, ma'am?"

With that poke, he tenders the note as an exhibit for later identification, then sits, mumbling an aside to Hugh, who is sitting taller, squaring his shoulders.

"We'll take the break now." Judge Luckwell frowns at me over her glasses, a teacher urging me to pull up my socks or fail: this could have been avoided, she is saying, had you taken depositions. "Do you wish the witness to remain on the stand?"

"No, Your Honor. I will call Ms. Struthers to testify as part of my case."

As we recess, Beatrice looks so mournful I want to take her in my arms. With as much fortitude as I can muster I tell her she deserves a medal.

"I assume I wrote it. I just don't remember it. I'm sorry."

Beatrice cannot stop apologizing: she should have gone to the police, a college counselor, a friend. She can't understand why she returned to the offices of the *Daily*, can't fathom why she would want to see Hugh again or to write that note. I must assume she hoped to vent her anger at him; she needed words from him, contrition, a plea for forgiveness.

"It's odd that I remember so little. I'm very sorry. But I remember the rape so clearly that I still have nightmares."

Maybe Bill's examination was too effective, because my mind again is infected by germs of doubt. Innocent Beatrice, wrenched free from her sterile past, reveling in her freedom, seduced by falsely whispered intimations of affection.... Surely Bea would not invent such a serious assault. Reconstructed memory? I simply will not accept that.

Both Bill and Hugh are watching me for reaction as the next witness is announced: Johann Krueger. They will not read surprise this time. I have prepared myself for him, but I am not confident and am slipping into one my blue moods.

Johann walks sternly up the aisle in his clerical collar, an advertisement of virtuousness. Was it only a few days ago that I watched him fight tears while turning in two members of his flock on a back-country driveway? I felt such empathy for him, held hope that he was finally daring to leap that gap that separates us. But no: I see the old acerbity in his face.

After being introduced by name and occupation, he asks if he may stand. I think he feels more in charge that way: the witness box as pulpit.

Bill leads him through a brief resumé: born in Oklahoma sixty-eight years ago of German immigrant parents, a minister for forty of those years, a graduate of Baptist Christian College in Louisiana. Served pastoral communities in Texas, South Dakota, then Washington, first in the Okanogan Valley, then in Lynden. Married forty-six years, one begotten child, "an unanticipated blessing from the Lord."

I feel my gloom continue to thicken as I listen to Johann's large persuasive cello of a voice; it carries to the farthest corner of the room. As far as he may be concerned, Beatrice and I could be on the moon: he has not looked at us once. I wonder if jurors will be persuaded by a man of the cloth who preaches against his own daughter.

Bill leads him briefly through Bea's upbringing, a sketch that doesn't quite capture the tedium of those years of insulation from the world: we hear instead of a willing and dutiful Beatrice at picnics and pot-lucks, helping with chores of church and home, a bright high-school student who herself taught Sunday Bible classes and was forever giving her parents pride.

"However, you began to have problems with her, did you not?"

He is silent for a moment, wrestling with his answer. "I have to say that at some point we began to worry that all was not well with her."

"In particular?"

"As a child she fantasized constantly." And why not? She was trying to overcome the drab realities of her boring life. "During her teenaged years we observed signs of growing disobedience and an unwillingness to tell the truth. She began to lie about certain social gatherings she would attend, deny knowing young men whom she was seeing surreptitiously. Not that we would necessarily object, but dishonesty was not a sin tolerated in our home."

I had hoped he might dilute this spiteful account of her growing up, but I am not about to shout any objections. Let the jury see how petty he is: as possessive of his daughter's sacred virtue as if it were his own. So I sit tight while he relates several minor instances of her reckless truancy, such as having the gall to spend evenings at parties at which *boys* were present, then claim she was with her good Christian girlfriend.

Bill knows he cannot slide in the hearsay about how Beatrice was fired for theft at Baptist Missionary and Social Services, but I am not sure if I would mind that either: exposing such a trivial episode would seem mean-hearted.

Ruefully, Johann allowed his grade-skipping daughter, just turned seventeen, to attend the University of Washington on a scholarship. She would often come home weekends, but they (Johann presumes to speak for his wife) observed changes in her: a restlessness, a spirit of rebellion. I want to interject: that's perfectly normal, she was seventeen.

Bill brings his witness forward to March 1971: "Beatrice was healthy and doing well, according to the reports I received from the good people at Rice Hall. We were expecting her home the last weekend of the month, but she called us with the excuse she had to study for examinations."

"She didn't mention any weekend sailing venture?"

"No, she did not."

"When did you next hear from her?"

"She phoned several days later. She sounded quite normal, though it was Amy she spoke to, my wife."

"Then let *her* testify about how normal she was," I say, with too much temper.

"If that's an objection, it's sustained."

The judge is grumpy, too, as we near the end of this long day. Bill looks at the clock: he wants to send the jury off to their dinners on a resounding note, so he quickly brings Beatrice home to Lynden: mid-April, long after the rape.

"Describe her appearance."

"She was unkempt and distraught."

"I understand she complained of a sexual assault."

"She insisted that a few weeks earlier she had been beaten and raped. I did not see any of the cuts or bruises she claimed were inflicted upon her person, nor did Amy, who conducted a less superficial examination."

"And what was your feeling about all of this?"

"I firmly believed she was prevaricating – lying in the face of God."

"Has anything since happened to change your mind?"

"No."

"We'll resume in the morning," says Judge Luckwell. She may be wondering why I have not been objecting to these baseless opinions – when is *belief* admissible evidence? But I want the jury to know what Beatrice has been up against all her life, to appreciate her loneliness, to understand the forces that pushed her to insanity's brink.

Surely the jury feels uncomfortable about Johann, wary of him. But I can't tell. As they file out, their eyes are fixed at a point behind me. I turn: Beatrice is in her husband's arms, sobbing.

I slink into my office just before closing time. Mattie sees I am in a sullen mood and knows enough not to ask about my day. She puts a consoling arm around me, and leads me to my mail and messages.

A bunch of cards. I had forgotten: today is my official birthday. Happy birthday, Liz: in two years, the lonely spinster enters her thirties, the desperate years. I'll be ready to take on anyone, the guy who wants to suck my toes.

I had hoped the publicity of the trial might prod other women upon whom Hugh Vandergraaf had preyed to come forward, but not so far. On voice mail, a miffed Yvonne Fairhurst: "Thanks a lot." I add guilt to my burden of dismay. I should talk to that ex-bailiff again, Juanita

Calvo; maybe she knows other victims of the predator – but who would want to be dragged through this?

"Shit is flying over the Vradjik divorce," Mattie says, "Curtis is trying to duck. There was a totally mean scene between him and Franca in the lounge, and a few minutes ago he roared out of here."

Junior will be apoplectic, and as for J.J., I worry about his heart. The office is thick with gossip: a messy divorce, adultery, swinging bridge players.

I call Ann Boorstein to brief her and seek her attendance in court. "I've just had an absolutely foul day, and tomorrow won't be better. They're moving into the medical evidence, and I think they found the nurse."

"Be brave." She will join me tomorrow.

At home, a greeting has been scrawled on the fridge with a felt pen: "She's 28, still great, don't wait, home late." Nick is with Stephane at his place on Mercer Island, and I can only hope he is pacifying him. I can't get involved, I have my own problems, the worst of which are niggling whispers of distrust: be wary of firmly held belief, of maintaining blind faith in your client.

Oh, God, what if I have wrongly maligned Hugh Vandergraaf? I will unravel if I allow such doubts to haunt me . . .

The Wandering I *tilts hard to starboard, the masts bowed by mainsail and mizzen hardened taut against a keening wind that funnels up the Strait of Juan de Fuca. The pale morning sun is behind the boat as she dips into the trenches, climbs the summits of the sea, a dot upon the vast domain of God. This is freedom, untempered by the cold restraints of law, that cruel mistress with her whips and chains, her complaints and pleadings, her punishments.*

A lonely passion, the sea. It is in our blood, yours and mine. A dreamboat, you seek, sixty feet long with a mast. Thirty-five won't do? Ah, you have such a way of diminishing a man.

Tell me, when did your resolve begin to weaken? I knew it would, so I watched you and I waited. On the first day, you held up — not surprisingly, given how obsequious were the gifts of praise tendered by my partisans and patrons. We had several others hiding in the wings, but I told Christiansen to send them packing.

Oh, but we need Fairhurst, he said. (Let me share this with you, my innocent, as I do all former secrets: one of our jurors is wed to the ambitious manager of his plastics division.)

I remonstrated: We've made our point, Bill, I don't think he'll add anything.

Don't be ridiculous. He's flown all the way from Tokyo to be here.

I saw you sneak a glance at me. Did you observe the signs of anus-clenching tightness? How did you uncover this furtive affair? And knowing of it, why didn't you shove the knife in all the way? Was the killer instinct lacking, was this a sign of weakness? Or were your veiled hints (as the chair of the Symphony Society was exhorted to believe) merely the flailing swipes of a dastardly opponent?

Ah, when would she come to us cap in hand? we won-dered. What madness motivates this stubborn, pretty pit bull? But you held on, despite the disputatious pastor, despite preen-ing, bumptious Dumbo, despite . . . my final suppurating weapon of defense, which I prayed I'd never have to unsheathe.

But I hold yet another secret, a way to certain victory. You can-not defend against it; you cannot win. I rejoice in knowing that.

It was not until Beatrice took the stand that the cracks began to show in your pietistic faith in my guilt. You had the look of one falling down an elevator shaft as you read that ancient note. A victim of rape who seeks to keep the lines of communication open. . . . How could this be? Did no, then, not mean no? Was that little syllable — enshrined as the great neg-ative gospel of the Movement — even uttered?

Consent: how blurred a concept; how coded is the lexicon of love. Say no, Beatrice. Say no, Helen. Say no. My ears aren't plugged; I hear. How soft and sibilant is that wondrous other word. Yes, yes, their bodies whispered, however silent were their voices. Must it be shouted to the rafters?

You do not deny, Elizabeth, that the body speaks with other mouths, truer than the tongue. But your own mouth now opens in a wide, shocked oval. Sparks fly from sapphire eyes. I have said the unacceptable, the truth, an ad hominem thrust to the heart.

Damn it, I felt Beatrice's desire, Elizabeth. One would have to be insensate not to feel that, to know it. Yes, there was anger, there was passion, and the heat from both was over-whelming. . . . And Helen Mazur — do you really think our quarrel was over an issue as base as politics? That it didn't spring from the need and longing neither could express? It's odd, isn't it, how human wants become confused and mangled, then erupt in acrimony.

But bury that; it's done. Let's put the past to rest. Forget, forgive; the time of strife is over. We have the sun, the sea, the cloudless heavens; and forever (though you cry a stubborn no a thousand times) we have each other.

Because we are each other, bonded in the bone. In death only do us part. In death only.

Ah, suck in the cold salt wind that wildly blows the hair and stings the eyes. It gives us strength, and soon the day will warm and melt our frozen tears.

Escaping from the rain into the courthouse, I find myself behind two of our jurors at the metal-detector lineup. Each looks at me, and nods unsmilingly. Maybe they are shy. Or maybe they are already lost to me, weighing their award in damages: eight million isn't enough; we must teach that hussy a lesson.

They wait until I'm safely within an elevator; they refuse to be trapped inside with me – they might catch something. My malaise, maybe, which is still sitting like a lump in my gut.

Vandergraaf is outside 941, and again a few women are ogling him: middle-aged, weary of the celluloid soap operas at home, opting for the real thing.

Beatrice is already in court, looking so dragged out that I wonder if she slept. Laconic Thomas, beside her, looks not much better, but he offers a kindly smile. Which is about as much as he ever allows himself: he so rarely opens his mouth. But he exudes quiet strength, and in inhaling it I feel somewhat repaired.

Ann Boorstein shows up just before we get under way, and I seat her beside Beatrice. Upon seeing us confer, the plaintiff's team huddles: if they don't know who she is, they will soon find out.

Johann, stepping into the stand, bows to Judge Luckwell as she enters, bows to the jury. Is this an affectation, the courtly manner he assumes? He still won't look at us.

"Just a few more questions, Reverend Krueger." As Bill rises, Vandergraaf looks at me with one arched eyebrow. I didn't want to do this to you, he is saying; you had your chance. He has been eyeing me intermittently, maybe with a growing knowledge that he creates an uncomfortable effect, that he makes my skin prickle. Or creep.

"Now, after your daughter came to you with this story of being raped, did you observe any changes in her?"

"Yes, her mental and emotional condition continued to worsen. She was given to long bouts of crying and rarely moved from her bedroom. She was in a state of such acute depression that we thought it wise to seek professional care. We arranged for her to enter the Faith Baptist Hospice for a long-term stay."

"And this was in Everett?"

"Yes, not far from home. I still regularly visit there to offer healing to its residents, many of whom are in distress."

"Go on."

"We would visit her from time to time, of course, and often take her away for a day here and there. She seemed to be improving at first, more placid, not raising her voice at us any more." The first indication she had done so: he has skipped over a few details. "But then there occurred . . . well, her attempts to leave this world for what I feared would be . . . let me rephrase that. Her attempts to end her life."

He clears his throat. For some reason this part of his tale seems to cause him strain. As if he's hiding something.

"And so it was suggested that she, ah, might be better off moved well away from the Seattle area and into an environment that would not be charged with so many unhappy thoughts and memories."

"That's when you placed her in a home in central Washington."

"Yes, the town of Okanogan. An older couple lived there, the Wilsons, whom I knew from my days of working for the Lord in that community. We thought Beatrice was well enough to provide home care for them – they were blessed people, but infirm – and this would at least keep her body and spirit occupied. But after Mr. Wilson had a stroke, she was returned to the hospice, where she remained for two more months before we took her back into our home. Much recovered, I must add, due to the ministrations of time and the aid of the Lord."

Bill has what he wants and seems about to sit, but Johann has built up one of his heads of steam.

"To say we were relieved is to underrate our feelings. We were proud, Mr. Christiansen. Once her troubles were over, she enlisted in Jesus's service, training for our worldwide missionary program, and worked with the impoverished natives of many foreign lands. Beatrice turned out to be everything that we had prayed for. Engagement to a hardworking Christian man, a happy marriage . . ."

"Thank you, Reverend Krueger –"

Johann talks through him, louder, reaching for a crescendo: "That is why we grieve to see her suffering this latest relapse. Sadly, in the last year and a half, certain influences have been exerted on her, supposedly modern and enlightened but foreign to all which righteous men believe, a baneful abomination in the eyes of the Lord. Dark forces are tugging at her spirit, my friends, seducing her from the righteous path –"

"Mr. Krueger," Judge Luckwell interrupts, "I think Mr. Christiansen has finished questioning you."

Jurors are squirming, embarrassed at this tirade. Bill, who has long since taken his seat, appears most uncomfortable, sitting small in his chair, trying to hide behind Vandergraaf, who is staring at the ceiling. They had obviously hoped to keep their witness on a tighter leash.

"Do you wish to have the sermon struck from the record, Ms. Finnegan?"

Suddenly, with Johann going off the wall like that, I

am feeling much more chipper. He has inspired me; the spirit is infusing me, a spirit of righteous anger. "It's all right, Your Honor, he was talking about me. I'm the devil incarnate as far as the good reverend is concerned." I turn to him. "Isn't that right, Mr. Krueger? We've had it out in these courts before, over the abortion clinics you enjoy picketing."

"There is no joy in it, Miss Finnegan."

"I'm over here, Mr. Krueger." I want to force him to look at Beatrice and me, but he insists on staring at a fixed point on the wall behind me. What is the jury making of him? I don't mind them knowing there is enmity between us: can you trust the word of a father who is filled with so much rancor that he is prepared to sit in the lap of the man his daughter accuses of rape?

"Do you recall having some words with me in this building a little over a year ago? I told you I would pray for you to *my* God, who is a compassionate God."

"Yes, I believe you claimed you were a Christian."

"Well, I am."

"I harbor some doubts."

"What's wrong, can't you look at me? I'm over here near your daughter."

Finally, he turns in our general direction, but cannot hold my gaze.

"Why do you want so badly to believe Beatrice wasn't raped, Reverend Krueger?"

"I don't quite understand the question."

"You feared she might be pregnant, didn't you? And that she might seek an abortion."

"That option never crossed our minds."

"You didn't want to face that awful possibility, so you accused her of lying. You rejected her at the most traumatic time of her life and so unsettled her that you were able to throw her into the prison of your hospice where you wouldn't have to deal with her, and I'm accusing you of that, Mr. Krueger."

My own voice has raised. I must maintain control, must not sound shrill.

"We loved our daughter," he says weakly.

"It seems a very controlling sort of love: she was forbidden television, movies, parties, even relationships, wasn't she?"

"I'd prefer to say she was given a good Christian upbringing − strict, yes, but it did not expose her to temptation. You must remember, Miss Finnegan, that in the nineteen-seventies there were many wild socialistic ideas floating about, and there were drugs, people running naked −"

"We'll get along better if you just answer my questions." I must snip his answers; he seems bent on running off in directions of his own choice.

"The answer is we did our best according to our tenets."

"You said she went out to social functions against your wishes. How do you know that?"

"We were given information, and, ah . . ."

"What?"

"She kept a diary."

"I see. She told you you were free to look at it?"

"It wasn't our view that permission should be required."

"Is that one of the things you fought about?"

"Some words were exchanged, I believe."

"Yes, she was furious, wasn't she? And you had many other fights with her, too, didn't you? This is what you call her attitude of rebellion and disobedience."

"May the witness be allowed to answer at least one of those questions?"

"Yes, Ms. Finnegan, that would be desirable."

I actually welcome Bill's interruption: my engine is racing too fast. I take a breath, then proceed at a more deliberate pace into the scene where Beatrice tearfully begged her parents to believe she was raped. I sense there is profit to be made, that the jury is as alarmed as I am at this cold reception to her account of a brutal assault.

"Without checking into this at all, you accused her of lying."

"I'd prefer to say we pleaded with her to look into her heart."

"Oh, come, you had a horrible fight."

"Miss Finnegan, what can I say to convince you I loved my daughter and wanted only the best for her? I had no ill feelings toward her and I was quite in control. Regrettably, she wasn't."

"These angry exchanges continued, didn't they, through several succeeding days?"

"There was no rancor on our part."

"Your wife will speak for herself, I hope. I just want to know what you did, saw, and said."

"There were a couple of other sessions during which she lost control, yes." Control. It is a mantra.

"Because you wouldn't believe her."

"Miss Finnegan, why would it take her over two weeks to tell us of this episode?"

"Obviously because she was afraid she'd be subjected to the very reaction she got." I can't keep the anger from my voice. But it's mine, it's real; I have to be myself. Surely his evasiveness is palpable; he still won't meet my eyes for longer than a second. "You couldn't deal with the fact you'd accused her of lying, of shunning her pleas for care and understanding, isn't that so?"

"I don't follow you."

"Oh, I think you do. That's why you shut her up in that hospice: you wouldn't have to look her in the eye."

"That is utterly false. She badly needed professional care."

"How professional it was I suspect we're about to find out. She didn't want to go – you committed her."

"On the advice of Dr. Chalmers, a saintly man who has been long sent to his reward. We were with her most weekends and there were many outings. I'll not have you say we abandoned her." Finally, we are eye to eye, in each other's zone of fire.

"But I *am* saying it. You continued to accuse her of making up a story of rape, continued to berate her, even during your visits, during those outings, and you decided to move her even farther away, to the other side of the Cascades. Then, of course, you wouldn't feel obliged to travel all that way to see her, would you?"

"I reject that completely."

"You didn't visit her once out there in Okanogan, did you? You or Amy?"

"There was, perhaps, some thought that we might do better apart for a period."

"Because of the terrible ill feeling between you."

"Very well. If you wish."

That satisfies, but it is like pulling teeth. I pause long enough to let this reluctant admission settle in with the jury, and Judge Luckwell seizes the chance to order the morning break – though I would rather continue: the heat of the fray has fired me up, evaporating my blues.

Beatrice, however, is still in distress: it cannot be easy to see her father – perhaps for the first time in his life – on the receiving end of a public scolding. Trembling, she leaves the room on the arm of Thomas, her caring shepherd.

Vandergraaf catches me looking his way and smiles calmly back as if to tell me he is enjoying this.

Ann Boorstein is contemplative. "What do you think?" I ask her.

"He never wanted Beatrice; he never wanted children."

Of course. That phrase: "an unanticipated blessing from the Lord." A child unplanned, unwanted.

When we resume, Johann seems out of countenance, tugs at his collar, which may be becoming tight. He glowers at me, assumes a combative stance. I decide to steer a different course. "Last year, after she told you she was going to make public her complaint of rape, you made every effort you could to block it."

"I felt she would be making a rash error of judgment. I believe we would have dissuaded her if she hadn't made the mistake of seeking other, ah, counsel."

"Legal counsel? You mean me?"

"To put it quite bluntly, yes."

"That evil influence who believes in a right of choice. Yes, you redoubled your efforts to sabotage her quest for justice."

Bill snorts an objection. "This isn't a bear-baiting contest, and she doesn't have to stand nose to nose with him."

I am *almost* doing that. I wasn't even aware I had been advancing on him.

"This is cross-examination, Mr. Christiansen," says Judge Luckwell.

"You spoke secretly to prosecutors, tried to undermine her quest for justice, isn't that so?"

"I gave them information I doubt they would have got from you."

"You volunteered yourself to the plaintiff's lawyer. You gave them a sales pitch: you told them Beatrice had been emotionally unbalanced and dishonest. You tried to direct her to another attorney."

"And what good advice did she receive from you? Look at where we are, young lady." His voice a clap of thunder. "This abysmal trial, human lives being cast upon a sea of uncertainty and rumor, reputations facing ruin. Perhaps *you* should have gotten some advice."

I am nicked by his flailing sword, but the throb eases as I wait for his reverberations to still. I am a few feet away, locked hard onto him. I want him to look into his unbending heart, to give me something. Repentance.

"Do you want to know why we're holding this abysmal trial? Because of your rejection of Beatrice. Had you consoled her, believed her, been some kind of father to her, do you think it would have come to this? She had to cleanse herself of a wound that you rubbed salt into. That's what we're doing here today; this is her way of becoming whole again."

"I don't know if Miss Finnegan is offering testimony or just making a speech, but I object to the constant badgering of this witness."

"Drive with caution, Ms. Finnegan." Judge Luckwell is stifling a rare smile; maybe she finds my style of cross-examination amusing. I back off a few feet, closer to Beatrice.

"Didn't you understand that your daughter loved you? That she couldn't bear the burden alone? That she finally came to you because she needed you?"

"I prayed for her."

"That's not enough! You can't just pass the buck to God! You're her father!"

He leans back from me, red of face. "That sounds of blasphemy."

I turn to Beatrice. Her eyes are clouded and she has a handkerchief at the ready. But she was always tougher than anyone knew, and her resilience is even greater now. Ultimately this can only help her heal.

Vandergraaf continues to stare at me – a puzzled frown, a pursing of lips. It is as if he doesn't believe this is happening, that I could be doing this to him, persevering in his destruction.

I soften my voice, offer an olive branch. "I think it's fair to say you are dedicated to your calling."

"I am dedicated to the service of God."

"Yes, and you're an extremely hardworking man, aren't you, Reverend Krueger?"

"The Lord, in his wisdom, never gives us enough time to do the things that must be done."

"And that doesn't leave room for much in the way of family life, does it?"

"It is one of my greatest sorrows."

I pause, further soften my voice. "You never wanted to have children, did you?"

No answer. An extended, pained silence.

"As you say, you were dedicated to the service of God."

"Amy wanted a child."

"In your case, Beatrice was unwanted."

No response.

"Pastor Krueger, we have heard you rail against dishonesty, you do not tolerate the sin of lying. Now tell the truth, here in this courtroom, before God."

And still he can't. "No child should be unwanted." His voice has dropped, hoarse with the sadness that I have finally brought him to.

"I agree with you completely." His lack of answer is answer enough. I slowly sink onto my chair. The court is eerily still.

"Do you have any redirect?"

Bill says, "No, Your Honor."

Johann looks about, not ready to believe that his day

in court is over. "She was brought up with proper care and good Christian values. Yes, we removed temptations from her. Is that wrong? If all in the world were properly taught at home, would we see the juvenile crime that is rampant in our communities?" Nobody is attempting to dam this flood. "Would we see the depravity and dissolution, the shame of a people blind to the Word, unheeding of the gospels? Would we see the blood-filled ghettoes, the stench of poverty, prostitutes on every corner, obscenities scrawled on every wall? I want you to look upon the streets and into the homes of America and tell me I have raised a child carelessly!"

It seems like several seconds before the echoes rumble away into a stark silence.

"We'll resume at one-thirty."

As I turn to watch the spectators file out I am startled to see Helen and Wilkie Mazur rising from the back row. She is wet-eyed. He is sullen.

I overtake them as they make their way out into the crowded hallway. "Helen, I'm sorry, witnesses aren't allowed in court until they testify."

"Oh, we didn't know. We were curious. That cruel, spiteful man."

Was Wilkie also moved by Johann Krueger's wrath to feel sympathy for Beatrice? But he merely scowls.

"It doesn't look like we'll get to you until next week, but I'm afraid you'll have to stay in Seattle." I ask her softly, "Will you change your mind, Helen?"

"No, she won't," Wilkie says. I want to snarl at him but hold my tongue. "It's too late, anyway," he adds.

What does he mean by that? But as he grabs Helen's wrist and starts to stalk off, she twists her head around to look at me. She nods emphatically.

The message is obvious. Johann's mean caviling against his daughter has turned Helen around. I want to cheer.

But I'm not allowed to engage them further because

Wilkie guides her quickly toward the elevators through the mill of press and spectators.

A slurred voice behind my ear. "Now you're starting to click." Harry Crake, grinning, half in the bag already.

I talk expansively as I escort Ann Boorstein to my office. I am puffed with self-congratulation; I have Helen onside. Harry, old sport, we are going to kick a few touchdowns. And now Johann has exploded in their face. My efforts did not achieve the high summits J.J. regularly conquers, though I was damn good.

But Ann gently pricks my bubble: let up on the scornful tone, already. Keep the voice low, modulated: the paternalistic society still disapproves of high female voices. And what's with this constant eating of pencils, an oral deprivation?

We have an hour for a final analysis of their expected medical evidence, and pore over copies of old histories and medical records from that *maison de folie* – all typed out and signed by the hospice nurse. I am learning a lot about drugs, especially tranquilizers.

"They fed Beatrice enough tranks to choke an ox," Ann says. "It's no wonder she can't remember; she was in a chemical straitjacket."

My session with Ann was so concentrated that I find myself running into court, arriving five minutes late. Everyone is waiting for me, including Judge Luckwell, who gives the impression she is tapping her foot. "We were just about to go on without you."

"I'm so sorry, I truly lost track; I was absorbed with a witness." I do not want to rile this punctuality-obsessed woman. Not that I think she is bending my way, but she seems to be granting me reasonable slack.

"Let us proceed."

"Call Mrs. Olive Ewanschuk."

She walks in with a serene expression, a tall, well-attired woman. After she takes the oath, she draws a small New Testament from her bag and kisses it, a showy gesture. In a soft voice one strains to hear, she relates the vital statistics: a nurse, fifty-six, flew in all the way from Uganda, a Baptist mission for AIDS victims. I can't help but wonder if Johann Krueger helped to track down this dignified and depressingly saintly woman – in comparison, my own witness from afar, the cocaine mule Thalia Pfeiffer, will look like something spewed up from the netherworld.

She tells us she was newly graduated from nursing school when she started work at the Faith Hospice; Beatrice was one of her first patients. She was also in charge of seven other patients of the rest home. Dr. Chalmers would visit about once a day, or come on call.

"You were there when Ms. Krueger was brought in?"

"Yes, I admitted her on . . . my notes say the sixteenth day of April, 1971."

"Describe her condition then."

"She barely spoke. She was extremely depressed. I'm not sure she even knew where she was."

"What caused her to be sent to you?"

"It was expressed to me as a possible psychotic episode."

This is hearsay and I am about to object, but turn to Ann, who warns me off with a gesture of her hand.

"What about her physical health?"

"It was difficult to tell. As I recall, whenever I tried to examine her, she resisted. I almost had to force her to eat."

"I see, but when she initially came in, did you make a physical examination?"

"I believe so." She dons a pair of spectacles, gaudy with gilt and curlicues, and peers at her twenty-eight-year-old records. "It says she was a frail girl, otherwise healthy-looking, and there were no bruises or lacerations or even scratches on her body. Oh, I have here one old bruise, but it was on her anterior right thigh." She must give me this gift: I spotted it in my copy of the notes. Beatrice told me Vandergraaf had pried her legs open with his knees. When Thalia Pfeiffer takes the stand, bruises galore, fresh and purple.

"And that you can get from, say, accidentally bumping into a table or chair."

"Or a fence. Anything." She has been well programmed.

"Did you examine her genital area?"

"I wrote down, 'No external damage or inflammation.'"

"Did she have any vaginal infections, venereal disease, anything like that?" Now *why* would he ask that?

"No."

"Did she complain of any problems in that, ah, area?"

"She did not."

I take a flash at Vandergraaf, who is sitting back, his arms folded, frowning, as if for some reason displeased at the nature of these questions.

Much aided by her records, Ms. Ewanschuk recounts Bea's uneven history of recovery: "At first, she rarely got out of bed except to go to the bathroom and to attend prayer meetings. It would appear she had a relapse in June; that's what my note says. 'Violent episode,' it reads. I think that's when she screamed at me while I was attempting to feed her. She threw some porridge in my face."

The first suicide attempt came soon after that, the attempted overdose of Thorazine. She vomited; her stomach was pumped. She cut her wrist a few weeks later, a deep knife slash that sent her to a hospital for a week: the psychiatric ward, the witness takes care to tell us.

As far as I can determine, that was the only time a

psychiatrist did attend on her, and Ms. Ewanschuk can't recall his diagnosis. Her records also show many grants of parole: when Johann and Amy Krueger fetched her away. Before picking her up, he would conduct prayer meetings with the staff and patients. The local minister also visited occasionally. More prayer meetings, followed by private sessions, efforts at counseling.

"I don't have many notes after July – I think she spent a good deal of time that summer with her parents. She was readmitted that fall and I have it here . . . January twelfth, 1972, it says, 'again in a state of dementia.'"

She remained for two more months, ultimately crawling from her pit of despair, and in late February, according to Ms. Ewanschuk's final note, was "released into the loving care of her parents," her "sensibilities" restored.

Ms. Ewanschuk's direct testimony concluded, we break for ten minutes, and I find a quiet corner to confer with Ann Boorstein, whose view is that Beatrice was lucky not to have suffered brain damage at the hands of Nurse Ewanschuk in the snakepit that was the Faith Hospice.

"Get dirty with her," she says.

"Stomp on Mother Teresa? The jury will love that."

"Ask about her qualifications. Carl Jung, she ain't. Those dosages of chlorpromazine were close to being lethal. And I can't see Bea as a psychotic – that's a pile of bull."

But it is what the opposition hopes to portray, of course, a picture of a delusional teenager obsessed with a rape fantasy. Nurse Ewanschuk is a dangerous witness, and I must knock her halo askew.

I begin by asking details of the day-to-day care she provided to Bea, and I soon realize that without those old worn notes she is lost at sea. Vague phrases multiply: "I can't be specific" and "I'm afraid I didn't write that down."

But I cannot wipe that beatific smile from her face. The jury sees her as self-assured, so very . . . nice. I fear she is one of those fundamentalist persons so firm in belief they can never admit to error.

"When she first came in, you saw an old bruise on the front of her right thigh. Probably just a few weeks old?"

"I couldn't be sure."

"Could have been caused by bumping into a fence, you say."

"Anything."

"Does anything include the point of someone's knee?"

"I suppose it could. You could knock against someone."

"Or you could be assaulted."

"Well, that's true."

"You say you examined for vaginal disease?" I am still wondering: why did Bill ask about that?

She fumbles through her notes. "No inflammation or sores, I did write that down."

"You really don't have much of a memory of Beatrice Krueger, do you, Ms. Ewanschuk?"

"It was a long time ago. I had many other patients."

"And what do you remember of *them*?"

"Let's see. A young man, who, ah . . . well, he claimed to be speaking to the Lord. And two other young women, and one older . . . I'd have to look at the records."

"I guess it wouldn't be surprising if Mrs. Struthers had poor recall of that time as well."

"I suppose not."

"Especially since she appeared to be in a severely drugged state most of the time."

"Well, yes, she had to be on medication."

"Phenothyazenes." Have I pronounced that right? Ann Boorstein nods her assent.

"Pardon me?" says the witness.

"You don't know what those are?"

"Dear me, well, the physician did the prescribing."

"Phenothyazenes are powerful tranquilizers used to sedate schizophrenics."

"My notes show Equamil and Thorazine."

"Those are trade names, Ms. Ewanschuk."

"I see." A tiny sign of fluster finally.

"Sodium amytal. Reserpine by injection."

"Again, I don't see that in my notes."

"It's marketed as Serpasil. Do you see it there?"

"Oh, yes."

"I take it you knew of the dangers of these drugs?"

"I was told there could be side effects. I think convulsions was one of them."

"What else?"

"Drowsiness?" She is asking me?

"What else?"

"I'm not sure."

"Phenothyazenes and reserpines are extremely ill advised in depressive cases, are they not? The depression may be made more severe. There's an extreme danger of suicide."

"I suppose that would depend on the dose. I just did what I was told by Dr. Chalmers." I glance at Shayne Wells, the nurse on the jury. This usually affable woman is making a sour face.

"Was he a specialist?"

"He had a private practice in addition to his work at the hospice."

"Was he a specialist, did he have psychiatric training?"

"No, Miss Finnegan." That smile has wilted.

"And how long prior to all of this had you finished nurses' training?"

"I was about six months out of residence."

"You weren't a trained psychiatric nurse?"

"No."

"Did your studies include counseling?"

"Of the physically ill, yes."

"But not of persons with emotional problems."

"Not . . . not too much of that."

"Did you ever study psychology, Ms. Ewanschuk?"

"As part of my nurse's training I took a course dealing with the mentally disturbed."

"What do you mean when you use the word psychotic?"

"Extremely deranged. Out of touch with reality."

"You talked with Beatrice about many things?"

"Oh, of course."

"And although depressed and heavily drugged, she knew what was going on around her?"

"Well . . . yes."

"She read, watched television, that sort of thing?"

"We didn't allow television."

"Oh, and I don't suppose you had many books."

"Well, we had the Scriptures, of course."

"That's *all*?"

"Many would feel that's enough, Miss Finnegan."

From the corner of my eye, I catch Shayne Wells slowly shaking her head.

"Delusional – that's another word in your notes. Did she have hallucinations?"

"I'm sorry, I can't remember."

"Well, why would you put that down?"

"I think . . . I believe one of her parents mentioned that, and it was confirmed in some of my conversations with her."

"What kind of delusions are we talking about?"

"She apparently believed she had been, ah, physically molested."

"Raped."

"Yes."

I have finally driven Bill Christiansen to his feet. "I object, it's hearsay."

"She claims Mrs. Struthers was delusional; I'm seeking the source of her opinion."

"Overruled."

"She told you she was raped?"

"That was her . . . story."

"I thought you said she barely spoke."

"At the beginning."

"You heard her arguing with her parents."

"Yes, but . . ." She trails off.

"Perhaps she was too exhausted from that to speak to you."

"I will concede she would get vocal at times. Later on."

"I take it you didn't believe her account of rape."

"I was informed it was inaccurate."

"By whom?"

"By Pastor Krueger. Her father."

"Did she tell you who raped her?"

"Yes, she —"

"I most *strongly* object." Bill wasn't expecting me to draw this from her. Nor was I, frankly.

"The objection is still overruled."

"Your Honor should at least warn the jury that these answers don't go to the truth of any rape complaint, that they can be used solely to assess whether Mrs. Struthers was truly delusional."

"I intend to do so."

This legal bafflegab goes completely over the jury's heads, of course. What they are hearing is that Beatrice told her story to yet another witness with closed ears.

"Who did she say raped her?"

"A law student. I don't know if the name was ever mentioned."

I glance at the plaintiff: he is doodling on a pad.

"Where did she say this happened?"

"On some kind of boat, I believe."

"You didn't make inquiries to confirm this?"

"No, I wouldn't doubt Pastor Krueger."

"I see. And what other delusions did she suffer?"

She stops to think. "Well, one thing I do recall is she thought she was being kept a prisoner at the hospice."

"That doesn't sound like much of a delusion, Ms. Ewanschuk."

Now I am winning response from the jury, a chuckle, a grunt of approval. Vandergraaf takes a packet of aspirins from his pocket, washes one down with a glass of water. He realizes I have seen him do so and returns to his writing pad, continues to doodle.

"Did you argue about her complaint that . . . well, basically that she was locked up in your asylum?"

"Objection."

"Rephrase that, Ms. Finnegan."

"Beatrice had been committed there by her parents, right?"

"Yes."

"And at some point she felt she was well enough to leave, and permission wasn't granted."

"She was often a difficult patient." An odd, unresponsive answer: clearly the two of them related poorly.

"Was it during one of these discussions that she threw a bowl of porridge at you?"

"I can't recall that."

"Any other so-called delusions?"

"No," she replies. Resistance has been broken; she is docile now, has lost that righteous look. The judge is giving me the eye and I glance up at the clock: it's day's end. Maybe time for one more touchdown.

"Are you telling me then, Ms. Ewanschuk, putting aside her concerns she was being kept a prisoner, that you determined she was delusional solely because she maintained she was raped?"

"That was a factor."

"And if that was no delusion at all, if she indeed *was* raped, you will agree, will you not, that she was hardly psychotic, in fact totally sane?"

She looks down at her hands. "I can't really say."

"Thank you, that's all."

Bill Christiansen leans to me. "Textbook," he says.

Franca Crabtree, who had dropped into court early during my cross-examination, has persuaded me to play hooky from the weekly office meeting and we are sipping wine at McCormick's Fish House and Bar, up the street from the courthouse.

"It was a demolition derby, Liz. Did you see Hugh's face? Our about-to-retire judge is in pain." She squeezes Vandergraaf's imagined gonads between her bony fingers. "I'd love to see his expression when Thalia does her bit for God and country."

But I am not so unpitying. My mind's eye still pictures Hugh Vandergraaf walking from court in brooding thought. He is definitely worried. But though that knowledge cheers me, it has also made me pensive. I must not feel pity for him, to fall into that woman's trap of empathy for the fallen wounded male.

We move on to a less savory agenda: Vradjik versus Vradjik. I urge my case: work it out, keep it in mediation, away from the prurient press.

"Stephane insists on custody, so fuck mediation, we're going back to court. I don't know what else I can do."

"You can withdraw from the case, Franca. It's all too incestuous. You can't go filing papers naming your own law associate as some kind of hedonist."

"Well, Jesus, Liz, I can't leave my client in the lurch either. It's like switching captains while your boat is heading for the rocks. It's a fucking emergency, we're going by way of short notice, and maybe it's *Curtis* who should withdraw. And keep it in his pants instead of poking it into orifices where it doesn't belong. This is a big issue: better those kids are with a caring bisexual father than a depraved mom."

Here's Franca Crabtree, the man-eater, prepared to go to the wall for one. But Stephane is the kind of male she would do this for: he doesn't pose the standard male threat. And she is like me, stubborn, finds a cause in every case.

"Depraved? Look, I think she's just a little sexually starved. Which, by the way, is a topic I'm becoming an expert on."

"So go buy a vibrator. Curtis says he's formed a bond with her kids, claims he can provide some kind of father role. He's just *asking* for it, Liz. I have to tell the court he's been playing with too many bridge partners."

"Curtis is just going through one of his . . . self-exploratory phases."

"*Self*-exploratory? It is to laugh. No, we're in court tomorrow. Mr. Kaplan will take his lumps. Hey, don't worry, your name won't come up."

She can offer no guarantee against that: slander defendant's gay roomie named in custody battle following orgy. This is beyond awkward, a distraction forced upon me at the worst possible time.

The ego warms me on my cold morning walk from Washington Shoe Building to courthouse: after a stumbling start I have blunted the worst of the plaintiff's case, Beatrice's alleged delusional illness. And now I am punished by guilt for having held misgivings about her.

I must be over the hump of this trial. Who do they have left? Amy Krueger, who I doubt will be as unbending as her mate, then Hugh's chum, the man known as Dumbo. Plus the plaintiff himself; the jury will have to decide how underhanded a liar he is.

Their testimony will amply fill the next two days, then I am owed one well-earned free night: the office Christmas dinner tomorrow. For the rest of the weekend I will add last touches to the case for the good guys: a final run-through with Beatrice and with surprise witnesses Helen Mazur — assuming she has joined my cause — and Thalia Pfeiffer. They will pursue Pfeiffer doggedly, but what reason would she have to lie?

Bill Christiansen is outside the Third Avenue entrance, puffing on a cigarette.

"Didn't know you smoked."

"Only during trials like this."

He is tense? Life can be difficult even for someone earning several thousand dollars a day.

"Offer's open for five minutes more, Liz. We might even be prepared to scale it slightly down." He is hinting: make a counter-offer. "This is the point of no return."

"Can't do it."

"You'll wish you had." He says this with a self-assurance that sounds menacing. But I am sure it's a bluff.

"Why? How many other secret witnesses do you have?"

"One of them won't be Amy Krueger. She's feeling poorly, so we're calling her off." He is afraid she may say the wrong thing. "But we have a couple of mystery guests."

"Who?"

"Won't you be interested to find out."

Now I'm perturbed. Brashly overconfident, I may have erred in my strategy of not trading witnesses' names: Mazur and Pfeiffer for the mystery guests.

As court is called to order, Bill announces his next witness: "Mr. Dwight Plum."

Who? I could have sworn he said Dwight Plum. It is no joke: he comes rolling up the aisle, the delightful windbag in a three-piece suit. It comes to me now that this mystery guest was likely subpoenaed to attest to my malice against Vandergraaf, my revenge-seeking rhetoric after my dressing-down in his court. But why didn't Junior tell me?

I am chewing furiously on my pencil as Dwight delivers his encomium about noble, caring Hugh: a rebel in his student days, but a stern advocate of nonviolence. One of the finest men he's been privileged to know.

"You are the managing associate of J.J. Plum and Company, the firm which employs the defendant?"

"I am. With the greatest of respect, if I may be permitted a digression, let me say I take no delight today in performing my duty to this court, finding myself in the unenviable position of dividing my affection and loyalty between two persons for whom I hold nothing but fond feelings. Miss Finnegan is a particular favorite of mine in the office – no one works harder or with a greater dedication to her clients' welfare."

At the conclusion of this hypocritical after-dinner

speech, he peeks at me, sorrowful, seeking charity and forgiveness. What a pontificating ham. Is Vandergraaf looking embarrassed?

Asked how I reacted to my rebuke from Vandergraaf in court, he says, "If I may be forgiven, I'll repeat her words: 'One day I'm going to get that pretentious son of a bitch.' This vow was announced at a regular office meeting. However, may I say in her defense she is a woman of volatile temperament, and often will speak incautiously and with a rancor soon regretted and forgotten. I myself have been the victim of Elizabeth's overly dramatic tongue, but . . . well, one has to know her."

Judge Luckwell is starting to fidget, growing weary of his oratory. You have to know him, Mavis.

"Let me take you back to the spring of 1971. You were then a classmate of Hugh Vandergraaf?"

"We were in second-year law at the University of Washington."

Now what?

"You socialized together?"

"Frequently. We shared many enjoyable times."

"Did he have a girlfriend?"

"At the time I think we're speaking of, no. He had just broken up with a young lady."

"And you?"

"I was occasionally seeing a Miss Cynthia Rosella, an economics major."

"On Friday, March 26, 1971, were Miss Rosella and you at a party on a schooner tied up near the campus on Union Bay?"

"Yes."

I can't *believe* Dwight wouldn't have told me this. He is, of course, the one who saw them kissing: "I suspect they didn't know we were in the vicinity, but I felt awkward just the same. When their lips came together, I immediately led Cynthia away." Lest we think he's a voyeur, he wants us to believe he ignored this spectacle.

"Had you and Mr. Vandergraaf made any weekend plans?"

"Yes, we thought we'd go sailing. Hugh's father owned a thirty-five-foot ketch called the *Wandering I*, that's I as in the first-person singular. He kept it at Friday Harbor."

I have stopped writing, am slow to comprehend: Hugh's abrasive crony, the nosepicker . . . my God, he's *Dumbo*. I am sure everyone reads my astonishment, which is so intense as to blank out a few minutes of his testimony. When I come to, still gaping at him, he, Cynthia, Hugh, and Beatrice have embarked on the *Wandering I*.

"It was a brisk spring day and we were all in good humor and there was much spirited conversation, though I'm afraid that after almost thirty years I can't recall any of it specifically."

I scribble furiously, willing my mind to concentrate, trying to stifle my anger. How bad is this likely to be? Did J.J. know his son was to testify? I cannot believe that.

"Miss Krueger had little to add to our debates about the issues of the day, and though mostly silent was extremely attentive to Hugh, to the point that . . . well, she seemed almost unaware of the existence of Cynthia and me." I am reading resentment, and I sense a kind of jealousy as well.

Junior's memory of events on South Pender Island is spotty: their act of illegal border-hopping had made him nervous and he'd had a "tiny" bit too much to drink, both on the boat and in the Bedwell Harbour bar. There, however, he recalls that Beatrice continued her relentless pursuit of his bosom friend. "To put it as innocuously as I can, she was crawling all over him, touching him, once going right onto his lap."

Again I read jealousy. I once kiddingly accused Junior of sheltering an unhealthy affection for Hugh;

maybe it's no joke. What have we here, someone hiding in the closet where the mocking green-eyed monster lurks? One failed marriage, no sustained relationships.

"Miss Krueger consumed alcohol in that bar?"

"Yes, and that made me a little nervous, too. I believe she was under-age."

"And breaking the law."

"Yes, sir."

"Please continue."

"It became apparent to Cynthia and me that Miss Krueger was seeking a romantic interlude with Hugh, so after we returned to the boat we announced we were going for a stroll. Hugh surprised me by insisting most vehemently that they join us, and they went down into the cabin to get their jackets and soon after that I heard some heated words being exchanged: it was clear some deeply felt issues were being aired."

"Did you hear any sounds to suggest a violent act was occurring?"

"Absolutely not. No fighting or scuffling or anything like that."

"Did she call out for help?"

"No."

"Any screams of pain?"

"No, sir."

"Calls for him to desist?"

"I heard none."

"All right. Did you make out any of their words?"

"Yes, ah . . . there was an open porthole, and I could hear her say, 'I don't care. I just want to be alone with you.' And I think Hugh said something to the effect that this was not a good time."

When Thalia Pfeiffer takes the stand we'll know that not only words were exchanged: those bruises were not self-inflicted. Nor was Hugh's neck bite; she drew blood. Will he remember that?

319

"More conversation followed in a lower tone. And some . . . rustling, shuffling about, that kind of sound. And since they didn't reappear, we merely carried on."

"How long did you remain there?"

"For about ten minutes."

Ten *minutes*? This sounds like *such* bullshit. But it is damaging testimony. I have been sandbagged, stabbed in the back. I *must* hold myself together.

I listen numbly as he describes a wander up a hill for a moonlit view through a madrona grove. On their return "after several minutes" they came upon Beatrice stamping angrily from the dock.

"What did you observe of her condition?"

"Aside from her demeanor, which seemed ill-natured in the extreme, nothing untoward."

"Did she complain about having been assaulted?"

"She didn't speak to us at all. Cynthia made a comment to me — which Miss Krueger must have heard — to the effect that someone, as she put it, appears to be in a snit. When we returned to our craft, we found Hugh in a disconsolate mood, and based on what he told me it would seem that Miss Krueger had deserted the ship. This had me greatly concerned, so Cynthia and I formed a search party but our efforts were to no avail. By this time I was growing anxious that we might run afoul of Canadian immigration officials for our unlawful entry into the country and I suggested we find an anchorage on our side. I hope no one will regard that youthful transgression as typical of the manner in which I deal with the laws of any country —"

"Just tell us what happened, Mr. Plum," says Judge Luckwell. Yes, Junior, you're not on trial. You should be. For perjury.

"Anyway, we cast off and spent the remaining hours of the night off Stuart Island, returning home on Sunday."

Bill turns to me: "Your witness."

But first the break, thank God — I need a respite to recover from the shock of Dumbo's treachery. And to sharpen my shears. He is lurking behind the plaintiff and his gang, not daring to look at me. Matters *could* be worse: he might have said he had an eye to the porthole and saw them making passionate love on a bunk.

I join Beatrice. "I am stunned. Before Hugh attacked you, did your conversation about his friends turn into an argument?"

"I didn't think it was that loud. They were so sneering toward me, and I guess I just said my piece. He asked if I wanted to join them for their walk, and I think I said, 'Why do we have to spend all our time with them?' Something like that. He spoke very loudly in their defense, and that's when he turned strange. Is it bad if we argued?"

"Maybe not. Maybe it helps."

I can see him becoming angry. Maybe it ignited into violence . . .

Judge Luckwell fixes Dwight in her sights with a long, penetrating look. "Your witness, Ms. Finnegan."

Junior improvises an expression both contrite and guarded as I stand. How is he going to explain his covert role as a witness? *I was under strict instructions not to speak to anyone, Elizabeth. You have to understand my position: I had no choice.*

"Okay, Dwight, you're a good, close, intimate friend of Hugh Vandergraaf — is that what you're telling us?"

"If that's an accusation, I must plead guilty." He makes that strained self-conscious laugh of his, *heh-heh*, but wipes his smile when he sees the judge's scowl. I don't think she likes him very much.

"You share confidences?"

"Oh, yes, we've told each other our various woes."

"And you'd back him up a hundred per cent if he was ever in trouble, right?"

The long pause tells us he is not sure how to answer. "That would depend on the situation."

"You were about the first person he talked to last year after I confronted him about the rape, am I right?"

He looks at Vandergraaf but is rewarded only with a composed shrug: so what?

"I think I know what day you're referring to. As I recall, you and I had a little to-do over it afterwards."

"What's the answer?"

"Yes, he telephoned me."

"Right away."

"Yes."

"To get you to persuade me to drop the matter."

"I disagree with that. He was merely expressing his concern."

"During our little to-do, you said in his defense that he used to turn them away from his doorstep and that he got all he wanted for free. Do you remember that?"

He turns a rosy shade. I have a witness, Curtis Kaplan, and he knows that. "Yes, but I think the implication was that Hugh didn't have to force his attentions on girls."

"And you said he never touched Beatrice Krueger."

"In the sense of rape."

"Well, there was a heck of a lot of touching going on on the boat and in the Bedwell Harbour bar and he was doing most of it, will you agree?"

"She was doing her fair share." A contortion of face muscles, like a twitch.

"Did that bother you in some way?"

He looks grievously offended. "No, of course not. Why would it? If Hugh found her appealing, why would that affect me?"

"Tell us about Cynthia Rosella. Where is she now?"

"I'm afraid you have me." His affected laugh. "The fact is, I haven't seen her since that day."

"How odd. Weren't you going together?"

"I'm sorry if I left that impression. It was more of a casual friendship."

"You didn't look her up after that weekend?"

"As I recall, we were deeply into examinations, and then the school year ended, and —"

"What's the answer?"

"No, I didn't look her up. I may have heard she married after graduation, then settled on the Eastern seaboard."

"You said Ms. Krueger didn't join in your animated discussions. What would they be about, politics, that sort of thing?"

"It was always politics with Hugh. He loved to debate."

"Would it be fair to say you considered her to be quite innocent and naive?"

"I would not call her worldly. Naive, yes, certainly in the political sense."

"Not really Hugh's type."

Another guilt-revealing twitch. The judge seems to notice, but does the jury? "I would let Judge Vandergraaf be the judge of that." *Heh-heh.* He hopes this is funny, but it clangs. I pause, stretching out the silence. He tugs at his vest.

"Do I understand that as you were eavesdropping outside the porthole, Hugh Vandergraaf said this was not a good time?"

"I take strong exception to the word eavesdropping —"

"Okay, listening."

"He said something to that effect."

"It wasn't a good time to do what? Engage in a quarrel? Cast aspersions on his friends?"

"I don't know."

"Though their voices were raised, that's *all* you heard?"

"Their voices weren't pitched quite that high."

"They were both arguing?"

"Yes."

"Did Mr. Vandergraaf seem angry?"

"I . . . couldn't say."

"You can't do better than that?"

"They both sounded angry."

"She could have been pleading with him?"

"That was not my impression."

"But you don't know, do you?"

"Frankly, I felt it was none of my business." Says the office super-snoop.

"And are you really trying to tell us you hung around there for ten minutes?"

"I wasn't staring at my watch. Thereabout."

"Oh, come on, Dwight, it was more like ten *seconds*, wasn't it?"

"Eight, ten minutes." Another twitch. A polygraph needle would be jumping.

"You stood on the dock all that time waiting for them to get their jackets? Really, Dwight. No one's going to believe that."

"It's my best memory."

"Yes, and you'd had a fair bit to drink, hadn't you?"

"I had my senses about me."

"You and Rosella went out walking for how long?"

"Oh, maybe fifteen minutes."

"Earlier you said several minutes."

"Well, maybe it was fifteen or twenty minutes."

"Or half an hour or forty minutes. The fact is you really don't know."

"I can only do my best considering the lapse of time."

I hope I have wedged open the window of opportunity for the rape. "However long it took you, when

Beatrice walked past you on your return, she was crying, wasn't she?"

"It was too dark to tell."

"Too dark to see her bruises, I guess."

"I object," says Bill. "That's taking a leap."

"Sustained."

"Assuming she was bruised up, you weren't able to see that?"

"Making that assumption, yes, it was too dark."

"But later you did see the bite mark on Hugh Vandergraaf's neck."

Junior pauses, frowns. "I don't remember any such thing." Then abruptly: "He was wearing a turtleneck sweater. He definitely did not complain of anything of that nature."

"He had changed into a turtleneck while you were out walking?"

"I . . . can't be sure. I believe so."

"See any blood anywhere?"

"No. I noticed the bedding on one of the bunks was slightly rumpled, that's all."

"Did you ever examine the bedding or the sheets for blood?"

"No."

This is not moving me far down the road. I try another route. "You left Pender Island in a bit of a hurry, didn't you?"

"No, I think not. We debated the matter."

"This was about ten o'clock?"

"Again, you have the better of me, time-wise."

"It could have been that early?"

"Possibly."

"And so you decided to leave Beatrice on this strange little island not knowing how she'd find her way home."

"We did search, but as I say we had this concern about not clearing customs, and —"

"What's the answer?"

"She apparently told Hugh she'd find her own way home —"

"What's the answer?"

"Yes, we left her there."

"Where did you search?"

"Cynthia and I went to the bar and looked around the buildings. No one was around who seemed to be much in charge of anything. There was little else we could do."

"Spread the word? Find someone with a car? Search for her on the road? You didn't do any of that, did you?"

"As I say, she seemed determined —"

"What's the answer?"

"No, we didn't."

"After a cursory search you abandoned this naive young woman, having parked her illegally on some foreign island with no idea how she'd get home, and you didn't consider that she might change her mind and wish to return to the boat. Do I have that right?"

"I can't add to what I've said." That is weak. I suspect he was pleased to be rid of her, wanted Hugh for himself. Vandergraaf, oddly, rarely looks at him: his eyes are constantly on me, steady and unsettling.

"Your hasty departure wasn't prompted by something your close confidant told you?"

Again, hesitation. "No, it was at my urging. Hugh had very little to say and I didn't pry. There had obviously been some difficulty."

"I might use a stronger word than that. No more questions."

I have done damage control, but not enough. I would be in a deep hole without Thalia Pfeiffer's corroboration of Bea's injuries.

Bill, who seems pleased enough with the mendacious

efforts of his surprise guest, says his next witness will occupy some time – Vandergraaf, obviously.

"I suggest we break early," says Judge Luckwell. "We can extend the afternoon to make up."

My noon constitutional takes me to the waterfront, where a ferry is churning to Bainbridge, gulls dipping and wheeling at her stern. The sun is now out. So are the Olympics, a vast frosted cake. A brisk and beautiful day that is lost on me: I am in a sullen frame of mind.

How bad was Junior's testimony? Judge Luckwell seemed to find him supercilious, and maybe the jury did, too – but that does not necessarily mean they rejected his story. Beatrice will say the assault happened quickly, following a quarrel that lasted a minute or two; Dwight's claim of being within approximate earshot for eight to ten minutes will be severely tested against her evidence. A verbal row followed by a rape: the jury will hear from Helen Mazur of a similar pattern. Did he attack these women through an angry need to control? Does he confuse the passions of heated quarrel and physical desire? Perhaps he sees rape as a virtuous act of war, choosing as his victims those he perceives as politically unworthy. How he confuses me.

We are nearing the moment of truth, the very core of this case: Judge Hugh Vandergraaf is about to testify. From the Latin *testis*, also the root of testicle (apparently because the presence of this potent gland gave clear testimony of maleness, to the relief of those assembled in the Roman birth-room).

Who is the other mystery guest?

"Judge Vandergraaf, would you come forward to be sworn?"

Hugh makes his way casually to the witness chair.

Despite the strain he must be feeling, he still looks a decade younger than his fifty years, and no less attractive than when I first met him. Focus that wandering mind; it must be as sharp and bright as a diamond.

He starts off confidently in that rich, plummy voice I hate to love, his enunciation so precise and crisp. We learn his father was a war hero, as was his older brother, Jerome, his platoon decimated by the banks of the Kan River. That event politicized him – "to the point I became a vocal opponent of the war." After a stint in the Peace Corps he felt impelled by his concern for society's betterment ("I hope that doesn't sound too grandiose") to pursue a career in law.

Throughout, he is unafraid to look at the jury. If he is at all unsettled, I am not seeing it. But there are butterflies in *my* stomach, flutters of concern that I may not be able to stand up to him, that I may founder in cross-examination.

Bill bypasses Vandergraaf's time in college, but pans leisurely across the ensuing years: ten with Owen Bristow's firm, then fifteen on his own, a practice inter-rupted only by a failed try for public office.

"You ran for the state legislature?"

"As an overly liberal Democrat in a conservative dis-trict. I got what I deserved."

The strategy is to paint him pink, to occupy some of my turf and elbow me out onto the lunatic fringe.

"And when did you decide to seek a judgeship?"

"I hadn't intended to do so, not because of its many grave responsibilities but because I would have to with-draw from a certain amount of social activism. I was enjoying my practice – though it wasn't as lucrative as yours likely is, Mr. Christiansen."

This draws laughter from the gallery and a waxen smile from me.

"But I finally succumbed to the blandishments of several rather insistent friends and offered my name during the 1996 elections. To my dismay, the operation was a success and I became politically neutered." More chuckles. Now he has Judge Luckwell smiling.

"And did you come to enjoy your work as a judge?"

"Yes, it wasn't as fearful as I had anticipated. In fact I've enjoyed it beyond all expectations. Some lawyers I hold in high regard tell me I have some facility for it."

"I believe we heard from a few of those earlier this week."

"It may be incautious to dispute their testimony, but the fact is I am still learning. As Your Honor knows, it takes at least a decade to master the complexities of achieving fairness and balance. It also demands a major commitment."

Surely Judge Luckwell is too shrewd to fall for this eyewash, but maybe it is a clever strategy: it doesn't necessarily buy favors, but does persuade her to stay firmly in the middle of the playground and not wander off to Lizzie Finnegan's yard.

"And have you made such a commitment?"

"Having run twice in two years for a four-year position, I would have to say yes."

"Tell us about that second election."

"When this allegation of rape first surfaced a year ago September, I felt the people of King County must have the right to decide whether I should continue to serve them. I resigned, then filed again for the November elections."

"And was your position contested?"

"Yes, it was a lively campaign. I recall seeing Ms. Finnegan, the defendant, passing out leaflets for my opponent."

He does? I don't. I only worked the Central District, not exactly his bailiwick.

I turn to see Harry Crake wandering in late. He is grinning. Where has he been?

"You're a bachelor?"

"Yes. It is the one great sadness of my life that I have never known the joys and comfort of wife and family. But I have been comfortable enough with a hermetic existence and I think better able to concentrate on my duties." Another gesture to Judge Luckwell, *feme sole*. I am not sure if I appreciate the way she is leaning forward, almost as if she is beamed onto him.

"You do maintain a social life?"

"If you mean, have I had women companions, yes. But my recreation tends more to the outdoors than in. Skiing and sailing, squash, a neighborhood baseball league. For which I hold the all-time record for errors at third base."

The laughter is especially merry from the area where his fans sit, women bored with their marriages, mooning at this glib, handsome rapist. He is superb, however: a calm, relaxed master of self-deprecation; the jury will forgive the hints of narcissism.

"How long have you known Elizabeth Finnegan?"

The witness directs those two blue lasers at me, unafraid, assured. He even dares to smile, and somehow this causes me to clench up. Perhaps, though, it is because I have to pee; my bladder is nagging at me.

"I think we shared a counsel table at a few brief trials several years ago. I recall complimenting her on a submission. She seemed very able for one so young." He intends to be seen as chivalrous in the face of my shrill feminism. I cannot believe how collected he is: the trial is a minor irritant, a mosquito bite, he has better ways to spend his time.

"And tell us about your first encounter with her in your role as judge."

This he recapitulates in an almost jocular fashion,

conceding that a wiser judge might have ignored my intemperate outburst instead of summoning me for an "old-fashioned scolding."

Bill then asks him about my visit to his chambers.

"She invited herself, ostensibly to apologize, which she did, and perhaps somewhat innocently I agreed to have lunch with her." It was *his* idea.

In summary, a pleasant time was had – until the cat bared her claws. "She suddenly dropped her mask of congeniality and accused me of raping a woman named Beatrice Struthers."

The photo ("rather tasteless, I'm afraid") becomes the next exhibit. It does not put him in a flattering light, a smart aleck looking down Bea's blouse, but Bill is doubtless anxious to give it a quick burial, though he must suspect I won't let the grave remain undisturbed.

"Did you recognize the woman known then as Beatrice Krueger?"

"After a couple of moments, yes."

He did *not*.

"And what was your reaction?"

"At first I thought I was on the receiving end of a tasteless joke. Then I realized Ms. Finnegan was being serious. I was dumbfounded." A quivering note of righteous indignation: "It was a disgraceful allegation to make, totally reprehensible. Nothing like that had remotely happened. Some terse words were exchanged, and I departed."

He looks at Judge Luckwell, releases a deep sigh. She straightens a wayward lock of hair.

"And what did you do next?"

"I spoke with one of our senior judges. Acting on his advice, I met that evening with the King County prosecutor, Mr. Schoenenberg, who took a statement from me." Then, too fast for me to react in time: "I agreed to take a polygraph –"

"Objection," I say, rising.

As Judge Luckwell sends the jury out I give Bill a cold look: he knows he cannot buttress a witness's credibility with results of a lie-detector. I am fully expecting the judge to give Bill a tongue-lashing, but instead she gives him her ear.

"While the result of the test may be inadmissible," he argues, "the fact that he offered to take one is a benign event that's merely part and parcel of his general denial of the rape."

I argue that Bill is flouting precedent, that Vandergraaf's testimony leads to an inadmissible inference. But to my astonishment, Judge Luckwell finds against me: Vandergraaf will be allowed to say he volunteered for a polygraph but not state the result.

"With respect, Your Honor, that is not *right*. The jury will obviously infer he passed it."

"It's a little too late to close the barn door, Ms. Finnegan. You should have anticipated this."

We take the break, and I hurry to the nearest jane to void the three cups of coffee I drank for lunch. I sit there longer than required, fuming. But I am more angry at myself than at the judge. I *should* have raised the polygraph as a prior issue; I never dreamed they would so brazenly slip it in.

Has the judge turned against me? It almost appears she is succumbing to Hugh's smooth pitch – maybe more than that, the way she stares at him and preens, fusses with her hair. Has she decided it is safe to buy a car from this salesperson? Some of the jurors, too, I have noticed, seem to be buying. It's the savoir faire, the cool quips, the calm injured innocence. Would a guilty mind not be tense, the palms sweaty?

In the corridor, I bump into Harry Crake coming from the stairwell. "Hey, some amazing stuff is going on in Judge Wiley's court. I'm trying to figure it out. Custody thing over a couple of kids, gay scientist versus a wife who took on all comers at this retreat for promiscuous couples. My own custody hearing's close to kickoff, so I'm learning as I'm being entertained."

I blanch. It's going to be all over the news.

I return to counsel table to find Vandergraaf in relaxed conversation with Bill and his assistant counsel – Pamela Adams is her name and her main role seems to be to hover lovingly about Hugh's person.

The jury shuffles in. I am sure they can see through the fakery of my smile. *I'm* the one with the sweaty palms.

"Just to pick up where we left off, you offered to take a lie-detector test?"

"Yes, I did that the very next day."

"I'm not permitted to ask you the result of that –"

I cut him off with a display of pique: "So he passed it. I wonder if Your Honor might explain that the polygraph is a notoriously unreliable instrument that has led to so many miscarriages of justice we can't possibly rely on it in court."

Luckwell frowns over her glasses at me, miffed because I am taking such vehement issue over her ruling. She is curt: "For several important reasons, polygraph evidence isn't admissible. Proceed, Mr. Christiansen."

"Let's go back to 1971, Judge Vandergraaf. In the spring of that year, you were twenty-two and completing your second year of law?"

"Yes."

"You were active in student politics, involved with the student newspaper?"

"The *Daily*, yes, I was on the editorial staff."

"And we know Beatrice Krueger was one of the reporters. Tell us about your dealings with her."

"I remember her as shy and hardworking, determined to prove herself. I helped her out somewhat, checked her copy for errors, and we often chatted about issues of the day. She was full of questions, curious about the world, and refreshingly naive, in a way I found quite compelling. She seemed to enjoy my company, if the increasing number of visits to my desk meant anything, and I often caught her watching me in a way that . . . well, I felt I was receiving a clear message, and I finally screwed up the courage to ask her out."

It is not this nervous suitor's courage that is screwed up. I guess he does not remember badgering Bea with invitations and being responded to with rejection slips.

"Before it escapes my mind, earlier that week she asked if I was still seeing Marjory Clayton, a former girl-friend. I told her we'd had a spat and had parted ways."

If that is true, Bea did not remember. The implication, I gather, is she was inquiring as to his availability.

Friday, March 26: beer and pizza in the *Daily* office, then that innocuous first date on the schooner where he boldly kissed her on the lips.

"I have, oddly, a specific recall that she seemed unsure how to do it, that she was not experienced with closeness to a man. She cast many oddly intense looks at me as I drove her back to her residence. When I asked her if she would like to go sailing the next day she was very quick in response, and I made arrangements to pick her up and I remember her jumping out, turning and waving, then running off somewhat jauntily to her door."

Borne away on the dove-like wings of her fluttering heart. His version may not diverge far from truth, but I am offended by the bold colors of his portrait of the lovesick schoolgirl. When I turn to look at Beatrice, she is blushing, embellishing the picture.

He is quite full of himself – but does the unbiased jury see that? Are the men recalling their own teenaged conquests, the girls who came across after the prescribed display of reluctance? And when I try to see within the minds of the women on the jury I realize I would have feigned *no* reluctance.

But not Beatrice.

Franca Crabtree is suddenly at my side, breathless, as if she had run from the office.

"Sorry, but there's some bad shit happening. Thalia Pfeiffer had herself bailed out yesterday, and she's split."

"Tell me you're joking."

"DEA arranged a safe house, but last night she slipped out the back door and into a waiting car. Bolted for Canada, I think."

"Who the hell would bail her out?"

"The guys she was in the process of ratting on, of course. She suckered the narcs."

"Is there a problem?" Judge Luckwell asks.

Problem? What problem? "May I have the court's indulgence for a moment?"

I confer hurriedly with Franca, imploring her to conduct full search and rescue. After she leaves I find myself stricken with a tight throat, a lump of lead in my stomach. And now, my brain anesthetized by this ghastly development, I have missed a long segment of Vandergraaf's testimony; the room is in a titter at some *bon mot* from the witness.

"And was Ms. Krueger also enjoying this sailing trip?"

"She was fine, smiling, rather quiet. She might have felt a little shy: she was a freshman; we were all older. She took a while to warm to my boisterous companions, who perhaps seemed to her rather imperious."

I am desperately trying to concentrate, but Thalia Pfeiffer's jolting act of truancy continues to becloud my thoughts. I do not even hold a deposition from her that I could try to file, merely an affidavit. I had not issued a subpoena for her: unnecessary, I thought, she was behind bars; risky, too, a subpoena might have come to the attention of the wrong people. Concentrate.

"What was her manner toward you?"

"I felt she was . . . clinging is not the word, but she rarely left my side, and I would often catch her staring at me in a way that frankly made me feel self-conscious."

"I understand the two of you had a brief conversation having to do with your companions."

"Yes, when we were alone for a few moments she apologized for being poor company – she felt she was unable to relate well to Dwight or Cynthia. I told her that being on a boat with strangers can be a testing experience, and she said – I remember clearly her words – 'Do you think we'll have any time together?'"

I am trying to retain focus, and am writing so furiously my pencil breaks.

"I can't deny amorous thoughts had not entered my head, though I was concerned that she was developing a feeling toward me that was – maybe infatuation isn't too strong a word. I won't pretend that as a young man I was either sexually naive or, to put it plainly, without a keen interest in the opposite sex. However, on that particular weekend – and you'll forgive me if I find this awkward – there was a more compelling reason for me to, ah, renounce the flesh, so to speak."

Thalia Pfeiffer – may she rot in hell – induces another lapse of concentration: why is he talking about an appointment with a doctor?

". . . who explained to me it was something venereal – gonorrhea, to be blunt. He prescribed penicillin, and I was still under medication."

Gonorrhea? Confusion compounds dismay. I remember: in seeking settlement, Bill had hinted his client might be forced to divulge something "awkward." But how can a sexually transmitted disease aid his client?

"The condition hadn't gone away?"

"Not quite."

Bill hands him a slip of paper. "Does this mean anything to you?"

"Yes. My name is on it. This is a copy of Dr. Soo's prescription."

"That will be the next exhibit, subject to Dr. Soo further identifying it." The other mystery witness. What game is being played here? "Was this problem explained to Ms. Krueger?"

"I was much too embarrassed to mention it. But of course my humiliating condition demanded complete sexual abstinence."

They did not perform the physical act, is that what he is about to tell us? Of course, *that's* why the nurse was pointedly asked whether Bea was suffering from any venereal infections. The flight of Thalia Pfeiffer is bad enough, but now it's abstinence and gonorrhea. Instead of playing games with Bill, I should have uncovered this unexpected alibi six months ago. My client does have a fool for a lawyer.

By the time I gather my wits, we are on Pender Island, in the Bedwell Harbour bar, devouring hamburgers.

"How much did you have to drink?"

"Oh, a few beers. We picked up a box of twelve for the boat, as well."

"And Ms. Krueger, did she drink?"

"Yes, it was the first time in my presence she had taken anything alcoholic. She drank a couple of screw-drivers, and I am afraid she became rather giddy. At one point she sat on my lap and put her arm around my neck. She was completely ignoring Cynthia and Dwight and I cannot blame them for assuming matters between Ms. Krueger and I were accelerating toward a romantic climax."

He tells of Beatrice's reluctance to join in the moonlit stroll. "She indicated she had to find something warmer to wear and she took me by the sleeve and led me down to the cabin."

That *really* sounds like Beatrice. Dear God, there is

not a doubting look on any juror's face. I have half eaten another pencil already.

"We found her jacket, but instead of putting it on, she flung her arms around my neck, held herself tightly against me, and kissed me on the mouth. I won't say I didn't respond – in fact, I felt a strong desire. However, in my mind Beatrice Krueger was far too nice a girl to . . . and, well, conditions weren't right for reasons I have stated. When I drew back and said we should do the polite thing and join our companions for a walk, she became, in a word, petulant. Perhaps it was the liquor that inflamed her disappointment, but she began speaking rudely of Dwight and Cynthia in a loud, animated voice. I am afraid I returned the fire and in doing so provoked a tirade of complaint about my allegedly snobbish friends, accusations that I was less interested in being with her than them, and regrets that she had not stayed behind to study for examinations."

Beatrice's temper tantrum (one struggles to visualize it) continued for some ten or fifteen minutes, after which she grabbed her jacket, announced she would find another route home, and flounced out. He followed her to the deck, remonstrating, but she ran down the dock. Dwight and Cynthia returned, then made their cursory search of the grounds.

"I was in a dark mood, and Dwight suggested we give up on her, and as I sat on my bunk, feeling both foolish and sorry for myself, he piloted the boat to an anchorage on our side, on Stuart Island. In the morning we sailed back to Friday Harbor."

And that, according to this distressfully credible account, is all that happened. No ripped panties, no broken hymen, just a broken heart, which was in evidence ten days later in the *Daily* office: Beatrice hovering about sadly, uncommunicative.

"I was waiting for an opportunity to be alone with

her to bandage some wounds, but she left abruptly. That's when I found the note in my typewriter."

Bill has him identify it: *I don't understand why you won't speak to me.*

"You kept it all these years?"

"I have this terrible habit of keeping all my old notes and letters. I tried to look her up shortly after that, but she had disappeared, left campus in fact. The next time I saw her was twenty-eight years later at the commencement of this trial."

"Judge Vandergraaf, did you ever assault Ms. Krueger?"

"My answer is an unequivocal no."

"And what do you say about her accusation of rape?"

"It is entirely in her imagination."

"Thank you." As Bill sits I can almost hear his sigh of contentment. The court is still, except for my beating heart and a respectful cough from the gallery.

"What are your wishes, Ms. Finnegan?" Judge Luckwell asks, looking at the clock: five minutes to go. I must react quickly and vigorously if I am to reclaim any of the ground lost today.

"Thank you, Your Honor, let me at least begin." Heedless of consequences, I let fly, hoping to ambush him.

"Do you remember a woman working at the *Daily* named Helen Collins?"

He frowns. "I can't say I do."

"You went out with her. Helen Collins, now Mazur."

"Perhaps her memory is better than mine."

"Can I can refresh yours? You raped her in a country lane in the fall of 1971."

The sound of many lungs sucking air, then total turmoil, Bill rising in loud complaint, Vandergraaf shouting over him, "That is an absolute falsehood!"

"Members of the jury, you will entirely disregard

Ms. Finnegan's accusation," Judge Luckwell says in a taut voice. "You are dismissed for the day." As they file out, she glares at me as one might at a person who had committed a terrorist act. "I'll hear argument."

I am so stunned at her muzzling me in such an abrupt and arbitrary way that I hear Bill Christiansen's long objection as a disconnected garble of phrases: "no foundation laid whatsoever," "grossly prejudicial," "scandalous and disgraceful."

Then the judge, addressing me: "This is a very grave matter, Ms. Finnegan. I should have expected an offer of proof of this very serious allegation to be tested before me on a voir dire. There isn't a hint of it in your pleadings and it's too late to amend them. You shall not pursue this line of cross-examination."

I completely lose my temper. "But that − with all respect − is . . . it's wrong! It's totally unfair! Your Honor, I should have every right −"

"Hold your tongue! I will not hear further submissions." Teeth gritted, she slams her gavel, abruptly rises, and pauses to look at Vandergraaf with such eloquent intensity that I know he has won her to his side.

By the time the elevator disgorges me onto my floor I have slipped into a quicksand of disconsolation. Pfeiffer on the lam, gonorrhea, now this insane ruling that emasculates what is left of my case. The judge has denied me a key witness, I have been deserted by another. I am doomed. J.J.'s words haunt me: *You are damned prideful. It's by far your worst quality.*

I was too prideful, all right, an arrogant presumptuous brat. How had I persuaded myself I had the skills for this trial, the smarts, the toughness, qualities honed only by experience?

Now comes the voice of God himself: "Come in here!" A bellow from down the hall. J.J.'s door is ajar; I can see Curtis Kaplan within – he has been summoned, too.

J.J. slams the door behind me, looking at me as if I am some odorous substance that has been excreted onto his Persian carpet. I gather the strength to welcome him back. "You look really good."

This goes ignored. He stares me into a chair, and shouts, "Is this a law firm or a goddamn circus?"

"Easy, J.J.," says Curtis. "The old ticker."

"We have Bozo the Clown here, specializing in erotic pratfalls for the delectation of divorce court, and over here we have Minnie Mouse, flailing away with a rubber bat at some dickhead with a testosterone problem."

"You haven't mentioned Dumbo."

"Dumbo who?"

"You haven't heard?"

"No, young lady, since I've come in I've been occupied with Franca. She left here with tail down and ears curled back after a tirade which has almost – not quite – exhausted me. What dirty dishes must be washed from *your* kitchen-sink drama?"

"You didn't know Dwight testified today?"

He greets this with utter shock. As I explain, he slowly goes white. I have killed him.

I step toward him but he waves me away, a weary toss of his hand. "Leave us, Curtis, we'll be some time. Franca will explain to you how we're handling matters. Oh, and call the court reporters. I want an expedited transcript of all the testimony in Elizabeth's case, whatever it costs, even if they have to work all night."

After Curtis leaves, J.J. says, "Begin. Everything."

I bring out my file, my penciled notes. There follows two hours of impassive listening, a death-like quiet broken by only the occasional question, comment, or cuss.

("You did *not* have a subpoena served on this Pfeiffer woman?" "She was in *jail*." "Who's this Cynthia Rosella?" "Dwight's date." "He had a damn *girl*friend?")

At the end, he says, "Settle it."

I think of trying to explain doing so to Beatrice. I think of the women who marched, of all the abused women to whom I would deny courage and hope. I wonder if he has any conception of how impossible it would be for me to entertain such a notion.

"I'm sorry, J.J., I can't."

"You've made a hash of it, Elizabeth."

"I know." And I start to weep, and I have never done that in front of him before.

21 | Friday . . .

The wan, dejected warrior in the bathroom mirror needs a coat of camouflage, makeup to hide the eyes' red rims, those tired lines and sallow skin. How horrible that I cried in front of J.J.; how hurt he was that I so bitterly rejected his words of solace. I cannot cave in, I told him. I would rather die than be a traitor to my principles and have them bought so cheaply.

He showed compassion; he did not accuse me, as I thought he might, of having adopted a mindset of dogged faith in Beatrice, of being willfully blind to a clear alternative, Vandergraaf's innocence. Please, he urged, let me work something out. "Whatever I can devise, it's your call; I'll respect that." Go home, he ordered. Get some bloody sleep.

It was indeed a bloody sleep: a sluggish flight on bleeding hobbled legs, a gored body floating on the ocean's wash. I woke, I slept, I woke again.

As I dress – something demure in sackcloth? – J.J. phones, in the office already at a quarter of eight. Or he has been there all night, reading those expedited transcripts, risking that weakened heart.

"You might want to put off your cross of Vandergraaf. I've arranged a little chinwag with the foe this morning."

What does he expect can be accomplished? I know he means well with his efforts to steer me from the precipice, but I will not bend my course. How can I settle without surrender, without disgrace? I will let the fates carry me where they will.

"I'll see you at the courthouse. *Non carborundum illegitimus.*"

Too late. The bastards have already ground me down.

I stare morosely out the window: the clouds are thick and slung low, shedding giant snowflakes. We are in for a taste of winter on this cruel frosty Friday. Maybe I should simply not *go* to court today. Disappear like Thalia. Live like a hippie on some remote Micronesian island. String shell necklaces and sell them to the tourists. And hope no one recognizes me. . . .

Nick lurches into the kitchen, awakened by the smell of coffee. I realize I have not seen him for days – he was sleeping when I returned last night.

"An acne-pitted Nazi dropped over yesterday and thrust this ridiculous piece of paper at me." He tenders a subpoena from Maxine Vradjik's lawyer inviting him to Judge Wiley's court this morning. "May I assume it's something that may be safely wiped and flushed?"

"At your own peril."

He slaps his forehead. "God have mercy. I am about to be torn to shreds by some snarling homophobe –"

"Oh, God, stop whining! I'm a wreck, I'm ruined, I've blown it." He looks shocked and hurt and I regret my harsh tone. "Come on, coffee up and get dressed for court. No pink ties or aquamarine socks, please."

I bundle Nick up to the tenth floor and deposit him with Stephane and a glum Franca, who is still licking wounds inflicted yesterday by the master of the house of Plum. J.J. is now closeted with Judge Wiley in chambers; I assume he sat the parents down and reminded them they are intelligent beings. The trial is on hold: all concerned know matters have gone too far – except perhaps Harry Crake, wanting more, hooked on marital discord.

He is busy with his laptop, and I leave before he can spot me. I do not care to hear his analysis of Hugh's all-star performance. *She's not getting up, Dan. Let's look at that injury again, Al.*

I wait outside 941 for J.J. to join me from upstairs, and when he finally arrives, the clock reads fifteen minutes after starting time. Though court is not in session, Judge Luckwell is standing by her chambers door, looking irked. "Is the jury going to be kept waiting much longer?" she demands of me. When she sees the rangy older gentleman ambling up the aisle behind me, her demeanor abruptly changes, softens.

"Good morning, everyone," J.J. says heartily. "What do you say, Judge, if we let the jury go off to do their Christmas shopping? Just for the morning. Getting awfully close to the day of giving, I'm sure they'd appreciate it."

Vandergraaf must be pleased to see him: the defendant is in trouble; the boss is galloping in to rescue her, or at least to salvage what he can of her scattered pieces.

Luckwell tells her bailiff to excuse the jury until one o'clock. She is aware now that talks among counsel are to commence, and it is obvious she would like to put this monster to bed. "I'd like to see counsel in my chambers." To J.J.: "I take it you'll join us?"

"Why, sure, I got the time if the coffee's free."

She smiles. "Still sugar and milk?"

"Still sugar and milk."

J.J. confers for a moment with Bill, who instructs Hugh to stay outside and brings instead his assistant counsel, Pamela Adams, about my age, teased dark hair. She has been flitting about Vandergraaf like a hummingbird all week.

Luckwell ignores the rest of us, moves to J.J., pecks him on the cheek.

"Don't get me too excited now, Mavis, I've got a weak heart."

"I heard, but you're looking damn good, Jeremiah, perky as ever."

Jeremiah? Nobody calls him Jeremiah.

"Guess the Lord doesn't take all the sinners. How's the farm? Still keep a few black Angus?"

This colloquy carries on for a few minutes while the bailiff speeds off for coffee and we all find chairs. Bill has managed to compose the pallid smile of someone stumbling into a private party. I do not feel invited either, and am certain the judge is still put out at me, so I quietly gaze from her chambers window; it overlooks the old Smith Tower, almost obscured by a veil of falling snow.

"All right," Luckwell says, "what's the plan of attack here? Are we talking settlement, and if so is there anything I can do to help things along?" She pours for J.J., milk and sugar, the way he likes it.

"That's a mighty kind offer, Mavis, and, yes, there is something. The ruling you made yesterday, this Helen Mazur business: I thought I might ask you to reflect on that a bit; can't help wondering if you were just a little fast on the draw. Now, of course it came at the tail end of long, stressful day, and Liz here got up your spine a little, but, heck, you don't want an appeal court sending this whole mess of dog food back for a retrial. If she can't cross-examine about the sexual misdeeds of the plaintiff, how does she prove her case? He preys on women, Liz says. Well, maybe he does and maybe he doesn't, but the Constitution gave us juries to decide those things."

And J.J. carries on like this for a while, cozy, persuasive, bluntly arguing that if she wants this case settled she cannot strip me naked, can't take all the bullets from my gun. No more difficult task is faced by a lawyer than asking a judge to reverse herself, though I have begun to sense Luckwell is uncomfortable about her mistake. But there is a Maggie Thatcher quality about her and I do not expect her to relent.

My hopes plummet when she says she will not

change her mind, but rise again when she says she'll amend her ruling: if the defendant lays sufficient groundwork of a propensity to prey on women, she will hear further argument. Luckwell directs a meaningful look at me: she has dealt me a break; I am to use it to bury the hatchet with Vandergraaf.

"I'll leave you to it," she says, finishing her coffee, rising. "You can stay here; I'm going to do *my* Christmas shopping."

Bill confers for a few moments with Pamela, then abruptly turns to J.J. "I think we should stop playing peekaboo. What have you got?"

J.J. turns to me. "Let's end the suspense, Elizabeth, what do you say? It's not fair to these folks."

"Sure." Let him do it his way. I am almost ready to let him take over the trial if he wants. It is a tempting thought: I have proven what *I'm* capable of.

"Well, Bill, the fact is young Vandergraaf wasn't just sowing wild oats; he was sticking his plow into every little patch of grass that came his way. My friendly advice is that he discontinues this action before Liz here finally chops it off. Sometimes they can't sew it back on."

"J.J., don't hand me that guff; I've been around the block a few times. I told Liz: full unabashed apology, her best offer against a million in damages. That was a minimal figure that we proposed to avoid bringing up this sorry business about the gonorrhea. That awkward evidence puts paid a lot of dreams for Hugh: he was in line for a federal judgeship. So our offer is scrapped, it's out the window. She had her chance. I warned her."

He is being hard-nosed, negotiating from strength.

Standing now, pacing, J.J. shakes his head and pats me on the shoulder. "This young lady will not be going down on her marrowbones for some dissolute goat, so you can forget about either an apology or damages."

I am no less taken aback than Bill: J.J. is displaying an

almost reckless confidence. I am grateful that he staunch-
ly refuses to sell me out.

"Come on, J.J., Hugh is totally innocent of this and
you know it. Sure, he's going to get hit with all the crap
you can fling at him, but he's not going to evade, he's going
to be damn straightforward about it all; the jury will respect
him for that. All you've got is an amnesiac woman with a
history of mental illness who writes love notes after the
fact. She didn't contract the clap. You're faced with high
marks on a polygraph. And you have your own son's honest testimony that he heard nothing to indicate a rape."

J.J.'s face clouds – Dwight's role must be a deep
embarrassment for him.

"Convince me otherwise."

J.J. thrusts Helen Mazur's affidavit at him. "Decent, honest family woman. No question she'll be allowed to say her
piece; you saw how Mavis is coming around on that one."

Bill seems merely to glance at it. "Unadulterated
bullshit. Pamela, do you have that file we opened on
Mrs. Mazur?"

They have already done their research. I listen with
growing alarm as Bill reads from a page of printed notes in
front of him: "'Having given further consideration to my
interview with Miss Finnegan, I now realize I spoke too
hastily in describing the incident as being in the nature of
an assault. Though I was taken aback by the suddenness of
his approach, I cannot say I denied myself to him.'"

"That sounds *so* made up. Where did you get
this?" Unlike J.J., I am rarely able to hide my consternation behind a veil of composure, and am seething
with exasperation.

"Since we're finally being open about this affair." Bill
hands me the sheet. "Transcription of a verbal statement
made to her lawyer. Came in this morning."

The source notation at top: "Per telephone conversation with Wilkie S. Mazur, C.A., Friday, Dec. 10,

8:47 a.m." The initials "P.A." Pamela Adams offers me an almost condescending smile.

J.J. reads it over my shoulder: a forced recantation that implies Helen's encounter with Vandergraaf was but a pathetic tumble in the bushes. J.J. is aware Wilkie Mazur hired a lawyer to wheedle a false version from his wife. I have also told him about her emphatic nod of acquiescence.

"She's in a state of absolute serfdom to her husband," I say. "This isn't her talking, it's something written out by the lawyer." The lofty feminist, Lorna Beale.

Bill leans comfortably back in his chair. "In the doubtful event that she's permitted to testify, I hardly care which version she gives. She has recanted and the jury will give her no credit whatsoever."

"Well, I'm sorry, Bill," J.J. drawls, "attorney-client privilege attaches to this here extorted statement. Made to her lawyer. Absent her consent, it's inadmissible."

"I guess we'll have fun with that one. What else did he say when you phoned him back, Pamela?"

"Mrs. Mazur is seeing a psychiatrist. And she's been placed in care a couple of times, for some kind of depression thing."

"Another supposed rape victim with a history of mental disturbance," Bill says.

I warn myself: hold the anger. "I am astonished, Bill, that you would stoop so low."

He takes on a regretful look. "Sorry you feel that way, Elizabeth, but if there's to be all-out war, we have an indication you enticed the statement from Mrs. Mazur by offering her daughter a job with your firm."

I will not explode.

"What else have you got, J.J.?" I am ignored; Bill somehow assumes Finnegan has been taken off the case.

"The name Thalia Pfeiffer — that mean anything to you?"

"Nothing."

"Thought so." J.J. reaches into his briefcase, pulls out a photocopied sheet. "I don't mind telling you, she got caught bringing up drugs from Panama and now we have to bring her down from Canada, but we're hoping to set that right."

Finally, Bill loses his poise, almost choking on his coffee as he reads Thalia's affidavit. "In what sewer did you find *her*?" He passes a note to Pamela, who quickly leaves on a research mission.

J.J. continues to lay my cards on the table: "Plus there's a couple of other folks who might not mind telling their anguished tales. His former bailiff, for instance, Juanita Calvo: toyed with, seduced, a victim of her boss's dissolute cravings. And Mrs. Yvonne Fairhurst. Hate to see your client provoke a messy divorce involving one of his upstanding character witnesses. And there's more of the same: Liz and I are working on it."

"If this turns out to be a snow job . . ." Christiansen looks slightly bilious; he may be having digestion problems.

"Nope, but whoever's in charge of the weather out there is sure doing one," says J.J., watching the thick flakes descend outside. "Anyone heard the forecast? Hell, how am I going to get up my hill? Maybe we should be talking about getting out of here early. Liz, if they abandon, you won't be claiming costs, will you? That might be like rubbing it in."

I am heartened by the tough stance J.J. is taking. Listening to him pitch Bill, I almost sense the dim light of hope.

"It's the Canadians he's worried about, isn't it?" J.J.'s tone is solicitous. "Folks up there don't feel time forgives sins the way we do. Maybe what we ought to figure out here is some way to spare poor Hugh the rigors of extradition and trial. But there'll be no groveling at his feet."

"Let's adjourn this for an hour or so," Bill says. "I'll need to go over some of this material with Hugh."

After Bill returns to the courtroom to confer with his client, J.J. heads wearily for a chair. He is exhausted, trying not so show it. I lead him to the couch. "Lie down for a while, okay? And thanks. Whatever happens, thanks."

He lies back with a sigh. "Don't expect too much. Two-thirds of that evidence I mentioned is either unavailable or inadmissible and they'll find that out. Liz, don't bite my head off, but what about some blandly worded apology? Get Mrs. Struthers to drop her complaint up in Canada."

"Let's see how that works. A guy commits a rape. You accuse him of it. He sues you for slander. He agrees to drop his suit if you pay him off and beg for mercy. So you withdraw your complaint, and we all go home happy that justice was served?"

"Okay. Let me take him on then, Liz. There's some fire left in the belly."

"I'm more worried about the heart . . . no, that's a cop-out. I have to do it, J.J. I have to finish it."

He nods. I know he understands. He has not mentioned Dwight once, though I sense he is galled that his son tried to sabotage me. I kiss him on the cheek and return to the courtroom, where Vandergraaf's group is in a huddle, talking low and earnestly.

"We'll be a while," Bill says to me.

"I'll go for a walk."

As I stroll by, Vandergraaf is frowning at me, and I cannot decide whether he is peeved or perplexed.

Outside, all is a white and silent gloom, the streets smothered under a thickening carpet. Rarely is the city struck by a major snowfall, but on such occasions it is brought to a slippery halt, its twelve hills littered with abandoned cars, suburban refugees trapped in the city's core, waiting in a daze for a bus that never arrives. I might normally enjoy the stillness and the dreamy peace: the white muffled city, innocent, unready.

I slip and slide down the hill to home, bring out my dress for the party tonight, funereal black but slinky, low-cut, skin-tight, slit to mid-thigh: daring, but I intend to look good at my funeral. I pack the dress in a suit bag and climb into my snow gear – all-weather boots, thick ski jacket, and mitts – then head back uptown.

Our office building seems in the process of being evacuated, secretaries, clerks, accountants, lawyers, all fleeing for hearth and home. On the thirty-third floor, I search for Junior, but he, too, has bailed out. He will face my wrath tonight, at the Christmas party.

My fellow J.J. Plummers are jittery: if this snowfall swells to a blizzard, how is the staff to toil their way to the dinner at Canlis? The restaurant is two miles to the north, beyond Lake Union. Maybe I should have brought my skis. I am determined to show my face; my absence would be read as the shameful admission of an ignominious defeat.

Curtis Kaplan steps tentatively into my office. "The judge let the kids decide. Michael will go with Stephane and Janice stays with us. Nick's subpoena was canceled and we're wrapping it up this afternoon. How's the trial going?"

"It's in the toilet."

"I'll come by the courthouse with some moral support." He cannot deal with my gloomy emanations and flees.

Mattie tells me Bill Christiansen's office called: all parties are to meet there at twelve-thirty. She has a slew of voice mail, mostly well-wishing pals, some media types. *The National Enquirer*. I don't *think* so. *Good Morning, America* is keen to get me on camera.

The only message I listen to is a breathless speech from Mother: "How *is* that trial going, dear? I can't make head or tail from the news, it's all such a mishmash. Darling, it looks like that stock is taking a little tumble, so Jake is unloading it . . ."

I click off the machine; I don't want to hear more. Nipigon Goldfields has bottomed out. I may call her tonight after a bracing drink.

I slump in my chair, stare morosely at that photo on my desk: Mom and me, graduation day. *Darling, we'd better send you to law school so you can exercise that big mouth of yours.* And over here is Dad. So handsome with that hank of dark hair over his eyes. Girls must have gone gaga over him. Almost glad he's not around to witness this debacle.

Mattie on the speaker: "I have Sergeant Duff." She has been trying to reach him.

"Miss Finnegan?" A stammer: he sounds nervous. "Before you say anything, that Pfeiffer woman wasn't supposed to get bail. Either someone down there goofed or her lawyer was brilliant."

"Sergeant, I hope you didn't set this whole thing up."

"I guess you don't know me very well. Miss Finnegan, I wouldn't do that."

"Oh, are police more ethical than lawyers?"

"Happens that I *am* a lawyer. Dalhousie, '87. Though you probably think I'm saying that to impress you." I have made him defensive, and regret that; he sounds sincere. "We have a nationwide alert out for her, but after talking to some of her crowd, we think she's hanging around here in Vancouver. If I find her, I'll have her down there faster than a blink . . ." A gulp. ". . . of your pretty blue eyes."

I am no longer denying the signs: on brief acquaintance, this shy Mountie has a slight crush on me. Is that why he bumps into doors when in my presence? I remember the intense way his eyes were fixed on me in Victoria. His interest is warming, even flattering.

"You know, Sergeant, when I first saw you, I

thought you were brought in because you can run a tape recorder. What's External I? External investigations?"

"Yes, ma'am, I set up the extraditions. That's why I was there."

"If you call me ma'am once more, I'm *not* going to buy you that drink. It's Liz."

"I get Nat. Short for Nathaniel."

"Okay, Nat, well, I'm dying here. Up to my pretty blue eyes in mud. I don't know how things could get worse."

Hesitation from his end. Then he sighs. "I'm afraid that could happen, if some of the DEA's wiretaps get into the wrong hands. They had a tap in Panama, it turns out. They have her talking to you."

"Saying what? She basically volunteered to give her testimony."

"The transcript has: 'Just get me out of here; I'll say whatever you want.'"

God has no mercy.

Bill Christiansen's firm is a factory: the top several floors of a high-rise near the courthouse. Our meeting is in a penthouse boardroom that is glassed in like a solarium, snow-blurred vistas below us. As I enter, I see Vandergraaf, off by himself at the far end of the room. His only greeting is an arched and cryptic eyebrow. J.J. does not look too happy. It appears the trial is going ahead.

Bill is stern and businesslike: "Sorry, Liz, but the DEA says this Thalia Pfeiffer is a supreme con artist and a pathological liar. Frankly, I wouldn't mind at all having a go at her, but unfortunately no one knows what rock to look under. Anyway, she was apparently ready to lie through her teeth to get her passage paid up here."

The old boys' network has been busy; the drug-enforcement people gave him everything. Did I put too much faith in Thalia Pfeiffer? She seemed so credible. . . .

"Her amazing story was also prompted by an offer of free legal services from your office. That will be our position." Bill hands a paper to Pamela Adams. "Make the changes and have it printed out. It's the final offer."

"Up to you, Liz," says J.J. No doubt he has done all he can.

"What's this final offer?"

"Four hundred thousand, payable over ten years. This is worth one hell of a lot more, but Hugh insists on being magnanimous. A full apology, then we put the whole thing aside."

"I'm out of here."

I rise, but so does Vandergraaf. "Damnit, Elizabeth, sit down." With what seems a profound weariness, he slowly walks to Pamela, who has stopped on her way to the door. He takes the paper from her hands and rips it in half. I am standing, my hands flat on the table, staring at him in confusion.

"Forget the damages." He turns to face me, a fierce look now. "I don't want a dime from you. I want your *remorse!*" This demand is shouted; I feel its vehemence like a shove of hot wind.

Bill and Pamela seem taken aback. J.J., too, but he is studying Hugh intently.

"You are the most willfully stubborn person I have ever had the terrible misfortune to know, Elizabeth. I am *not guilty*. Yet you stand there in front of me in all your pitiless pride, having accused me with utter falseness and malice of being a multiple rapist, and I find myself pleading with you to do the fair and honest thing. Tell me you're *sorry*, damnit! Show just one tiny goddamn *ounce* of contrition for what you've done to me. A million dollars, eight million, do you think that will stop the sniggering, the jeers and taunts behind my back?"

"Hugh, I think we have to talk about this," Bill says.

"We've had enough talk," Hugh says. "Reword it. She doesn't have to kowtow. God knows I'd *never* expect Elizabeth *Finnegan* to get down on her knees and plead for forgiveness. A bland concession to the effect she now entertains some doubts about the matter and won't pursue the complaint. Just scribble it out, Bill, and let's bring this atrocious farce to a screeching halt."

Vandergraaf walks back to his chair. He swallows another aspirin.

They are waiting for me to respond. I am to grasp at this offer. My mind is reeling.

"It is Beatrice Struthers's decision whether to lay charges," I say.

Vandergraaf's voice softens: "Mrs. Struthers is a charitable woman; just ask her to say she regrets this whole thing happened and wants to get on with her life."

How can I ask Beatrice to knuckle under, even to save me from financial devastation? After all she and I have been through, I would carry a burden of failure and appeasement all my life. I am feeling faint and weak-kneed. No breakfast again today, no lunch. I turn to look out the window, not wanting them to read the despair my face must reveal. The snow has temporarily let up, the inlet waters appear as a purple bruise on white skin stretching to all horizons.

"I can't ask her to do that. And I can't say I'm sorry. I can't."

"Don't do this to yourself, Elizabeth." I am not sure whose voice this is, maybe J.J.'s. I am undergoing a terrible struggle against tears.

"I can't." And I rush from the room.

I lapse into a blank stall after I leave the building, and stand on the balustrade in the snow, pulling deep gulps of cold air into my lungs to revive me. The snow continues to slacken, though traffic is sluggish, a few heavy trucks and four-wheel-drives churning through the slush.

Pull it together, Liz, don't fall apart. How am I feeling? I am hungry and depressed. Why am I depressed? I am staring at certain ruin: possibly several million dollars' worth of ruin now that all offers are to be withdrawn. I am on my own; J.J. has written me off as incurably headstrong.

Why were you being so generous, Hugh? Was that an act? Are you scared? I cannot, *will* not, accept that Beatrice Struthers and Helen Mazur have told me false.

A figure looms beside me: J.J. I await his rebuke, but he remains silent, staring with me at the fluffs that fall intermittently from the sky.

"What happened after I left?"

"Hugh blew his stack. I thought you were the champion hothead around here."

I smile wanly, and I see he is smiling, too.

"There was a distinct odor back there," he says. "Did you pick it up?"

"Maybe . . . some concern. Fear."

"Good, your smeller's working. Most important sensory organ of the skilled cross-examiner. Hugh Hustle, campus lecher, work on that. You have a lead-in with the gonorrhea; ask him how he got it. Okay, Liz, I'm going to have a little chat with this Juanita Calvo – I don't think Mavis will be pinning any medals on Hugh over that conquest. Now you just go into that courtroom with a big flapdoodle grin on your mug and give 'em shit."

I hug him. I recite a quiet prayer and head to the courthouse. It will be a long afternoon. I had better stop somewhere on the way for a bagel.

On the ninth floor I plow a path through the disgruntled late arrivals who mill about the courtroom door.

Despite the snow, every seat within is claimed, and the air is thick with expectation. The gallery seems equally divided between women's-movement friends and Hugh's fan club.

I will myself to look at Hugh: he is staring at me with consternation, as if stunned by my unbudging defiance.

I take some strength from the smiles of Beatrice and Thomas. I have not mentioned the Thalia Pfeiffer crisis to them; I cannot bear to let them know how forsaken have become our hopes of victory.

"I had a little talk with the other side," I tell Bea. "They seem to think this can all be settled if I apologize and you withdraw your rape complaint. I told them to jump over the moon."

Bea smiles and squeezes my hand. "You know what? Sometimes you make me so proud that I just want to burst." That charges up my spirits. "When I pray for you I have this powerful sense the Lord is answering back. I know you have His blessing."

I need all the help You can give me, God.

Bill hands me a document. "In case you've come to your senses, you'll want to look this over."

I scan it quickly: "Plaintiff agrees to withdraw said action . . ."; "Issues to be settled without payment of damages . . ."; "Plaintiff declines to punish Defendant for having spoken in error . . ."; "Plaintiff accepts in good faith that Defendant truly believed to be accurate certain false allegations made by the following persons . . ."

I fold it and put it in my bag. "I'll keep it as a memento. Let's push on, Bill."

"You utterly amaze me."

As the jury straggles in I try on a smile, but I am sure they see that it masks dejection. I feel myself being studied speculatively by Judge Luckwell: why didn't you play ball, counsel? I let her down; I should not expect to be coddled any more.

"Ladies and gentlemen," she says, "we're watching the weather. If it gets any worse, we'll recess early."

Bill rises. "I wonder if we may defer for a few moments Judge Vandergraaf's continued cross-examination. Dr. Soo has travelled from North Carolina to be with us and I'd like to get him back before the airport socks in."

"No objection."

Dr. Ling Soo is prompted to the stand. He's a slight man of about sixty, a surgeon in Raleigh now, but for several years he ran a general practice in Seattle's University District. He has no specific recall of treating Vandergraaf for venereal disease, but that matters little since he is allowed to refresh his nonexistent memory from his old medical files. His testimony is brief – Hugh came to see him March 18, 1971, and Dr. Soo was quickly able to diagnose the cause of a "purulent discharge" and a painful genital itch.

I take a few minutes to study his notes before rising, then flip to a page of a medical text I have armed myself with.

"Doctor, one gets gonorrhea normally from sexual contact?"

"In the large majority of cases, yes. Ninety-five per cent."

"And that's likely how Mr. Vandergraaf contracted this infection?"

"Very likely."

"It doesn't follow that the disease will be transmitted to ninety-five per cent of persons who come into sexual contact with a carrier?"

"No, the percentage could be much lower."

"So there's a chance of infection but not a certainty."

"A strong chance."

"But that would depend on the extent, duration, and frequency of sexual contact with the carrier."

"I will agree."

Shayne Wells, the nurse, nods vigorously: I think she may still be on my side, but she is only one of the ten I need.

"The condition may not be quite as noticeable in women as in men?"

"That's true."

"And in women it may often clear up without treatment?"

"That's also true."

"And you're not supposed to drink alcohol while on this medication?"

"Quite true."

"You would have warned your patient not to take liquor until he was off penicillin?"

"Absolutely. If it was to be effective."

"Your notes say that Hugh Vandergraaf made a return visit to you on Wednesday, March 31, 1971?"

"Yes."

"By which time he seemed pretty well cured."

"Yes."

"You have no idea whether he was still taking penicillin four days earlier?" The date of the rape.

"I do not."

Maybe this gonorrhea is not such a handicap to me after all. Hugh might have been wiser claiming Beatrice consented than constructing his case around the handy fact he had venereal disease.

I turn to see Franca and Curtis seated behind me. I assume the custody hearing is finished. They still seem cool with each other.

As Hugh Vandergraaf steps calmly to the stand, I perform some control breathing, then rise to face him. A long pause as I stare into those blue icicle eyes. I feel ripples of unease, and wait till they settle.

"While the topic is fresh, Judge, how did you get infected with gonorrhea?"

"I have to assume from sexual contact."

"With whom?"

"A friend of brief acquaintance."

"A woman."

"A woman." A faint smile to show he's not offended. He has pulled himself together for this cross-examination: calm, direct, unwavering eye contact.

"Who?"

"I'm not able to bring back her name. Someone I met at a demonstration. Not a student."

"Exactly how brief was the acquaintance?"

"One day."

"Brief interlude."

"Indeed."

He has been told to be candid, not to excuse himself or hedge. I must restrain an instinct to adopt a scolding tone.

"In the course of a single day the two of you met, you went off somewhere, and suddenly you were engaged in intercourse?"

"It was an anti-war rally. There was a get-together later at which some of us . . . well, the two of us slipped away and, yes, we had relations. In a vehicle."

"Your old Volkswagen van?"

"That's right."

"When was this?"

"About mid-March, I can't recall the date more exactly. It was on a weekend."

"Two weeks before the incident we're concerned with here?"

"Perhaps a week."

"You were protesting the war – speeches, placards, that sort of thing?"

"Yes."

"And you went about in a T-shirt, I'm told, that announced your opposition to the war?"

"One with a very angry and immature message."

"What did it say?"

"'Get the fuck out of Vietnam.' You must forgive me for that, Ms. Finnegan, but I suppose I hoped to shock people into an awareness of the wrongfulness of that war; I was many years recovering from the loss of my brother."

"And you never saw this woman after your sexual encounter?"

"No."

A whisper behind me: "Slam bam." It's Franca. She had better not create any distractions.

"You're not absolutely sure it was she who infected you, are you?"

"I'm assuming."

"Could have been someone else."

"That's doubtful."

"But you'd had sexual relations with many other women, hadn't you? You got all you wanted for free, according to that college chum of yours we heard from yesterday. Was that reasonably accurate?"

"Dwight might have found a less offensive way to put it, but, yes, I was more sexually active than might be considered acceptable by the mores of other times. In the sixties and seventies, however, young people were widely experimenting with a new-found sexual freedom. Perhaps it had something to do with our felt need to rebel, to break restraints. AIDS was unheard of, and unwanted pregnancy an insufficient deterrent to the reckless. I usually tried to be careful."

When he lectures in this manner, it is as if he's talking down to us from a high pedestal. Does it annoy the jury? Hard to tell: no frowns, no fidgeting.

"You didn't seem to be that careful with this woman whose name you can't remember. You obviously didn't use a condom."

"Ah, no, she said it wasn't necessary."

"Did you have one at the ready?"

"I object. Is all this private detail really necessary, Your Honor?" I am getting to Bill, at least, if not the unflappable witness.

"I'm sure Ms. Finnegan will exercise due caution, but she's entitled to explore an issue the plaintiff raised himself."

"Your answer?"

"I happened to have a condom, yes."

"You normally carried a few of them in the event of similar chance meetings?"

"No, not at all. I just happened to be . . . armed. So to speak."

The first hint of discomfort. J.J. was right: this dose of the clap has opened unexpected avenues.

"*Why* did you just happen to be armed?"

"I was seeing a young woman and we were intimate."

"That would be Marjory Clayton, whom you've described as your girlfriend?"

"Yes. We had been dating regularly for three or four months."

"And was she your girlfriend at the time you were enjoying sex with the anti-war demonstrator?"

"Well, yes, she was."

"I see. So what was your arrangement with her – she didn't mind your making love to other women?"

I do think that is a blush. Yes, it is a small dilemma, Hugh: you can choose to be a deceitful sexual partner or a shameless free-love adherent.

"I spoke to her about it and apologized."

"She took it in good humor, did she?"

A pause. "No, I'm afraid not. We broke up over it."

"Is that because you infected her?"

"Regrettably, yes."

I wonder why he is admitting to this unseemly history. Maybe he thinks I might locate Marjory Clayton. And I realize they have no idea how many nasty skeletons I may pull from the closet.

"You infected her despite the condom?"

He runs a hand through his hair. Time lengthens. This is proceeding more smoothly than I had hoped: some of the jurors are looking at him reprovingly. "The, ah, problem showed up elsewhere."

"I see, and where was that?"

Bill is on his feet again. "What has any of this to do with the issues we are debating?"

Judge Luckwell beckons us forward and we join her beside the bench. "If you're having a problem with this, Bill, I'm sorry, but you raised the issue."

"That doesn't mean she's entitled to snoop into every aspect of his private life. Let's turn this around: were this a woman being cross-examined – a rape complainant – such manner of questioning would be considered harassment of the most prying, indecent, and irrelevant kind. What other men did you sleep with, what manner of sex play did you indulge in? *You* would be justifiably outraged, wouldn't you, Elizabeth?"

I am finding it no easy task to answer this. "Yes, but this is not just about rape. It's also about whether he's a sexual predator."

"So far you haven't even come close, Ms. Finnegan," Judge Luckwell says. "Go on to something else."

It does not look as though I'm winning her back to my side.

I return to my station disgruntled, and boldly fling out, "Okay, so you infected her elsewhere, we'll leave it at that."

Is it possible to contract gonorrhea of the mouth?

Let the jury wonder. And a couple of jurors *are* looking slightly disgusted. Poor Beatrice seems discomfited: one doesn't read about such indelicacies in second-year English literature.

"While you were dating Ms. Clayton you were also pursuing other women, isn't that so?"

"Ms. Finnegan, if you have checked into my student history you have learned I had little time to indulge in dating rituals."

"Oh, please, you were hunting women down relentlessly."

"Rumors of a person's sexual activity have a way of expanding under their own power."

"Do you remember what they called you – Hugh Hustle?"

"I don't think I ever heard that."

"It's fair to say, isn't it, that your sexual attentions were not always welcomed."

"I was never given such an indication."

"Do you deny you had intercourse with several women without their consent?"

Though I am expecting an outburst from the plaintiff's table, Bill is mute. He may seem overprotective if he continues to coddle his client.

"That is entirely untrue."

"You're saying you didn't commit any sexual assaults?"

"That's absolutely preposterous." He assumes an indignant air that seems almost overdone.

"You were actively pursuing Ms. Krueger for several weeks."

"That's not quite true."

"You were coming on, telling her she was gorgeous, importuning her for dates. Do you deny that?"

"I suspect you have much embellished my brief history with her."

"You suspect? You do not remember it?"

"I was preoccupied with many other things, Ms. Finnegan."

"When I spoke to you a year ago last fall you didn't even remember her."

"That's incorrect."

I retrieve a copy of the April Fool's photo and hold it to his face. "I asked you if you remembered going sailing with this woman whose breasts you're staring at and you said, 'Damned if I do.'"

"I was being confronted with something that occurred three decades ago. Forgive me if it took me a few moments."

"You had relations with several other women pictured here?"

"I object," Bill says wearily.

"Are you going anywhere with this, Ms. Finnegan?"

"I'm doing what you asked, Your Honor."

Judge Luckwell ponders. Though irritated at me for not agreeing to settle, she knows she cannot easily retreat from her ruling permitting me to lay groundwork for the Helen Mazur assault. "You're on a short leash, Ms. Finnegan. Carry on."

I randomly point to one of the women in the picture. "What about her? Did you have sex with her?"

Hesitation. He is wondering what I know. "I can't remember if I went out with her."

"What about this one?"

"I may have dated a few of these girls."

"Seduced almost every one of them, didn't you?" So said Gayle Mitsuka.

"I find such a characterization offensive. Any episodes involving sex were freely entered into."

"What about Gayle Mitsuka here, the editor? Did you go to bed with her?"

"I think there was an occasion, yes."

"She wasn't interested but you insisted, you pushed yourself on her."

"If she told you that, she made it up." Is that a slight sheen of perspiration on his forehead? Some jurors are looking troubled.

Now I point to Helen Mazur. "And this woman?"

He peers closely. "I have no memory of her."

"You went out with her a couple of times in September of 1971."

He studies her photo. "I think I recall her now."

I do not think he does — the tone is faltering. I am resisting a compulsion to fling the facts in his face: you grabbed her, Hugh, you threw her into the bushes, you pinned her, you stripped off her underclothes, and you violently penetrated her. But have I laid the groundwork to make such a blunt accusation?

I cautiously ask, "Do you remember a sexual episode with her?"

"Not really, no."

"Do you remember afterward telling her she'd gotten you too hot?"

"Objection," Bill snorts. "This is cross-examination by innuendo. Your Honor may wish to warn the defendant her continuing malice risks vastly increased damages."

But Judge Luckwell's attention has been drawn to the back of the courtroom: J.J. is standing inside the door with an innocent smile. And beside him, Juanita Calvo. Hugh turns slightly red.

I shrug. "Since Mr. Christiansen seems so terribly worried, let me put the matter aside — for the moment. You used the phrase sexually active, Judge."

"Pardon?" His mind is elsewhere.

"Are you still sexually active?"

"I have had recent relationships."

"With anyone you see in this room?"

"I see you have invited Ms. Calvo into court. She was my former bailiff."

I am wondering how far Judge Luckwell will let me go. "You were her boss?"

"Yes."

"Last year you got her so drunk she passed out, right? And then you had intercourse with her."

Bill slaps his hand on the table. "I object to this!"

Judge Luckwell looks at Juanita, now at the witness; her expression is unreadable, though facial muscles are stiff. I cannot tell whether she infers indescribably bad behavior on Hugh's part or considers my tactics odious and high-handed. "Can anyone tell me what the weather's like?"

"Snowing hard," says J.J.

"All right, I will decide this weekend whether I can allow Ms. Finnegan more leeway." Her nostrils flare as she gazes down upon me. "Court is adjourned."

It is five-thirty, and I am getting high on alcohol and anxiety with Curtis and Franca. At a far table in McCormick's Fish House and Bar sit the enemy, Hugh, Bill, and Pamela. This is the only nearby port in the storm that is not shut down. A *tempête de neige* is under way outside.

But a blizzard will not divert me from the office Christmas party. I will make my way there even if I must walk the two miles. Will I remember it as a pre-victory bash or a condemned person's last dinner? Whatever may be the ultimate verdict of my trial, tonight I intend to tilt Junior's bowl of soup onto his lap. I have earned this party, though maybe I am too well started on it. Two wines, two martinis.

The enemy camp are deep in discussion, and have

been so since we came in an hour and a half ago. I have performed commendably enough against Vandergraaf – so far. J.J. gave me pats. It is touch and go, he said. Hard to read the jury, hard to read Mavis Luckwell.

I told him the judge was looking very sourly at me. Not to worry, Liz, she always looks that way.

If Judge Luckwell does not give me the green light to proceed full speed after Hugh, sell me a ticket for the next bus out of town. Even if I am allowed to call Helen Mazur, even if Thalia Pfeiffer miraculously reappears, they may be laughed out of court. One has told two different tales, the other is a low-life trafficker with motives to lie.

With too many drinks in them, Curtis and Franca are back to bickering over the Vradjik trial. "You made me out like I'm the Marquis de Sade," Curtis whines. "My name is mud."

"Well, you were rolling in it, Mr. Mud. Shit sticks."

"Stop it, you guys."

"I'm going to take a pass on the party," Curtis says mournfully. "I don't intend to be the latest lawyer joke."

"Well, I'm going," I say.

"By dogsled?" Franca doesn't sound too keen either. "It'll be a fiasco – who's gonna sow up . . . show up?"

"Come on, the walk will sober us up."

Franca shakes her head. "I don't need to get laid that badly. Obviously you do. Love that dress. You're really showing off the goodies."

I changed to my dragon-lady outfit in the court-house. I am made up, decorated, silver necklace and drop earrings. The only missing touch is my black heels, still in my bag with cellphone and other accouterments. Nobody at J.J. Plum particularly twangs my bowstring, so what is the point? I am unsure. I just want to feel corrupt tonight.

Franca leans toward me: "Look, they're deserting poor old Studley. Here's your chance."

Pamela is standing, straightening her skirt, slipping into her coat. Now Bill rises too, and out-duels Hugh in a battle of gold cards. As he works his way to the door, he pauses at our table.

"Nice work, Liz, but I think Mavis wants to shut you down. Got the impression the jury's beginning to resent the tactics of smear. I'll try not to pull the same stuff on Mrs. Struthers."

He has had a few drinks: his bluster is showing.

"Just stay the case, Bill. Explain you don't want to put my witnesses through the pain of testifying. I'll accept that."

A resigned wave, and he leaves.

"How can he act for that prick?" says Franca.

I glance at Hugh, alone now, staring out the window at the swirling snow. I am drinking martinis on an empty stomach and he is pouring back the Scotch – we are deadening our mutual pain; we are partners in adversity.

Curtis slides back his chair. "Somehow I've got to find my way out to Alki Beach. Maybe they're working on the freeways."

"Give Maxine a big mooshy kiss for me," Franca gaily calls out as he leaves.

The waiter comes by with another wine and double martini. "That gentleman over there," she says.

A gift from Hugh, who also sends a cryptic smile our way. Franca grins and raises her glass to him. "Accept it," she says. "It's his token of surrender, a tribute to Caesar."

"I doubt it." Who does he think he is impressing? I tell the waiter to return the favor, a double of the best. "I think he's written me off by now."

"He's been checking you out all evening, in case you didn't notice."

"Maybe he's putting the make on *you*."

"So introduce me to him."

"Sickos turn you on? Shrink calls it a wolf complex."

"Maybe the guy just needs some penis-restraint exercises. I bet he's really hung."

"Franca, you're obscene."

"It's a crime to imagine? He's pretty hot-looking, you have to admit."

Franca constantly astounds me. She's perverse — so down on the opposite sex yet drawn to them, or at least to one of the more useful tasks they perform. But have I not myself succumbed to romantic vagaries? Ann Boorstein says I ought not to blame myself for my fascination: he is interesting, quick-witted, an enigma.

Franca is no less fascinated than I about the inner workings of Hugh Vandergraaf. We decide he is a complex construct of his upbringing. When he was on the stand, I picked up a real sullenness toward his military dad. Is he simply another tragic victim of paternal neglect? One of those father-wounded sons who grow up insecure about their masculine identity? Can he find proof of it only in a bed or a back seat or a clump of bushes?

Yet something more compelling — and fundamental, I think — bothers me about him; I have a notion it relates to his mother. Only once in his testimony did he make mention of her, a passing reference to her descent from a "proud line" of military officers. In interviews that I have read he seems to shrink from the topic of his mother. An unloved child, or even, like Beatrice, unwanted? That must be horrible. Menacing as well, if it translates into anger at all women.

Why is he not leaving this restaurant? It must be a test of strength being in the same room. I am certain he abhors me; if he stares at me, it is with hatred. This trial, whatever the outcome, has likely ruined his chances for high judicial office, a sad consequence, in a way. He would be persuasive, perhaps dominant, in argument on civil-rights issues with the curmudgeons of the U.S.

Supreme Court. Though he could turn into his father, join the old guard.

The latest martini seems to have gone directly to my head. I must not arrive inebriated at the party, or too late for dinner: Canlis is an hour's trudge through damp, heavy snow.

I pluck an olive from my empty glass, pop it into my mouth. "You coming or not, you wuss?"

"Walking all the way there and back? No way. I'm gonna snuggle in with a book." Franca, whose down-town condominium is only a five blocks from here, is not the outdoors type.

I stand and pull my coat from a hook. "Okay, I'm off."

"Jeez, Liz, Hugh's coming over here."

I turn. He is working his way slowly, visibly tipsy, stepping carefully. He shrugs into his cape-like coat as he gains our table.

"I came to collect my scalp."

"Yeah, it's a tough one." That sounds positively intel-ligent. What am I expected to say, jam it up your nose? But his cordiality is disarming, and I cannot understand why he seems so calm when I have been accusing him all day of being a moral deviant.

"I'm Franca Crabtree." She thrusts out a hand. "Maybe you remember me from that armed robbery at the Wallingford Seven-Eleven."

"Of course I do." A smile wide enough to show teeth.

"Hey, how about one for the road?" She indicates a chair. I am standing directly behind her and nudge her in the back: Franca, do not fraternize with the enemy. Wine has made her overly playful.

He glances down at her in an abstracted way, then turns the high-beams on me. "If anyone would like a lift, I have four-wheel-drive and chains."

"I'm just a downhill slide away," Franca says. "But,

really, stay for a drink."

"No, thanks, I'm well beyond my limit. Elizabeth?"

I find myself thinking: if he is going home to Ballard, a minor detour takes me to Canlis. But a poorly functioning part of my brain is at work. A keener sense warns: you are half in the bag.

"Thanks, but I need the fresh air."

He frowns at me. "Where the *hell* did you come from, anyway?"

"Place called Coalsack, Idaho."

"Coalsack. Jesus."

I am still standing, holding my coat. He is blocking my way. I lose focus on his eyes, see double. "Where did *you* come from?"

"Lackland, Texas, Air Force Base."

My eyes remain locked in blurred grip with his. I feel confused by what I see in them: dejection, yes, but yet a glint of humor, reinforced by that smile. It is as if he is sharing something, an understanding that the two of us are playing our parts too well in this tragic drama.

And there is another quality I see in his eyes, a mystery I cannot decipher.

"Who are you?" I ask, though I am not certain what I mean by the question. "Who the hell are you?"

His answer is as enigmatic as my inquiry. "Dark forces, Elizabeth. Dark forces." And he bows in proper Pastor Krueger style and turns and makes his way to the door without a glance behind.

"Dark forces?" says Franca.

I share her confusion and shrug, and I make one last half-hearted try. "You're not coming?"

"And get back how? On my high heels in ten-foot drifts? Hey, listen, Liz, I think this is one of those typically dumb, stubborn ideas of yours. It's not safe out there. I've seen you before when you've had too many. You get stupid, you go into a fucking altered state . . ."

I am on my way to the door. Pausing there, I turn to blow her a kiss.

But as I step outside my mind is on dark forces. Was he speaking of himself? Perhaps not – Johann's courtroom speech comes back: *Dark forces are tugging at her spirit, my friends, seducing her from the righteous path.*

I look around. Hugh and his car are not in view, nor are any pedestrians. The snow has suddenly started to melt and it has turned heavy and wet. I scoop up a handful and place it on my tongue. Not much protein. Who said that? What's-his-name, that Inspector Clouseau fellow, Nathaniel Duff. I smile at the way he nearly choked trying to compliment me.

I proceed out onto the street, where tires have beaten slippery pathways. Though in boots, I must hike up my dress so it will not get wet. I skid here and there, but the way is not that difficult through the downtown, and heavy vehicles are making it through.

Managing to retain Franca's stern advice about safety, I politely decline two offers from male drivers. Now comes a plow truck behind me, creating a wide path; the walking will be easier. It slows upon approaching me.

"Give you a lift anywhere, lady?" Bodybuilder, broad chest and shoulders. Lascivious grin.

"No, I'm a block from home."

He looks me up and down: the mascara, the bright lipstick, the sheer hose below the lifted hem. "Nice girls don't go out alone on nights like this. You a nice girl?"

"Screw off."

His face sets and he pulls away.

That incident apart, by the time I complete a traverse of the business district, I feel refreshed and sobered by the crisp air, which is now several degrees above melting point. A warm Pacific front must have shouldered its way in. Am I even a third of the way? I pause in my tracks. What if this party has been canceled? I have not been using my alcohol-addled head.

When I connect with Canlis on my phone, I am relieved to hear boisterous voices in the background. Mattie is summoned and tells me at least two dozen showed up and others are still arriving. Dinner has been delayed.

"Is Junior there?"

"In the flesh."

"I'm on my way."

But as I press forward, suddenly I hear that old, ominous tinkling of bells, and I am beset with the sense of a presence lurking near. When I look behind I see nothing but snow and shadows and distant oncoming headlights. Why are my invisible specters again making visitations? Maybe that trucker ruffled me more than I thought.

I am tempted to give up this expedition, return, seek sensible refuge in my warm loft. Think clearly, Liz — attacks by strangers are rare media events. I shall not succumb to my illogical fears, and as if in defiance of them I form up a snowball and toss it at the nearest street sign. I am bold, I am fearless. I have been on a ride through hell this week and I will not let it subvert my sanity.

The drinks have not only muddled the brain but filled the bladder, and I search for a facility that is open. But a gas station is closed, and so is an eating place at the next corner, and yet another. But forested Denny Park offers privacy; as I set out for it, a truck's headlights catch me tromping into the deep snow.

I find refuge behind the spreading skirts of a fir tree and wait for the truck to pass, but it stops on Denny Way and idles. I am frozen by the sound of the door slamming shut and male grunts of exertion. Someone is plowing through the deep snow toward me, and I realize with increasing horror that my premonition should have been heeded: I am in physical danger.

In growing panic, I attempt to run but the snow is thick as paste. I whip off my heavy gloves and dive into my bag, foggily trying to remember if I brought the pepper spray. My hand emerges with only the phone.

As I make my way around the fir tree, I see the idling truck: two-ton plow and dumper, the one that stopped for me, the leering muscleman. I glance behind — he is gaining on me. *You a nice girl?*

By now I have dialed 911. "Assault in progress!" I shout. "Denny and Ninth! Denny Park! Two-ton plow truck!"

The man flings himself toward me. "This is what you really want, isn't it, you little bitch."

Leaping, he catches me by the ankle and I topple into the thick snow. He scrambles up, and I trip him in turn, and fling the phone.

"Fuckin' whore, I'm gonna get mine."

I am on my hands and knees as he lands on my back, pressing me into the snow; he is grunting, I hear his fly unzip, and now he is tearing at my dress.

From my phone, a distant, muffled voice: "*Hello? Please state your name.*"

"Shit!" He sits up, seeking the source of this voice. I don't move.

"*Please give precise location. Hello. Hello. Are you there?*"

He quickly rises, wades into a snowdrift, searching for the phone.

When he is five feet away, I am in motion again, my skirt hiked up, leaping like a jackrabbit toward the street. No oncoming cars.

I glance behind — he is pursuing me again. But by now I have reached the traveled lanes of the street, and make swift progress toward his truck, its cab and plow blades facing me, lights off, but the engine still idling. As I reach it, my feet slide out from under me, and I clamber up just as he gains the street.

Lock the doors. Too many gears in this rig. Emergency, where's the release? This is it. Fear's adrenaline has made me sober. I am driving this machine.

Its regular operator is in my way, standing on the street, waving frantically. I find a higher gear and accelerate toward him.

He dives to the side and I roar past him.

I turn south, find my way to Third Avenue, and go straight to the Public Safety Building.

22 | Saturday . . .

I awake to the sensation of bright light outside, disorienting sunshine, and sense a fleeting, powerful nightmare – I do not want to remember it. For a moment I am confused about the recent past, one of my bouts of temporary amnesia.

Orient. I am in my bed in the Washington Shoe Building. It is Saturday. I am in the middle of the trial of my life. I had too much to drink last night . . . I was assaulted, nearly raped.

The night floods back: the attack, my escape, my flight to SPD headquarters, the long, testing interviews.

My trauma was added to by embarrassment. Though I was applauded for my brave escape, Detective Ellen Oversmith looked at me queerly when I admitted to embarking on a two-mile trek to Canlis Restaurant. I think: how insane was that? I was impaired by my own foolish stubbornness as much as by alcohol, refusing to heed Franca's admonitions. Censor that. Don't blame yourself.

My assailant hightailed his way by foot, and had not been apprehended by the time I was driven home. In panic, he had thrown away the phone he had worked so hard to retrieve; it has his fingerprints. The 911 center recorded a snarling voice: "This is what you really want, isn't it, you little bitch."

I sit up to look out the window and am momentarily blinded by sun reflecting off melting snow on Occidental Walkway. Icicles hang from my window frames. People are on the street; the shops are coming to life; Seattle bounces back for the final week of Christmas trade.

Those were not jingle bells I heard last night. What is the point of possessing such power of intuition if one does not heed it? But again, I am blaming myself.

I shudder as an image returns of that brawny trucker leaping at me like a jungle carnivore. A close call, but relief is mingled with anger. Thankfully I vented much of it last night, at the police station, at home where I dragged Nick from bed, shocked him awake with my tale.

Now it will be difficult to put my mind back in gear for my trial. Yet I must stow this event in a back compartment, locked away. I must confront the fears that feed paranoia.

It is ten o'clock. I don my robe and rise, tracking the scent of fresh-brewed coffee. Franca is with Nick in the kitchen – I had called her last night, but told her not to come until the morning.

"They get him yet?" I ask.

"I don't know," says Franca. "When they do, I'm going to shoot his balls off."

"Did you sleep well, princess?" Nick hugs me and smoothes my hair, stands back to admire me. "Hail Elizabeth, queen of the truck drivers, my lionhearted little Lizzie. Henceforth, I will not complain about washing your coffee cups every morning; I am *proud* to wash them."

He pours one for me as I phone Ellen Oversmith. While I wait for her to connect, I silently question myself. My personal security checks had failed me. Alcohol-impaired, weaving down the street, gilded with lipstick and mascara, I was an open target. *Never* blame yourself, I kept telling my audiences; it is the basest thing you can do to yourself. Strangers don't rape, friends do: how pretentious I must have sounded as I tossed off *that* smug formula.

I feel tense; maybe it is my hangover, maybe my fury.

Finally, Ellen comes on. "Perpetrator is one Mark Branco, who is known to us as a result of past violent acts. He drives for Olympus Sand and Gravel; the city brings in contractors to help the emergency crews. At first, he claimed he had mistaken you for a prostitute."

"That was his *defense?*"

"He declined to co-operate further after we played the recording of his voice. He is in the bag. Attempted rape."

"My name hasn't been released, I hope."

"You're Ms. X on the report sheets, as you asked. But we can't keep the public in the dark for long, Liz."

"After my trial is over."

It may be a short one. This weekend, Mavis Luckwell will decide whether to curtail my cross-examination of Hugh; if she rules I am merely stirring up irrelevant mud, then I have overreached, lost my wild gamble. My career, my fortunes, are in the hands of a woman I have offended.

Last night returns and my body shakes. Damn all rapists to hell.

You, too, Vandergraaf. I will find a way to bring you to ruin.

For the remainder of the morning, I concentrate as best I can, reading evidence transcripts I have brought home, planning my continuing cross-examination of Vandergraaf. I phone Mattie, then J.J. They greet my harrowing tale with shock first, then relief. I urge them to tell no one else of last night's near-atrocity. After lunch, I set out for the office.

The halls of J.J. Plum and Company echo hollowly on this Saturday afternoon, but a few coats are hanging in the vestibule. Mattie Crooks is here, and tries to distract me by recounting a lesser abomination that occurred last night. "A disaster. We all sat around and got totally polluted wondering if we were ever going to get home. I never even got groped, it was so bad."

"And Junior? Did he dare show his face?"

"He dropped by to fill it; a hurricane wouldn't keep the scrooge from a hundred–a–plate dinner already paid for."

"How did he look?"

"Really scared and nervous, and then he got all morose and drunk and telling everyone he admires Liz Finnegan like no other, but he had to do the right thing." She imitates his false laugh: "*Heh-heh.*"

I can imagine the bluster. Everyone in the office is on my side, Maggie tells me. The split between father and son has caused a buzz.

"There's a bunch of phone messages from yesterday. Nothing that can't wait till Monday. Your mom."

She will be put out that I have taken so long to call her. This evening, when she is comfortable, sitting down.

"Beatrice Struthers a couple of times. Amy Krueger."

"And what did *she* want?"

"Wouldn't say. To talk to you. She sounded strained. Oh, and Bill Christiansen fifteen minutes ago. J.J. is waiting for you in the library. He doesn't look too happy."

Heavy casebooks are spread on the table before him, and he is jotting notes. Volumes of my trial transcripts sit nearby. He rises, grasps both my hands, and tentatively kisses me on the forehead. "You are one lucky lady. Tough in the clinch; I'm proud of you."

"What are you up to in here, J.J.?"

"Just exploring a few possibilities. See if we can come at Mavis from another angle."

His smile is tense; he has something urgent to say but cannot push it out. I assume the worst. "Please tell me if you have bad news. I can take it."

"She's cutting you off, Liz."

This is the final ghastly fillip to the worst twenty-four hours of my life. I sag into a chair. I listen numbly.

Mavis Luckwell called an hour ago with this ruling:

"'The Defendant's cross-examination relating to non-violent sexual acts falls short of being probative of a propensity on the part of the Plaintiff to engage in them. The Defendant unwisely risks escalated damages as a result of the opprobrious nature of her attack.'"

"My *attack*?" I am astounded at her harsh choice of words. She has gone overboard.

"There's worse. Helen Mazur's evidence will not be admitted. 'The evidentiary foundation is not in place with regard to an event of insufficient nexus to the crime alleged against the Plaintiff.'"

This is the end; I cannot win if I am gagged and the jury is denied access to Helen Mazur. "She won't hear further argument?"

"She said no. She was as cranky as an old dog with fleas, and wasn't in the mood to chat even about the quirky weather we're having. I didn't tell her what happened to you, Liz. I don't know why you're so insistent about that."

"I don't want the jury to know I was nearly raped. It would seem like a cheap appeal to sympathy."

"Nonsense. It's a fact."

"It doesn't feel right. I won't pander. Also, they took a blood sample; my reading was point-one-three. Do I want them knowing I was drunkenly wandering around in a snowstorm? They'll think: if she was dejected, if she's lost faith in her case, why should we maintain any?"

J.J. ponders this. "We still have to tell Mavis. You'll need a continuance of several days."

"No."

"Liz, the jolt of such an episode will stick a bit, emotionally. You need a few days off. You can't drive yourself on spunk alone."

"I will be in court on Monday." I must call Beatrice to tell her she will be taking the stand in the morning.

"I'll take the blame for this." J.J.'s pretended good

spirits have failed him. He sits and stares lugubriously at his hands. "It was a mistake bringing Juanita Calvo into court; I reckon that somehow got Mavis's dander up. Too close to the judicial bone, alleging liaisons with bailiffs. I thought I knew Mavis."

"Just how close were you two?"

"Well, we shared a long trial or two." More than that, I suspect.

"It wasn't your doing, J.J. The judge reacted like a person scorned." I tell him my theory: she knew we were a breath away from a settlement that got me off the financial hook – I have no doubt word of it was leaked to her. She was infuriated not at my cross-examination but my rebuff to an agreement costing me nothing but pride.

"Well, maybe that's so, Liz, and maybe she wants to back you against the wall, force you to take their terms of surrender. But, hell, I don't know if that deal is still open."

"The one where I apologize." My throat tightens at the thought. But I feel my anger, too. Branco, Vandergraaf, they are kin, the same aberration.

I cross the room to the phone. I dial Bill Christiansen at his home.

His mood is upbeat. "Off to take the kids sledding, so I'm glad you called back so promptly. Liz, I'll be blunt. I told Hugh: take no prisoners, Mavis may even find a subtle way to hint to the jury that damages should reflect – how did she put it? – 'the continued gross impugning of Plaintiff's character.' My view is we should go full steam ahead after your client. She has a history of lying, Liz, and I can produce someone from Baptist Social Services where she was fired for theft."

"That's a bluff, Bill. You're too shrewd to affront the jury with something so picayune."

He takes a while to digest the unappetizing fact that I am still defiant. "Liz, you haven't a snowball's chance."

"Maybe not in Mavis's court. But I'll win a new trial

on appeal. Guaranteed if she *dares* comment to the jury on the evidence."

"Stalwart in defeat. I told Hugh his character has been so damaged he has nothing to lose by continuing; his name could be salvaged by a handsome verdict. But this is the good news: as lunatic as it sounds, he wants to me reiterate our last offer. We must ask, under the circumstances, that your apology be stated in firmer tones than we originally proposed."

"I'll get back to you, Bill."

After I hang up, J.J. asks if the offer holds.

"If I crawl."

The long angles of late-afternoon sunlight reflect yellow and harsh from the glass facings of the city's towers. A cold breeze from the ocean ruffles my hair as I huddle into my parka. I am strolling deep in thought along streets thronged with shoppers; I am hidden in this mass of humanity, anonymous, without particular destination. In part, I am putting myself through a test: I must quickly conquer a fear of walking alone in the city.

The sidewalks have been swept bare of the melting snow, but rushing streams fill the gutters. People swim past my eyes, hurrying from shop to shop, smiling, bantering, on a high of seasonal joy. At a department-store window I pause among a crowd of noisy children to watch elves cavort around Rudolph and his blinking nose. At another window, Father Time, his scythe in motion, clicking off the seconds of these last disastrous days of the millennium.

I know I must concentrate on the decision I must make, but the horror of last night regularly visits my thoughts. I do not block memory of that leaping monster tearing at my dress; I stare hard at it. It seems the best therapy.

I board a train at the Pine Street monorail station and am silently swept off to Seattle Center, and there I alight to wander through the old exposition grounds, the amusement park at the foot of the Space Needle, that towering symbol of the city I had grown to love and now feel trapped within. Elizabeth Finnegan will find no escape here from the sneers and sniggers. If I could simply board a train or plane to nowhere I would do so, find some hidden corner of America where crow will not be on every menu.

Here at the rim of the Expo site is the Opera House, where Maxine Vradjik and I entertained at intermission, a burlesque, a light farce, an event made trivial by the despair of impending shame which I will soon wear like a coat of nails.

The Opera House fiasco was at the beginning, after I had met Beatrice, as I was eagerly putting into motion the chain of events that would lead to this hopeless end. So presumptuous was I, so brimming with noble purpose, so heedless of consequence.

Despite my brave talk to Bill, I have little hope of winning in appeals court; when in doubt, judges will side with an otherwise respected brother, and Vandergraaf has many friends up there.

But I must pull myself together.

Twilight has arrived and only the great bulbous platform of the Space Needle remains in sunlight. At home, friends wait anxiously for me. I must phone Beatrice, though I am not sure what to say to her. If I give up, how will I summon the strength to look upon her face, to see the sorrow she would feel for me? If I call her to the stand, Bill will attack with cutting finesse. Why should she suffer such a distressing experience when a simple signature from me would write a finish to the whole calamity?

Surely, Bill bluffs with his threat to trot out that old theft from Baptist Social Services. I still find it odd that

Beatrice had been so embarrassed over it, so reluctant to speak of her youthful error.

I must also call Mother: having struggled almost to the end of this day and taken some deep breaths of fresh air, I now feel a compelling need to connect with her.

I turn south to the waterfront, and watch the sun die briskly behind the Olympic Peninsula. Alaskan Way is a ceaseless flow of home-going traffic, the shopping day over. I pause by the rail and look out over the frigid waters of the sound, a tugboat hauling a barge of wood chips, an incoming trawler, gulls wheeling and screaming above it.

Below, my wobbly reflection talks to me: you surely are not going to cave in, are you? I think of the brute who tried so callously, violently, to use my body, and I decide I have no reasonable doubt about what I must do. A person must live with herself. I turn and increase my pace to home.

Nick has bought a coho at the Pike Place Market and is stirring a marinade. He masks his relief at my late return with a brusque manner. "We'll be eating early, dear heart, and then I'm tucking you into bed. Ten minutes more and everything would have been in veritable ruins. And now we have to *stretch*. A calm dinner for two has become a raucous affair for three. Ms. Crabtree awaits within."

I find Franca in Nick's studio staring at a work-in-progress, a new phase, less abstract, almost representational: a young woman on her knees in a field of flowers. She is holding a cross, her head uplifted, the wind tossing her hair wildly.

"That's me. Praying."

"Jeez, Liz, she does look vaguely like you, except for the long hair and a bit of plump."

For some reason, the painting disconcerts me, an unsettling, almost physical sensation.

"What's up?" I ask. "You're smiling."

"I just had a very interesting chat with that Mountie you met, Nat Duff. He called from a pay phone down the street, and I met him for a beer."

"Did he find Thalia Pfeiffer?"

"No, but –"

"Not much else matters, does it?"

"Yeah, it does."

"Bear with me for a moment." I lead her to the living room, where I dial Mother's home in Coalsack. Jake Bjorklund answers.

I express myself with fake cheer. "Hi there, Jake, it's the daughter of Charlene. So what happened to Nipigon? What's the bad news?"

"Well, looks like some damn fool fouled up the assays. 'Fraid we took a bit of a rubbing there. Forty grand."

I am too preoccupied by other concerns to critique his investment skills. It could have been worse. "Take it out of my share. Nothing from Mother."

"Real sorry about that, Liz, but I'm gonna make it up to you tenfold and more, you wait. I can't count the irons I got in the fire. You caught me outside as I'm grilling some heifers. I'll just pause with my duties here and take the phone in to your mom."

"No, Jake, just tell her I'm fine, absolutely fine. Stay out there with your steaks. She can call me after dinner. Give her my love."

I return to Franca. "Okay, Sergeant Duff."

"He called, I said you were out, and we had a real cozy conversation across the street at the Brewing Company."

I am glad I was not present. This awkward, gentle police officer would have read my dismay at how my trial has collapsed around me.

"The narcs have been on a rampage ever since Pfeiffer skipped town. Apparently they ran a check on a certain bail-bond firm on Yesler. Seems someone came in and plunked down fifty thousand in cold cash, which was strange. Why go through a bond office? You listening, Liz?"

"Sure." I have an image of Sergeant Duff earnestly explaining this, his angular smile.

"The person who put up all that cash was a lawyer by the name of Susan Marks. Ring a bell?"

"I'm not sure."

"Think, Liz. She was one of Hugh's character witnesses."

Susan Marks comes back to me: Vandergraaf's buxom booster, his campaign manager last year. "What does all of that mean?"

"Shake the cobwebs, Liz. Do you think the Colombian mafia would hire *her?* Someone else put up the dough, someone who knew your key witness was under arrest here in Seattle. There's been this whole conduit thing happening between Drug Enforcement and the county prosecutor's office, and I'll bet the boys uptown were desperate to get Pfeiffer *out* of town."

"Who gave her the fifty thousand?"

"She's not talking. Attorney-client privilege, et cetera, so there's no way really to trace this to Hugh Vandergraaf. But she's real scared, Liz. This was a stupid thing for her to do."

A flickering light at the end of the tunnel? "Where's Nat Duff now?"

"I'm meeting him for drinks tonight. He's kind of cute, don't you think? *So* Canadian. I like the shy ones. He's pretty non-threatening for a cop."

A date . . . I guess he has given up on me. If I were in normal spirits, I would be able to laugh at this.

Franca quickly changes the subject: "Bill Christiansen has redrafted the settlement, sent this over."

She hands me a manila envelope, my groveling *mea culpa*.

"He called to make sure it arrived. When I told him about Susan Marks putting up Pfeiffer's bail, he got downright anxious, and begged me to believe Vandergraaf had nothing to do with it. He'll try to talk to Hugh about it – the predator is on a fucking sailing trip; he keeps his boat up at some marina on Whidbey Island."

Nick enters. "Mesdames, dinner is served."

The salmon having been consumed, compliments having been passed about the meal, and permission denied to help with the dishes, I am dispatched to my bedroom. I sit in brooding silence, staring outside at the twinkling Christmas lights, still hearing the echoes of stunned silence after I told Mother about the attempted rape.

"Why didn't you *call?*"

"I didn't want you to come rushing out." She would have sped recklessly to Spokane for a late flight. I want her to come tomorrow, though; I need motherly affection. She will catch a noon flight. Franca will pick her up.

From the hallway comes a murmured conversation of departure: Franca leaving, off on her date with the Mountie. More cheerless news for me; I rather liked him. Now the soft hiss of the shower, then Nick's feet padding past my door to his room.

I change into pajamas and I try to sleep, but cannot. My rag dolls sit on their shelf staring down at me with solemn inquiry.

Hours pass, and as my mind processes the trauma of twenty-four hours ago, I feel somewhat restored. Attacks by strangers are less personal, more random, easier to work through: this is a mantra I have recited many times, and I sense its truth. Beatrice's tragedy was greater, indelible: she had been infatuated with her assailant and the assault must have damaged her in ways I can barely comprehend: the betrayal of trust, the years of self-doubt and hurt and confusion.

Outside, the city slowly stills; moonlight and shadow play on the deserted streets below. A distant wail of siren, rap music from a passing car, laughter from a strolling couple, and then just the inner sound of my beating heart.

I have lost this trial.

I had expected to keep my stubborn pride intact, but now with expectancy of imminent failure, it lies about me in a thousand broken pieces. And suddenly I am afflicted not only by a feeling of dejection but by that old sense of not knowing who I am, of being ungrounded, lacking connection. Who are you, Elizabeth Finnegan?

It comes to me that last night I had asked that same inscrutable question of Hugh Vandergraaf. Who the hell are you? Dark forces, he answered. What were we trying to convey to each other?

And what majestic irony springs from that tête-a-tête in McCormick's bar? Had I accepted his offer of a ride to Canlis I would not have been attacked by a stalking truck driver. I held no concern for my safety with Hugh, beyond doubts about his ability to drive. His offer, generous in the harsh circumstances, would have spared me from conflict with the dark forces he foretold. I am not sure what lesson to take from that.

Where had everything gone wrong with my crusade against this man? Was I simply damned from the start? Tunnel vision. J.J. was right: I was obsessed to the point of blindness with a compulsive drive to avenge Beatrice. I am like Johann Krueger, dogmatic, fanatic. And I was out of my league, trying to play with the big boys with all their power and connections and wiretaps.

And damn Thalia Pfeiffer with her "I'll say whatever you want."

Still, Hugh's teammates had pulled off an extravagant

and risky venture in helping Thalia disappear. If they were convinced he had not attacked Beatrice, why would they take such a chance? Were they afraid that Bill, with all his facility, might not sufficiently damage her credibility? Perhaps. Thalia *had* told me her story with little prompting, and it accorded well with Bea's.

Not placing her under subpoena was a monstrous miscalculation. So many errors. But why am I trying so vigorously to convince myself I have blundered into a hopeless dead end? I cannot simply give up.

Amy Krueger wants to speak to me. That could be important; I must return her call. Why did she beg off from giving testimony? She was clearly becoming distressed with her muted role, chafing under Johann's stern direction. Only once, at her home in Lynden, she rebelled: "Do the right thing," she told him. "This time, do it."

This time . . . Do they share some sinful secret? Or was that exhortation spurred by her shame at their heartless treatment of their daughter? She sounded strained, Mattie told me. . . .

That sterile Baptist hospice . . . then that long banishment to the town of Okanogan, six and a half months during which they did not visit her. Johann thought they "might do better apart for a period." Was that the real reason?

My mind is crowded, moving in circles; I am too alert – I should not have had two cups of coffee at dinner. My clock is ticking off to midnight: another week begins.

Unaccountably, my thoughts jump to that strange painting by Nick, the woman praying on the grass. I am troubled by it, and do not know why I want it to speak to me . . .

I sense a pulling need to hear its voice. I climb from bed and walk in slippered feet to Nick's studio, where I am surrounded by the dim and busy shapes he has created. Abstract beings in motion, all but one: the praying woman.

I flick on a light so I may closely examine the painting. The woman wears a filmy gown draped across a small rounded belly. From where within the maze of the creative mind came this vision?

As I peer more closely at her face – unfinished, lacking detail – I realize she is young, maybe in her teens. But somehow familiar.

"Do I know you?" I say softly.

"I think it's Beatrice," says Nick, and I turn and see him in his pajamas at the doorway. "I couldn't sleep either."

"Beatrice?" The resemblance comes clear, as if replicated from old photographs. Nick had seen the one in the student newspaper; she had long hair then, as here. He has captured her innocence, her devoutness. "So strange. Why, Nick?"

"I don't know, pet. Maybe it's a statement. We are seeking answers from above while the truth lies within us. Maybe it's Beatrice or maybe it's just a girl praying uselessly to the wind. Are you feeling all right, princess?"

"Yes. Exhausted, though." I cannot stop gaping at this strange portrait. "The truth lies within us. . . . What truth is that, Nicholson?"

"The living truth, princess, that lies within the womb, not the soul."

"Within the womb . . ." The concept stuns me. My mouth drops.

"What's wrong, pet? Why are you looking so astonished? It's just a painting."

I again study the canvas, her swollen belly. My mind whirls back to last week, to the day I was preparing Beatrice for the witness stand. I asked if she had told me everything. "No, not everything," she said. When pressed, she was inexplicably troubled, and finally admitted to a minor misdeed. Was that just an escape hatch? I accepted it, and did not probe further. Should I have seen a more agonizing truth hidden behind the rose of her blush?

Count the months. From March 27, 1971, to her return to the hospice, nine plus two weeks. Nine months! Nine! My God.

Did Hugh Vandergraaf impregnate Beatrice? If so, he has brazenly lied on the witness stand. And if such falsehood can be proved, his credibility will be damaged beyond repair, his case will shatter like glass. I am suddenly dizzy with the impact of this profound notion, and I stagger. Nick secures me, holds me upright.

"Princess, you've been under stress. I think it's back to bed with you."

He lifts me into his sinewy arms and carries me to my room and lays me gently on the bed, where I clutch his hand with both of mine, unable to stop shaking.

I try to persuade myself I have made a mistake. Why in the name of the God she loves would Beatrice have kept such a secret from me?

Waves chop and swirl, explode in foaming spray as the Wandering I *bucks and shifts and fights the tide, close-hauled to the ceaseless wind of Juan de Fuca. The shores of Canada grow closer. . . .*

It must be nearing nine o'clock, but the miserly winter sun gives no more warmth than my morning snort of malt-laced coffee. I am no longer alone with you and my scattered thoughts. In the certain knowledge that misery loves company, several smirking dolphins, barely able to hide their contempt, dance about the bow, confidently leading the way, too sure of my destination.

And so before time runs out, before whiskey further dulls the brain, I must conclude this rambling peroration. Let me put the case for my angry, confused young client in terms that might yet wring a grudging tear from your eyes. Young Hugh stands before you bowed, repentant, a callow youth of twenty-two. Shall I say he comes from a good family, or would you prefer to hear he bears the scars of a broken home? Which works best? No juvenile record. Indeed, an unspotted past, if one ignores the petty deeds of youth: the six-pack filched from his dad's garage, a joyride in his Jeep, trespasses quickly paid for by a few swipes of a belt and forgotten – or remembered with a smile of pride. That's my boy. . . .

You squirm impatiently. You've heard it all before, the standard text, the usual forensic whitewash. I hear you bark at me: get to the point, counsel. How do you defend the crimes of which your client stands indicted? Count one, the rape of Beatrice Krueger. Count two, Helen Mazur. Youthful excess, do you say? Boys will be boys – is that all you can come up with?

Do you think I have not tried to understand? I have sought answers everywhere to who this young man was, what pressures stained and twisted him. I have read, I have studied, I know the jargon. Inability to cope with frustration, lack of impulse control, an unconscious need to fulfill the role of dominant male foisted on him by inescapable tradition. Overcontrolled in childhood, insecure about his masculinity, a life of living a father's lies, of feeling motherless, abandoned. A mind and soul warped by the death of one too dearly loved: Jerome, whose violent end sent young Hugh lashing out in blind insensate anger at the world. . . .

An intrusive memory has been badgering me of late. I am screaming at my mother, furious, beyond reason, blaming her, hating her. . . . She had loved him more than me. Yet she had sent him to his death. "We have had soldiers in our family since the Civil War," she told him. She had done the enlisting; Jerome, who shared my antipathy for Father, had no ear for his career advice. Ah, but Mother . . . how she loved Jerome; and how guilty he felt about that, returning a love diluted with pity and shame at her alcoholic serfdom to Father. Jerome would do anything for her. And did. And paid.

I suppose I have suppressed Mother in my mind for many years — she would occasionally pop by as an afterthought (am not I, too, the second son, an unintended afterthought?), but her flickering image has become more frequent in the last few days of stressful trial. I try, I try, but cannot blot her out.

She never spoke to me after I refused to enlist, to pick up Jerome's dropped sword. . . .

What force is ordering me to about-face and confront the past? Why does a mother's visage so bedevil me?

But I see you are glancing at the clock, impatient, fretful. You are weary of my insipid struggle for insight. How much more must you listen to before you march the monster to his cell and blithely throw away the keys?

In the end, these are just words in the wind, aren't they? Inane excuses, puerile empty pleas. I crave only your understanding, not forgiveness (how impossible for you), and perhaps just the slightest twinge of sympathy. I pray your memories of me may never be so foul and rank that you cannot abide the taste of them.

Who are you? you asked, *looking at me with all that hazy intensity.* Who the hell are you?

How did I take that question? Rhetorically? Socratically? As an exordium to philosophic discourse? Neither of us knew the answer would be so unadorned and simple, or that it would come with the blunt force of a battering ram.

But now the wind softens. I must let out the sails and pour another potion for my pain. Soon will come peace. . . .

23 | Sunday . . .

On yet another December Sunday, I am wending my way on a country road toward Lynden, this time with Mattie Crooks in her Honda. It is a gray morning; thick drizzling clouds have rolled in from the ocean, washing away the murky snow that mottles field and meadow.

I slept poorly last night, perhaps two or three dream-haunted hours. Nick awoke me as I was calling out. Don't lie to me, I cried, don't lie to me. Whom was I entreating?

The numbing hunch that came last night, was it only the product of a weary mind in too much turmoil? I cannot shake it free; it clings like a burr. I had often felt a vague but inexplicable uneasiness in my encounters with the Krueger family, perhaps missing the clues that were in Beatrice's eyes, in the shame and guilt her parents tried to hide from me.

But what would have stopped Beatrice's lips? We had shared such closeness, surely she had loosened those fundamentalist bonds of shame. After Vandergraaf's testimony, his false denial of coitus, could she not have known she held the secret that would salvage victory for both of us?

Or was there no birth at all, but an earlier miscarriage, or even — a possibility weighted with cruel irony — a medical abortion? Or a backroom job, some rheumy-eyed whiskey-breathing wretch with a bent coat hanger? Is that the unendurable secret that the Kruegers share? If Johann arranged it, he has much to say to God in the privacy of his prayers.

And maybe that is why Beatrice cannot speak of it. How could she live with that, the taking of fetal life? And if it did occur, one should not wonder at the gravity of her breakdown and the long extent of recovery.

But it is Amy Krueger with whom I must speak first. I must gird myself for Beatrice; I will be better able to confront her with my brooding suspicions if they are confirmed.

As we approach the town, we are greeted by the chime of bells and then, from a side street, a carol, voices raised in celebration of the birth of Christ, of the virgin mother and her child. . . .

And now we are proceeding down the main street of this pretty postcard town with its manicured winter lawns and gardens, its tidy dust-free homes adorned with Christmas lights. Not many people are about the streets, but few here do not attend one church or other: Dutch Reformed mostly, though many Baptists, too, as appears from the number of cars outside the True Gospel Chapel.

We squeeze in between a pickup and a van, and Mattie turns off the engine, and we sit for a moment in silence as I gather strength for this encounter.

"Coming in?"

"Are you kidding?" Mattie says. "I'd cause a riot."

Possibly. With her nose rings, her saucy scornful bralessness, her Nelson Mandela T-shirt. For my part, I am as neatly attired as any churchgoer.

As I approach the steps to the church door, I can hear from within – and almost feel – the vibrating voice of Johann Krueger, purging his flock of their sins.

I enter to the sound of his foghorn: "Look not thou upon the wine when it is red; it biteth like the serpent, and stingeth like an adder. And therefore the Apostle Peter commands us thus: be sober, be vigilant." At least a dozen heads turn my way, but, probably because I am silhouetted in the light, Johann does not seem to make me out. "Be vigilant, because your adversary, the devil, as a roaring lion walketh about, seeking whom he may . . . devour."

He falters now, watching me slide into an empty pew at the back. He sends a quick glance to Amy, who is standing front and center in the chancel, among the choir. On seeing me, she puts her hand to her mouth.

Johann seems to lose direction, has trouble picking up the thread of his entreaty to shun the allurements of Satan in his many guises. He seems fixed on his allegorical savage beasts: "There is a lion in the way! A lion is in the streets, my friends!"

And he finally peters out and riffles through his hymnbook, then announces a selection. An organ pumps and whines. The choir starts off awkwardly, in ragged harmony, Amy staring at me now, not singing.

Her body wavers, and she suddenly looks faint, but recovers, stands erect, raises her eyes to the vaulted ceiling, then closes them as if in prayer. Without a look at Johann, she walks quickly out a side door.

Some seventy singing heads of women, men, and children turn from her to me as I rise and step outside.

Amy is at a rear door, near a walkway. She beckons me in: it is the church kitchen, and the counters are laden with cakes and pies.

"Good morning, Elizabeth. I had to slip out to help with the bake sale."

She fidgets anxiously at trays of cookies and cakes, tends to a coffee urn. I help her lay out cups and saucers, put a kettle on the stove for tea. We work at these tasks for a few minutes without speaking, listening to the muffled sounds of song.

I touch her arm; she flinches.

"You have something to tell me, don't you, Amy?"

She turns to me with a weary sigh and nods, and I know now she holds the key that solves all riddles, a key to a past she has tried to lock away.

She speaks hesitantly. "Judge Vandergraaf . . . he said in court that he did not have relations with Beatrice?"

"Yes."

"I wasn't sure. Johann won't talk about the trial. He has cut himself off from it. No newspapers or radio . . . but I spoke with someone who heard."

"Beatrice became pregnant, didn't she?"

She nods again and lowers her head. Her tiny body shudders. We sit on facing wooden chairs. I wait for her to pull herself together, and she finally begins to speak in a tight, nervous voice.

"It wasn't until July that we realized. She was so thin, but the signs were there. No one talked about it, and I don't think the nurse was aware."

That seems not at all unlikely. Ms. Ewanschuk had complained that Beatrice resisted whenever she tried to examine her.

"For a long time, I think, Beatrice refused to accept the fact that she was with child. We . . . didn't know what to do. Johann still couldn't be persuaded she was violated, that she hadn't lied to us. He saw only the embarrassment and scandal that would come to her. And to us – I must be honest about that. And Beatrice was removed to the country. The people she stayed with, the Wilsons, understood the need for discretion."

I listen rapt to this soft outpouring: a circumspect local doctor, a delivery in a clinic near Okanogan, and a baby girl had come wailing into the world. Arrangements were quickly made for adoption – Baptist Social Services had a long waiting list for children. The names of the chosen parents were never revealed; state law forbids such disclosure.

"A young couple in the area, that's all we know."

And Amy begins to weep, and I don't know how to comfort her, and we sit together in silence.

Where is the child born of Beatrice? A simple DNA test would prove paternity, that he lied about the rape. Yes, Hugh, somewhere your progeny walks this earth, clear, living evidence of your guilt.

*She was far too nice a girl. . . . Conditions weren't right
. . . .* You perjured yourself, Judge Vandergraaf. You raped
Bea. You raped Helen.

But can that birth be proved? Baptist Social Services
. . . another sudden illumination: yes, yes, Beatrice and the
stolen files! Oh, Beatrice, I hope you did not destroy
those birth or adoption papers that you took away with
you. State adoption records are sealed from public view.
Could I get a court order for their release?

The hymn-singing has long since ceased; Johann has
been leading the congregation in prayer, and now his
voice stills. In a few moments he enters, quickly closing
the door behind him. His face is pinched, white, and he
is trembling, as much with anxiety, I suspect, as anger.

"Why are you upsetting my wife in the midst of my
service?" he says in a voice he strains to keep low. "Why
must you ask us to continue to wallow in every indeli-
cacy of your salacious trial? You are not welcome in this
house of the Lord. You defile it by your presence."

I rise, furious. "How do you *dare* speak to me in that
manner? *You* defile your church, you corrupt it with your
lies. Oh, yes, Johann, I know the truth, I know it now."

He advances on me, his voice still low, but barely
controlled. "Lies? You who have served as a courtesan to
the Antichrist speak to me of lies? I've told no lies!"

"You hypocrite!"

"*Hypocrite?* Because I tried to protect Beatrice from
the greater shame to which you now seek to expose her?
Is she less a sinner that a child was born of her act of
blind and careless vice?"

Amy abruptly rises, tears streaming, and her voice
has the force of a whip: "The shame is ours, Johann! She
was raped! Our daughter was raped! Oh, Johann, Johann,
for God's sake, open your heart to her!"

Johann seems frozen into place, staring at her, his
mouth open in a shocked oval. I do not know when the

door into the church opens behind us, but when I turn I see bewildered white faces.

Johann whirls, looks at them, at Amy, at me. His mouth moves; no words come out.

A silence falls upon us that is so thick and heavy I can barely breathe.

Then suddenly the kettle whistles, like a shriek of denunciation. Johann slaps his hands to his ears to dim the sound, and his face is twisted as if from unendurable pain he feels inside. He stumbles to the door and flees outside into the rain.

"Forgive him if you can't forgive me," Amy says.

"Why do I learn this only now? Why couldn't you tell me?"

"Beatrice made us promise . . . we were never to speak to you of it. She begged, Elizabeth, she begged."

I follow her outside, where Johann is kneeling on the rain-soaked lawn, shaking, weeping, praying. "Oh, almighty Lord, save this wretched sinner. Lead me to the rock, lead me to the rock."

Amy bends and comforts him.

Mattie encourages me with a smile as I get out of her car in front of the Struthers house in Madison Park. She will wait.

Through the porch window I see Beatrice stooping before a Christmas tree, smiling to herself in the soft twinkling glow of multicolored lights. From a box beside her she removes a large silver star and a winged angel. She studies them, twirling them, comparing.

When I rap on the glass, Beatrice starts, but smiles as she sees me. At the door she hugs me.

"Liz, where have you been all weekend?"

"Up and down, here and there." I do not want to upset her by telling her about Friday night.

I shuck my coat and join her in the living room, where a large box of decorations sits open by the bushy fir tree. From the workshop in the basement, a muted whine of an electric saw. Thomas with his tools.

"Which one, do you think, for the top?"

I tell her I prefer the star; it is simpler.

As she reaches up to fix it to the tree crown, I gather up long filaments of silvery icicles, and loosely hang them from the boughs.

"I must have tried to call you three or four times," she says, squatting beside me. "I'm having a few jitters. Stage fright. I also wanted to tell you again how proud of you I was. It's going well, isn't it? The trial."

I shake my head. "It has been a bumpy ride."

"Oh, I thought . . . then it will be up to me, won't it?"

"Yes. Entirely. The judge knocked both knees out from under me. But maybe now that's not too important."

"I'm afraid I just don't understand all the legal rigmarole."

I am not sure how to begin this, what to say. I stall. "How was the service this morning?"

"All Christmasy and earnest. Reverend Lucas *does* become tedious. I think I miss the fire and brimstone. Father literally used to scare the Jesus *into* us."

"He hasn't lost his touch. He was carrying on this morning about stinging adders and lions in the streets."

A frown. "He . . . I'm sorry, what do you mean?"

"I just returned from Lynden, Bea. I talked to them. Mostly to your mother."

I bite my lip, waiting, wanting it to come from her. She cannot seem to find words, but slowly reddens. Her hand is shaking.

I ask her softly, "Why didn't you tell me?"

"Oh, my . . . I'm feeling very flustered. I think I . . . would you like a sandwich?"

"Maybe later."

"Tea? Oh, of course, coffee, that's what you . . . I'll make a fresh pot."

She tries to rise, but I pull her by the wrist back to the carpet. "Stay right here, I'll make the tea." I squeeze her hand. "No more secrets, Bea."

As I reach the hall to the kitchen she calls to me in a trembling, breaking voice, "It's only because I love you so much."

I falter in mid-step. "What do you mean?"

"Elizabeth, how do I beg your forgiveness?"

"Simply by being honest with me."

"There's much more to forgive, Liz. My rejection of you. My abandonment."

I am puzzled, and my progress remains arrested in the hallway. "I don't recall anything like that. When?"

"Because I didn't fight for you. It was as if you were *their* baby, *their* mistake, they wanted rid of you. I loved you, but I hated the memory of how you were conceived."

I move forward, toward the kitchen, feeling disoriented, unable to comprehend what she has said, and then I stop, stumble, grab the counter for support, knees buckling, almost giving way.

Bea has followed me, and her face is streaked with tears. "I was dishonest with you only out of love. I wanted to shelter you from the trauma of discovering you were adopted."

The mind is numb, stunned, still unbelieving, as her quiet words of explanation and contrition float through the air, not quite sticking or even alighting, my fingers gripped so tightly about my teacup that it could shatter in my hands. How long has she been talking this nonsense? How long have I been sitting rigid by this Christmas tree?

"Do you remember when I first showed up at your

office? That lovely day in September, and you were dressed for outdoors, and you never got to enjoy it? I came to you because . . . well, I'd been to your panel discussion on rape, and you were so quick with your mind, so beautiful and . . . I was confused by the ache I had felt for all those years to be close to my daughter. I felt a need to connect with you, and I had an excuse. I was afraid of shocking you, but thought I should confide that I was your birth mother. Not right off the bat, after we got to know each other, after we talked a little. And I expected you would advise me what to do, perhaps send me to a colleague who would not be so personally connected. I felt I needed your permission to take any action."

I will not hear this; it is a mocking, cruel fantasy. I dare not allow myself to go where reason demands, to take that final impossible leap of logic. For if Beatrice is my birth mother, then my father is . . . This is a thoughtless joke. . . .

"And then . . . you told me about your mother, Charlene, your other mother, the one you more truly deserved. And – do you remember? – I was looking at that photo on your desk, your graduation day, Charlene hugging you with all that intense love and pride."

That time comes spinning back, Beatrice entranced by the photograph. *You're lucky. She sounds like a wonderful person.* But then that memory dissolves into vapor, and my mind is again flailing, fighting, denying. This cannot, *cannot* be. . . .

"And then you said something that just . . . it changed everything. It stopped me in my tracks. I remember so clearly. 'My super long-time-single mom,' you said. You told me you owed everything to her – your entire existence. Of course I'd assumed you *knew* you were adopted, and I didn't know what to say; I was totally discombobulated. And I couldn't tell you the truth, I didn't dare. You loved her so deeply; I thought I would hurt you terribly. So I have continued to live quietly and alone with that, with the secret of your birth. . . ."

The dam I have tried to build against this outpouring is collapsing, and I am drowning, drowning.

"And, so . . . you and I just carried on, I suppose, and things kept building and building, and it became impossible to let you know the truth of your origins. . . . I wanted him to pay for his crime; I still do – he had robbed me of so much of life. And I simply decided you would never know he was . . . well, what he is. There was no way you would find out; I had destroyed all the records."

She fades into momentary silence. My eyes are closed, my body is clenched.

"If I had been asked in court, I would have committed perjury, lied before God. But I believed I would never need to face that prospect. The trial seemed to be going so well."

"It was *not* going well. . . . You didn't know. . . . I couldn't tell you. Everything was falling apart." I am stuttering, barely able to speak.

"I'm sorry, I saw it differently. . . . Was I so wrong, Elizabeth, was I so terribly wrong?"

When she puts her arms around me, I want to shrink farther into myself, but I can no longer hold myself so tight, and my body trembles, shaking itself loose, and my eyes flood with the tears I cannot keep inside.

We have parked on South Jackson Street, across from my building. I think it is about four o'clock. Christmas shoppers are thronging the streets. Everyone seems happy, boisterous. Their energy rattles me.

"Should I stick around?" Mattie asks.

I say nothing for a moment, just sit, all emotion drained, my ears ringing, my eyes raw. Mattie is badly shaken, too, by what I have told her.

"Yes, please. Go on up." It is a struggle to speak these simple sentences. I clear my throat. "Sit down with them. Explain it all to them." I have such a terrible headache.

I can see someone in vague outline at my bedroom window. Mother. She is waiting for me. How long was I at Beatrice's, an hour, two, three? Bewildered and shattered, desperately holding myself together, I finally fumbled my way to the phone and called Mother, but I could not talk to her. So Beatrice took over. I think that is when I wandered in a daze to Mattie's car.

I work my way into our crowded corner pub, a micro-brewery. In the women's room, I wash my face, touch it up, try to do something with hair matted with sweat and tears. I stare for a few moments at my sickly reflection: I know now who I am, and I can hardly bear it.

As soon as I am back at the brass-railed bar, a man offers me his stool, and I am too weary and abstracted in thought to argue about that or to refuse his offer of a drink. I stare out the window at the Washington Shoe Building, sipping a pint of honey ale, not even pretending to listen to the man's chatter about a Seahawks football game, only poorly aware of him.

That is Franca looking out the kitchen window. Others are with her.

The beer begins to soften the headache, maybe even the pain of revelation. But I am still in a state of shock, my senses dulled. The man is still talking, but his voice comes only dimly to my ears. I hear Beatrice instead. Was it only two days ago? *Sometimes you make me so proud that I just want to burst.*

Our first meeting in my office some fourteen months ago drifts back: that sensation of having known her from the past. But it was I whom I was seeing, my face in hers, my body. She had followed my career, she said, and knew I was raised as a Baptist. I had not stopped to think: how would she possibly have learned that?

March 27, 1971. My date of conception. December 8, 1971. My date of birth, three weeks' premature. I failed to notice the coincidence. Or that the town of Twisp where I was born was not far from Okanogan.

Johann Krueger is my grandfather . . . one of them. The other is . . . I cannot work this through, I cannot handle it.

I must. I will fly apart if I do not. I am a child of rape.

I had been pulled to him in ways I did not understand. An unhealthy distorted desire, I had thought. But something else impelled me, deeper, more elemental.

There were aspects of myself I must have unconsciously seen in him, besides the color of eyes and hair. Did I inherit the ambition, the vigor, the acuteness of mind? The hot temper, certainly, the short fuse. But surely not those other unwanted parts of him, the immoral and the cruel. Nurture transcends nature.

His parents damaged him. Mine offered love. That is where the true difference lies.

Memories and faces whirl in muddled tumult through my head. Johann . . . I had once asked if his deity would deny an abortion to a woman who was raped. *God does not discriminate. He granted you a wondrous gift you would selfishly deny to others.*

The irony is almost too terrible to contemplate. I exist because the Kruegers adhered to a rigid moral doctrine I oppose with an equal fierceness. I am because of them. I owe them my life!

The Seahawks fan is looking at me oddly. And I realize I am making a sound, a slightly manic laugh. Is this the hysteria that comes before the breakdown? No, I cannot allow myself that; it is too easy, a cheap escape. I am more resilient than Beatrice. I can survive this inner turmoil and confront who I am. I must.

"Born of violence, born of evil."

I realize I have said that aloud. The man beside me quickly departs.

I close my eyes; I have been inconstant in my faith, and God owes me no favors, but I pray.

I feel a slight settling, a calm. My breathing becomes less labored. It is almost as if, through exhaustion, perhaps, or laying on of unfelt hands, a sense of acceptance comes. What has happened has happened. These faint stirrings of hope and renewal, of *élan vital*: whether they come from above or within, I do not know. Maybe from God, maybe from that innate willfulness that has so often been my undoing.

I pause at my fourth-floor landing. The door is ajar and I can hear shuffling, softly spoken words, an exclamation, a hush, more conversation, earnest and anxious. I straighten my dress, run my fingers through my hair.

A flurry of movement as I enter. Nick and Stephane are preparing dinner. Franca is also in the kitchen, Mattie elsewhere, maybe with Mother. They stare at me, and fall silent, afraid to approach, to touch me, as if I would shatter on contact.

"Don't everyone speak at once."

Finally Nick steps forward, takes both my hands, and bends and solemnly kisses me on the forehead. "Are you ready for your martini, princess?" Business as usual. I offer a smile.

"Do you know what I would like? I'd like everyone to stop standing around looking like an alien has just walked through the door. Remember me? I'm Elizabeth Finnegan. I'm working through it; I'll get over it. I just need a little calm support. Thank you all for being here. Thank you for caring."

Mattie emerges from the hall. "Charlene is in your bedroom. We'll let you be alone."

"Go on out for dinner. You're not to worry. I'll be okay."

Nick hands me the martini; I don't really want a drink and take it to my bedroom. There, Mom is lying down, a wet face cloth over her forehead. She struggles up, groans, and I brace her head with a pillow.

"Looks like you need this more than I do." I hand her the martini, and she takes a sip.

She looks at me, then lowers her eyes. "That awful man didn't hurt you?"

"No. I've just been delivered another shock that is harder to bear."

"Baby, I'm so sorry."

"I have had my fill of sorrow. I need understanding."

"Don't stand there looking so . . . so calm. You're not. I can tell you're fuming and you're trying to hold it in — I *know* you."

I have never been able to hide from her. Stripped of my placid disguise, I ventilate: "Can you even *begin* to grasp how jarring this is? My world is upside down. I am entangled in a vitriolic feud with my . . . my *birth* father! I've accused him of raping the woman who bore me! He is suing me down to my shoelaces."

She swallows the martini in one gulp, takes a breath. "Liz, please, how could I have known all this would happen? No one told me how you were conceived, who your birth parents were."

"Damnit, that's no answer, Mother. I need to know why I have lived a lie all my life. Your lie. *Everyone's* lies. I feel I have been conspired against, denied my reality. I have been haunted all my life by feelings of being lost, of not knowing who I am. Could you not sense that, could you not have helped me find myself, make me whole?"

She covers her face, and it is some time before she speaks, her words coming in gushes between sniffles.

"I suffered everything but the birth pains; I changed

your shitty diapers, nursed you through measles and chicken pox and all your flus and colds. I strung your mittens and patched your old jackets. I drove you to school and made you do your homework every night. I lived through all your crises, everything from acne to knee scrapes and broken hearts. We didn't have much, but we made sure you never wanted. You are who you are because of me, not because of someone who didn't love you enough to keep you. I'm sorry if that sounds so defensive."

"But why, *why* had you never told me?"

Another snuffling silence as she seems to grope for words. She clears her throat, begins again, a softer voice.

"We both wanted a child. We really tried. Six, seven years, nothing. I don't know whose fault it was."

"It's not a question of fault."

"Whatever. And the pastor said we should register with the church adoption agency, and suddenly . . . there you were. A miracle. And, oh, God, you were so beautiful. So incredible. So perfect. And I think we just tried to convince ourselves you came from us. It seemed so easy to do. We moved from Twisp when you were still just a little thing, and that's when your dad opened up his garage in Coalsack, and everyone said you had my nose, his chin, and we never explained; we just carried on as if you were our natural child."

I am sitting beside her now. I cannot tell what I am feeling; I can't bring myself to touch her.

"And as you grew you began looking so like me – it's not like you were on your way to being a six-foot redhead – and it was almost like we forgot we were pretending: you were our own, our very own. When you grew old enough, we promised each other, you'd be told. And when you were only six, your father died, and you don't know what I went through – you became my total reason for being. How was I to tell you then? You were traumatized. Should I have added to the horror you felt?

I was ashamed, too – my neighbors, my customers, I would have been mortified if they found out I had lied to them. But mostly, Elizabeth, I was tortured with fear that you would stop loving me. That would have broken my heart."

"Didn't you tell your own parents?" I hardly knew them, these mysterious sources of Christmas and birthday presents.

"I told my mother. She just kept quiet about it."

"I don't know what to say. It's like a life of false pretenses . . ."

"But it's a damn better one than many you could have had. I didn't give you life, but I gave you something life is meaningless without. I gave you love. Maybe too much; I know I spoiled you, that's why you're so headstrong. Little Miss Smarty-pants, I used to call you. You were *loved*. You *are* loved. More than I can bear to admit."

"You should have told me, Mother. I would never have stopped loving you. How could you not have known that?"

Her tears come, and my eyes flood, too. I can barely see, and I grope for her, wrap my arms about her, pressing myself into her so firmly I am hardly able to breathe.

I don't know how much time passes as we remain entwined, maybe half an hour, but eventually we separate, and I coax a smile from her. She holds a tissue to my wet nose, and I blow, a child again. She runs a hand through my lank, untidy hair.

"We have to do something about this."

"Remember when I dyed it orange?"

"Oh, God, I almost fainted."

"And the principal sent me home from school?"

"What an ass."

We laugh, we remember. The closeness brings comfort, forestalls the demands of new realities: a man who does not know he has a daughter is suing her for slander.

Who are you, Hugh Vandergraaf? The answer has come thudding home to me. Now you must face that same truth.

An evening wind has shredded the clouds, revealing moon and stars, and I am alone in silence as the taxi pulls away. Hugh's bungalow, which is in an old residential area of north Ballard, is in darkness. It is a quarter to seven, and likely he has not returned from his weekend sail. I will wait.

What state of mind am I in? Numb, I think. I have been on overload; the weight of events has finally dulled emotion. Maybe some protective inner self has raised barriers against anguish and pain.

I stroll about the yard: rolling lawn, a twisting yew tree, hydrangeas and rhododendrons asleep for winter. The house seems recently restored and is handsome, faced with gray-stained cedar, three tiers cascading to the waterfront. The front door is locked, the adjoining two-car garage as well. I slip around the back, where the lawn slopes to the lapping waters of Puget Sound. A small cruise ship festooned with Christmas lights plows by and from it comes the merry music of a marimba band. A tug toots as it passes the other way. The evening grows dark and cold.

Extending from the back of the house is a solarium, and within it a low-wattage bulb glows. Indoor plants, all well tended to, pools of water beneath hanging baskets. Access is by a thick glass door, and it is a fraction of an inch ajar. When I pull the handle, it opens – the lock had not quite clicked shut.

I am untroubled about entering: I am without dishonest intent – and would Hugh balk at his offspring seeking shelter from the cold while she awaits him? Tiled steps lead beneath an arch and into the house proper. I find a panel of switches, click one on, and inset lights glow in the living room. It is immaculate, not a speck of dust. Well-placed art on mahogany-paneled walls, antiques.

Here is his cushioned place of repose: a Chippendale wing chair and needlepoint hassock, a book lying open on it, *The Theatrical Works of Galsworthy*. A line from a play, *Justice*, is marked with a penciled exclamation point: "There is nothing more tragic in life than the utter impossibility of changing what you have done." A sad truth that has clearly been afflicting him.

I wander, explore. Extensions lead to a dining room, a library to the other side, with a corner study near a glassed wall of first editions. Elsewhere, history and philosophy tomes, Nietzsche, Marx, Havelock Ellis; the complete Dickens, the complete Balzac, Dostoevsky, Hugo, Thoreau. Thinner books, poetry new and old, a section devoted to it.

On his oak leaf desk, a scatter of journals and transcripts and documents, and just as in his chambers there is that sense of intellectual untidiness, of a mind hard at work. Beside a computer, a few chewed pencils, evidence of our unsavory common habit. Weaned too early.

A foolscap note in his handwriting sits on this clutter: "Dear Mrs. Gossens, please do not as much as touch a dust cloth to this desk. A reminder: check the back lock; it tends to spring. I shall not be home until Monday." Where would he be this evening? He had driven to a marina on Whidbey Island.

His answering machine blinks at me. My hand hesitates over the replay button. Why not? Hugh and I no longer keep secrets from each other. He has not erased his last several messages. His mechanic: "We can take the Romeo next Thursday afternoon, Judge." From Whidbey Island: the Mainsail Marina has gassed him up and pumped the bilge – the *Wandering I* awaits him. Bill Christiansen, twice, urgently seeking audience. Stan

Grogan: "Hugh, something's come up we hadn't wanted to bother you with." The bailout of Ms. Thalia Pfeiffer coming home to roost. Bill, again: "Certain parties have pulled off a dumb stunt, Hugh. Call me as soon as you get home."

From a bottom drawer of his desk, I remove several envelopes of old snapshots. Here are my roots, those missing parts of me. This is my paternal grandparent, the air-force general in his uniform, erect in bearing, cold unsmiling eyes, but robust and handsome. His wife is short and thin, bright lipstick, a troubled smile. I know nothing about her; I must learn. Opal was her name: how odd that Hugh devoted so few words to her in court. Such a cogent omission. It impels one to think she may have exerted a more potent influence even than the general in the shaping of his psyche.

There are not many pictures of Hugh as a child. But this is he in late adolescence: sardonic grin, knobby knees, tennis racket, a background of palm trees and desert. Another showing him slightly older, laughing, about to jump into a swimming pool, another tropical setting.

But in most photos he is with his brother, Jerome, somehow always in his shadow. There are many other snapshots of the brother, often in the company of young women. My deceased uncle seems happier than Hugh, smiles more easily.

Here is one of Opal and the two boys. Hugh is looking down at his shoes; she is smiling at Jerome.

In other drawers, I find old letters, diaries, scraps of paper, the undiscarded memorabilia of his life. In a filing cabinet, thick files of correspondence extending back thirty years. I resist a compulsion to pack it all away, to take his past home with me, dig into it, an orgy of self-discovery.

I check the kitchen: a tiled island, an inset oven, a copper collection. On a hook above the kitchen counter, a set of house keys and also to the second car, the Alfa Romeo, which I assume is in the garage.

His coffee maker has been shut off but is not empty – enough for a cup, which I place in the microwave to warm. I sit down on a barstool and stare outside at the flecks of moonlight dancing on the waves of Puget Sound.

It is after midnight, and I am skimming along on deserted I-5 north, the Alfa Romeo in full-throated growl, music sweeping from the speakers, the Sibelius second symphony, searing violins, woodwinds resonating with lyric pain, intensifying a mood of felt tragedy. Among the glove compartment CDs: the Mahler eighth, the Brahms first, the Emperor Concerto – these are the soaring plush sounds Hugh enjoys.

It is a solemn, empty night, the sky huge and patched with stars above the Skagit flatlands. Whidbey Island, says the sign, and I sweep around a curve to the road that takes me to the island bridge.

On a long-ago October day a Volkswagen van toiled down this road, bearing Helen Mazur to a scene of violation. How could he not have felt abased, no less humiliated than his victim? He must have felt guilty afterward: he apologized, however crudely.

And I soar over the bridge, above the black, boiling waters of Deception Pass. . . .

The marina is on the northwestern shore of this narrow, looping island, by a small store and restaurant near which I park. Here is his Toyota Land Cruiser – I assume he plans an early start for Seattle and the courthouse.

Decorative electric lamps light my way along an asphalt path to the docks, where sailing vessels bob in the wind and bounce against their fenders, most of the boats deserted, tied up here in refuge for the winter months.

The night is cold, the wind brisk and cutting. I hear the echoes of my footfalls on the planks, and suffer a flash of memory: the nightmare in which I was running naked along a dock. I shrug it off. A memory uglier, more real: the attack of two nights ago. That is harder to dismiss. I still my tremors; I will not be afraid.

The *Wandering I* is near the far end of the floating dock, a classic wooden ketch, details in brass and mahogany. No lights are on within, so he is asleep.

I pause before going aboard, and drink of the cold rushing air, which helps revitalize me. I will rest when this is over, reassemble the scattered remnants of my life. I shall make resolutions: no more mindless debauches, no fits of temper, no stubborn arrogance. All that foolish pride has seeped away.

The boat gently lurches as I step on board and into the open cockpit. The door that leads below is not latched, and swings open on soundless oiled hinges. The air is warm inside: a stove is giving heat. Its occupant emits a raspy snore from a bunk at the bow.

I find a flashlight by the door, then send a beam through the cabin. In an alcove, a small desk with a laptop, a tape recorder, books. Thucydides. Goethe. *The Collected Works of Whitman.* Some magazines: *Harper's*, *The Nation*, and . . . I am taken aback: *City Living Magazine*, me on the cover. Why is this here?

A fifth of Glenlivet, a third full, an ounce in a glass. Another unopened bottle on a shelf. I roll out a chart that is set beside the books. The Gulf Islands of British Columbia. Is he planning to sail there? To revisit the past, as if doing so might make it different, or somehow go away?

I throw light on the forward bunk. He is bunched

into an unzipped sleeping bag, his naked legs protruding. Long, narrow feet, high-arched like mine. He groans as if in tortured dreaming. The light disturbs him, and he rolls over. Then after a few seconds of stillness he sits bolt upright, banging his head on the beam above.

"Who's there?" A voice husky with sleep, perhaps with drink.

"Elizabeth Finnegan."

"Eliz . . . That's impossible."

A bedside lamp is switched on, emitting a soft yellow glow. "Jesus almighty — it *is* you!"

He sits up, rubs his head, and brushes back the hair that has fallen over his eyes. He looks at his alarm clock. One in the morning.

"This is an ungodly hour — even for strange visitations. Have you gone mad? What are you doing here?" He continues to stare at me with amazement.

I make no response, and sit on the starboard cot as he stands in his T-shirt and undershorts and pulls on a pair of jeans.

"You appear to be unarmed, so I take it you are not here to seek some sudden primitive form of justice. You seem to be making a profession, Ms. Finnegan, of being unpredictable. How did you get here — by bloody bicycle?"

"I came in the Alfa Romeo."

"You *what*? How? Please convince me that I am awake."

"I was in your house. The solarium door, as you know, doesn't lock too well. Bill is trying to reach you. Stan Grogan, too. I've had a very busy day, and I'm afraid everything has turned upside down."

"Elucidate." He is still standing, his arms folded. His eyes seem troubled, raw, as if he has been struggling with emotions.

"This is where it happened, isn't it? Where I'm sitting. The starboard cot, Beatrice said." Here I was conceived.

"How do you expect me to respond to that, with impassioned umbrage?"

"It happened, Hugh. You perjured yourself when you denied intercourse. Particularly for a judge, that seems no less serious a crime than rape."

Slowly, he sinks onto the cot opposite me, and leans back into the shadows. His eyes have lost their former brilliance, are strangely soft, speaking silent words which mystify me. His smile seems inappropriate to this occasion.

"How does one plead innocent to deaf ears? As you may recall from law school, perjury requires corroboration —"

"Please don't patronize me."

"Forgive my sins of pedantry. Kindly tell me, why are you are storming through my life, my privacy, in this way? If you have thought, as a desperate measure, to gull me into some offhand admission of guilt, I can only admire your audacity."

He says this rather lightly, more composed now, more intrigued than agitated.

"Tell me the truth, Hugh." I cannot understand why I feel such an urgent want — even need — for him to end his mendacity; he is being offered a chance to do so before the harsh light of apprehension comes. The proof of perjury is staring him in the face.

There is sadness behind that smile; it is a mask for pain. His face is grizzled, two days of beard.

"Tell me, Hugh."

"I am searching for words and finding only questions. Are you here to resolve our fractious trial? Am I to save my mangled career, or my reputation?"

"I don't think so."

He nods, still smiling. His eyes are locked on mine, still sending those odd emanations. "Then let me speak of something that may seem rather bizarre. Preposterous, even. Are you ready for this?"

I suspect I am not, though I have no sense of what he might say. Maybe he is not ready, either, because he reaches across to his glass of whiskey. He points to the bottle.

"Shall I pour one for you?"

"No, thank you." I wonder if he has been doing more drinking than sailing. "What is it you want to tell me?"

He sips, then tilts the glass, lowers it, and sighs. "You want the truth? Let me for a few moments struggle with that fragile concept. Perhaps this is not the confession you expect. It has to do with . . . us." He leans forward. "Let us wander back fifteen months to that day of our stubborn contretemps in my court. I bullied you, and came out the loser. At least, I *felt* vanquished – and in an odd way. Twisted up. For days after, I kept thinking of you, how you stood up to me, the spunk. You were me, the same lawyer half a lifetime ago, even grittier."

I am uncomfortable. I do not want to hear more.

"It is no wonder, I suppose, that your accusations of rapacious thuggery came like such a wounding blow. Yet as the ensuing months went by, as the trial loomed, I actually grew *concerned* about you, about the damnable risk you were taking, and I couldn't understand why."

"Don't say this. Please."

"It will be said, though to no good purpose: I do not expect reward or conciliation. 'Who are you?' you asked, and I wasn't sure. And I began to contemplate. All those months of confused emotions, of hating you – and myself more, for being drawn to you. Was I in furious denial? I thought, my God, do I hold *feelings* for this outrageous woman? Is it only by dint of willpower that I have maintained my justifiable animus toward her?"

"Please don't joke with me. I am begging you – be honest."

He wards off this protest with a raised hand, and leans closer to me. "Listen before you judge. I asked myself: however beyond the pale, however mockingly ironical a concept, am I attracted to the woman who seeks to destroy me?"

"*Attracted?* You don't know, you haven't the faintest idea . . ." I am horrified that, ignorant of our consanguinity, he can express himself in such manner. I stand. "Tell me you raped Beatrice!"

"Will that make you happy?"

I wildly swing my open hand and slap him fiercely, and he recoils, his face widening with shock if not with pain. As he gains his feet, I lash out again, my hand stinging.

When he retreats, I pursue. "Bastard! Liar!" I slap him again, and once more, and yet again.

He does not defend himself, does not move. He stands, his eyes closed, wincing as he is hit.

I wheel from him, spent, breathing heavily.

He makes a sound at last, a gasp or a choking sob, I am not sure, then turns away from me and with an unsteady hand splashes another ounce of whiskey into his glass, stares at it for a moment.

"Courage," he says, and drains it, then speaks with lowered voice. "I have intended to give you satisfaction. I had hoped this weekend to summon the strength, and on Monday to withdraw my suit."

I sit, shaking, nursing a wrist which I have lightly sprained. That is sufficient admission of guilt – I want to leave now. I cannot bear to face him with the final truth that proves his crimes. But I have decided: no more secrets, no more lies.

I force it out: "You impregnated Beatrice. I am your daughter."

My words do not connect for him; he stares blankly at me. "Excuse me . . . I – what did you say?"

"I was born of you and Beatrice."

I recount what I have learned – the concealed pregnancy, the adoption, Beatrice's reasons for coming to me

– but my words seem not at first to register. Now he begins to shake his head furiously, as if rejecting all I have to say. He trembles as acceptance comes, and his face takes on a terrible haunted look.

Then we are in silence but for the quiet creaks of the *Wandering I*. He shudders and closes his eyes, rubs them. Without a word or whisper he picks up a pen and sits, writing on a legal-sized pad. He pauses in thought, counting with his fingers, as if making a list. The silence creeps in around us: just the wind outside, whining past the rigging and the halyards, a harp-like sound, out of tune. The *Wandering I* rolls and strains against her moorings.

Ultimately, he rips off three pages and seals them in a manila envelope, on which he writes the name of Bill Christiansen. He hands it to me.

"I am beyond redemption," he says.

He slumps behind his desk and covers his eyes with his hands. I rise and flee.

I wonder if the dolphins which escort me divine my purpose. They are well known to be intelligent mammals, capable of conveying emotion and perceiving it, and maybe they sense how stricken is this drunken wanderer of Juan de Fuca.

Oh, God, Elizabeth, how wracked I am. I have built a wall of lies around me of such poorly mortared bricks that one swipe of truth has brought them crashing to the ground. I am buried in them, broken, dying.

Why was my anger so commingled with my lust for those women? But who can comprehend the chemistry of sex and anguish? It seems a potent mix in which the one is a catalyst to the other, firing the body, closing off mind and senses. Twice it happened in my life, only twice, and this I beg you to believe. I went into some demonic state outside myself.

Oddly, I do not remember Beatrice biting me, though she must have − I covered up the evidence of it, the blood upon my neck. Did I then slap her? Is it possible that I forgot, that I, too, suppress what lurks frightened in the shadows of the mind? And when she left that note in my typewriter, here was the proof my conscience hungered for: she had consented! I was innocent after all!

And such self-deception took root and grew and produced the evil-smelling blossoms of tortured denial, of a life of deceit. When the detritus of that life is cleared away, all that is left is the stinking fact of guilt. I am twice guilty of rape, and of multifarious counts of perjury.

Guilty! Guilty! guilty!

And as I scream this final judgment to the churning empty seas, the dolphins disdainfully flip their tails at me, and swim off, unanimous in their verdict; the case is closed.

Yet I might have swallowed the obloquy, the dishonor, even paid the price the law demands. But I would expire more often that way, more cruelly each time I saw your photograph or heard your name (which will be as large and famous one day as mine is small and mired in infamy). I cannot face my daughter again. I cannot hide from you. There is nowhere on earth I can hide.

Maybe you saw the volume on my desk: Whitman, who wrote so sublimely of night, sleep, death, and the stars. Praised be the fathomless universe, praised be sweet love, praise for the sure-enwinding arms of cool-enfolding death. Ah, well, let the poets create their tragic songs of America. I am but a footnote, a smudge upon the page of history; I have left no other mark.

That is the failing with which I cannot live. Errant and futile love, shame and ignominy: these prick at me, cause pain, draw blood. But wasted dreams sap the heart of appetite for life.

So do not feel in any way accountable for this. No bruised conscience, please. I will simply be repaying a debt of failure for having left the world no better than I found it. That goal, a just and gentler world, I bequeath to you.

The masts bend to the low-slung winter sun as wind and tide urge me toward distant tree-clad shores. I am surely in Canadian waters now, in the busy sea lanes below Haro Strait. A cheery wave from the mate of a passing dragger. A roll and dip in the wake of a cargo vessel, low in the water, laden with lumber, churning toward Japan.

I must pause to let down the sails and lower the anchor . . .

It is eight-thirty as I leave the Washington Shoe Building – the Alfa Romeo is where I left it on Jackson Street, soon to gather tickets. Court commences in an hour and I have again slept only briefly – three hours – then up at seven, awakened by my own thrashing.

The bleakness and sorrow of last night's confrontation remain deeply with me. I still see Hugh's face, lined and gray with shock. I see his bowed form in the play of shadows from the cold morn-ing sun.

I order my mind to banish such images, yet still feel uncomfortably tense, as if I am denying pain.

After ducking into a coffee salon for a latte to go, I make my way to the office, needing the comfort of familiar spaces, of routine, but also to reaffirm that the world is still spinning, that I am still a working cog in its machinery. But I must also thank J.J., who has been so unswerving in his support.

All the staff have not arrived, but God is at his desk. I can see him down the hall, past his always-open door. As I proceed that way, a large object blocks my path in the form of Junior Plum, emerging from his office. We gently collide, my elbow making contact with his middle.

He rears with fright, as if under attack, then blushes, tugs down his vest, works up a smile.

"Just the person I wanted to bump into," he says. He adds his "*Heh-heh.*"

"Good morning, Dwight. I hear you tied a good one on at the party Friday night."

"Guilty as charged. One might say I was a little too full of Christmas spirit."

His manner toward me suggests that his father has

not confided that I am Ms. X. This is confirmed as he begins talking in a staccato fashion: "Actually, I was hoping to see you there, maybe clink a glass, let you know we're still warriors on the same team. Professionals. Above it all, I'd like to think. No grudges. My, you really had me hopping on that witness stand. Made me feel like an uncaring brute. It went your way, no question. I was of no help to Hugh at all."

"Not so, Junior. The jury lapped it up. You shouldn't be so modest."

"I said what transpired, no more, no less." He bends to my ear. "They had a gag order on me, Liz, a no-disclosure oath in an affidavit I signed without absorbing the implications. I couldn't even tell Father. You can't believe how trapped I felt."

"Don't worry, Junior, this hasn't changed my feelings about you one bit."

Relief envelops his face as he straightens, pulls at his vest once more.

"And, ah, I was wondering – as a favor – if you might perhaps try to, ah, intercede with the old man. This whole unappetizing business has created some distance –"

"I'll tell him I don't blame you."

"That's my Liz." He gives my shoulder a playful squeeze. "Good luck in court. Hope it goes well for you."

In a strange way this joshing tête-a-tête has relaxed me, created that aura of normalcy I seek. No one has changed. Dwight is Dwight and Liz is Liz. Heaven is in its place. The sun still shines.

J.J. rises from behind his desk, always the old-fashioned gentleman. He asks how I am feeling. Well enough, I tell him. He again tries to dissuade me from appearing in court until I am well recovered from Friday night's trauma. He will appear for me. He will explain all to Mavis Luckwell.

"The file is about to be closed, anyway," I say. "It is all over."

He misunderstands. "Nonsense. I've opened up some new avenues." He hands me a sheaf of documents. "I slapped together a brief on the admissibility issues. We're entitled to a voir dire on the Helen Mazur matter."

"Oh, God, did you work all weekend on this?"

"A labor of love." He looks embarrassed. Love is not an easy word for him to say, even in that figurative sense.

"J.J., you are the sweetest man. I just wish . . ."

Wish what? I cannot formulate it. Do I wish I had been born decades earlier? He looks flustered, clears his throat, continues in his stern admonitory way. "Mavis will realize it's a point of appeal, so don't let her off the hook."

"Sit down, J.J. Listen to what I have to say. By the way, I want you to forgive Dwight, okay? He was possessed by uncontrollable forces." I find myself smiling, though I cannot think why.

He leans back on his swivel chair. "Well, you seem in an . . . unlikely mood."

I do feel strange. I wonder if I am fighting hysteria. Too much has landed on me too quickly. What happens when the witches of despair come knocking at my door?

"J.J., the trial is over."

"You've settled?"

"No. They'll be withdrawing the complaint."

He frowns, not understanding. "You mean you've won?"

"I guess so. I guess I've won."

I feel little sense of triumph.

I jog to the courthouse, arriving fifteen minutes late – I talked too long to J.J., a river of words, laughter, tears, a manic performance, and I almost had to convince him I had not gone mad. Though maybe I have, slightly.

J.J. was, of course, flabbergasted. "You? Hugh? His

daughter? That is more amazing than a two-headed six-legged barnyard cat." He called in Junior, who, upon my brief retelling, seemed almost to lose critical bodily functions, and had to lie down. To give him credit, Dwight insisted that the firm pay all my trial expenses.

Standing outside the Fourth Avenue door is Pamela Adams, scanning the oncoming traffic.

"I don't imagine he'll be showing up," I tell her.

"Hugh? Why?" She glances at the envelope in my hand, addressed to her boss. I have resisted the temptation to tear open and read this client-lawyer communication.

"I had a little talk with him."

"You met *secretly?* Are you putting me on?" A sly look. "You've settled. Sanity prevails."

"Let's just say we reached an understanding." I add nothing to that.

The ninth-floor hallway is crowded, people whispering to each other, now falling into a hush as I pass by.

I open the courtroom door a crack. The gallery is crammed, but the jury seats remain empty. Mavis Luckwell has decided to put the delay to use: two lawyers are arguing a civil matter before her. Bill Christiansen is shifting restlessly on the counsel bench, and he frowns as Pamela bends to his ear. Beatrice looks tight and nervous, primly sitting beside her Thomas.

"You're in deep shit for delay of game," Harry Crake says from behind me. "Why do I feel something's gone kerflooey? Hugh hasn't shown, and Christiansen is jumpy."

"No comment."

Helen Mazur is alone in the witness room, looking pensive. But she smiles as I enter, and when she stands she seems less stooped, her shoulders straighter.

"How was your weekend?"

"We went home – Wilkie had to catch up on his work. We had some discussions. They weren't very comfortable. I decided to hold my ground."

"And how did that feel?"

It is a question to which she cannot seem to find the answer. Then she smiles — the first time I have seen her do so. "I called him a thoughtless s.o.b. It felt . . . yes, it felt good."

"And what did he do?"

"After we had words? Nothing. That was the strangest thing. Well, Terry interceded; she had a long, quiet talk with him. And . . . we carried on, we ate dinner, and he just sat there moping, and he went out to walk the dog, and I decided to join him, and . . . it was okay. He even helped with the dishes. This morning he drove me to the airport."

She had never stood up to him, but now has fought for and earned respect. I never thought he would leave her. Who would cook his dinners and wash his clothes?

"Why don't you phone him and tell him that by being tough you helped me win this trial. Your subpoena is canceled."

A look of relief sweeps across her face. This ordeal has caused her as much affliction as anyone.

"You've *won*?"

"We've won, Helen. You, Terry, Beatrice, all of us."

As I walk into room 941, a cranky Judge Luckwell is railing at a hapless lawyer about his sloppily worded pleadings. "This is utterly incomprehensible. I'm striking out paragraphs three, five, six, and nine. Come back with something the court can decipher."

As the victim of her wrath beats a sorrowful retreat, she turns sourly to me. "Is your watch adjusted for the Pacific time zone, Ms. Finnegan?"

"Please accept my apology."

"Don't be sorry, be on time. I intend to finish this

trial before the expiration of this millennium. Are counsel ready?"

Bill hurries to my side. "May I have a moment, Your Honor?" As I hand him the envelope, he speaks gruffly and low: "Pamela said you reached an understanding. You had the gall to meet with Hugh behind my back? Where is he? He might have had the courtesy to phone me. These are the settlement papers I sent you? I'll want to read this into the record, then we can dismiss by consent."

"Your moment is up, Mr. Christiansen."

"Your Honor, an accord has been reached. I don't think the development will come as any great disappointment to the court."

I whisper, "Bill, read it."

He tears the envelope open, pulls out the two sheets of longhand. He frowns. "This isn't the right . . . Holy Lord."

His face stiffens through an ensuing silence.

"What have you got there, Mr. Christiansen?"

"Ah, instructions from my client. Excuse me, I'm not sure if I . . . this can't be right."

"I think I'd better see counsel in my chambers."

Bill, still reading, follows Pamela Adams in while I join the Struthereses. Thomas looks baffled, Beatrice apprehensive. I motion her to the counsel table while her husband busies himself in a *Popular Mechanics* magazine.

When I tell her that Hugh has all but admitted his guilt, she says nothing. A tentative smile, but she has difficulty looking at me.

"I talked to my mother. She explained, and . . . it was hard, but everything's okay."

"I was on the phone to her again last night. I'm sorry, Elizabeth, if I could undo . . ."

"You can't, Bea. Nothing can change it." But I cannot adjust to this new reality, and I still feel stunned, sensing the full impact is yet to come. And I find it difficult to forgive Beatrice her sin of omission. The lies of the mothers.

"Have I ruined our friendship?"

"It's . . . altered, that's all."

She bites her lip. "What will happen now?"

"You've won, I've won. Conviction in Canada for rape is certain. He may also face prosecution here for perjury; I don't see how it can be avoided."

The trials will be grueling, and I will endure cold comfort in being the instrument of my father's downfall, but I do not think either Beatrice or I will ever find it in our hearts to forgive Hugh; a part of us will always be angry. Perhaps such stubborn implacability is in the Krueger genes.

"You've been through so much. Are you able to take some time off?"

"I'll probably go skiing for a few days."

"Charlene invited me to her wedding. I didn't know what to say."

"Just come."

In chambers, Bill is slouched in a chair, still dazed. Beside him, Pamela Adams looks in shock. Mavis Luckwell, though, greets me with some kindness in her smile as she looks up from Hugh's composition.

"I'm sorry I was so sharp with you, Elizabeth. I didn't realize how hectic and . . . well, strange it's been for you. Please sit."

I do, by the window, through which the morning sun sends slanting rays of light. Rainier is out, white and majestic. There will be deep snow at Crystal, good powder. I need to escape the madness of the city into the lonely solace of nature.

"It's in the form of a confession," Mavis says. "He admits to the two rapes. The facts are bluntly stated. The remorse expressed is unambiguous and genuine."

"He wants it filed as an exhibit," Bill says. "He's instructed me to do so. He has also ordered me to apply for a directed verdict and formal judgment by the jury in your favor."

"What condition was he in when he wrote this, Elizabeth?" Mavis asks.

"He was in a terrible state. Emotionally."

"He was in control of his faculties?"

"I . . . think so."

"I almost hate to tell you this, but I wasn't intending to allow you much more latitude in his cross-examination. Perhaps an error of judgment – thankfully it never had to be made – but I'm not sure if you know how close you were to a crushing damages award."

"Did you believe him?"

"I thought some of his past behavior was beyond rakish. Graceless, in fact. But, yes, unfortunately I did. And if I read the jury right, so did all but one or two." Mavis again studies the first few lines Hugh wrote. "Your instructions seem absolutely unequivocal, Bill. He wants it done today."

"Then let's not take any time over it. If he feels he owes it to Elizabeth, I must accept that." He smiles at me sadly, offers an apologetic shrug. "I do accept that, Elizabeth, sincerely."

Mavis adjusts her glasses, turns over the last sheet. "What about this last page, Bill? It seems to be in the form of a will."

"There's a third page?" Bill abruptly rises, takes it from her, and examines it. "Christ *almighty*. Elizabeth, where did you see him last?"

"A marina on Whidbey. I have the number."

"Pamela, get onto them right away. And the police, or the coast guard. Was he acting suicidal?"

A chill runs through me. "No, but . . . maybe. He was terribly despondent."

I had not thought of suicide. I should not have left him. I suffer a spasm of self-blame and fear. And I am suddenly aware that despite everything that has passed between us, that whatever else he may be, he is blood to me, the only father I have left.

I am in emotional disarray as Pamela tries to reach someone in charge at the marina. We do not wait, and I find myself being gently ushered back to court, which is abuzz with noise until order is called. We all stand for the arrival of the jurors.

Mavis addresses them slowly, deliberately: "The first two pages of Judge Vandergraaf's statement will become the next exhibit. The last page isn't relevant to these proceedings." I did not ask to see it; I am too preoccupied with worry. When I left him, I had been overwrought with the effort of collecting my scattered thoughts: I had not fully grasped what an appalling state he was in.

Mavis is speaking again. "I hope, members of the jury, you will not think your services and your many sacrifices have been in vain, but the plaintiff has admitted to wrongdoing sufficient to defeat all his claims. Accordingly, I direct you to bring in a verdict for the defendant Finnegan and against the plaintiff Vandergraaf."

Behind me, an uproar of gasps and exclamations. Mavis gavels the room into silence. "I don't want to have to clear this court." She briefly summarizes Hugh's admissions of guilt, then tells the jurors, "You will do justice to this court, and even more justice to Ms. Finnegan and the two women whose cause she has so courageously championed, if you will retire quickly and return with your verdict."

We recess and head for her chambers, leaving the tumult behind, reporters jammed at the door, fighting their way out. A few women remain seated, in shock, one weeping. Others, women's-movement friends, seem pleasantly stunned.

Pamela is speaking into the phone. "Yes, a ketch. The *Wandering I*. No, I don't know when he left, probably during the night. I'll hold on."

She covers the receiver. "I'm talking to the coast guard. The people at the marina say his boat's not there. His car is. That's all they know."

I have propelled him to this. . . .

Quickly we are summoned into court.

As foreperson the jurors have selected Shayne Wells, the nurse, who rises to give the verdict. "We find for the defendant for sure." A few of the men nod sheepishly. She turns to me and raises high a closed triumphant fist.

And when I turn to the back I see a score of women in the room, all standing, all returning that salute.

In my own heart, there is emptiness. He is the father I have never known.

The whiskey has run out, and so has this tape, and time is running out as well for me to complete the course our night of revelation has set me on. The drag from the anchor will halt the Wandering I, *if no one rescues her first. I do not want her to founder. She has been in our family for two generations, and of course she passes down to you.*

As does all else.

I'm not sure what I'm worth — it's mostly by inheritance. Thirty million, forty? My accountant can figure it out.

I have taken a few moments to redraft my hastily scrawled will to add a few more good causes, though how generously you wish to endow them is left to your discretion. ACLU, *Vietnam Veterans Relief, and, closer to home, the Puget Sound Literacy Project (which I proudly helped get off the ground), and the Downtown People's Law Center. You will have your own favorite charities as well: women's hostels, rape-relief center, Abortion Rights Union. Do with the rest what you will.*

Oh, and can you drop the Alfa Romeo off to my mechanic (oil and lube, engine's idling fast)? And call my dentist, tell him I won't need that crown after all. You'll find their numbers in my to-do basket in my chambers. Make sure you pay Mrs. Gossens's bill — she comes in every Wednesday and Sunday and if you decide to keep the house you won't want to lose her.

I'm sorry to complicate your life in this way, but I don't have anyone else. Isn't that odd? After fifty years of life. . . .

The anchor's drag has slowed the Wandering I, *though she still drifts toward a rock-strewn Canadian shore, groggily rocking in the slap of waves. They seem eager for me. Find peace, they cry, find peace in the arms of Poseidon.*

PART THREE

2000

The old order changeth, yielding place to new . . .

— ALFRED, LORD TENNYSON

I open my eyes to the new millennium, stretch my arms, turn to the window: a sunny, cold day, the Coalsack River caked with ice, blue and deep, criss-crossed with skating scars. Some of them are mine.

How am I feeling? No hangover. (Ann Boorstein says — no surprise — I may have a problem with alcohol. Moderation is part of the new code of conduct.) Overall, I am much improved from a week ago, comforted by the familiar surroundings of childhood: my upstairs bedroom — the poppy-patterned wallpaper, the Toulouse-Lautrecs, the one-eyed panda bear in its place of honor on the bureau. I smell coffee; I hear happy voices.

The breakdown finally came calling for me — in all its glum majesty — three days after the trial. I was skiing at the time, at Crystal, fortunately with friends from the office, and was leading them down a steep run when the tears began to pour.

I braked, I sat, kicked off my skis. I was taken to J.J.'s chalet, and made to lie down. In my disintegration, I sensed a dreadful sharing of the emotional illness that had afflicted Beatrice Struthers many years ago.

Ann says she is amazed at how long it took for exhaustion and stress to take their toll. "You were due. It's proof you're normal. You'd have to be a walking robot not to break down under the kind of pressure you were under."

I lay around the loft for five days, Nick clucking like a hen, Mom flying in to nurse, to serve up the hot clam chowder she insists I like. Ann visited twice a day, working me through Hugh's cool-enfolding death. Sure, grieve, she says. But when all the travail and torment is done, more important concerns await in the in-basket of life.

My pieces slowly reassembled. I woke up one morning to find my rag dolls grinning down at me while gulls swooped by my window and the skies drizzled – that seemed important. It was normal. This was Seattle. It rains there.

I emerged from the cocoon of my room. I delved into the pyramid of letters Mattie brought from the office: carefully selected by her, supportive, cheery. I went for a walk arm in arm with Nick. I laughed at his jokes. I vented.

Ann said home care in Coalsack was the best medicine she could prescribe. I have been here a week, but soon will return to work. Clients are lining up at the office door (I am a celebrity, how macabre).

In the meantime, I am toiling to give away Hugh's money. I do not know why I feel such urgency. Maybe I believe I can erase events that way, to buy quick, over-the-counter forgiveness for having abandoned him that night. Why did I flee so abruptly from him? It is unhealthy to reproach yourself, Ann says, the doing was his. Seeking reassurance, I listened again to his last words: *Do not feel in any way accountable for this. No bruised conscience, please.*

I have compiled a long list of worthy causes to remember on his behalf, and most of the remainder I will allot to education, law scholarships, endowments for women's studies. Of course I will set aside enough to ensure my mother's comfort.

I shall sell the house in Ballard, but may keep the *Wandering I*. It has so many sad memories, but to part with it would seem a betrayal; Hugh particularly wanted me to have the boat – it was in "our family" for two generations.

Our family. The Vandergraafs. Grandpa and Grandma and Uncle Jerome and Dad. And I suppose I am truly my birth father's child, ambitious, career-oriented. I do not expect to have children. I have goals to accomplish, places to go. I have felt a gnawing need to move from law – with its minor victories, its sideline skirmishes – onto some grander field of combat.

I suspect I am being driven there – by unfathomable force – to pay his debt of failure. *That goal, a just and gentler world, I bequeath to you.*

Hugh's mentor, Senator Loovis, phoned, inviting me to Washington. A handshake with the president, talks about my future, the need for "able and spirited" women in politics.

Also, I have twice had visits from suppliants of the Idaho Democratic Party. The Second District, that is where they want to nominate me, here, this land of my childhood. It is a Republican stronghold, of course, and I am not much convinced by their assurances I will benefit from a strong women's vote: do the readers of those supermarket tattlers that featured me on the cover vote Democrat?

I have always told myself that conventional politics is an insider's avaricious game; the power structure buys people, saps their idealism, compromises them. But then I think: if one can just retain enough nobility and purpose, maybe one can nudge the system in the right direction, even enough to make a difference.

I am almost embarrassed to admit that I am considering that Washington trip. I will not sell my soul to them, though; I won't cop out. But maybe I owe something to Hugh's memory. *Take the helm, we give it all to you, our legacy of poverty and war.*

The *Wandering I* had been towed into a town called Sooke on Vancouver Island, and Nathaniel Duff led the team that went aboard. He brought the tapes to me that evening, and soon fled. (So apologetic, so overcome with clumsy-footed embarrassment).

The body was found a day later, washed up on a rocky beach. I felt nothing at first. I went skiing at Crystal. I unraveled.

Later, recovering, I listened to those tapes incessantly, needing to understand him, seeking the route to forgiveness. I played them for Ann, who agreed that the young Hugh suffered depressive illness after his brother's death, that he lost his controls while grieving for him.

"But it is only a partial answer," she said.

The rest of the answer seems almost laid bare by that old snapshot: adolescent Hugh staring at the ground, Opal showering Jerome with smiles. He hated her for pushing Jerome into the services, to his death. He hated war. He hated the military. Get the fuck out of Vietnam.

But mostly, during that year of his rage, he hated women. "To get Freudian about it," said Ann, "Beatrice and Helen were his mother's surrogates." Both held beliefs in reaction to his, Beatrice a fundamentalist Christian, Helen a staunch Republican, a supporter of Nixon, the war. That was a trigger that may have set him off. I am prepared to accept that he exploded within, that demons seized the controls.

Can understanding bring forgiveness? I am not sure but feel less divided, not trapped within a dichotomy of hate and love. I can allow myself to feel the emptiness, to accept that at the end I felt caring, however confused I was by it, however abruptly I fled from him.

Where might have wound the paths we followed, the dreams we separately dared? I have found myself asking that, too: how might I have been shaped by the guiding presence of this driving, cultured, tortured man? What did I miss out on?

I rise, dress, brush my teeth, comb out my hair, which I have decided to grow longer. New image. New me. New year, new millennium, new life. I have resolved to slow down, think ahead, to love more and anger less.

It is twenty degrees below freezing as I head off down the Coalsack River, slipping and sliding to town. I enjoy the bite of the mountain air, a fine day under a haze-hidden sun, the hills and valleys clogged with snow from the December storm.

Several boys and girls are playing hockey with a tennis ball where the river widens behind the Palace Hotel. Once the pride of Coalsack, built in its short-lived boom, this grand lady is no longer able to keep up appearances, looks frumpy and forlorn. But the townsfolk use its ballroom for big occasions; here will be the wedding and reception.

Jake has undertaken to supervise the decorations crew, but I find him in the restaurant, enveloped in cigar smoke, entertaining a captive but willing audience of Stephane and Nick – who can never get enough of Jake – and Curtis, who looks happy but exhausted. I think he was relieved to get away from Maxine for a few days.

"Well, now, there's no sound more fearsome than the beat of jungle drums as you're cowering in a kraal not sure whether they're going to eat you or marry you to the chief's first-born daughter." Jake is wearing a rented tuxedo – he cannot wait for the wedding to show it off – his bow tie askew, his cigar roaring.

I do not interrupt, slide in beside Nick, who looks resplendent in Tyrian purple and primrose yellow. Though he will be moving in with Stephane, he plans to keep his studio in the loft. Franca is to be my new roommate, a change of energy. She must have just checked in, for here she comes down the stairs, cool and beautiful.

Why isn't Nat Duff with her? However nervous he was when delivering the tapes, he was also gentle and kind, and I sensed there was a moment when, if I had said the right thing, we might have done more than shake hands. But of course Franca, not aware of my interest, had shouldered in front of me.

They are more of a match, anyway, both tall – he does not have to stoop a foot and a half to kiss her.

I wave Franca into a chair beside me. "You didn't bring your boyfriend?"

"Who's that?"

"Nat."

"You mean *you* didn't invite him?"

I frown. "No, why?"

"You really are a blonde, aren't you?"

Maybe she is right: I don't follow.

Jake finishes recounting his miraculous escape. Nick applauds. Jake winks at me, letting me know his tale was decorated with his usual inventions. My new father.

Almost all of Coalsack shows up for the wedding. The luminaries: Mayor Crockett, Sheriff Weekes, Doc Fairbanks. Mom looks ravishing in the dress I bought her at Nordstrom's. Jake strides about like a British baron, with his cigar and cummerbund.

Beatrice and Thomas, who arrive just before the ceremony, do not know many guests and feel out of place. I spend as much time as I can with them, making introductions.

Beatrice does summon her courage to join Mom and kiss her – it seems an awkward moment. I suspect there will always be a stiffness between them. I have forgiven both for having kept my past from me, but none of what happened had to happen.

I do, however, retain powerful respect for Beatrice,

for her determination, her courage, her flowering as a strong and independent woman. I am proud to have her as a friend, and have told her so. She understands where my deeper affections lie.

Both she and Mother are disappointed that I remain stoutly for choice, but they understand how I feel: it would be selfish to desert my beliefs. Think how lucky you are, Johann Krueger told me, to be a beautiful, breathing, thinking human being. But is not every marriage of egg and sperm a matter of luck? All humans conceived are trillion-to-one chances, and I cannot betray a principle merely because many insist on seeing me as a walking billboard for the anti-abortion lobby.

Much of the ceremony wafts past me as I stand on the stage, a bride's proud daughter, making no effort to follow the circumlocutions of Reverend Bell. He is taking advantage of the full house to deliver a twenty-minute oration.

I suppose I should cry as vows are pronounced, and I feel rather guilty that I can only smile. Nick makes up for me, wiping his eyes with a silk peacock-blue handkerchief.

A typical Coalsack snafu occurs. The best man — Jason Sims, manager of the local bank — drops the ring on the exchange, and we are in crisis. Members of the wedding party scramble on hands and knees; Jake finally fishes the ring from a crack on the wooden stage. The bride gives the groom a nuptial kiss for rescuing it, and Reverend Bell says, "Wait, I'm not through. I have to declare you man and wife."

Outside, Franca, who has the reach of a basketball player, eagerly snatches Mom's thrown bouquet, then winks at me. Why the sly look?

As the band warms up — the Idaho Silver Miners: fiddle, accordion, lap steel guitar, and the sultry voice of our own Wanda Zeigler – I see a tall, gangly man enter. It is Sergeant Nathaniel Duff.

Franca pokes me from behind. "He's all yours, sweetie."

I turn to her, speechless.

"I tried, but you were always in the way."

"You *did* invite him."

"On your letterhead."

The Silver Miners strike up a polka as Nathaniel, that wonky grin lighting up his lovely bony face, comes shyly toward us.

"Ask him to dance." Franca sidles away, leaving me to deal with him, and suddenly I am as nervous as he must be.

"I'm late. Freeway carnage."

"I'm so happy you came."

For a few moments, we stand mutely staring at each other, then I stand on tiptoes and kiss him. He blushes and his eyes grow wide.

"Can you dance to this?" I am throwing a challenge: I know he has two left feet.

"I doubt it, but I'll do my worst."

As we gallop around the floor – with more exuberance than grace, tripping over each other's toes – I decide that today I will bury my sadness. Let me come stumbling into the twenty-first century. I am ready.

About the Author

William Deverell has combined careers as a journalist, civil rights lawyer and activist, and author of prize-winning novels. His first, *Needles*, won the $50,000 Seal First Novel Award, and since then, he has published nine novels, including *Street Legal: The Betrayal; Kill All the Lawyers;* and *Trial of Passion*, which won the Hammett Prize for literary excellence in crime writing and the Arthur Ellis Award for Best Crime Novel. He is also the author of *Fatal Cruise*, a true account of a bizarre and high-profile murder case in which he himself served as defense counsel. He created the popular CBC television series "Street Legal." He is a founding member of PEN Canada, the Screen Writers Guild, and, while writing *Slander*, served his second term as chair of the Writers' Union of Canada.

William Deverell lives on Pender Island in British Columbia, and winters in Costa Rica.

ALSO BY WILLIAM DEVERELL

Trial of Passion

Arthur Beauchamp is Vancouver's leading criminal attorney. He's also an alcoholic with an unfaithful wife and a desperate need for solitude. So when he turns his back on his life and settles down on an island off the Pacific coast, it looks like a premature but very permanent retirement. Then one last case draws him back. The dean of law at a local university is charged with the sadomasochistic rape of one of his students. The evidence against the defendant is overwhelming. And he's lied again and again – to the police, his therapist, his attorneys.

If anyone can save him, Beauchamp can. But first, Beauchamp has to save himself – from the memories of his painful past and the torment of his inner demons. And then he has to face the choice that has haunted him throughout his career: does he serve his client – or tell the truth?

Seal Books / ISBN: 0-7704-2781-2